LAWMAN TURNED OUTLAW

Across the plaza, in front of the Sacramento House, they could see Corey Lane already in the saddle. Jacky stood in front of him, his left hand raised in the air in an odd mirror image of the way he had looked when the clerk had sworn him in. His right hand was curled just above the bone handle of the revolver strapped to his hip.

"Please, Corey," he was saying. "It's the job you taught me. *Don't make me draw on you.*"

"Get out of my way, Jacky. No one holds me here now. *No one!* Understand?"

"I've got to stop you, Corey. I've *got* to. You know that."

"I sure hope you won't make the try, Jacky. Now stand aside." He dug his spurs into the chestnut's sides, and the big animal moved forward.

Jacky Jameson's hand went to his gun. The move seemed fast enough, but the hand never got there. He was dead before his body crumpled to the caliche dust.

COREY
LANE

Norman Zollinger

BANTAM BOOKS
NEW YORK • TORONTO • LONDON • SYDNEY • AUCKLAND

This edition contains the complete text
of the original hardcover edition.
NOT ONE WORD HAS BEEN OMITTED.

COREY LANE

A Bantam Book / published by arrangement with
the author

PRINTING HISTORY
Ticknor & Fields edition published 1981
Bantam edition / April 1990

ISBN 0-553-28362-6

Published simultaneously in the United States and Canada

Bantam Books are published by Bantam Books, a division of Bantam Doubleday Dell Publishing Group, Inc. Its trademark, consist-
ing of the words "Bantam Books" and the portrayal of a rooster, is
Registered in U.S. Patent and Trademark Office and in other
countries. Marca Registrada. Bantam Books, 666 Fifth Avenue,
New York, New York 10103.

PART
ONE

"You are all resolved rather to die than to famish?"

I

New Mexico Territory—1879

The storm came in the morning, not long after daybreak, the clouds crashing hard against each other above the *malpais*, the ancient lava-flow which splits the Ojos Negros Basin north to south for more than forty miles. For two brutal hours they jostled each other, and the sound of thunder rocked the far Oscuras and bounced—perhaps a bit more faintly—off the distant mountains farther west. Once in a while, when one great thunderhead tried to shoulder another one aside, the sound came from behind the town, too, from the steep piñon-studded slopes of Cuchillo Peak. The big eastern mountain, bone dry after two months without a snowfall or even a drop of rain now that May had come, seemed with its stony echoes to be grumbling mightily that the dead wasteland on the valley floor should be glistening like a long, black, shining lake while its own parched flanks thirsted in the morning sun.

If the storm had waited until the afternoon, it would have caught the west wind which rises from the Jornada del Muerto desert every day this time of year, and it would have reached the town, only twenty miles away, but as the sun angled higher its strength grew by leaps and bounds, and by ten the blackest of the clouds had been put to flight or scorched away. "Rain before seven, clear by eleven" had met the test with time to spare.

In the town of Black Springs it just got hot. . . .

*　　*　　*

The thick adobe walls of the office of the *Chupadera County News* kept it cooler than the sun-baked plaza where the mob was gathering, but Jim McPherson—only five months the editor and owner of the *News*— found he was sweating all the same.

"Sam," he said to the gray-haired cattleman beside him at the window, "is this the way the start of a lynching looks?"

"Not exactly, Sonny Jim—but this mess could sure end up like that, only with one hell of a lot more dead than in any lynching I ever seen or heard tell about."

"Do you think they really mean to make a fight of it?"

"Hard to tell." Sam's grizzled face was tight, worried-looking. "If they do—and if they go up the mountain to face Will-Ed Martin and the other ranchers and their riders— there's a sight of them won't come back down tonight. Not under their own power anyhow."

Jim McPherson studied the older man standing next to him. Sam Riordan was probably the only stockman in the basin who could have ridden into Black Springs unchallenged on this ungodly hot May morning. Outsider that McPherson still knew himself to be, he was well aware how high feelings in the town were running against the cattlemen since Will-Ed Martin had thrown his new earthen dam across Sinuoso Creek, strangling the farms of the Rio Concho lower down. Sam, all but retired from his own stock ranch, spent most of his time in town now—a good deal of it at the long bar of the Sacramento House at the corner of the plaza—and in his entire five months McPherson hadn't met a man or woman who didn't genuinely like the old boy.

"Yep," Sam was saying, "there he is, all right. Granby Stafford. *Thought* we'd be seeing his grouchy old kisser. Likely he's the one who stirred this ruckus up. Can't exactly blame him. If them Concho farmers go under, Gran and his feed-and-seed store will probably go under with them. Damned shame at that." It was like Sam to look at things on both sides of the argument. The other ranchers McPherson had asked about the effect of the dam on Black Springs hadn't seemed to care, if they'd thought about it.

The editor looked for the merchant, but couldn't find him at first in the milling confusion of the crowd which almost filled the space between his window and the sheriff's office across the plaza. Then he saw him, facing the two young deputies who flanked the door of the adobe jail. Stafford was about the same age as Sam (upper sixties, maybe even seventy, it was hard to tell with these sunburned, weather-wrinkled older men out here) and he was built like the rancher, too—short, stocky, but by no means fat. The difference was in their faces. Granby's look was as pinched and suspicious as Sam's was open and warmly generous. Still, Jim McPherson had heard good things about the merchant. Even those of his fellow townsmen who didn't care much for him grudgingly admitted that the huge amounts of no-interest credit he extended the Mexican farmers of the lower Rio Concho had pulled those *campesinos* through some pretty rough times in the past. That was why so many of the homespun-clad silent men of the Rio had rolled into town in their rickety mule-drawn farm wagons for this morning's protest. They were the only quiet members of the crowd, these Lopezes and Sanchezes and Romeros. The angry shouts and curses beginning to fill the air of the dusty plaza came from the Black Springs folk—anglo to a man.

"Can those two youngsters over there handle things if this turns ugly, Sam?" McPherson asked.

"*Youngsters?* Hell, they ain't much younger than you are, Jim." Sam chuckled. "Sure, they can face up to it. Kids grow up fast out here. Besides, they been trained pretty damned good. Notice how they've left their guns inside? Ain't a man out there would make a mean move on them— not with them unarmed."

"That mob is sure carrying enough in the way of weapons," McPherson said.

"Yeah, but look at them, would you? Them antiques they're toting been gathering dust a lifetime. I can't see a firearm out there looks even as reliable as this beat-up old Navy Colt of mine."

Even to Jim McPherson's untrained eye it was a pathetic arsenal. Jammed into the belts or slanted over the shoulders of the Black Springs men was a dismal collection of single-shot rifles and scatterguns, pistols with corroded percussion caps, nothing more up-to-date than the odd Hawken gun or a battered Sharps. The Concho men were outfitted more pitifully still, often with only a grass-stained machete in brown hands, no more than three or four of them with anything as threatening as an heirloom Spanish flintlock.

"I sure don't like to think of them going up the mountain to face Will-Ed and his crew," Sam said. "There are eighty to ninety good shots up there behind that dam, every one of them sporting a repeating rifle. The braver the amateurs in this crowd are, that many more of them will die—and Lord knows these damned fools *will* be brave!"

The din outside the window was getting stronger. The mob wasn't quite out of hand, but it soon would be if whatever they were waiting for didn't happen quickly. That they were waiting for something—or, more to the point, somebody—was clear even to newcomer Jim McPherson, and it was clear to him, too, just who that somebody was.

He looked, as he had looked every day since he'd been here, at the sign hanging from the *vigas* of the porch roof above the door the two young deputies guarded. It hung from the thick timbers on short lengths of chain, motionless in the dead-calm, heavy, oven-hot air trapped in the little plaza.

COREY LANE—SHERIFF, it said.

The sign was severely weathered, its white background peeled and cracked where it wasn't pitted from the sand hurled against it by the rough winds of spring, the letters themselves graying out until soon nothing would be left but a ghost image of the name it carried. In spite of his growing nervousness at the situation in the plaza, Jim McPherson smiled as he remembered his first day in the *News* office and the deceptive effect the sign had had on him. For some reason it had led him to expect a rustic old-time frontier-lawman right out of the worst of the penny dreadfuls. Sam Riordan here had dislodged any such notion that night, but twenty-four hours would go by before Jim first set eyes on Corey Lane.

If the first fanciful picture he formed of the lawman didn't hold, no new one came to take its place. He felt as if he was meeting Corey Lane for the first time every time he met him in the months that followed.

"Where is the sheriff, Sam?" McPherson asked.

"Blamed if I know. I figured he'd be here by now. Ain't like Corey not to be around if there's trouble brewing."

As if their speaking of the sheriff had been a signal to the mob outside, McPherson could hear the questions being bellowed at the deputies: "Where's Lane?" and "Where the hell is he, Jacky?" Tempers were rising. Very likely the heat out there wasn't helping, either. The crowd was getting noisy—and mean. The sheriff's two men were holding up well, though—so far.

Granby Stafford had taken up a position in the center of the plaza and was standing facing the sheriff's office, his arms folded across his chest. Something about his stiff back shouted a monumental defiance, and yet despite his tenseness he was calm—the only one of the anglos in the crowd who looked composed at all. Sam was right: Stafford must be the ringleader of this show, but if he was, he was making no effort to bring the others under his control or hold them back.

Beside him was another man McPherson recognized, a slim dark Mexican from the Rio Concho named Eloy Montoya. The editor knew him only because Montoya's was one of just half a dozen Spanish names on the subscription list of the *Chupadera County News*. The farmer was as soft-spoken as the other Mexicans who came in once a month to pay their paper bills, but he seemed to have a quiet confidence none of his fellow *campesinos* shared, a belief in himself and his abilities which shone through his courtly Hispanic manners. Someone had told McPherson early on that Eloy had engineered the *acequias* of the lower Concho, the ditch system which had held such promise for the small-patch farms along the river until Will-Ed Martin's dam had choked off the main feeder stream, the Sinuoso. "Damned smart, Eloy—for a greaser," the man who told the editor said. Montoya's stake in this affair must be nearly as big as Stafford's.

"Well," Sam said, "as long as those two don't lose their heads—Granby and Eloy there— there's still a chance to keep a cap on things, at least until Corey gets here."

"Could *he* stop this war? It sure looks grim to me, Sam," Jim said.

"Sure he could. Squash it like a June bug!" Sam grinned. "That's right! You never seen Corey Lane take charge, have you? Something to watch, Sonny Jim."

There must have been two hundred men jammed into the plaza now. It was a wonder to the editor that there could be so much motion in the crowd. And except for the Concho farmers seated in or leaning against their carts and wagons, every one of them seemed to be talking—shouting, really—as they moved about. The hot air was fairly shaking with angry voices, but as yet there had been no concerted ʼmove of any kind.

Then, just when McPherson had begun to think that perhaps the mob was leaderless and this noisy show would come to nothing, Granby Stafford pulled his watch from his vest pocket and looked at it. He said something to Eloy Montoya and mounted the two steps to the porch of the sheriff's office. The deputies stiffened, and the hand of the older of the two, Jacky Jameson, moved to the hip where a gun normally would have been. He blushed, and Bill Talley, the other boy, smiled sheepishly, but neither of them relaxed even when the merchant turned to face the crowd.

"I say to hell with waiting one second longer! Let's get up the mountain *pronto* and do what we have to do!"

Stafford's face was red from the effort he put behind the words, but his voice carried clearly into the office of the *Chupadera County News,* only dying when a great roar from the crowd drowned any echo out.

"Hell's bells!" Sam Riordan said. "Come on, Jim, I reckon we'll have to take a hand ourselves. This is sure going to put a crimp in the serious drinking I planned to do today."

The shock of hearing Sam say "we" almost kept McPherson rooted behind the window. This was serious, he thought, if Riordan was willing to forgo his usual Saturday-morning start on a long weekend in the barroom of the Sacramento House. Then he took himself to task for even thinking there could be anything comic about this situation. Shaking, he followed Sam through the door, unsure as to what good purpose he might serve, just in time to hear the old rancher yell across the plaza to Granby Stafford.

"Hey there, Gran! What's the rush? Ain't you going to wait for Corey?" The hubbub died quickly at Sam's last word—the name.

The merchant looked across the plaza, squinting in the bright light as if he was having trouble making out the speaker.

"We've waited, Riordan. He said he'd meet with us at ten o'clock. It's getting on for noon!"

Granby, so steadfast earlier, seemed suddenly alive with an attack of nerves, almost twitching. Was it simply the appearance of Sam Riordan, the editor wondered, or was it, as it had been with the crowd, the mention of the sheriff's name?

"Just what are all these people doing here anyway, Gran?" Sam asked. His smile was disarming. McPherson could almost believe Sam didn't know.

The merchant snorted. "For that matter, Sam Riordan, what are *you* doing here? How come you ain't up on Sin Creek with Will-Ed and his pack of wolves?"

"Come on now, Gran! You know it ain't no hair off my old hide what's going on up there. I don't get my water from the Sinuoso side of the divide, remember? Ain't my problem."

"Then this ain't your fight, either."

"I reckon not. But, Gran, I reckon it's my concern if my friends and neighbors are setting out to get themselves all shot up—and while breaking the law at that!"

"Don't try to stop us, Sam!"

"Wouldn't think of it, Gran," Sam said. "I just want you to think about how bad it will be. Oh, my God, it will be bad!" This last was said in a hollow agonized voice that came right from his boots. McPherson recognized that the old rancher was a consummate actor—except that this wasn't any act.

The plaza was hushed now. Jim McPherson suddenly felt sick. To this point the whole affair had been at least as interesting as it was frightening, but the groan in Sam Riordan's voice had stripped away everything except the sharp peril shaping here. For the first time McPherson realized the carnage sure to come if this ragtag army lumbered up the mountain in their carts and buckboards and on the backs of their sad old wagon-horses. Even if their weaponry hadn't been so feeble, there was still the question of the fighting skill of these simple workaday men. Sam was right. If they challenged Will-Ed and the other ranchers and their "eighty to ninety good shots," it would be slaughter.

"Besides," Sam was saying now, "it's only for a little while. I hear tell Will-Ed's promised to open the headgate as soon as the stock tanks are full." He seemed to be gaining confidence as he went along. "You know how bad the run-off's been this spring. The crop ain't gone yet from the Concho, but the cattle in the basin will start to die damned soon, and the ranches with them, if—"

"Señor Riordan." It was Eloy Montoya. Compared to the harshness of Stafford's voice and even the gentle gruffness of

Sam's, his was soft, almost a whisper. "Señor Riordan, why is everything always for the ranchers? They are like *un gran estómago,* a big belly that swells bigger and fatter every day. Always *their* appetite must be considered first. *Por qué?*"

Riordan smiled. He seemed grateful to be able to direct a remark at someone other than Granby Stafford. "You got a point, Eloy. But the *real* point—long as you brought up the subject of anatomy—is that you got to feed a belly first to do the rest of the body any good. Hell's fire, man! The ranches *are* the stomach of the Ojos Negros. If it wasn't for them, there wouldn't be no Black Springs, no Concho farms, no business—*nothing!* It's cattle will bring us a railroad some-day. Yes, sir, cows just got to come first—for a while at least."

"That is *muy bueno, señor,*" Montoya said, "but, like any belly when it's through with food, all the *campesinos* get is *mierda!*"

Laughter echoed through the plaza. Some of it was tinged with bitterness, but it *was* laughter. *Good work, Sam, keep it up.* But before McPherson could truly begin to hope, Granby Stafford erupted into the tail end of the laughter.

"It's *shit,* all right! I say let's get going!"

There was no mistaking that the groundswell of mutter-ing rising now to a heavy tide was approving.

"Hold it!" Sam Riordan shouted. It was a frantic cry. The mantle of confidence he had tried to drape about his shoul-ders had suddenly slipped away. "Won't you wait and hear what Corey has to say at least? Don't you owe him—and yourselves—that much?"

Again the crowd quieted like magic at the sheriff's name.

"No, Sam," Stafford said, but not with the same sure violence as before. "No point in waiting a second longer." Then, as if forcing himself to something more, "He'll only side with them water thieves anyway—if he ain't already up there behind that dam with a gun in his hand."

"Shame on you, Granby Stafford!" It was the only trace of anger Sam had shown, and it lasted but a second. "Far as siding with the ranchers goes, I suppose he will . . . if it's the law."

"Law? What about *justice,* Sam?" If Granby, like the others, had been momentarily awed by Riordan's invocation of the sheriff's name, the awe was gone now. "Little too late to mouth off about the law. That bunch up on Sin Creek and the other Ojos Negros ranchers like Will-Ed been hiding behind the law long enough. And so has Corey!" The merchant took a deep, visibly painful breath. "We don't owe him one God-damned thing. Do we?" he shouted.

A full-throated chorus of angry voices roared back: "Hell, no!" and "You tell them, Granby!" and for one terrible moment the editor was sure they would move right then. Only the somber men from the Rio Concho had held themselves in during the outbreak. He found the face of Eloy Montoya. The Mexican looked thoughtful, his eyes fixed on Sam Riordan.

"Granby! All of you. Listen . . . *please!*" Sam's tone was nearly pathetic now, all semblance of sureness gone. McPherson could see that the rancher was readying himself for one last try, and he prayed it would occur to Sam to make the try with Eloy. Stafford didn't look as if he could be budged with a charge of blasting powder. "I think you *do* owe Corey something," Sam went on. "When old Mangas was whooping it up out on the Jornada, it was Corey—and the ranchers— that was all there was standing between Black Springs and a lot of bloody Apache knives. Why, if it hadn't been for Corey back then—"

"Cut that out, Sam Riordan!" Stafford was nearly screaming now. "That was seventeen years ago, man! He can't live on that forever. There's a limit to the boy-hero stuff you feed everybody all the time." The merchant's agitation shook him like an aspen leaf.

"Granby—" Sam said. His voice was weak and the words which followed were lame despite the force he tried to put behind them. "They could come again. You know they could." Sam was beaten, and his suddenly ravaged old face showed it. Stafford, still fuming, but steadier again, was getting ready for more, and the cloak of confidence Sam had lost covered him instead. He looked to the crowd now, rather than at the rancher.

"Corey Lane's treated almost every man, woman, and child in this town like they was plain dirt. Like I said before, we owe him nothing!" He was sure of himself, all right, but there was still something nervous in his manner, something bordering closely on hysteria, at odds with his cocksure look. In a flash of understanding Jim McPherson came to a strange conclusion: There was a different truth here than the one he had thought he was looking at and listening to.

The real truth was that none of this was concerned with Will-Ed Martin's hated dam—no matter that it was a genuine peril to the lives and fortunes of the angry, restless men gathered in this hot sun. The truth was that for Granby Stafford, perhaps for Eloy Montoya, too, and for most of the Black Springs men and even for some of the mute farmers of the Rio Concho, there was something more central to the final defiant thing they were beginning here today. The truth was that these men feared and hated the man they had elected (twice, wasn't it?) to enforce their laws. It wasn't for anything Corey Lane had said or done, despite Stafford's outcry, but for what he was.

"Well, what do you men *say?*" Granby shouted at the crowd. From the answers howled back at him—the torrent of "Granby's right!" and "We'll show the high-and-mighty sonofabitch!"—the editor knew he was right. Then someone yelled, "Let's go!" and from the edges of the plaza cries of "*Vamonos!*" uttered with possibly a bit more dignity but with no less determination, were beginning, too.

"Did you hear that, Jim?" Sam said. "If the Concho men are ready now, there just ain't no saving the situation. The only hope we got is if Corey gets here."

"My God, Sam! From what I've heard today, he'd only be adding fuel to the fire if he showed up now."

"No such thing." There was a kind of whimpering stubbornness in Sam's old voice. "You just plain don't know him, Jim." Well, that was true enough.

The crowd was beginning to form into something like a ragged marching order, men moving toward the hitchrails around the edges of the plaza, a few of the carts already groaning as mules leaned against the traces.

Then Eloy Montoya mounted the porch and stood beside Granby Stafford. He held up his arms for silence, waiting patiently until all the men who had begun to move spotted him and stopped. "*Uno momento, amigos, por favor.* One moment, please." His voice was lifted, but it wasn't a yell or shout. He turned to Granby. "Señor Stafford," he said, "let us give the sheriff just a little longer. Until noon, no? Then we will go, I promise." His face (a fine face, McPherson thought) was as impassive as if he were hoeing a row of beans.

A struggle began in the features of Granby Stafford. Finally, even while he was still shaking his head, he managed to speak. "All right, Eloy," he said. "Noon. Not one second longer."

The editor looked at his watch. Twenty-seven minutes. When he returned the huge brass timepiece to his waistcoat pocket, he swore he could hear it go right on ticking, something he couldn't remember ever being conscious of before. He heard it all the while he watched the farmer and the merchant leave the porch and join the mob.

"Let's get over there and see if Jameson and Talley know anything we don't, Jim," Sam said, pointing across the plaza to the deputies. Like a sleepwalker, the editor followed the rancher through the crowd. It was furnace-hot, but McPherson couldn't tell whether the heat was due more to the searing power of the sun or to the anger he felt in the men they passed. All the muttering and grumbling had stopped, but somehow the silence only made the tension worse, and it was but small relief to reach the shelter of the porch.

"Where is he anyway?" Sam whispered to Jacky Jameson.

"Plain don't know, Mr. Riordan," the boy whispered back. He sounded like a mourner at a funeral.

"We ain't seen him since Wednesday afternoon," Bill Talley, the other deputy, said. "He *said* he was coming in yesterday, was going to spend the night here at the office so he could be on hand for this." His voice was as hushed and hollow as Sam's and Jacky's.

"That's bad, real bad," Sam said. "Hell, Corey's never one second late for *anything*. Something's sure gone wrong." The old rancher looked out over the plaza. "Get a load of them damned fools. Why do you suppose they're in such an all-fired rush to die?" He shook his head. For the first time since he'd known him, Jim McPherson thought Sam Riordan looked every one of his long tough years. "If he don't get here to stop them," Sam went on, "half of them will be dead or dying hard before the sun goes down."

In the square the Black Springs people and the Concho farmers were moving about a little. Eloy and Granby had their heads together, the two of them speaking in such low voices their words didn't reach the porch. A few of the anglos drifted through the door of the Sacramento House. Some of the *campesinos* hauled sacks of food from their carts and found places in the scant shade of the two dusty cottonwoods on the east side of the plaza. If a stranger wandered into town today, the editor thought, he would think this was just another ordinary cowtown Saturday—until he realized there wasn't a woman or a child in sight. Yes, it looked normal. There was a dice game under way on the steps in front of the barber shop, and two of the Black Springs men were nodding at the buckboard for sale just inside the open door of the livery stable. The only telltale sign that things weren't right was the constant repeated pulling of watches from pockets in every part of the plaza and the turning up of faces of the men who used only the sun to tell the time. McPherson could still hear his own watch ticking, racing, but he fought back the urge to take it out again. He would know without looking when noon had come.

God, but it was hot, even in the shade of the porch. On the ground in front of the steps he could see the shadow of the sign hanging overhead, a black rectangle in the gray caliche. When it reached the first splintered floorboard of the porch it would be time. A crazy thought struck him. Why not race for a shovel and dig it out before it touched? He didn't realize he had laughed out loud until the other three on the porch turned toward him and Sam said, "Something funny, Jim? Let us in on it. We could sure *use* a chuckle now."

His face flushed and burned with nearly as much fire as whatever was eating at his stomach. He shook his head. "Sorry, Sam," he said. "Nerves, I guess. I'm scared."

Sam nodded. "Me too," he said. "Trouble is we can't get the right people to be as scared as we are."

Granby Stafford and Eloy Montoya had stopped talking and now the merchant pulled the watch from his pocket again, and McPherson could no longer keep himself from checking his.

Two minutes. When he slipped it back in place and looked at Granby once again, he saw Stafford was still staring at the one he held, studying it with such intensity McPherson wondered if the merchant's was ticking as loud and fast as his, the sound of it echoing inside *his* head, too, like so many rifles being cocked.

The shadow of the sign was still a foot shy of the porch they stood on, but it was ridiculous to suppose it could be an accurate sundial. He wouldn't look at it again.

The drinkers were coming out of the Sacramento now, and the lunch sacks were all back in place in the parked wagons. The dice game had folded up, and the buckboard in the livery remained unsold—and everything was quiet.

Granby Stafford returned his watch to his pocket, took a deep breath and cleared his throat.

"Let's go!"

No! No! No! It hammered back and forth in Jim McPherson's head like the clapper of some monstrous bell, but, try as he might, he couldn't get it out.

Eloy Montoya looked at the four men standing on the porch, shrugged his slim shoulders in a gesture that seemed like an apology, turned to the row of carts nearest the *Chupadera County News* across the way, and—simply, oh, so softly—said, *"Ahora, hermanos . . ."* now."

McPherson couldn't hear his watch ticking any more. He couldn't hear a thing.

Then a single gunshot, from somewhere in the plaza, shattered the silence, and Jim McPherson could swear his heart had actually, physically, literally, stopped. The shot echoed off the wall behind him and from everywhere, and for a second he didn't know where to look. When he finally forced his eyes to search, and when at last they focused on the southwest corner of the plaza where Estancia Street began, he saw him—Corey Lane.

He was mounted on the big chestnut horse with the white star blaze on its nose, and his right hand still held the Peacemaker Special pointed at the sky. Powder smoke was still billowing in a cloud around him.

Even with the dust of whatever trail he had ridden into Black Springs thick on his face, and with most of his hair hidden by a weatherbeaten hat, he looked as blond and brilliant as the sun hanging in the sky above him. His face, with the cornsilk-yellow mustache masking the mouth, seemed cool enough, but even across the plaza Jim McPherson could see the powerful gleam of the blue eyes—could feel their heat.

"What would you have, you curs,
That like not peace nor war?

II

"Why am I looking at so many guns in my town on a peaceful Saturday?"

Corey Lane's voice wasn't loud, but it pierced every corner of the plaza like the clear notes of a trumpet, and if a few of the men and carts still moved a little after the echo of the shot died away, the sheriff's words stopped every one of them. It was as if a dust-devil had whirled into the crowd of moving men, gathering them up like leaves and flinging them helter-skelter until they came to rest, shocked out of any movement whatsoever. McPherson could swear there was a strong, bad smell in the air, something heavy and sulfurous which didn't come from the gunsmoke eddying around the man and the big horse as they began to move toward the very heart of the plaza. The revolver was back in its holster, returned in some quick movement the editor couldn't remember having seen. The whole place looked strangely like a battlefield, and if none of the bodies he saw fell or bled, he couldn't shake the picture from his mind.

The smell came again, even stronger and more sickly, and McPherson knew it for what it was: fear. It came in waves, filling the plaza like a gas, and he almost choked on it, amazed then that one lone man over by the Sacramento House, probably one of the drinkers who had lingered a little longer than the rest, broke the silence.

"It's our town, too, sheriff—and we're fixing to fight for it!" The voice was thick with whiskey.

Corey Lane snapped his head in the direction of it, a

16

reflex so quick and mercurial it seemed impossible there wasn't some sound to it, something sharp and arresting like the cracking of a whip—or the sound of a gun. The sheriff's right hand, so recently emptied, flashed toward the holster, then stopped halfway there, the thick tough fingers curved almost delicately, an odd thing to see on so big a man.

"Fight?" Corey Lane's voice was acid, seeping even into the vitals of Jim McPherson. The sheriff had reined the chestnut to a halt in the dead center of the plaza. He placed both hands on the horn of his saddle and stood in the stirrups, rising as if forever, never stopping, looking around him as if he was assessing the damage done. "Fight, you say?" He wasn't smiling, but he looked as if he could rock with laughter at any moment, and McPherson was struck by the thought that laughter from this giant might be something terrible to hear.

"Why, there's no more fight in this mangy crowd than you'd find in a colony of pocket mice—even supposing any of you had a right to *start* one."

Lord, what a show! Corey Lane towered above the plaza like Gulliver, and even the horse seemed to share in this display of domination. There wasn't the slightest toss of head or quiver of flank or swish of tail, animal and man welded together in one solid mass of strength. McPherson looked at the faces of the men around the sheriff and saw pale, frightened looks where but half an hour ago he had seen red anger and determination. Could these possibly be the same men who were willing to risk their lives against Will-Ed Martin's eighty or ninety well-aimed guns?

The lawman was settling into the saddle once again, and McPherson looked for Stafford and Montoya, found them right beside the sheriff's horse, where they had been all along, lost to him in his complete fascination with Corey Lane. The lawman knew they were there, too, and they knew he knew it, the consternation, frustration, and fear mixed with fury on the face of Granby Stafford contorting him until he looked like a shriveled elf, his ordinarily firm stocky body sagging and deflated. The editor felt no surprise at his appearance. Granby had known all along exactly what would happen if this invincible, supremely overbearing man showed up. Why then, McPherson wondered, had Granby shown that early patience? Why hadn't he rushed his men up the mountain after the first few minutes of the sheriff's tardiness? And why, above all, had he assembled his shaky forces here in town today where Corey Lane could get at them and work this brutal sorcery? Maybe there were precincts in Granby Stafford's mind the merchant didn't know himself. Maybe, like some delinquent children, he craved punishment or, more likely still, wanted to be stopped before he went too far too fast. To the man's credit, he was looking at the sheriff, and not to turn away must have taken all the will he could muster.

Eloy, too, was looking directly at the man on horseback, but his back was to the editor, and McPherson couldn't see his face.

No one spoke, but the plaza wasn't completely silent as the sheriff sat his horse. Some of the men, those far enough away to feel they wouldn't draw attention to themselves, were shuffling their feet in the caliche dust, and across the plaza, unmindful of the chestnut's superb example, one of the mules in the ragged line of wagons trumpeted a distant echoing reminder of the defiance so suddenly gone in hiding.

What was it he had told himself before he left the office? McPherson asked himself. Oh, yes—that every time he saw Corey Lane was like seeing him for the first time ever. Today was no exception, but McPherson had the feeling that he was at last seeing him more closely to the way he truly was than at any time before. The intensity, the heat, the consuming pride he looked at were light-years beyond mere arrogance or ego—things more monumentally feverish than he'd seen in any remembered encounter with another human being. *And I wondered what Corey Lane might find to say to calm the crowd that waited so grimly for the stroke of noon.* Why, the few words the sheriff had so far uttered hadn't even been needed. It was the presence of the man which made all the difference.

Corey Lane turned now and looked at the four men on the porch. There was a look of faint surprise on his features, as if he hadn't really expected them to be there, and (was he imagining it? McPherson wondered) was there a hint of disappointment, displeasure, at not being alone against the mob he had so utterly cowed?

"Seems like the petitioners I heard were coming here today have lost their tongues," the lawman said. "Can one of you tell me what these people are doing here? You, Sam?"

"They've planned a little jaunt up the mountain, Corey, to persuade Will-Ed Martin to turn the Sinuoso water loose."

Corey Lane said nothing. He looked from one man to another in the frozen ranks facing him, as if memorizing each face, and then even the scattered shuffling on the farthest edges of the crowd stopped, and even the noisy mule remembered its manners. When his eyes had made a full sweep of the plaza, he laid the reins across the neck of his horse and turned it toward the porch, where Sam and the editor and the two deputies stood as fixed as everyone else in sight. When he reached it, he tossed the reins carelessly over the chestnut's head, and Jacky Jameson leaped forward and caught them smartly as the sheriff slid from the saddle, the whole thing done in much the same manner a great lady will let a priceless fur wrap slip from her shoulders without warning and without a backward look, confident there will always be someone, lord or lackey, who will never let it touch the ground.

He stood there for a moment, his back to the plaza and all its guns, as Jacky led the horse to the hitchrail alongside the porch. He stretched languidly, rubbed the small of his back with his gun hand, beat the trail dust from his pants with the other, nodding gravely to each of the three men and to Jacky when he returned, taking time with each of them. The performance was an insult—was meant to be.

"They realize, don't they, Sam," he said then, "that Will-Ed's got a proper legal document from Santa Fe for everything he's doing?"

Now there was the sound of someone stirring in the crowd, but with the sheriff in the way, McPherson couldn't see who was causing it. When he heard Granby Stafford shout, his heart threatened to break right through his ribs.

"God damn it, Corey! Don't give us none of that legal-document stuff: These people got rights that go way beyond Lew Wallace's cockeyed notions about the law." The defiance in the voice couldn't hide the agony and fear behind it, and it forced from the editor a half-nod of respect that poor Granby, scared out of his wits and badly burned, could still make the try.

Nothing changed. The editor moved a little to see Stafford's face, and when he found it, he wished he hadn't.

"I won't have it, Sam," Corey Lane said. He looked at the deputies then. "Jacky, Bill—if this mob doesn't clear the plaza in fifteen minutes, I'll lock every man of them up if the county has to rent a barn to put them in."

"Corey!" It was Granby again, screaming now, but the voice, strong enough to begin with, faded to a whimper as he finished. "COREY! *Look at me* . . . when I . . . talk to . . . you."

The sheriff did turn then, but he still didn't look at the merchant or any one man in particular. His eyes swept back and forth across the plaza—and only then did he let them rest on Stafford.

"Go home! All of you," he said. His voice was even and level at first hearing, but it held an aftersound, not quite an echo, something so filled with threat, so close to violence, it wouldn't have surprised the editor if Granby Stafford and even Eloy Montoya, standing with him, withered before his eyes. The feeling was so strong he was stupefied when Montoya spoke.

"Is it because, *señor*, you are a rancher, too, like Señor Martin and his people?"

By God, this farmer is unafraid. The simple question had come easily, without effort, as if he were asking about the sheriff's health. McPherson watched Corey Lane's eyes shift from the merchant to Montoya.

"May well be, Montoya." The fierce heat was still there, and Corey Lane's voice still pounded like a hammer on an anvil, but there was something different in it. With Eloy, the contempt was gone. "But let me tell you," he went on, "even if I sold yard goods in the smallest store in Black Springs, I'd still be telling these people what I'm telling them now—and for the last time. *Go home!*"

Eloy didn't move, nor—in some last anguished effort to keep himself there just one second longer and maybe regain a little of what he'd lost—did Granby Stafford, but the crowd, that hapless army which it had taken all the long hot morning to bring together, suddenly, and without a word or the slightest sign of protest, began to melt away. The old carts went first, wooden axles groaning, then the few horsemen, finally the men on foot, the exodus leaving the editor blinking at its speed and silence.

The sheriff watched the plaza as it emptied, with eyes

now strangely impassive. Try as he might, McPherson could discover no triumph in them, no hint of gloating. His job done—for now at least—Corey Lane looked as empty as the plaza was becoming. The editor wouldn't have blamed the lawman if he had betrayed some small pleasure at his victory, but perhaps his routing of the mob had been too easy, and McPherson could see that indeed it was—for Corey Lane. He could guess that the sheriff must be honest as well as proud. There would be nothing here for him to boast about.

For a moment longer Corey gazed out over the Black Springs plaza, completely vacant now save for the spent figure of Granby Stafford and the immobile one of Eloy Montoya, the one looking as if he had been severely beaten, but the other, amazingly, as unruffled as if he'd just arrived in town and had taken no part in what had gone on. The only expression on Eloy's smooth, seamless face looked to be equal parts curiosity and faint amusement.

Then Eloy nodded to the sheriff, took Granby Stafford gently by the arm, and began to lead the man away.

"Wait!" the sheriff said. "You two stay for a bit. I've got something important to talk about. In my office." He turned away from them, turned back again. "Nothing to do with this nonsense here. Something of *real* importance."

The contempt was there again for an instant when he said "this nonsense here," and McPherson thought, *Good Lord, that baleful old stone brute Ozymandias and his "sneer of cold command."* Nonsense, that. This man was no ruin.

Now the sheriff turned fully toward the four men on the porch. McPherson was baffled when he saw the lawman's face. He had expected to find the same almost idle, blue-eyed, unfocused look with which the sheriff had watched the last of Granby's and Eloy's army as it slunk away in silence, or if not that, some slight rekindling of the heat which had burned across the square earlier, like a fire on the *llano*.

Something had changed. It wasn't quite a smile lighting Corey Lane's face yet, but the masklike look, caused by the caked trail dust and the dried white salt of some sweat which had come much earlier—certainly not from any exertion here— was beginning, not to soften, but to show signs of some new and very human feeling.

The sheriff beckoned Eloy and Granby to the porch with a sweep of his arm, and by the time the merchant and the

farmer reached it, with Eloy still holding Stafford's arm,
guiding him, McPherson had come to a conclusion about the
look on the lawman's face. He had been looking far too
deeply, searching for something dark and hidden in every
shift of mood the sheriff made. What the editor was seeing
here was a simple thing, an open expression of uncomplicated
happiness, and for a moment he felt cheated because he now
was half-convinced this titan wasn't immune to the vulgar
frailty common to ordinary men. Corey Lane *was* exulting
over his victory in the plaza, and he wanted to parade his
laurels in front of these two poor devils he had beaten.

McPherson was crushed, and the sick feeling of letdown
was promising to get even worse, when the sheriff, speaking
to them all, began to talk.

"I got a message at the ranch yesterday," he said, "from
Harry Jackson over at Fort Craig."

At the sound of the sheriff's voice, McPherson was elated
and relieved. The unbridled ecstasy he heard, whatever might
be its cause, couldn't come from what had happened in the
plaza. This was something new and different. Corey Lane was
trying to contain himself, like a man who has been told he
has won a king's ransom in a lottery, and who won't let belief
quite take hold of him until the treasure is in his hand, but
who wants fortune's touch with such desperate fervor that his
joy outruns his will.

"Colonel Jackson's chief scout rode through the night to
get it to me," Corey Lane was saying. The editor had to force
his attention to the words, and away from the refrain racing
through his skull, *I was right! I was right!*

"According to Colonel Jackson—" the restraints were
still there, but slipping, slipping fast—"more than a hundred
fighting men with their women and children, mostly Mimbreños
and bronco Mescaleros, but with some Staked Plains Comanches,
too, broke out of their *ranchería* at the agency south of Zuni a
week ago!"

The afternoon wind was beginning to rise, and the caliche
dust rippled in the plaza like tiny waves on a dead gray lake.
The wind keened through the wires bracing the sign above
the Sacramento House at the corner of the square, the gusts
making the humming of them rise and fall like an orchestra
tuning up. Something, a deep bass drumming, was playing a
heavy counterpoint to the other sounds, and Jim McPherson

realized it was his beating heart, and he realized, too, that it didn't have its genesis in him—it was something he had surely caught from the great joy welling in the chest of Corey Lane. Something more was coming, something even bigger, something even the great stone-vessel body of the sheriff couldn't hold.

"They've been raiding up and down the river ever since they made their move. Bad, bloody depredations. This is easily the biggest war party since we tangled with Mangas Coloradas and Cochise seventeen years ago."

The sheriff drew a breath, a deep one, waited for a moment, and then let the last of it spill over them, the words gushing out like some wild torrent.

"And get this," Corey Lane said. "Victorio is leading them! *Victorio!*"

*"He is a lion
That I am proud to hunt."*

III

Back in his office after the conference with Corey Lane and Sam Riordan and the others, Jim McPherson took a blank sheet of copy paper from the sheaf on the rolltop desk. The words were there all right, but he couldn't get them down. It was as when he was a child back in Puckett's Corners, New York State, on those bright summer days when he would lie belly-down on the grassy bank of Gill's Run, trying to catch just one of the minnows which gathered not ten inches beneath his nose. It should have been easy, the way the schools hung quivering above the sunlit pebbled bottom, jammed together as thickly as the herring salted in the barrel at Jones's store, but the most careful or daring scoops of his hands, slow or sudden—it made no difference—would scatter the dark darting slivers in a silent and shadowy explosion, and he would come up with nothing.

Well, the words floating in the half-light of the little office were like that, and, as with those long-ago minnows, he had no net to gather them.

And he should write *something*. What he had witnessed in the square two hours ago, and what he had heard in the sheriff's office, was the stuff of legend, the kind of story Jim McPherson had dreamed about when he left the East for a climate dry enough to cure the borderline consumption that had laid him low in raw, damp, gray New York. Instead, he had filled the columns of the *Chupadera County News* with church socials and legislative records, nothing more heart-stirring than the odd wedding or obituary or cattle auction or

any of the other dull if lovingly worded dribblings he was
half-sure no one really read. The worst of it was: out here
where "men were men," the unrelieved diet of beef and
beans meant there weren't even any fish to wrap in the paper
he labored so feverishly to bring out every Thursday afternoon, as if his deadlines mattered to anyone but him. At least
that much use could be made of the *New York Sun*—where
he'd actually gotten three bylines before his health sent him
West—even on the dreariest, most uneventful day.

Now his big story had burst on him with all the incan-
descence of the fireworks display at Battery Park last Fourth,
and he couldn't find the words to get it down on paper.
Outsider that he still felt (hell, *knew*) himself to be here in
Black Springs, the things he thought today, and *could* find
words for, would likely result in his being laughed right out
of town by the simple, honest, tough, far from stupid but
manifestly unsophisticated folk who made up the subscription
list of the *Chupadera County News*, circulation four hundred
and eighty-seven. He smiled bitterly at the thought that the
sheriff's arrival, late as it was, had probably kept him from
losing a monstrous fraction of that precious circulation at one
bloody stroke.

Outside, he could see that the inevitable afternoon wind
was blowing unchecked through the deserted plaza. Its hot
spring breath had peeled enough gypsum from the flats west
of town to fill the air so thickly it seemed as if the pure
peerless New Mexico sky had become a clouded overcast.
Tumbleweeds, great, round, bushy juggernauts, were chasing each other through the square with startling regularity,
and across the way the sign which had hung so motionless at
noon was swinging rapidly back and forth, buffeted by the
wind the way some Fancy Dan boxer hammered the light bag
at O'Ryan's gym on 37th Street.

Even above the wind's howl he could hear the lengths of
chain which held the sign creaking against the rusty eyebolts
in the rough-hewn *vigas*. It was as if they were giving voice
to the dim legend on the sign itself, making sure that those
who couldn't read (there were enough of *them* in this be-
nighted town) would have no doubt who held sway in this
suddenly forlorn and, for the moment, empty crossroads,
shrieking over and over again, in maddening repetition, *"Corey*

Lane, Sheriff . . . Corey Lane, Sheriff . . . Corey Lane, Sheriff."

Corey Lane! Something nagged at McPherson's memory as he thought of the sight of the tall lawman riding into the plaza in the broiling sun of noon after firing that single warning shot—and then imperiously quenching the flames licking at the very structure of the town itself. Quenching? Bad metaphor that, the editor thought. *Quenching* wasn't any part of it. The sheriff had put the fire out with an even more consuming backfire of his own. And hadn't McPherson seen all this, or a scene very like it, once before? Yes. It was when the doddering old drama critic on the *Sun* had slipped McPherson two free tickets to the theater and he'd taken his Brooklyn landlady's daughter to see the great Booth. In the opening sequence of the play, the actor, in a flowing toga, had harangued a Roman mob and driven them from the stage like the wind which was sweeping the tumbleweeds across the plaza. McPherson shook his head. On second thought, this wasn't the same at all. For one thing, no matter *how* Booth had created the magic of near-reality behind the flickering oil-lamp footlights that enchanted night, it was only drama, *play-acting.* Jim had been able to forget what he'd seen the moment the curtain closed, turning his full attention on the simpering, unlettered, but oh, so willing charmer in the seat beside him. What he saw in the square today was *real,* and, too, the turbulent bombast, the raging brutal poetry the tragedian had unleashed to defeat *his* enemies, had little in common with the understated detonation of Corey Lane's "Go home!" Still and all, the effect on the sullen men of Black Springs and the Concho—and by association on McPherson, too—had been remarkably the same. The fight with Will-Ed Martin was over now. Or was it? No matter. The proud, ruthless man now planning a more important battle in the office across the way would doubtless crush the next attempt on the rancher's dam with the same haughty ease when and if it came.

Well, even if McPherson's heart bled for the gut-justice of the cause of Eloy Montoya and cantankerous Granby Stafford, there was no doubt in McPherson's mind that the problem of this Victorio was paramount. McPherson's blood raced, thinking of the name, not even having to hear it aloud, and the fear came again as it had when Corey Lane had breathed it out so passionately. The fear wasn't even connected with the Apache leader, actually. The first tremor had come when the editor grasped the almost erotic rapture with which the lawman spoke the Indian's name.

Corey Lane had motioned them all to seats—there weren't enough chairs, but McPherson found an old wooden box —once they were inside the office.

"Is he headed our way, Corey?" Sam Riordan asked.

"Don't know yet, Sam," Lane said. "I hope so." It had the breathless fervor of a prayer, and McPherson felt his stomach churn.

"Wasn't Victorio with Mangas and Cochise back at Apache Pass, Sheriff Lane?" Jacky Jameson asked.

"Yes." Something dreamlike came into the lawman's eyes. "He was a great warrior even then. He's older now, of course, nearly fifty, I guess, but still strong as a buffalo and even smarter than he was. From what Harry Jackson says, he's a lot better armed now, too. Instead of those old Henry repeaters he used to get in trade from the Mexicans, he's somehow gotten hold of brand-new Winchesters, and plenty of them. What's more, word is he's trailing three horses for every one his men are riding—so he'll be traveling fast, no matter where he's going."

"Corey—" Sam Riordan's voice was mock plaintive— "how come you didn't spill this out when you rode into town today? I like to had a heart attack when you faced that crowd out there. They would have gone away meek and mild if you'd told them about all this. Not that they didn't anyway, but it would have been a whole lot nicer if—"

"Because," Lane broke in, "this news had absolutely nothing to do with that out there. They were about to break the law, and *that* had to be settled first."

The editor glanced at Montoya and Stafford, and saw Granby wince, while the Concho man actually smiled a little. When McPherson looked back at the sheriff, he saw that Lane, too, had picked up the smile on Eloy's face and was answering it with a strange look of his own, one filled with respect, but it was the respect one gives a potential enemy. McPherson wondered if he could have faced it back with anything like the farmer's coolness or if he would have worn the lingering, wan look of defeat Granby Stafford still wore, in spite of the new turn of events in the sheriff's office.

"Governor Wallace," Corey Lane said, "is sending some major down here with a couple of troops of horse militia, volunteers, although what good they'll be if Victorio gets into the Oscuras is beyond me. All the regular cavalry is west of the Rio Grande, played out and needing remounts. Pity they can't *steal* horses from the Mexicans like Victorio can. What it amounts to is that we've got to raise our own force, keep track of the Apache until those Santa Fe soldiers get here, and then hit him hard." Corey Lane's hands were flat on the top of his desk, hands strong enough and big enough to choke a steer, McPherson thought, and yet with the strange look of delicacy he had seen when the lawman made that frightening half-reach for his gun in the center of the plaza. A pulse was visible between the thumb and forefinger of the right one, and it rose and fell as the sheriff talked. "I rode out over the *malpais* at first light today," Lane went on, "trying to cut some sign. My guess is Victorio—if he comes our way, and that does make sense—will be so full of beans he won't be *hiding*. I thought maybe he might have outriders ahead of him, but I didn't see a thing. I left that half-Zuni wrangler of mine, Mike Calico, camped between the two main water trails across the lava beds. He's got a second pony with him, so he can ride one clear to death if he has to come in fast with any news." He stopped and looked at his listeners. "Sam," he said next, "I'd appreciate it if you'd ride up to Sin Creek and break the news to Will-Ed and the rest of them. Bring them in. We'll need every gunhand up there. Tell them their dam will be as safe as if it was in God's pocket until we look after this." He looked at the merchant and the Concho farmer. "Won't it?" It wasn't exactly a question.

Granby nodded weakly. Eloy's calm, brown face didn't betray a thing, but the editor wasn't worried. Something told him Montoya wasn't the type to stab anybody in the back.

"Corey—" It was Granby Stafford. Speaking seemed an effort for him now. "What can *we* do, us folk here in town, and Eloy's people?"

Corey Lane raised his head and looked at Stafford as though it pained him. Then he shook his head from side to side. "I don't want your people, Granby," he said at last.

"What?" Stafford was bewildered.

"I don't want them."

McPherson was staggered, but he got the full implication

of the refusal through his head even before the sheriff began
again. "If they can't stand up to one lone man, they'd never
last a second with Victorio and his *fighting* men."

In the silence McPherson could hear the wind beginning
to pick up speed outside.

Sam Riordan coughed. "Guess I'd better hightail it out of
here and see Will-Ed and the others. Don't suppose"—he
looked wistfully at Corey Lane—"I got time to stop in the
cantina for a snort or two?"

"I don't suppose so, Sam." Lane said. His face broke into
the first real smile since they'd all gathered in the office. As if
on signal, Jacky Jameson and Bill Talley began grinning, too.
The editor wasn't sure whether it was at the slight anguish on
the old rancher's face or at the harrowed discomfort and
shame on that of Granby Stafford.

Outside, McPherson had stood on the porch with Granby
and Montoya, and watched Riordan hurry through the smoky
dust of the plaza to where his horse was hitched.

"Eloy," Stafford had said, "how come I can know I'm
dead right and still that man can make me feel but two inches
high and wrong as wrong can be?"

Montoya had shrugged. " *Vanidad!* Pride, *señor.* This
Lane has enough of it to fill the Ojos Negros five times over.
It will bring him low someday. Perhaps we shall have to help
it, but not quite yet. All things go his way—*por el momento.*"

Jim McPherson crumpled the unstained sheet of copy paper and hurled it with all his force at the window of his office.
The wad made only half the distance, fluttering to the floor in
an erratic arc, leaving him frustrated again and feeling foolish
that he'd spoiled a perfectly good sheet of paper.

Hell, if he *could* write this, who would he write it *for?*
As always, when he tried to picture his audience, the craggy
good-humored face of Sam Riordan came to mind. Old Sam
wouldn't begin to fathom his words if he wrote of the pride
and passion of Corey Lane in the way he wanted to, and if he
spilled it out bluntly enough for the rancher to grasp his
meaning, the good old cowman might fortify himself enough
at the Sacramento to march into the office and set in motion
the time-honored tradition of horse-whipping the editor. He
smiled. *Serve me right, at that.* Sam Riordan had befriended
him before anyone else in Black Springs. No fool on almost

any other matter, Sam had a blind spot where Corey was concerned, something which had wormed its way into the editor's thinking in subtle ways for weeks now. An attack on Corey, however mild, would be like an attack on Sam.

So much for the editor's vaunted neutrality and journalist's detachment. He wasn't much of a newspaperman after all, it seemed. First he'd wanted to throw his support behind today's protest and had neatly, conveniently, effectively talked himself out of it. Now he wanted to hang the arrogance of the sheriff high enough for everyone in the county to see, and he was letting friendship for Sam talk him out of *that*. Or was it something else? Fear? Might as well be honest and admit the probability. Oh, it wouldn't be physical fear, of course. Corey Lane surely wouldn't stoop to doing violence on him; but he'd seen today how the terrible force of the lawman's contempt could reduce sturdy irascible Granby Stafford to jelly with little more than a look. Would *he* fare like that? Again—was it too much to hope that he could be something like Eloy Montoya? He was sure it was.

No, damn it! He wasn't afraid, not that afraid anyway, but he did have to know a good deal more before he wrote, and he had to go over everything he already knew about the sheriff, right from those first things Sam had told him, in the very beginning.

Riordan had been just about the first citizen Jim McPherson had met in Black Springs except for his landlady, Addie Hepburn, the rancher's widowed sister. Sam had come to call the first evening the editor spent in the house on Estancia Street, making no secret of the fact that he was there to check on the new boarder, see if his "kid sister" (she was sixty-five if a day) was safe with this foreigner, and this despite the fact that Addie looked thoroughly capable of stopping a stampede squarely in its tracks. Satisfied she was in no danger, Sam had stayed to play some chess and split the bottle of perfectly God-awful sherry Addie ferried out from the kitchen she barred to relatives and paying guests alike.

After Sam, with the white, mated on the thirty-ninth move in that first chess game (McPherson had played a diplomatically weak defense without actually *trying* to lose), the rancher had settled back with a cigar and the execrable sherry and filled the editor in on "a few of the things and people you'll have to know in order to get along in this here burg." He began with Corey Lane. The unholy light of un-questioning worship in the rancher's eyes should have given McPherson a clue right there that he wasn't getting an en-tirely objective view.

"Finest man in the territory. Watched him grow since he was born—thirty-three years ago. Swear he became a man at twelve, the very second that last shovelful of caliche covered his pa, Jason Lane. When he was sixteen—that was in '62—his ma shipped him off with us to fight Mangas Coloradas and that Chiricahua fellow, Cochise. The Army wanted to keep him out of the battle at Apache Pass, figuring him for a kid. Hell, he was leading some of their old-hand troopers before the day was out. Took three slugs and still climbed that canyon wall where this Mimbreño tiger named Victorio had a whole troop pinned down. Turned the scrap our way for keeps."

McPherson had thrilled at this. He'd have to drag more detail out of Sam someday, but right then it had seemed best just to listen quietly.

"Then the Civil War got hot here in the territory, and Corey signed on for a while with Chivington and his Colorado bunch. Collected enough medals at Glorieta they had to cart them out to his ma at the X-Bar-7 in a Wells Fargo box. Fought at Val Verde with Canby, too. Might have made a career of soldiering, but he got plain disgusted after the California column took over and Carleton's bluecoats mur-dered old Mangas at Fort McLean when he was a helpless prisoner. Cut out for home quick, then."

At this, McPherson couldn't wait to set eyes on the paragon Sam was describing.

"Corey came back and ranched the Lane place hard as hell until seven years ago, when some of us ranchers talked him into running for sheriff of Chupadera County. Won hands down. Mite closer three years ago." Riordan had chuckled then. "Don't suppose he'll make it next time out. He's ridden hard on some of the folk in town, but, by God, he's given us law and order, even though I don't think he's ever drawn that Peacemaker Special of his seriously."

McPherson met the sheriff the very next day. It was hard to find in him the man Sam had described.

The editor had spent a lot of time with Sam Riordan, whose small ranch was almost out of business now. With the seventy-year-old's wife dead a dozen years, and with Riordan's one married daughter moved up to Colorado, the rancher spent most of his time drinking cheap bar whiskey in Black Springs. McPherson soon learned that things weren't as happy in the seemingly well-run town, whose "pipsqueak of a mayor" never ventured into any controversy. The mayor spent most of his time in Santa Fe, trying to wangle a job with the Territorial administration. That didn't help with the trouble brewing between the cattlemen with their demands for even more land and water on the one hand, and the merchants, who, with the farmers of the nearby Concho, worried about equally vital needs. Sam, although his whole workaday past here meant that he had to keep at least one of his pigeon-toed booted feet in the camp of Will-Ed Martin and the ranchers, was as fair-minded as he was good-humored, and the editor relied more and more, as he settled in, on the old timer's background and saddlebag of gossip for the news stories and strong editorials he'd fully intended to write for the paper he'd spent every last cent of his New York savings on.

He blushed now in the accusing silence of the office as he faced the truth of the matter. Oh, he'd *touched* on the troubles in Black Springs (maybe "skirted" them was a better way of putting it), but there hadn't been more than a hint of the things which really should be said.

He blushed, too, at the memory of how Sam had saved him from deep embarrassment just one week after he'd met Corey Lane. He'd been in the dry-goods store, ordering shirts more serviceable than the ruffled dress ones he'd brought west with him, when he discovered, standing next to him, the most incredibly stunning young woman he'd ever seen.

She'd smiled easily at him, and although Jim McPherson had no illusions regarding his attractiveness to women, his heart had thumped wildly, the surge of blood making him bolder and suddenly more confident than he could ever re-member being. It had been a long time since he'd been with a woman, and nothing he'd seen so far in Black Springs had made him count the days. Even the youngest women in town—once they were out of pigtails—dressed in the same sacklike Mother Hubbards, their plain weathered faces shad-owed under the brims of monotonously identical poke bon-nets. The striking creature standing at the counter with him wore a black, broad-brimmed, flat-crowned hat of the Spanish riding style, with a band studded with turquoise and a small but jaunty feather in it. Under a trimly tailored buckskin jacket he could see a cream-colored blouse cut excitingly deeper than any he'd seen in town. Surely the smile wasn't enough to go on, but in a sudden rush of desire he'd easily convinced himself that the two of them must have much in common. An insane wish to run his hands through the thick dark hair under the smart hat was easy enough to check—after all, he *was* a civilized adult; but a search of the smoothly tanned face, open and friendly in the extreme, had him on the point of extending some kind of invitation which would have revealed his intentions and his feelings clearly. Luckily, before he'd made a complete fool of himself (the look on his face surely had that process under way already) Sam Riordan appeared at his elbow.

"Virgie," Riordan had said, "I don't think you've met our new editor yet. Jim McPherson . . . Mrs. Corey Lane."

They'd chatted for a few minutes about things whose details McPherson couldn't remember in the slightest, with Sam, of course, doing most of the talking. When Virgie Lane had made her purchase, nodded goodbye, and left the store, Sam and the editor had gone to the Sacramento for a drink. Sam had begun to laugh. "I saw that look in your eye, Sonny Jim. Better remember that Virgie Lane is a *very* happily married woman." Sam had taken another belt of the rotgut which passed for whiskey and laughed again. "I sympathize with you—from memory. Reckon the only thing a young fellow can do, with the situation on worthwhile females in these parts being what it is, is to take himself and his problem up to Santa Fe or down to El Paso from time to time— along with *mucho dinero* and a damned strong stomach."

Well, he hadn't needed any introduction to Alicia Lane, Corey's mother.

He knew who the fierce spare woman was the first time he'd set eyes on her. She had the same hunting-hawk look of her son and, small as she was, the same look of incendiary pride and strength. When she came to town to market, she disdained the buggy or the buckboard the other ranch ladies favored. Alicia Lane handled the big mare she rode as well as any man, for all that she sat it sidesaddle, her white hands delicate on the reins, deceptively delicate in the same way Corey's were. Alicia? He hadn't called her that, and likely never would. The only soul he knew who used "Alicia" instead of a very respectful "Mrs. Lane" was Sam Riordan, and McPherson was sure he'd heard something tentative in the rancher's voice when he did.

In her dealings with the people of Black Springs the older woman showed her contempt for all of them even less subtly than did her son. It was a more general contempt than Corey's, too, one which didn't discriminate in any way among the different skins or languages, or among the different levels of what might loosely be called society in the town. Ranchers, farmers, merchants, the pastor of the one church, even the harried little mayor, Wilson Blaine—she seemed to despise them all. It struck McPherson as strange that he never heard a word of criticism of Alicia Lane for this—until he realized that, for some unexplained reason, *he* couldn't bring himself to dislike the woman. He guessed it was the fact that her patent arrogance was a thing apart, an unreasonable and therefore paradoxically accepted pride of *being*, not one of mere fortune or even accomplishment. It was easy to see in her the woman who had "shipped" her only son off to fight the Indians.

If it had only been that easy to "see" the son who had apparently gone to war so gladly.

It was almost pitch-dark in the office now, but the plaza was glowing golden from the slanted rays of the setting sun. The wind had stopped, and the sign on the sheriff's office was hanging motionless again. The sky outside must have cleared to the deep gradients of turquoise McPherson, even in his darkest moods, felt made his self-exile from the more stimulating city worth almost any amount of loneliness.

He saw the two deputies leave and walk across the plaza. The light in the sheriff's office was on. Corey Lane must still be at *his* desk, too. McPherson should touch a match to his own oil lamp and get about the business of writing. There was enough time before supper to get a few rough paragraphs on paper, then stop at the Sacramento for a quick drink and see if Sam had come down the mountain from Sin Creek yet. The old rancher would need a drink badly after his ride. His weekend diversion was now half a day behind schedule.

Then McPherson saw the light in the sheriff's office go

out. A few moments later Corey Lane emerged, locked the door behind him, and stepped to the front of the porch.

The sun hit the lawman's figure directly and with all its force, and if he had seemed golden when he rode into the plaza at noon, now he fairly glittered. He looked westward, his eyes narrowed against the glare, unreadable slits at any distance, impossible from the editor's seat here in the dark.

It wasn't the sun or the darkening western mountains Corey Lane was looking at. It was the Apache somewhere out there. Suddenly Jim McPherson knew that if he would ever understand the man he was looking at, he would have to see and understand the other, too.

". . . we shall ever strike
Till one can do no more."

IV

The man called Victorio climbed over two ridges of the black rock, and the noises of the camp were finally lost behind him. He would post lookouts after the evening meal, but now he wanted to make the first survey by himself—and in silence. His legs ached from the long ride, and walking the uneven ground would help to pull the knots from them. He grunted. There had never been any aches back in the days when he'd ridden with Mangas, but since then he had taken three wounds in those scarred legs, two from bullets (one was still stubbornly trying to kill him after all these years) and one from a saber cut. Even better than the other wounds, he remembered how that one had come. Sometimes at night, when sleep came hard, he would summon up the face of the soldier with the long, gleaming blade, and he could drift away easily, seeing again the look of the man, the blue-eyed disbelief as the lance had run a bloody tunnel through his chest. That had been a splendid fight. Better far than all this thundering nonsense they had to make with guns. The sharp, cutting sword and the long, true, bright-beaded, feathered lance made the combat and the good quick killing at the end as close and hot as the first time he had taken the woman, in the sweaty heat of that marriage wicki-up back at Ojo Caliente so long ago. He smiled. There was never any need to conjure up the woman to get to sleep. She was still with him, and always there. To him she was everything and nothing, which-ever one he needed, and with an instinct that never failed to tell her which way to be. That was why he had never gone with any other, not one of his many captives, nor any of the Chiricahua girls nor the ripe Pinal maidens the other young men chased laughing through the *bosques* in the long summer nights, not even in the times she carried the seven children, of whom only the one strong boy, man now, and the stunted girl with the crazy distant smile were left. The other men had laughed at his fidelity when he was young. It hadn't bothered him then, and didn't now.

The woman would come soon, when his food was ready. She would pad through the rocks behind him like a mountain cat, and would hold her face away from him in silence while he ate. Then, when he nodded, they would talk. Until he was ready she would be that nothing which gave him space to think. Then, when he signaled, she would become everything, as she always did, and they would sit together and talk a little while the hot wind died and the sun sank behind them.

He wouldn't touch her, not here or in the shelter she would have built by now. If his loins turned to flame, he wouldn't touch her. Even though the camp was resting now without an enemy within a half-day's ride, they were still at war, on the raid—the longest he had ever led—and to touch her before the raid was over would bring medicine as bad as the black-green bile which bubbled from the horses they had killed this morning, the used-up animals they had ridden until their hoofs had splintered like yucca spikes.

He wondered if he would *ever* know that bow-strong body that way again. This raid, as well as being the longest, might very well be the last, one that would end for him in death. Death, of course, was not bad medicine. It wasn't medicine at all if it came quickly and cleanly—in a battle.

But that was enough of this blanket-headed thinking. If a man, a war leader, crowded his head with the past, the almost forgotten fights and, yes, with the woman, too, none of the things which should get done would even be begun. He must plan the rifle pits, pick a better place for the extra horses the women and children had brought into the camp in the train of the mounted warriors. If they kept them in the deep, narrow, box-ended arroyo where they were now, there would be no way to get them out if an attack came and it went badly for them and they had to run for it.

All in all, though, he was satisfied with this camp. There

was only the one likely way anyone could come upon them: they would have to ride across the table-flat alkali wastes which stretched away from the *malpais* to the north and west as far as even the keenest young eyes among his scouts could see. Unless they walked them (and what white man would ever show the patience *that* demanded?) their horses couldn't set hoof in that sea of chalky dust without spewing up a cloud seen long before they could reach the slopes beneath the camp. He could place his men the way he wanted them with deliberate calm, avoiding the rush which might cause mistakes.

If a small force came, he could hold them off forever (he had water, and that alone would make forever come very soon for the attackers), and even should they number twice or three times the men he led, he could retreat up the mountainside from pit to pit, sneak his riflemen through the deep rock scars one by one until all had topped the high saddle in the range behind them, keeping the hot thirsty enemy pinned down on the searing flats below. Maybe, if the soldiers were as foolish as they usually were, they would have ridden, with their simple-minded courage, right to the very edge of battle, bringing their horses within the range of his new fast-shooting guns. He could kill some of the horses first, before the white man who was their chief ordered them taken to the rear. Then he could slip his band over the saddle to where their own fresh ponies waited. The women and children, pack-animals, and riderless spare mounts would be long gone by then, and once the warriors were in the saddle or on their riding-blankets and their horses' bellies were awash with water, he would salt the sweet spring, ruin it for his enemies, and wave his men down the trail to yet another camp.

Ah, but if there were *two* armies after him, and if one of them was even now gaining the pass to the west he had seen when they came riding in, and if they were circling even now at their leisure to block his planned escape—what then? Very simply, he would die. It would happen this way someday, somewhere, why not here? No shame to die except through carelessness.

He was content. Nothing had been forgotten. He smiled. Even death itself must be considered part of his careful plan.

"*Como está, mi esposo?*" It was the woman, with his meal. She had come up so quietly behind him he hadn't heard her, and for an instant he felt alarm that his senses had betrayed him, even if his perch on the rocks was so completely safe. He growled and then hoped she wouldn't think the irritation in his voice was meant for her. It was good she had remembered to speak to him in Spanish. A week ago, when they began these frenzied rides, he had given orders that the hated language was the only one they would use until the day came that the fighting ended for a while. It would go some small way toward wiping out the differences between his own Mimbreños with their Mescalero cousins, and the maverick Comanches and Navajos who had joined them after their midnight flight from the agency.

He ate from the tin plate which had been issued to him at one of the forts before this last one, sometime so far back in one of the tortured journeys the soldiers had forced them on he couldn't exactly remember where or when. The meat was stringy, tough, and tasted of the thin bitter grass the cow had fed on before they had run it off from that small *estancia* north of Fort Craig, where it had taken them half the morning to storm the adobe house and kill the Mexican rancher. The wife had been so old and fat none of the warriors had wanted her, and even the women had decided against taking her for a slave. There had been no children at the *estancia*, and it was just as well. If they were returning to some secure established *ranchería*, young captives for slaves or ransom would be good, but on the march like this—no. The wife had shrieked herself into such a state they couldn't be sure she wasn't truly crazy, and they had let her live. They had ridden off with her screams still white in the air, and from some distance out they could see her racing wildly around the house, whose ceiling and roof smoked against the blue sky from the fire that Mescalero fool Nariz Roto had set before they could see if there was anything inside worth taking.

A sack of corn would have been good, or flour, or a squash or two. It would be good to have something to eat besides this strong sour meat. For more than a week now he had had nothing but beef or venison or mule, and he could smell his own powerful stink high above even that of all the others in the band. Still, a man could not sneer at fortune. He remembered too many rides in the past where all they had had for days was roots, or only the same weak grass this cow had chewed.

He handed the tin plate to the woman when he finished,

and stood up and stretched the last of the day's kinks out of his legs and trunk. The time for talking would begin now, and he must be very careful to play their game by the rules which had worked so well since he bought her from her people at Cañada Alamosa so long ago.

He wouldn't ask her any questions, and she wouldn't give advice—not in words. To take counsel from a woman was a taboo so powerful that breaking it would cost him the respect of every warrior in the band, and very likely his place as leader, too. It wasn't that he wanted the leadership as much as he had when he was young, but who else was there? The wise sturdy son, the one the white men called Washington after some long-dead chief of theirs, was languishing at the agency near Horse Springs under the watchful eyes of so many troopers he couldn't put his nose outside his wicki-up without an escort sticking as close as wood ticks. Nana and Loco (even if he could somehow spirit them out of the clutches of the agent Russell up at Stanton) wouldn't do, the one too old and the other too often given to acting like his name. Well, perhaps Nana; what he lacked in strength now he made up in shrewdness. Maybe Nana.

No, for a while *he* must lead. Nothing could be allowed to weaken his grip on what might be the last set of reins. His talk with the woman must be guarded. Honor demanded that his behavior be impeccable whether anyone else was there to witness it or not.

"Some of the warriors back at the fire," the woman said, "say that Victorio sees ghosts, that no one rides from that way." She pointed east, and his eyes followed. There was still one lingering snowfield on the summit of Sierra Blanca, the great mountain which leaned over the agency where most of the Mescaleros still fattened on the agent's beef, all struggle given up. The snowfield was beginning to redden in the low-angled rays of the sun sliding down beyond the mountain wall behind them, but it seemed more of a reflection of the flame which touched his cheeks. Yes, he could have guessed they would question his prediction. They had ridden south all day with that emptiness stretching away on their left all the way to the other range of mountains. Except for the dust-devils which whirled in before the general wind picked up just as they reached this camp, not a thing had moved. There had only been that one small glint of light coming from the

dead lava-flow lying along the valley bottom like a sunning
snake, monstrous, black, endless miles long. Someone there
had watched their progress, perhaps had even watched long
enough to see them settle here.

"Some of them must think the leader right." It was a
statement, not a question.

"Most of them," she said, "and even the doubters think
Victorio wise to be so careful.

"Then," he said, "they will fight well."

Little by little he drew her out about a number of things
which had to be considered: the mood of the women and
children as well as the men; the state of health of every
member of the band; the level of food supplies; and when
they would have to begin the raids again; and all of this by
long-practiced indirection. He would talk, watching her, and
she would nod or just look wooden—never saying "No" to
him.

One thing on his mind would not come out in words,
even though she knew about *it*, too.

His eyes traveled from the twin summit cones of the
white mountain piercing half the sky, scanned the lesser
peaks to the north of it, and jumped over the wide-topped V
of the Concho Valley, fifty or sixty miles to the north and
east, to the huge bulk of slab-sided Cuchillo Peak, not as
towering as Sierra Blanca with its two high summits, but just
as imposing in its lower snow-free blackness. Under its massive brow was the town, and somewhere just this side of the
town was the sprawling *estancia* of the man who *would* come
after him, no matter what the young men said, if not tomorrow, someday soon.

"*Qué pasa, mi esposo?*" the woman said. Had his face
given away enough for *anyone* to see, or just for her?

"*Nada, mujer.*" His reply was foolishness. It wasn't *nothing*
and she knew it.

For seventeen years he had thought about the man who
would soon come riding out of that dark valley on the hunt
for him, the young white chief who had made such a big
difference for the troopers in the battle at the pass. He had
seen him four—no, it must be five—times since that first day
when he had surrendered to him without a word, only pointing to the many dead warriors lying like broken pots around
him. The next sight had been during the "time of shame"

when the soldiers from the land beyond the deserts to the west had murdered great Mangas in the fort and even mighty Cochise had been helpless to take revenge. The young white man, Lane, had aided the other bluecoats in restraining him and the few others who had tried to fight, but the young chief's disgust for his fellow white men was plain to see.

Another time, two or three years after that it must have been, Lane had driven a small herd of provision cattle into the agency at Selden when the Mimbreños had been quartered there before the bad marches, sometimes in shackles, to San Carlos and all the other foul places they had been sent over the years he wished to forget but couldn't. Lane had refused to leave his beef in the care of the cheating agent, but had herded his stock right into the encampment and stayed to watch it divided among the people. It was a fine thing to do, and all the Mimbres people—Victorio, too—would have made much of him, but he hadn't gotten off his horse, hadn't smiled, hadn't allowed himself to be approached. He had just looked at them with those terrible hot blue eyes as if measuring them all, and Victorio in particular, against the day when the blood would run again.

He had been clean-shaven then, and his corn-yellow hair had curled out under his hat, framing a face burned as dark as any Mimbreño's, the mouth a straight hard cut under a well-shaped nose. The mustache he had worn in the three times they had seen each other since hid the firmness of the mouth with its faint look of cruelty, but nothing could hide the eyes. They weren't the cold empty blue of those of other white men; there was something burning about them, like certain sky-stones, a look of hot pride so intense it was hard to believe one man could hold it all.

And there was a little something wild and restless about him, too, as if this fat easy time of peace sat uncomfortably on the strong wide shoulders.

They had never spoken together, not so much as a single word. When this white chief and he had words for each other—he had thought this many times—they would come as battle cries. One of them was the bringer of the other's death. He knew this better than any shaman knows these things. Enough. Thinking of this man too much before they met would do no good.

"Now, woman," he said, still looking to the darkness

across the basin floor, "it is time to go back to camp and send the lookouts to their places."

Almost reluctantly he took his eyes from the place in the distance the man with the blue burning eyes would come from.

"To a cruel war I sent him, from whence he returned, his brows bound with oak."

V

"Can I get you another cup of coffee, Mr. McPherson?" Virgie Lane said. The editor shook his head carefully, as if in fear something in his stiff neck would crack. The younger woman was trying, despite her own obvious tension, to put him at ease, but Jim knew it wouldn't work—not as long as that fierce haughty-faced old empress Alicia was in the same room with the two of them. Then he thought, ruefully, of the quite different nervousness he would be feeling if she weren't.

Good Lord! As a green repotter on the *Sun* he had interviewed the New York City police commissioner with a good deal less thumping in his chest, and he didn't even have to write a story about *this* talk, not yet anyway.

The feeling of coming up short had been there all the way out on the long ride from Black Springs to ask Corey Lane's permission to tag along on the expedition going after Victorio next week. It had mounted alarmingly when he rode into the compound of the X-Bar-7 and found a ranch entirely different from any he had yet seen in the basin grasslands.

It wasn't sumptuous or grand; in fact, it was almost classic in its simplicity. Adobe walls, plastered smooth by hands more severe than loving, were almost devoid of windows. There were just a few long narrow ones set high under the pointed *vigas* jutting out from below the straight roofline like gigantic spears, the unbroken expanse making the façade appear even more massive and monolithic than it was, and more closely rooted to the hard stony ground. Certainly it was an *hacienda*, and certainly Latin in every respect, but to

44

the editor it seemed more Roman than Spanish and much more fortress than dwelling-place.

Everything about the house turned inward, and it made him wonder more about the lord of this citadel, and about the two women who were its ladies, when he was ushered into the room where they sat, needlework in Virgie's lap and, improbably, in Alicia's, too.

He felt that Alicia Lane viewed him with that same disdain he'd seen her display toward the people in Black Springs when she came to town. She tipped her head back and gazed at him down the length of the nose so much like her son's. The nose wasn't all she shared with him, either. Perhaps it was just as well Corey wasn't there, Maybe he wasn't ready for the two of them together yet.

The "sneer of cold command" was on her face, too, but, like her son, she was no Ozymandias. There were no signs of ruin on those fine sharp features, and certainly none of the "despair" Shelley's glum colossus prophesied.

"My son," she said, when the editor had settled himself on the very edge of a gigantic hide-covered armchair, "will be home in about an hour, Mr. McPherson. I suppose you'll want to wait." *She supposes nothing of the kind,* Jim thought. He knew an order when he heard it. *My son,* In all the talk that followed, that was about the only way Alicia Lane ever referred to the man they waited for, the possessiveness in her voice raising the level of it almost to the cry of an eagle. For a moment he couldn't figure out quite why she should be so determined that he wait, but a deeper assessment, once he had gotten over his first awe, reminded him that he was, after all, a newsman and had some slight value to this astonishing Amazon and her pride. That she didn't care for him much or rate him very highly remained as plain, though.

"If it's any of my business, and *please* just tell me if it isn't," Virgie Lane said then, "what was it you wanted to see Corey about, Mr. McPherson?" Oh, what a difference here. The voice was gentle but not at all timid, and the editor almost blushed at the warmth invested in the "Mr. McPherson." Jim eased back into the big armchair, suddenly comfortable.

"I wanted to ask the sheriff if I could go with him next week, Mrs. Lane."

The older woman's frost seemed to thaw a little, and a

tiny careful smile appeared on her lips. *Well, there's a point for my side*, Jim thought. Obviously she had dismissed him as an all-out gunshy non-combatant, and probably a coward and weakling in the bargain. If she only knew how close to right she was, she would have him out the door before the coffee Virgie had asked the Mexican maid to bring could reach a boil.

Now the chill seemed to have shifted from Alicia's face to Virgie's, but something told him it had nothing to do with *him*, only with what he'd said. She was afraid, and the particular kind of fear he saw behind the sudden cold told him something else as well. He hadn't seen Virgie Lane and her husband together since he'd been in Black Springs, but he didn't have to now in order to know how much she loved him, and how deeply the prospect of the looming war terrified her.

"For God's sake, get that look off your pretty face, Virgie!" Alicia said.

Jim was surprised to discover that this high-handed demi-harridan could display something so close to sensitive awareness. It would never pay to underestimate Alicia Lane, that was clear, and it was clear, too, that if he would ever know the son, he would have to know the mother first, almost as much as he would have to know the Apache. He wondered what it might be like if the sheriff ever slipped the bonds of self-restraint which girded him like armor. What kind of rage could storm forth then? The thing in the plaza Saturday hadn't been the final test, not by half.

He pushed these considerations away when Virgie spoke again.

"I know you won't have it, mother," she said, "but Corey says this will most likely be a bad, *bad* war. A lot of men will die, maybe Corey."

"Not *my son*." *Oh, yes*, Jim thought, *they've been down this road together many times*. What amazed him was that the younger woman, for all her seeming mildness, showed not the slightest sign of being affected by her mother-in-law. On second thought, he realized his amazement was far from justified. Of *course* Corey Lane wouldn't have married a woman who couldn't face up to life on terms he could deem acceptable. Still, the fear was there. For Corey. A little sadness welled up inside the editor. There were times, during and since the cavernous emptiness of New York, when he'd worked his beat at night, that he had felt real loneliness, but not like now. Could there ever be a woman like this for him?

"If Will-Ed and the other men going out weren't such Indian-haters, mother," Virgie said, "and if they didn't always push Corey to the front so much, it might be different. Somehow they'll make him do more than he should, take chances that might—"

"That's the way it *should* be!" Alicia snapped. "Not one of them's got a smack of sense compared to *my son,* not Will-Ed Martin nor the other ranchers—and particularly not that tin soldier from Santa Fe. Corey will *have* to do the leading, and most of the fighting, too. I wouldn't have it any other way."

"We're not all as immune to fear as you are, mother."

The powerful charge which had come into the air seemed to ebb a little then, and it gave the editor enough ease to take his first real look around the room. At first glance it had seemed intimate enough, but on closer inspection it revealed itself to be as austere as had the outside of the house. Only the warm presence of Virgie Lane, he decided, could account for that first impression.

The walls were bone-white and free of any kind of adornment except for a faded Spanish tapestry hanging above a wooden chest scrolled with the same crude carving he'd seen in the old mission church in Black Springs. Across from that, facing the chair he sat in, an arched fireplace scalloped the other wall like a gaping mouth. A wide window looked out over a patio locked on every side by the house itself, and above the flat roof opposite this sitting-room section he could see the blue knife-sharp ridge of Cuchillo Peak, actually some twenty miles away but seeming to thrust toward them with much the same tension he had felt in the room when he entered it. The light from the window washed over the wall above the fireplace, and it was there he saw the very heart of the home of Corey Lane. An Indian shield, the leather still tight as a drum, but with the earth colors dimmed to just a memory, and the design laced through with the faint blue veins or arteries of the long-dead buffalo, was crossed by a heavy wooden-shafted lance with a long rusted iron point like an excrescent fang.

"The shield's Apache—Chiricahua," Alicia said, "but the lance is Spanish." She must have been following his eyes everywhere. "My son took it from a chief in the fight at the pass." She surprised him with a laugh. "Corey had just begun to shave when that happened." The laughter stopped. "That war chief must have taken it from some Spaniard—anyway *they're* both dead and *my son's alive.*"

That last must have been for the benefit of Virgie. Sure enough, the younger woman answered.

"All I want is a husband, not a hero, mother," she said, "and a father for little Corey." There was no whimper in her voice, just a level assertion of her feelings. Jim felt they must have forgotten he was in the room when Alicia turned to her daughter-in-law, her slate-blue eyes suddenly glowing coals.

"That's nonsense, Virgie!" Her voice was piercing, a half-controlled low shriek—but the younger woman didn't flinch. "If my son were my husband, I'd a damned sight rather have him off rounding up this savage than home in bed with me, and make no mistake, I loved Jason Lane well enough that way, too." If Virgie hadn't flinched, Jim would have at this last, or turned red at least, except that he was certain now that the two of them no longer felt him there.

"Even when he was a toddler," Alicia went on, "and everyone in town was telling me what a *sweet* child he was, as if he was some picture I could hang on a nursery wall, I was planning a day when the whole Territory would know who he was. That old bearcat Mangas solved it for me. I sent Corey off to fight him, and got him out of the clutches of the schoolmarm and those fussy old biddies at Bible class. He came back from Apache Pass, and from running down the rebels with Colonel Roberts, as full of honors as a Roman general. I was alone all the time he was away, too—Jason had been dead four long years by then—and I was alone on that trip to Santa Fe, to talk old Governor Connelly into striking that medal that's on my bedroom wall."

I was right, Jim thought. The columns of the *Chupadera County News* would be sweeter, brighter-toned trumpets for Corey's fame this time than the lone horn Alicia must have blasted into the governor's ear in Civil War Santa Fe. It wouldn't surprise him if this shrewd woman knew of his wire-service connections with the papers in New York City.

"But what if he'd been killed, mother?" Virgie asked.

The question was only a whisper, but it brought death into the room as a more real and far more palpable visitor than McPherson felt himself to be.

"Then," Alicia said, "his reputation alone would have been my son. *That would have been son enough*—and *you* know how much I love him." She meant it, every word, and Jim winced. He looked intently at Virgie, uncaring if Alicia saw it or not.

He didn't know what to make of the face he looked at. It was much the same as the one which had greeted him when he arrived, the same delicately tinted cameo, warm, soft, a different sort of stone entirely from Alicia's, one that age might firm, but never harden. Never, he was sure, had he seen beauty such as this.

Her lips parted, and she seemed about to speak, when the maid who had brought the coffee appeared in the doorway.

"*Perdón, señoras,*" the girl said, "Señora Martin has come to call."

"Val? Here?" Alicia said. She seemed surprised, more than surprised, puzzled, and Jim wondered why. Will-Ed Martin's Diamond Four ranch was even farther out from Black Springs than Corey Lane's, and visits from Val Martin on her way to or from town shouldn't be unusual.

"Show Señora Martin in, *por favor,* Maria," Virgie said. She seemed to have a question, too, on that face Jim had begun to study just before the interruption. Was he wrong, or did he also see a tiny look of alarm? "What do you suppose brings her back by here again this afternoon, mother?"

"Well, she sure wouldn't ride clear over here for a cup of sugar, not after being in town only yesterday, and if she just wants gossip, she would have stopped here then."

Even the editor could understand the reason for their wondering now. Ranch people visited long and hard. Distances in the basin were too great, and travel, even by wagon or buggy with a hired hand to do the driving, too difficult and troublesome, for women to make spur-of-the-moment calls.

A big woman, somewhere between Virgie and Alicia in age, Valerie Martin rolled into the sitting room like a rampant gingham tumbleweed. Affable and outgoing, Val was a favorite in Black Springs, even among those who opposed Will-Ed and his dam so bitterly, and Jim McPherson was no exception to the general rule. He'd enjoyed her and liked her hearty boisterousness, and was pretty sure she liked him, too, but she didn't so much as look in his direction when he rose to greet her. Then he saw that she was shaking with excitement.

"Put away that sewing, girls!" It was almost a shout. "I've got the big wagon parked outside your gate. Get some clothes together, enough for maybe a week, and I'll have Porfirio haul them out for you. And pack party dresses, too. Bet we'll have a dance or some other jollification when they all get back!"

"What on *earth* are you talking about, Valerie?" Alicia asked.

"Oh, Lord, that's right, you wouldn't know. *I'm* supposed to be the one who tells everybody out this way." She stopped for breath. "Corey and Will-Ed sent the word out to me on account of we're farthest out from town. I got to let everybody know on my way into Black Springs. Figured the three of us could ride in together, as long as Porfirio had to hitch up the heavy team anyway. Corey wants our big wagon—to tote supplies, I guess. If we start now, we can reach Piedra Springs before—"

"Sit down, Valerie!" Alicia's voice rang like steel on rock. "Kindly begin at the beginning."

"All right, Mrs. Lane. I guess I ain't making much sense at that." (Yes, it *was* only Sam who dared the "Alicia" to her face.) "According to the message Matt Hendry's boy Tom brought out, Victorio's settled into a hideout in the Oscuras. Corey and the boys were going to let him be until next week, maybe get him to think nobody was really chasing hard, but the old devil hit a small place near the river day before yesterday, family named Cisneros. Ran off the stock and butchered the rancher and his wife and their three youngest. If the oldest boy hadn't been out riding one of the higher pastures at the time, we might not have known about it for a couple of weeks. Anyway, Corey's moved up the timetable— he's going after him at daybreak. He wants all the womenfolk between Black Springs and the *malpais* to grab up their kids and come into town until it's over, one way or another."

Jim McPherson had never claimed to be much of a horseman, and the livery-stable plug he had ridden out to the X-Bar-7 was certainly no candidate for any racing trophy, but it was embarrassing to see Alicia Lane fly by him as if he and his mount were standing still, with only the barest nod from her, and with no backward look when she reached the high ground forming the watershed between the Arroyo Concho and the Rio Bronco, still ten minutes short of Black Springs. Her full skirts, draped on the lefthand side of the saddle, flared in the wind at the top of the rise and then she was gone. He urged his tired horse to a little more speed. It would be impossible for Val Martin and Porfirio to pass him with the wagonload of women and children after stopping at the two ranches this side of Corey Lane's, but he couldn't chance another bout of shame. It was bad enough knowing that among the women and children in the Martins' wagon —and whatever others had started out by now—there wouldn't be any trace of Virgie Lane.

It hadn't been his place to plead with her after Val Martin resumed her journey to alert the other ranches, particularly when Alicia hadn't said a word, but he had tried all the same.

"No, Mr. McPherson. Thank you for your concern. I really *do* appreciate it, but I'll not leave here until Corey comes home again."

He felt a little better when Alicia announced that she would return to the X-Bar-7 once she'd said goodbye to Corey when he and the others rode out next morning. Nobody had ever said anything about whether or not Alicia Lane could handle firearms—just in case—but he surely couldn't think of a reason to doubt she could, and probably better than most men. There were two cowhands at the ranch, old men but determined-looking, and while, like crushed Sam Riordan, they were apparently not considered fit enough to go along on the sheriff's expedition, they were in all likelihood of far more use if trouble came than a deskbound editor could ever be. Corey Jr. *was* in the wagon. Any number of Black Springs women would be pleased to house the six-year-old until this was over, their feelings about the boy's father put aside while the wars went on.

Sheepish when he convinced himself that there was no way Val and her loaded wagon could catch him before he reached Black Springs, he eased the horse down to a slow walk and looked back over his shoulder, past the lava-flow to where the Oscuras were purpling as the sun settled behind the farther, bigger range of mountains on the rim of the basin world. The excitement he had felt that morning when he decided to ask Corey if he could go along was rising once again. Somewhere in that dark vastness he was looking at, Victorio waited. This might be the one real adventure of McPherson's life, no matter how small the part he played in it.

But—it was an important "but"—it would all have been so much better if he'd known that there was no need to ride to the ranch to see Corey Lane, that the sheriff could have been found at the militia's bivouac two miles west of Black Springs. He wouldn't then have known of Virgie Lane's decision not to seek safety with the other women, and he wouldn't have felt such a fraud when she spoke to him alone just before he left, while Alicia packed some things for her saddlebag to tide her overnight.

"You go on, Mr. McPherson—and don't wait for mother. If I know her, she'll prefer to ride alone. And, Mr. McPherson—if there's some way you can find to make Corey take care, please do it. You will, won't you?"

Like a fatuous ass, he'd nodded. As if he could tell Corey Lane a thing!

"Thank you, Mr. McPherson—and God bless you—and keep *you* safe, too."

"Thou mad'st thine enemies shake, as if the world
Were feverous and did tremble."

VI

It was a "cold" camp. Corey Lane had issued strict
orders against fires the moment they settled into it, and for
once Major Horace Lattner, the militiaman from Santa Fe,
hadn't argued, just braced himself, turned on his heels, and
walked off toward the tent his men were pitching for him,
looking every inch the "tin soldier" Alicia had said he'd be.

Two days out from Black Springs, Jim McPherson was
bone-tired, hot, thirsty, and still scared—something which
gave promise of getting worse the closer they got to Victorio.
Without a doubt the men around him were just as scared,
even the old veterans who had fought the Apache before
across the wastelands stretching in front of them, or deserts
exactly like them, but, in God's name, why couldn't they
have the decency to *show* it? From Will-Ed Martin to young
Bill Talley (Jacky Jameson had fretted at being left behind to
be the law in Black Springs) the Chupadera men all showed
the same easy determination on their faces, and even the
youngest of the troopers who had come down from Santa Fe
seemed more bored than fearful. Maybe he looked that calm
himself; he didn't know. It might have been easier if the
sheriff had let Sam Riordan come along.

More than all the others put together, though, it was
Corey Lane that McPherson watched. On the march out he
had seen the command of the expedition, nominally the job
of Major Lattner, shift to the sheriff. It wasn't a subtle or
gradual shift, either. Authority had passed from the soldier to
the lawman in great chunks, even if small things pried them

53

loose. When Lattner had wanted to send civilian scouts out
ahead of the column (actually, there were two columns, the
militia and the cattlemen), they'd turned to Corey openly for
permission, and when choosing the campsite both last night
and now, the major's own non-commissioned officers waited
for the sheriff's nod. Most of the time the Santa Fe man took
it without a word, but it was obvious he was chafing at this
loosening of his grip.

Corey himself was as silent as a statue, except for the
two long conferences he had held aside from all the others
with Mike Calico, the Zuni half-breed who talked only to
him, turning his masklike face away from everyone else in the
train. Calico came and went independently of even the other
scouts, reporting directly to Corey when he returned from a
ride, and then going off by himself, either to parallel the
route of march at a distance of nearly half a mile or setting up
his own camp apart from the main one, eating something
which looked like jerky and a corn mush he heated in a small
pot he fished out from his saddlebags. That had been the
night before, of course, before Corey's "no fires" order.

Calico was a stunted man, a gnome alongside the tall
elegant Corey Lane. McPherson had never seen him in town,
and he swallowed hard at his first close-up look at him. The
Zuni was dressed all in leather, much like sketches Jim had
seen of the old mountain men, a grease-stained suit of buckskin so ancient the fringes on sleeves and trousers had been
ripped away or worn down to tiny nubs. The wrangler's face
was as shiny dark as if it had been greased, too, and wrinkled
like a washboard, but in such a peculiar way it was impossible
to tell the man's age. Indeed, it was almost impossible to tell
where the costume left off and the skin began, except for
Calico's left hand—or what might at one time have been a
hand, now just a blackened half-claw with most of the thumb
and virtually all of the fingers missing.

"Shows you Mike wasn't always the smart old coot he is
today," Will-Ed Martin had said when he saw the editor
staring at the wreckage at the end of the leather-clad arm.
"Happened at Apache Pass. Mike was working for the Army
then, and carrying one of them murderous old Colt revolving
rifles. Guess he got so excited at his first good look at them
Chiricahua bastards he forgot to crook his piece across his left
arm instead of grabbing it under the barrel. Every one of the

chambers let loose on him at once and ripped off the best part of his mitt." Will-Ed *laughed*. "He went right on fighting after wrapping the stump in his neckerchief, but that night after the fight it swelled up like a pumpkin. Corey, with his arm in a sling and all shot to hell himself, grabbed him and dragged him to the cooking-fire and jammed what was left of that paw right into the coals. He's been Corey's man ever since. Don't ask me why."

Jim was almost sick at the horror of it. If he'd felt out of place before, now he wondered if he had any business at all on this adventure. The incredible toughness of these men, soldier and civilian, staggered him. They had fought this raw land to a standstill since birth, as some of their fathers had for a generation before them. The coarse humor and rough, almost cruel practical jokes of the past two days had been frightening, as when someone (he was half-sure it was Will-Ed, certainly old enough, you would have thought, to be past such a prank) had stolen Bill Talley's canteen when they'd saddled up this morning. Everybody in both columns seemed to know about it by the time Talley made his first mid-morning reach for it, and not a jeering soul would share his own water supply with the deputy, nor was he allowed near the water barrels in the mule train. When they reached camp, here in the lava-flow on the edge of the alkali flats, the youngster was seriously dehydrated, his face drawn and gray, like a man of sixty. After a brief salvo of curses, he hadn't complained or whined all through the march, and although McPherson wanted desperately to give the boy a drink, he knew instinctively he had better not. Bill didn't betray any elation, either, when the canteen appeared magically beside his saddle when the dismount order came. He even waited through ten minutes of what must have been pure torture before he took a pull at it.

Although the men, particularly the Ojos Negros men, were hard on each other this way, even their offhand gibes caustic and often brutal, they showed the editor very nearly the same respect they did Corey Lane, but with this difference: Corey had earned it, and McPherson hadn't, and knew he hadn't. He wished almost wistfully that they would try their clowning out on him; that would make a tiny start toward real acceptance.

He might not have looked Mike Calico over so thoroughly, except that with his eyes constantly studying the sheriff, he saw a good deal more of the little half-breed than he did of any other single man, aside from Corey, in either group. Calico was just about the only one who approached the lawman, at least on any regular basis. Like his wrangler, Corey rode separately from the rest of the column, even seeming to do so when he was hemmed in by other horsemen. None of the ranchers, not Will-Ed, not Talley, nor the major nor any of his troopers or junior officers, had bothered the tall man during either of the two days' rides.

With difficulty, given his suspect horsemanship, Jim managed to keep a fixed distance from the sheriff, behind him and a little to one side, where he could watch him carefully.

As they rode, he thought back to last Saturday's awesome scene in the sun-baked plaza. He could still feel the proud heat of the man as he slammed the crowd into silence and servility. Corey Lane was ten times the size of other men, no two ways about it.

Then, made uncomfortable by his own romanticizing, Jim tried to tell himself he was making a self-fulfilling fantasy out of his observation of Corey Lane. After all, the sheriff was just a minor law-enforcement officer in an inconsequential town on the edge of nowhere, an ordinary mortal doing a job made just a little bit extraordinary because of when it was being done, not why. If he wasn't careful, he would be imagining other things. He might begin to feel, for instance, here and now, that the heat he felt riding over the black rocks of the long-dead lava-flow came from something ages old, something primordial and therefore more threatening and deadly than what it really was—the simple direct heat of today's very ordinary, if scorching, sun.

It wouldn't wash. There *was* something infinitely larger than life about Corey Lane, and Jim McPherson wasn't the only one who knew it. As the riders passed near Corey, he noticed, their eyes never failed to take the man in, even if their gaze was no more direct than if they had been glancing at the sun.

Will-Ed Martin was a good case in point. Because the rancher had been spending so much time on the Sinuoso dam, the editor hadn't met the man during his five months in Black Springs. Jim had prepared himself, remembering the trouble Will-Ed had caused, to dislike him and had maintained a wary attitude toward him during the first day's ride, but there was something appealing about the raw-boned cattleman which for a while Jim couldn't understand. He should have been put off by Will-Ed's casual cruelty, revealed not only in the prank played on Bill Talley and the laughter when he told of the mishap to Mike Calico's hand, but by a score of smaller things.

Then he realized what it was that drew him to Martin. In talk and manner he was enough like Sam Riordan to be a younger brother (and oh, how Jim missed that whiskey-soaked old wit) and he was like Sam in one other respect, too: his regard for Corey Lane bordered on adulation. Maybe, with time, he would mellow as Sam had. The editor felt a stab of guilt, thinking that. Maybe all cowmen were alike.

When they had stopped for the noon meal today, and because of Will-Ed Martin, McPherson had made one more discovery about Corey Lane.

After he'd gone through the mess line, he'd found Will-Ed and two others of the ranch contingent eating in the shade of a lone cottonwood which grew like a freak beside a ravine splitting the lava rock. Will-Ed had called to him to join them, and he'd found the group deep in a discussion of the sheriff. Jim sat with his back against a big rock, facing the others.

"Oh, I think the major will grab the lay of things all right," Will-Ed was saying. "He will, at least, if he's got any brains at all. Corey's just plain *got* to run this show if we're going to have any chance at all with that red devil."

The sun was beating fiercely down through the half-grown new leaves of the cottonwood, but the editor was so intent on what was being said he didn't really notice it.

"Yeah," one of the other two broke in, "but this soldier boy's got a pretty large opinion of himself. No bigger than any other they could have sent down from Santa Fe, I reckon, but he ain't likely to relish letting Corey get all the glory out of this here little outing."

"Hey!" It was the third man. He was somewhat younger than the other cattlemen. McPherson knew he was a recent arrival in the basin. "Just how good *is* this Lane?"

The editor detected a subtle change in the light, and he looked up to the lip of the ravine to see Corey Lane standing beside the trunk of the cottonwood. From where the sheriff

stood he could look straight down into the little group, but
Jim had the feeling that he himself, sitting a bit apart from
the others, hadn't caught the man's eye, and just as surely
Will-Ed and the rest of them hadn't seen Corey.

"He's the absolute best," Will-Ed said. "Totally without
fear, but smart enough to smell out danger before it reaches
him. He won't think *like* this Apache; he'll God-damned well
think *for* him. He'll out-general him, out-maneuver him, and
if it gets right down to it, he'll out-fight him, gun to gun or
hand to hand, if need be."

McPherson's fascination with the man standing above
them was now such that he stared straight at him, not caring
if his look was seen. Corey Lane looked in ecstasy—almost.
There was something else trying to work its way into the
handsome face, but the editor couldn't quite make it out.

"Wish you could have seen him in action when I first
did, seventeen years ago," Will-Ed went on. "He climbed
that canyon wall like a catamount, streaming blood but breathing hellfire, dragging those troopers behind him until they
was heroes, too, in spite of themselves.

"He was like that at Val Verde when we rode with
Canby and Roberts, too," the other older rancher said. "The
Rebs didn't fare a bit better with him than Cochise's savages
did. And, my God, he weren't nothing but a kid—ten years
younger than you are now, Dan."

It went on in much the same vein for another five
minutes, Will-Ed and the other oldster regaling Jim and the
newcomer with exploits the editor would have thought fanciful before coming to this wide country, and all the while
McPherson kept his eyes riveted on Corey Lane's face.

". . . and, oh my, how he can stand pain. I recollect one
time," Will-Ed was saying, "at Perro Wells, it was, when we
was—"

"That's enough, Will-Ed!" the man standing by the cottonwood said. The voice wasn't loud, but it actually echoed.
Will-Ed stopped as if he'd been struck. Corey Lane turned
and strode away, his boots ringing on the rock.

Jim knew then that Corey Lane wanted, needed, *had to
have* praise—like meat and drink; when it came, it pleased
him well enough, but drugged as he seemed by it, at the end
he was revolted.

Jim carried this new insight with him to the first big war council in camp that night.

"Put them away, Major!" Corey Lane's big hand reached out and swept the field glasses down from Lattner's face, almost knocking them from his grasp. "With the sun that low you'll send a reflection right through the front door of Victorio's wicki-up." The rebuke was sharp. Jim McPherson gasped. "Besides," Lane went on, "we're still fifteen, sixteen miles from that saddle. You couldn't make out anything but rocks and more rocks from here."

The ridge line of the Oscuras danced and rippled in the last of the day's heat-shimmer, making the distant mountains look like the big rollers McPherson had often seen from Montauk Point. He had difficulty picking out the terrain features Corey talked about while the major pored over the map spread across the boulder in front of him. This country needed a special kind of sight.

"He's in that lowest section, just to the left of the conical peak," Corey said.

"You're sure?"

Lane nodded. "Mike Calico was there, or near enough to make it the same thing."

"Couldn't we just roll right over him? Storm that slope head-on without a lot of fancy strategy?" Lattner said. They were phrased as questions, but the editor knew they were meant to be much more. The militiaman wanted a cavalry charge. It was what he was trained to lead. Jim smiled when he realized he was half-hoping Corey would agree. By George, it would be something to see, all right!

"Sure," Corey said, "I guess you could. That isn't exactly an Ojos Negros pasture you'd be riding across before you got there. Victorio would have the better part of three hours to get ready for you, too."

"But *he* rode up there—and with women and children and baggage animals."

"Wasn't anybody up there shooting at him, either, major. Suit yourself. If you decide to risk it straight-on all by yourself, it's all right with me, but in that case the Chupadera men will pass."

McPherson could see the major struggling with himself, watched him as he won a close victory over rising exasperation.

"Look, Sheriff Lane," he said, "I'll gladly defer to your experience, I'm no fool. But I haven't heard you put forth a plan as yet."

No, McPherson agreed silently, this Lattner wasn't a fool. He must have watched Corey Lane as closely as had the editor while Will-Ed and others had given their advice. He must have seen the faintly contemptuous amusement on the lawman's face as he rejected strategy after strategy—and without uttering a single word. Yes, Lattner had doped out that Corey wanted to be asked, and the soldier was asking now.

"Well," Corey said at last, "there's a whole bunch of possibilities—just possibilities, mind you. Mike tallied ninety-three able-bodied warriors in that funny counting system of his. There may be even more. He wasn't sure if they were all in camp. That's a lot of firepower with the stacks of Winchesters Mike saw, and they're dug into the rocks on that slope as tight as ticks. This is no simple-minded savage we're up against. His defense is laid out well enough to do credit to a Lee or a U. S. Grant.

"Now, if you do try a frontal assault, major, starting from here, say, and if you succeed in making it stick, which is doubtful at best, he'd be over that ridge behind him and off to the south in the winking of an eye, and all you'd have to show for it would be a lot of dead or dying troopers, a few Mimbreño corpses—and we'd have it all to do all over again in three weeks or a month, provided we could track him and catch up with him. That might be the right way for you, at that, but *we* have ranches which won't run themselves forever.

"The best plan, if we could get a signal to Harry Jackson over at Craig, and if he could or would act on our say-so, would be to slip another force from across the Rio, a force just as big as ours, through that pass you can see a dozen miles or so down-range from Victorio's camp. He can't see it from where he is. They could block his escape and you could charge that slope to your heart's content. You'd lose most of your men, but in the long run it might be worth it."

Jim McPherson's heart froze.

"Only trouble is," Corey went on, "that might take upwards of a week, and we've got no way of knowing if Victorio will find out exactly where we are by then, or if he just plain gets itchy and decides to break camp on pure whim. Either way, he's gone and we start from scratch again."

All this was given out in dead-level voice, and Jim was almost tricked into marveling at the sheriff's "coolness," but every once in a while he was conscious of the heat beneath the surface. The editor wondered if he was the only listener who felt the heat.

"This Apache knows we're somewhere in the *malpais*. He most likely doesn't know precisely where we are, and he probably doesn't care. He knows we can't nose out of here without his seeing us. He doesn't really want a fight, but sooner or later, if he stays put, he's got to raid. If we can get just a little closer, like where the black rock juts out into the alkali flats, and be ready when he sends a party out, and if the party is big enough, we've got our chance. I say 'big enough' and that's important, for two reasons. One, it cuts his firepower by perhaps a third. More to the point, he might run if only a half-dozen or a dozen men were out of camp, but if maybe a third of them are gone, he'll never leave, not if we slaughter every one of them."

The voice wasn't level now. Little by little it was rising, then falling, soaring up in the next sentence to new heights, and with no attempt at coolness, either. The chill inside McPherson was gone, too, as if the heat of Corey Lane was contagious.

"So far he's only made one mistake. He's only crossed the *malpais* once or twice in his whole career. He knows the road we took yesterday and today pretty well, but what he doesn't know, and what Mike Calico does, is that we could sneak the Army of the Potomac to within five miles of him without him seeing us. That isn't close enough for what you had in mind, major, but it puts us in good shape if he sends his raiders out."

"Couldn't we move my command down into the flats by night just as well?"

"No! That won't do!" Corey was riding roughshod now, and the words were drumming like hoofbeats. "He wouldn't budge one man until you made that God-damned silly attack I can see you still have your heart set on. Pay attention, man. There's more."

McPherson couldn't bear to look at the soldier then, any more than he'd looked at Granby Stafford and Eloy Montoya after the gratuitous insult in the sheriff's office.

"While you and your militia are waiting, impatiently or

any other way you want to, I don't care, I'll take maybe twenty of my men and work even farther down the lava-flow. At one point it pushes a kind of rock peninsula within a quarter of a mile of the same ridge Victorio's on. When his raiding party busts out, and after you move into the flats and maybe he just has his eyes on *you*, we'll get above his camp and see if we can upset his plans for leaving. You can have your charge *then*."

Without warning he turned and walked away. When he had gone perhaps thirty paces, he stopped and turned back.

"Of course, major, *you* are in command here. These have only been suggestions."

I must have slept, surely I must have, Jim McPherson thought when the sun burst over the top of Cuchillo Peak, so many aching miles behind them. He couldn't remember if he really had or not. They had already been in the saddle for more than an hour, following the corkscrew trail through the very heart of the *malpais*. He had seen Mike Calico only once, in the half-light before dawn when they mounted up. The Zuni was somewhere out in front of the column now, with Corey Lane directly on his heels, the rest of the cattlemen and soldiers strung out over a mile of the grotesque landscape they threaded their way through. Now McPherson had to keep his eyes, if not his thoughts, on the rider right ahead of him. He couldn't seem to get the hand of trusting his horse to find a sure path through the jumble of twisted black rock as the others did, and he knew he was giving the poor beast a hard time of it, yanking on the reins in near-panic every time they seemed headed for one of the crevices which crosshatched the lava-flow. The tortured animal's mouth must feel like an open wound by now.

With the sun still but a few feet above the eastern rimrock, and lost to them when they were in one of the countless depressions he would have sworn would block their passage (and did until Mike Calico, unseen in front of them somewhere, led them around the chasms), today's ride had become like a journey through a disease-crazed mind.

Seen from Black Springs, the *malpais*, at least in certain lights, had a murky somber look of beauty. At that distance, its jagged contours softened by the slight haze blurring any faraway object in the basin, particularly during the summer months, it looked like a great black river, arrested, frozen forever in its course along the valley floor, lifeless and eternal.

Deep inside, it was quite another thing. To his amazement, these badlands teemed with life. Ocotillo, a score of other cacti and succulents, more wild grasses then he could name or even recognize—green, but a sickly green—sprouted from nearly every crack and sinkhole, and lizards as black as the printer's ink that stained his hands each Thursday morning skittered across the trail at every turning. He wondered what the devilish chemistry was that turned them the color of the forbidding rock they lived on.

While most of the stretches the men and horses traversed were as parched as the grainy desert to the east and the alkali flats stretching away to the Oscuras (and Victorio) on the other side, there *was* water, even if he heard it more often than he saw it. It occurred to him as they rode along (and he was finally learning to give his poor horse its head, if only gingerly, tentatively) that men *could* live in these monstrous, ungodly, exploded wastes—but they would have to be a special breed of men, perhaps a breed that had undergone something like the chemical change which had dyed the lizards such a hellish nightshade black.

All morning long the band of men wound between and around giant black monoliths on a trail spiraling and turning back on itself with such defeating frequency it took a good five miles to advance the column two. In places the trail narrowed between vertically walled gullies plunging into pit-blackness forty and fifty feet beneath them, sometimes thinning to such slender causeways the horses wouldn't go on, no matter how viciously they were spurred. Then the men were forced to dismount and lead the frightened animals to where the path widened again. Most of the march had been made in silence; it was impossible to talk, traveling in single file. During those times when they were on foot and gripping the leads of the horses, the men ahead of and behind the editor cursed, some of the curses raised to such a pitch and so full of references to hell he realized suddenly how close to at least one kind of hell the *malpais* was. Once, when the trail made a dozen quick switches back and forth through a particularly deep and rocky place, enough below the general level that the sun was lost, he could see where a mule from the baggage train behind him had slipped from the path, its sure feet pulled from the trail by a badly packed and now unbalanced load. The animal lay spraddled against the black stone under it, two of the ranchmen tugging mightily at its halter. McPherson's mind flashed back to his childhood and his first wide-eyed excursion through the Doré engravings in his father's Dante, particularly a dark miasmic one, "The Minotaur on the Shattered Cliffs." The mule was honking like a deranged earthbound goose, and the sound, mixed with the blasphemies of the men trying to help the animal, echoed off the walls around him like some Satanic oratorio. When he forced his eyes back to what lay ahead of him, he saw, four or five bends down the road, the heads of Mike Calico and Corey Lane. Their mounts were hidden by the lava folds, and their faces seemed to float, disembodied, serenely undisturbed by the bedlam loosed behind them. If the Zuni seemed even more of a gargoyle in this outlandish scene, the fair-haired sheriff looked like what?—some new-fallen Miltonic Lucifer, still proud, uncrushed?

McPherson began to laugh—silently—laughter to ward off evil spirits, he told himself, but more because of these purely literary imaginings assailing him. Of all the times in his life when he had wanted to escape his bookishness, this had to tower above all the rest. He didn't want to think of what the hard men of this expedition would say if they knew of the things running through his mind. If he was truly lucky, the fear of their opinion might drive away the deeper fear that was like an acid in his blood, an acid that polluted his body's fluids, ending up in his saliva, a burning sourness he didn't dare spit away in this desiccating heat, and one he couldn't swallow without risking nausea.

By one o'clock the columns reached a place where the lava-flow was wider, lower, and blessedly flatter than the part they had been riding through, thrusting what McPherson figured must be the peninsula which would be the jumping-off place for the militia when they made their move. Here the wild surface of the *malpais* had been somewhat tamed by the sand and gypsum which had drifted in from east and west on the fickle winds of ten thousand seasons. The sickening deep fissures didn't open on either side of the trail with such alarming regularity here, and if McPherson guessed this only increased their chances of being seen by Apache eyes, still it was a relief to be relatively free of the gaping black mouths which opened above throats and gullets waiting to swallow any rider whose horse made the slightest misstep.

He had been so intent on watching just the horse ahead of him it came as a shock to discover that the column had accordioned to a broad front under the pinnacles of a rock formation not part of the *malpais* proper. He could see where the molten rock had parted to make its way around this volcanic plug, already ancient when the lava had rolled and surged its way down the great flats of the Ojos Negros Basin. By the time the word had been passed back through the loose ranks of mounted men that they would camp here, he saw that Corey Lane and the Zuni had already dismounted and made their way up the steep talus slopes to where the topmost ridges of the outcropping were limned against the sky like the crenellations of some ruined Camelot.

He could see the tall lawman staring out toward the mountain saddle where his enemy was hidden. Mike Calico crouched on a rock ledge even with Corey's head, but from below it seemed that the Zuni was perched right on the sheriff's shoulder. He looked like a gnarled dark imp whispering in Corey's ear. Once again the image of the banished angel came to the editor's mind.

Behind the cattlemen unsaddling their horses, the cavalry was pounding in under the protection of the high rocks, the horses' and pack-mules' shoes hammering and echoing on the campground's sunbaked surface. Jim saw Major Lattner rein his pony to a stop and swing down to the ground.

The three-day march had taken some of the parade-ground starch out of the man, but clearly this soldier wasn't one to complain. He looked up the face of the rock to where Corey and Mike were staring out over the rim to the Oscuras. He started up the talus slope after an orderly had led his horse away, then apparently thought better of it, turned about, and walked—a bit listlessly, Jim thought—to where his two lieutenants and his sergeant-major waited for him by the mule train. *He's given up,* the editor decided; *from now on it's Corey's show.* The sheriff's scornful lecture of the night before must have left the major's sensitivities too tender to take any more right then.

Just as "cold" in the sense that no fires were allowed this night either, after supper the camp generated an inferno of activity that burned everywhere. Rifles and sidearms were stripped down and cleaned, the evening sun glinting off the bare metal parts as the men worked, clicks from the reassembled weapons sounding to the editor as grim and deadly as any shot. Riding-tack was cut to a minimum, saddles and harness trimmed and battened down for whatever swift action the next day might bring. Bedrolls and personal gear not needed for the attack would be left in camp. With even more diligence than the soldiers, the cattlemen were trying to sweat their baggage down until they and their mounts became true "light cavalry" like the Indians hiding in the mountains looming across the flats, no more than five or six miles away now, Jim figured.

There wasn't as much talk as there had been the night before—and no jokes. What little conversation there was turned on the outcome of tomorrow's battle—if it came.

"Ain't no law says Victorio's got to send his raiders out tomorrow just to suit our schedule," Will-Ed Martin said.

"What if he don't?" Bill Talley said. "Can Corey figure out some other way to hit him?"

"Sooner or later, I expect. We didn't ride out here just to look at scenery. If we don't punish this Apache on this trip, he'll get cocky as a breed bull in April, and a hell of a lot of stray killers will come flocking into his *ranchería*. Can't let that happen. Meantime, though, Corey will stick to his plan."

The militia officers and five or six of the ranchers met with Corey again after supper, and McPherson joined the gathering, watching Major Lattner to see if the man would make some move to regain control of the venture. And watching the man, too, to see if there was any bitterness in his face. There was no sign of either. What Jim did see was a look of awe much like the one he feared he wore himself when he gazed at Corey Lane.

Nothing new came out of the meeting, just a reprise of Corey's plan, outlined the night before, and one by one the men drifted off to their bedrolls until only the editor and the lawman were left together.

And just at that moment the enormity of the danger he was facing roared down over Jim McPherson like an avalanche, and he realized that the fears he had felt eating him since they rode out from Black Springs had only been the tiniest of nibbles. This was a monster bite of fear which could leave him chewed to shreds. He wondered if he was shaking as much as he felt he was, and if the sheriff saw it. What kind of insanity had prompted him into the company of men like Corey Lane and Will-Ed Martin—or Horace Lattner, for that matter? He *was* bookish, and didn't belong here. His place was back in the office of the *News*, rewriting the dispatches the sheriff—and if not the sheriff, certainly the major—would sooner or later send in from the field once they came to grips with the marauders across the flats.

Then—and the shock of it emptied him of all feeling—he heard himself say, "Sheriff Lane, I want to go with you and your men tomorrow—or whenever it is you go. May I?"

Good God! Had he really said it? And if he had—why? Surely it wasn't to impress Corey Lane. This god of battle who was looking at him keenly would give him no marks at all for cheap bravado, and Corey Lane would know if that was all it was. Maybe—he grasped at a new thought—maybe he'd said it to impress himself. Maybe he was trying to raise a tide of courage inside himself which would sweep him forward against all will and reason. Maybe—no, there was no maybe about this at all, just cold certainty—Corey could answer these questions for him better than he could himself.

"It will be a bloody business, editor," Corey Lane said. "We'll have it a sight worse than even the major and his troopers, in all likelihood. I should think you'd want to stay here in camp where you could see both ends of it, and write it up good and proper. Are you *sure* you want to go with me?"

Jim swallowed. The sheriff was letting him off the hook he'd sought so carelessly.

"No, sir. I guess I don't really *want* to go with you," Jim McPherson said. "I *have* to."

The sheriff nodded. "All right, then, editor. Bring that rifle I saw in your saddle holster. You'll use it if you go with me."

McPherson knew he was dismissed. He turned and picked his way across the compound to his bedroll, avoiding in the dim starlight the bodies of sleeping men. How could they sleep so soundly in the face of the terrible test to come? He knew *he* couldn't.

But he did.

*"If should tell thee o'er this thy day's work,
Thou'lt not believe thy deeds; but I'll report it. . . ."*

VII

"Can you *imagine* that little horny toad? Will-Ed said,
pointing to Mike Calico. "He sniffed old Victorio out from
right here where we're standing. I can't no more make out
that camp in them heat waves than if it was pitch-black."

Jim McPherson gazed up the length of the alkali flats,
boulevard-wide compared to the labyrinthine corridors of the
malpais they would leave if anything stirred in the Apache
hideout. After the confusing rides of the last few days he was
finally beginning to orient himself. Corey Lane's hand-picked
force was poised to go on the sheriff's signal. It was perched
on a corner of the short side of an isosceles triangle, with
Victorio on the other, two miles down the ridge on its left, a
serrated, ugly, broken ridge a quarter of a mile across the
flats. Major Lattner, waiting at the top point of the triangle
with the militia and the rest of the Ojos Negros men, was to
leave the shelter of the volcanic plug, five miles from the
Indians, and begin his march and assault as soon as a large-
enough raiding party left the mountain camp.

Jim had wondered, as they left their comrades before
daybreak, why Corey had decided the entire command
wouldn't move down to the narrows with them. To him it
made sense to attack from where they would be only two
miles away instead of five, but halfway down the *malpais* a
giant fissure opened across their trail, a crack so sharp and
deep he knew they would have to leave the horses, cross the
chasm (and the alkali flats, too, when the time came) on foot.
At least the major and the main force would still be mounted.

The horses were herded into a steep-sided arroyo, with a makeshift fence of mesquite thrown across its mouth to corral them. As they worked to secure their mounts he realized how well Calico, and Corey, too, knew this country.

Given his poor horsemanship, he thought it would be good to be on foot again, but they had barely climbed out of the crevice before he began to feel even more uneasy than he had while in the saddle. At first he thought that perhaps the solid bulk of the horse under him had given him more reassurance than he had realized.

It wasn't until they had settled into this present vantage point and he sat down on a big boulder with his rifle between his knees that he knew what the real trouble was. It was the rifle. On horseback the Winchester Sam had loaned him was safely in the saddle holster, away from his touch and out of mind except when Corey had mentioned it last night. The sun-warmed metal now seemed alive in his hands, as if it might at any moment twist from his grasp and go about some deadly business independent of him.

As he looked at the rifle, something occurred to him, not for the first time: that of all man's artifacts it was his weapons on which he lavished the most care and affection, the most time, trouble, and, above all, genius. Even from what little he knew of Indian handiwork this seemed true. He had seen some pottery and wampum beadwork in New York museums that had shown considerable skill, even art, but none of the things he was familiar with impressed him as much as the flint arrow point he'd found in the meadow behind Granby Stafford's store and had kept in his pocket ever since. He wondered at how hard it must have been for the Indian who had worked the intractable stone—with tools of the crudest kind—to fashion a thing of such finely chiseled beauty. It made him think of the faded but still magnificent Chiricahua shield above the fireplace in Alicia Lane's sitting room—and that made him think of Virgie, and he knew suddenly he had better derail this entire train of thought.

He looked around at the men resting on the black rock, huddled in what little shade they could find in this treeless lava rubble. Except that they were all sweating, some of them fanning themselves with their big hats, they seemed relaxed and easy, and once again he wondered if they shared his fear. If it weren't for the weapons (the rifles like his, the pistols or revolvers every man here carried except himself, the one bayonet he saw hanging from a belt in its black leather scabbard with the big *U.S.* tooled in its shiny surface), the sprawled men around him could have been a work gang stopped for lunch. But any fresh resentment he might have felt at these apparently calm cowhands was throttled when he tried to take a pull at his canteen and Will-Ed stopped him.

"Don't mean to mind your business, Jim," he said, his voice kind, even warm, the last qualities the editor had expected to find in the cattleman, "but I'd go easy on that stuff if I was you. If you think you're thirsty now, it ain't nothing like it will be after we fight—if we do. Besides, if you're at all like me, and irregardless of how much water you think you're losing in this sun, it's a good idea to go into a gunfight a mite on the empty side. First time *I* got a whiff of unfriendly powder smoke, I pissed my pants so much I like to filled my boots. 'Course, maybe you ain't as scared as I am."

Jim murmured his thanks, then stammered a question at the man. "Will they come out today, Will-Ed?"

"Don't know, Jim. Hope so. If they don't raid today or tomorrow, I guess we'll have to go back to where the major is. We'll need more food and water. Long as we've come this far, I'd as soon get it over with."

Jim found he felt the same way.

Will-Ed turned to Bill Talley. The deputy, as far as Jim knew, hadn't been bloodied in combat, either. What would the older man say to *him?*

"Talley, this ain't going to be like breaking up fights in the Sacramento House. Think you'll be able to handle it?"

Bill grinned, but then he licked his lips. Jim thought he could detect dryness in the youngster, too.

"I'll beat *you* into Victorio's camp, Will-Ed," the deputy said.

"Put some money where your mouth is, sonny."

"My horse against yours?"

"You're on. My, but you're going to get mighty sick of walking."

It was quiet for a while. The sun climbed above them and the alkali flats rippled like a white-hot sea.

Concerned with himself and the men closest to him, Jim discovered that he hadn't kept his eyes fastened on Corey Lane nearly as much as he'd expected to. The sheriff and

Mike Calico were seated on a point of rock away from the rest of them, fully exposed to a sun they had apparently made no attempt to avoid. The Zuni looked as if he were a part of the black stone itself. And Corey? McPherson stared at the lawman's broad back and the sweat-damp shirt tight across the broad shoulders. Outwardly Corey was as much part of the terrain as the twisted blackened little man beside him.

Through the long hot morning the men waited, and what talk there was dwindled to faint echoes of a boredom so vast, so weakening, that Jim wondered if they would ever be able to rouse themselves.

Then, just before noon, he saw Calico touch Corey's sleeve with his right hand while the withered claw pointed across the flats toward the unseen Apache camp. The twin movements were slight, and for a moment Jim was sure he was the only one who had noticed them, but then around him he felt the sudden alertness. Will-Ed got to his feet; then Dan Stone, who'd asked "how good" Corey was; then the editor and the rest; and they surged forward, behind and around the lawman and the Zuni. Corey Lane nodded. No one spoke.

Jim peered across the flats, but nothing had changed as far as he could see. The volcanic plug where the major waited with his cavalry poked its spires at the sky exactly as before. Jim couldn't detect the slightest sign of movement on Victorio's ridge, and between the two "the lone and level sands" still "stretched far away."

A minute passed. Then at last he did see something, and of course the men around him saw it, too.

At the foot of the slope where the Apache were, and where the rocks made their pell-mell meeting with the alkali flats, seeming in the shimmer of the heat-haze to bounce and bound, he saw a wisp of smoke, a tiny white plume of dust fanning out above the desert floor, and under it the dark hint of horsemen.

"He's sent them out!" someone said in a whisper, as if the riders pounding down from the enemy encampment could hear his voice.

Other voices broke around him.

"How many?"

"Can't tell yet."

"Enough of them?"

"Looks *like*—yep, it sure does."

Good Lord! How could they see so much? Jim struggled to make out the detail so readily seen by the others. It wasn't until he gave up straining against the reflections dancing above the two miles which separated him from the slope and forced to relax that he finally focused on the horsemen streaming out across the flats.

Now Calico was wiggling the fingers of his good right hand, slapping his leather pants smartly at intervals, clearly signaling Corey Lane in what must be "that funny counting system of his." Jim couldn't count the horses and riders he saw with *any* system. The tiny figures seemed to run together, break apart, wheel crazily in the swirl of snow-white dust.

Corey was nodding at the messages flashed from the dark hand of the little Zuni. Then they both stopped, and the sheriff turned to the men behind him.

"Victorio's turned loose fifty warriors, half his fighting men. Way too many for just a raid. If he's up to what I think he is, I hope the major tumbles to it, too. We'll have to wait and see."

Jim turned to Will-Ed, saw a nod of understanding, and hoped the rancher would share his insight. He wasn't disappointed.

"I think I understand what Corey's driving at. See that other ridge? Way, way, *way* up there, three, four miles beyond those hostiles? Most likely they'll ride out over it and then come screaming back once the soldier boys have made their move, catch them on the flank. Got to hand it to that old devil up there. He's thinking."

"What should Major Lattner do, Will-Ed, sit tight?"

"Not necessarily. If he's got sense enough to split off twenty or thirty skirmishers, they could hold that war-party off while he positions himself for his main attack. *Somebody* in the Ojos Negros crowd will tell him so—if he'll listen."

Corey had turned back to watch the activity at the foot of Victorio's slope. Now he stood up slowly, the movement looking to the editor like the one in the plaza when he had risen interminably in the stirrups. His back was rigid, and even if Jim couldn't see his face, he could feel the power being gathered and concentrated in the splendid body, as if Corey Lane were some giant magnifying-glass collecting the heat of the midday sun and narrowing it to one piercing ray.

Again Mike Calico tugged at Corey's sleeve, and again the sheriff nodded, the gesture more abrupt this time, and even Jim could see what was taking place. Fifteen or twenty of the mounted Indians, he couldn't count them yet, had turned away from the others and were riding straight toward them. Corey stared out over the flats for just a moment longer, and then turned to face his men.

"I shouldn't have to draw you a picture of how things stand," he said. "Victorio has guessed we're down here somewhere. That party coming at us is supposed to draw our fire. He's worked it out, too, that if he's wrong he's still not hurt. They'll just move a mile or two farther down, where they can't be seen from the major's camp, and then swing back when the militia moves onto the slope they're on—just like the larger party plans to do from the north. If Lattner moves, he'll lead his troopers, and those of our people with him, right into the Apache's trap. They'll hit him from the rear and from the sides at about the moment he comes under Victorio's guns. We'll lie low. Not a shot—understand?"

"But, sheriff—" it was Dan Stone—"if we take this bunch on, we can at least keep *them* off Lattner's uniformed ass."

"No!" The one word held a storm. "I'll kill the first man who fires, I promise you!" The blue eyes blazed, and for a moment Jim thought the lawman secretly wanted more resistance from the rancher so he could prove his point. Then he saw the fire in Corey's eyes subside a little. "The only chance we have is to get high enough on the Apache ridge to be above their camp, where we can start a little crossfire of our own. Victorio most likely doesn't think we'll try it. What he's up to now with all this riding around is to get us to change our minds. We'll stick to our original plan. It might turn messy if the riders we see don't go far enough past our position here. Then we may have to fight our way across the flats. That's bad enough, but it will be just as bad if every one of us makes the rocks on the other side. The firing will wake Victorio up. He'll know we're coming, and where we're coming from. All right, get back from the edge, well back, and out of sight. Nobody moves a muscle until I tell them to. No talking, no smoking, every handgun and rifle safetied—you're going to have to run with them, remember."

He waved his hands like a man brushing something away from him, and they scurried for cover.

Jim found himself sharing a depression in the black rock with Bill Talley and Matt Hendry, a quiet man whose ranch was situated on the lower reaches of the Bronco. He wished he could have landed in the same hole with Will-Ed Martin. He was sure his fear was plain for everyone to see, and it would have been easier to have Will-Ed looking at it than these two.

To take his mind away from that, he thought over everything Corey Lane had said. And then Jim heard them.

The hoofs of the approaching horses didn't hammer on the rock-hard surface of the alkali as he'd expected—the sound was more of a flutter, like a flight of buzzards beating their wings against the air. Suddenly panicked, he still kept enough of his wits about him to realize that there was a gap in the rocks above the hole which sheltered them, and that he could actually see out onto the flats, his field of vision in the center (half a city block away) perhaps twenty or thirty yards across. The fluttering grew louder, and he held his breath.

A spotted pony nosed into view, trotting easily. On its back was a short heavy-set old man. It shocked Jim to see the white hair puffed above and flared wildly out below a brilliant orange headband. This ancient rider was looking directly at Jim. It didn't matter that there wasn't a chance in a million he could be seen in the narrow slit he peered through; something squeezed his heart.

Then the old warrior turned and looked straight ahead of him, and by the time Jim permitted himself his first strangled breath, the rider and pony had moved on and disappeared.

Ten or fifteen seconds passed before any more riders came along, and then they came in bunches: two, four, five, then none for a beat of Jim's heart, then—he counted them off—eighteen in all. They moved easily, as the first one had, not rushing, not even the one who urged his mount into a canter in an apparent attempt to catch the leader. Quick fear returned for an instant. Had this one noticed something? Jim had to make his mind up from his observation of the others when the faster-moving animal left his sight. No, none of them looked any different. They still scanned the edge of the *malpais* warily, but there was no look of any special alarm in the way they rode.

And there wasn't a rider in the rest of the band as remarkable in looks as their leader had been—not until the last man came into sight. He was wearing a piece of headgear so outlandish that the sight brought the beginning of a laugh, despite Jim's fears. Tied onto the Indian's head by a yellow scarf, which made him look like someone bandaged for a toothache, was a dilapidated gray opera hat.

Then they all were gone. Somewhere, a bird—a raven, probably—screeched into the silence, and when it stopped, Jim heard—for the first time, it seemed—the hum and buzz of the insects which must have been livening the hot air, unheard above the fear in his chest. Had the fear gone now? It seemed so . . . until someone a hole or two away coughed a dry hacking cough and the fear flooded back.

Fifteen minutes went by, or twenty. There seemed little point in looking at his watch. They weren't normal minutes anyway. Then he heard Corey Lane's whisper, loud enough, but coming as if from another planet.

"Get ready. Mike will take one look to see if they've gone far enough. If they have, we go. Run as if the devil himself was after you."

Another measureless time of waiting; and when the order came, Jim didn't really hear it. He felt himself pulled, sucked forward as Hendry and Talley left, and then he was running, jumping from the last ledge of the *malpais* onto the sun-hardened alkali, running again, the weight of the rifle making his shoulder socket ache, every breath like swallowing flame, his lungs—the lungs he'd thought whole and sound again in this wide free-breathing country—suddenly as tight and pained as they had ever been. He ran hard, not looking to right or left, afraid he would find the enemy on his heels and an Apache lance aimed at his back. And then, at last, he was in the rocks at the foot of the ridge on the other side, sinking exhausted to his knees, only half-feeling the jagged stone he was kneeling on . . . and the thought came fiercely: *To hell with you, Will-Ed Martin! I'm going to have a drink of water if I piss a canyon full in front of everybody.*

But there was no time for that. Corey Lane was towering over them, roaring, "Don't stop now! Climb the rocks! Every man a hundred feet above the flats at least."

Jim was on his feet and climbing with the others, and no new feeling of agony came.

When they were high enough to suit the sheriff, they did stop to rest. No one had to point or speak; they all saw the new cloud of dust, where the major and his militia were leading the way out of the *malpais*, coming around the side of the volcanic plug. The thirty or so riders Victorio had sent north were gone, out of sight beyond the distant ridge which would shelter them until it was time for them to double back and catch the major (if Corey Lane and Will-Ed were right, and Jim was sure they were), and there was no trace of the smaller band which had trotted by their hiding-place. They must have disappeared to the south where the alkali flats made the sweeping bend around the same ridge the sheriff's men were on.

"But won't they see our tracks in the flats on their way back, Will-Ed?" Jim asked.

"Probably. But they can't follow us up here on ponies, and I doubt if they'll want to come after us on foot. They got to chase back up there to support them other devils."

"Could they signal Victorio some way?"

"Sure. They could start shooting—but that would let the major know they was there, too. They wouldn't want that."

Then they were moving again and Jim could see that indeed no mounted men could follow them. The stony way they traveled—it wasn't a trail—was a mere eyebrow on the mountain's face. For all Jim knew, they could be the first humans who had ever walked these high scree-littered barrens. He was pleased to find that, in spite of his effort to breathe, he had no trouble with the pace. Tough as they were, the cowpokes and ranchers who struggled along ahead of him (only Bill Talley came behind him now) had spent their lives in the saddle. They despised walking, and this wasn't exactly a saunter across the Black Springs plaza to the Sacramento House. He blessed the memory of the long hikes he had taken in the Adirondacks every boyhood summer, the hard wading through boulder-strewn trout streams, and if this dry ridge was hotter than the floor of hell, and if the rifle was a weight, he could manage. What came after this rocky journey was another matter. He'd have to deal with that however he could.

As they trudged along, climbing steadily, the heavy breathing up the line beating out the rhythm of the march, he looked down from time to time to check the progress of the militia and the rest of the Ojos Negros men. They had left the *malpais* in one long dark column, but now they were spread out across the flats in a broad attacking front, and the white dust drifted into the still air behind them. He listened for the tinny notes, however faint, of the bugle which would blow this smoldering line into a full-scale holocaust. It was much too early, he realized then. They still had more than two miles to go. At least he didn't *think* cavalry could sustain a charge from that far out, or could it?

Then he felt something tugging at his knee, and when he looked down, he saw the dark stain where his pants were sticking to it. Blood. He must have cut his knee when he'd fallen after the run across the flats. He hadn't felt it then and, strangely, didn't now; it couldn't be more than a tiny laceration, the merest scratch, nothing that would stiffen up and hold him back.

When Matt Hendry, the man ahead of him, stopped suddenly, Jim nearly climbed the rancher's back. Matt was about forty, not fat, but paunchy and clearly not in the best condition for a trek like this. Jim had heard the man's gasps and wheezes punctuating every step he took. For a moment Jim thought exhaustion had brought him to a halt, but when Matt sank to the ground, heaving like a beached whale, Jim could see farther up the line to where Corey Lane was signaling silently for attention.

"All right," Corey said in the same commanding whisper he had used earlier, "this may be the last planned order I give you." Mike Calico was nowhere in sight, Jim realized. "Take a look up there at that rimrock. It hangs right above Victorio's camp. When we reach it, the enemy camp will be about one hundred fifty feet below us and a little on our right. To the left the rim breaks downward pretty sharply toward the saddle they'll use to run for it—*if* everybody does his job. After our first volley—and I'll come to that in a minute—I want the slope leading to the saddle above the camp denied to every single one of them. If they reach the horse herd, we can't follow, and I'll guarantee the men with the major will be in no shape to either, even if things go well with them."

"Why don't we move straight there and block the saddle now?" It was Dan Stone again, and Jim didn't have to wait for Corey's answer to ask himself, *Doesn't this man ever learn?*

"Because the only way down there is on the rimrock."
Corey hadn't even looked at Stone. "To go on. There's a drop
of maybe a dozen feet just beyond where you can see. The
only other way down is around by way of the saddle. It's the
only drawback the place has as a hideout, and it's the reason
why we don't see lookouts on the ridge. You can be sure
Victorio didn't forget that detail, it was just something he had
to chance. Any sentries he feels he can afford will be over on
the saddle where the ponies are. That's where Mike is now.
If there are any lookouts there, where they could spot us,
they won't be there by the time we reach the rimrock."

Jim wondered where the oppressive heat had suddenly
gone. His spine was cold.

"Now for your orders." Corey Lane pointed to the ridge
again. "We'll spread out at intervals of five feet right under
the top there, on your bellies and a rifle-length back. There
will be no sign from me. At the first shot from the Apache
camp we clear the top. You'll be able to tell whether it's
Victorio or the major when the firing starts. Every man will
pick a target as close to straight ahead as possible—if he can
find one. If he can't, I want him shooting anyway. Three
rounds. *Fast!* I want noise . . . shock."

"What if we find a woman or a kid in our sights, Mr.
Lane?" Bill Talley asked.

"Kill them!"

Jim McPherson wondered if he would reach the rimrock
before he vomited.

"After the first three volleys, I want you shooting at
warriors. Cut down their riflemen. But that first time, *kill
anything you can.* All right, let's move."

Matt Hendry struggled to his feet. *He'll make it easier
than I will,* Jim thought.

"Talley," the sheriff said, "take Mr. Stone and one other
man and climb up behind that tall rock. If White Hair and his
party have decided to come up behind us, you stop them. If
they don't show in twenty minutes, you can join the rest of us
at the rimrock."

As they began to climb again, Jim heard Will-Ed laughing.

When Jim McPherson crawled into the line "a rifle-
length" back from the edge of the rimrock, he struck his
knee, the one with the cut, on a jutting stone, and this time

he really felt it. If the pain was sharp, it was welcome. He was grateful to be feeling anything. Since they began the last climb all his senses had deserted him.

Oh, Lord, how he wanted a drink of water—and how right Will-Ed Martin had been; he could feel the heavy pressure on his bladder way above the agony in his knee.

Two places away from him, he heard a boot scrape in the silence, and when he looked, he could see that the wearer had dislodged a good-sized stone. It was just at the moment the stone came to rest that he heard the first sound of firing, and he was astonished at how close it sounded, and how unreal, more like the popping of corks than the explosive thunder he had expected.

He stood up, took his pace forward with the others, went to his belly again, and poked the muzzle of his rifle across the edge. He wasn't even conscious of his knee as he pulled the trigger. When the first salvo up and down the line roared in his ears, he realized—to what he knew would be his everlasting shame—that he had forgotten to release the safety on his rifle, and then he saw, in the black V of the gunsight and not twenty yards away, the running figure of an Apache warrior he could not have missed. Before he could try again, billows of black powdersmoke obscured everything, and he knew he would have to wait for another chance.

The smoke cleared fast. There was a strong updraft coming out of the Indian camp, air rising from the cupped heat of the dish-shaped slope beneath them. Within seconds Jim McPherson got his first good look at the insanity of war.

Some of the Apaches, like the man he'd had in his sights and whom he couldn't find now, were running. Perhaps a dozen were prone behind a variety of rocks and firing back up at the attackers. Jim blinked and winced as their shots reached the stone face dropping away in front of the firing line and then whined off into the sky above it. There were some bodies. Most of them didn't move. In front of a rude shelter of some kind, one of many which dotted the scene below them, he could see an Indian—he looked to be no more than a boy—crawling in circles.

The firing from the men around Jim had slowed after the first crashing volleys, and he could tell that Will-Ed, Hendry, and the others were selecting targets now, not shooting wildly, and it was then he remembered he hadn't yet squeezed off a single round himself. The crawling boy was the easiest choice, but he passed him up and tried for a runner who had stopped and turned and was aiming back up the slope toward them. The stock of the Winchester slammed him hard in the shoulder and the barrel jumped as the report came, and then the black cloud swirled around his head. When it drifted off, the warrior was nowhere in sight, and to his surprise he didn't feel the relief he was sure a miss would bring. He barked, "Damn!" and amazed himself.

When he looked at the boy again, he saw dirt kicking up in a half-dozen places around him, and then he saw the one violent shake of the slight body which told him someone had found the mark.

The firing around him stopped for a bit. He felt someone slip into place beside him, and turned to see Will-Ed.

"How you doing, Jim?" The rancher's face was black as a minstrel's, and for a second he wondered if he looked like that himself, until he remembered Will-Ed had probably emptied a magazine already.

"The major's in a hell of a lot of trouble," Will-Ed said, pointing down.

Jim wanted to see where Corey Lane was, but he didn't know when another chance might come to size up the whole situation, so he looked where Will-Ed pointed.

In the flats he could see that the militia's and cattlemen's battle line had broken. The party which had ridden out of sight across the ridge had joined the action, and from the right he could see White Hair and Opera Hat charging up to hit them from the other side.

The troopers and the ranchers with them were all dismounted now, at least the ones at the foot of the slope facing the Apache fire. Most of the horses were drawn well back from the fight, but Jim realized that they were under fire, too. There were a number of dead animals, twenty or more, in the space between the main herd and the rocks where the soldiers and the Ojos Negros men with them were entrenched. There were bluecoated bodies dark on the white alkali, too, and enough nondescript, drably clad others to make him ill.

Above these men he could see the Apache riflemen in their pits. Ugly smudges of black smoke above them marked the regularity of their fire. Nothing seemed frantic.

Perhaps it was Will-Ed Martin's remark about the "hell

of a lot of trouble" the major was in (after all, what did he, Jim McPherson, know?), but suddenly he was deeply depressed. The outcome of this battle looked bad. Now he looked for Corey Lane.

He wasn't hard to find. While Jim had gazed down the slope, Corey had stood on the very edge of the rimrock with Mike Calico at his side, back from whatever he'd had to do at the Indian horse herd. Until then the editor hadn't noticed that the Apaches who had fired from the rocks scattered directly under their guns had disappeared, drifted farther down the incline. Now they were in a line behind the rifle pits, shielded from the embattled major and his forces and, while not out of range of the rifles on the rimrock, too far away for accurate fire.

Jim looked back at Corey Lane again. Some sixth sense told him a decision was necessary and that the tall man was about to make it. The sheriff was a towering colossus against the sky. The last ragged puffs of powdersmoke from the volleys and the steady rifle fire afterward were trailing away around the blond hair, passing in front of the lawman's face. The Winchester in his big hand looked like a toy.

"He's something, ain't he?" Will-Ed Martin whispered. "But I'll tell you one thing, Jim—he scares me. Nearly as much as them Apaches down there."

The firing far down the slope was getting more intense, the reports more frequent, running together in a crescendo of noise, with clouds of black smoke all but concealing the Apaches and their targets, the militia and ranchers burrowed into the rockfall on the edge of the alkali flats. With White Hair and Opera Hat and their men now fully engaged, the major was hemmed in on three sides. It didn't take a veteran to see how desperate their situation was.

"Why don't they close in and surround them completely, Will-Ed?" Jim asked.

"They want them to run for it—try to reach the horses. In the flats they'd slaughter them like coyotes."

"Can't we do something?"

"Far as I can see, not one damned thing. Any second now I'll expect Corey will tell us to get out of here and see if we can save our own skins."

Perhaps the grimness of their predicament was too much for Jim to take in, particularly since it was only imminent and

not immediate, but he felt no overwhelming dread, no terror.
He looked at Corey Lane once again, and when he did, he
knew why he wasn't terrified. Corey Lane would take care of
them. He would *do* something.

Corey was gazing down the slope with a different look
than before, not as wide-ranging, not the look of a general
reading the flow of battle. There was something selective
about his stare, as if he had chosen one particular thing or
person for his scrutiny, and if Jim thought he had seen fire
burning in the sheriff's blue eyes in the plaza, it had been a
weak guttering flame compared to the intensity Lane was
now directing against something in the Apache camp.

In back of the Indians in the rifle pits was a second line
of warriors, most of them prone but now beginning to rise,
apparently to advance on the white men pinned down in the
rocks, and in back of that line stood a lone warrior. This was
the man Corey Lane had fixed in his sight. Jim didn't need
anyone to tell him who it was.

The Indian leader was gesturing to his men, pointing to
routes for them to take as they moved down to annihilate the
major's force. Runners came to him and then departed after a
quick nod. Nothing about the man seemed hurried and,
though he was in full view of the soldiers and the ranchers,
he made no attempt to look for cover. Once in a while dirt
would kick up near his feet, but not the slightest sign of
flinching betrayed itself in a body Jim could see even from
that distance was strong and muscular, and half a head taller
than the others near him.

But as steadfast and solid as this Victorio seemed, it was
impossible that anyone could withstand for long the look
coming at him from the rimrock. He must have felt it boring
into his back. Sure enough, when he had finished his signaling and the last of his messengers had joined their comrades
in the advancing line, he turned slowly, deliberately, and
looked up the slope.

His gaze went right to the one man standing on the
ridge, and for what seemed to Jim like long minutes the man
of the Ojos Negros and the savage raider of the Jornada del
Muerto were joined together in a way he had never seen two
men joined before.

Then, and Jim would always wonder if he had really seen
it or if it had only been in his imagination, Victorio raised his

hand, the one with the rifle in it, and shook it two or three
times at the figure against the sky above the rimrock. The
gesture, provided Jim *had* seen it, was half-defiance, half-
salute. Then the Indian turned away from the ridge and
began walking away behind his warriors, motioning them
toward the white men burrowed in the rocks. He didn't look
back—not even when Corey Lane's voice trumpeted above
the sound of the gunfire echoing across the slope.

"*Not yet, viejo! We're not beaten yet!*"

The sheriff took one step forward, to the very edge of the
precipice, and looked to the right and left at the riflemen
lying flat on either side of him, guns silent now.

"All right!" the sheriff said, "we've got to get down there
now, take the pressure off the men in the rocks or Victorio
will finish *them* first and then turn on us. You can take his fire
head-on this way. If we wait until he's through down there,
we'll die with our wounds in our backs. Let's go!"

He leaped from the edge of the rimrock, his rifle high
above his head, hat flying away as the huge body arched
through the air. For all that it was a dozen feet down to the
rocky floor of the slope beneath them, he landed no more
heavily than a hawk settling to a kill. Then a dark streak
appeared in the corner of Jim McPherson's eye and he knew
it was Mike Calico. The little Zuni hit the slope rolling, and
in a second was standing beside Corey Lane.

Without thought Jim found himself on his feet, and in
another moment, just as thoughtlessly, he felt himself sailing
through the air toward the lawman and the wrangler.

Even before his awkward landing he knew it would be a
bad one. The injured knee had stiffened during the time on
the rimrock, and it was clear before his boots struck the
ground he couldn't flex it to absorb the impact. Pain shot
through his kneecap like the sharp report of the Winchester
he had fired earlier. Before he even tried, he knew he
wouldn't be able to stand, and he could see the knowledge,
too, on the face of Corey Lane, hovering over him.

The big man didn't waste any time examining him, though.
He was looking up the ridge they had leaped from, and Jim
saw that the three of them were the only ones who had
jumped. The edge of the rimrock still bristled with the rifles
of Will-Ed, Matt Hendry, and all the others. Bill Talley, Dan
Stone, and the other man who had lain in wait for White Hair

and Opera Hat had joined the rest of them, and it was these faces, at least a little known to the editor, that drew his eye. It shocked him when he realized that none of them had risen, nor intended to. They were going to stay where they were, behind the sure, if temporary, shelter of the lip of rock.

He wondered why *he* had sprung forward so readily, without a moment's doubt or thought. Stupidity was the only answer he could give himself, and stark terror gripped him when he realized suddenly how dearly he would have to pay for it. If Corey Lane reversed himself on finding that his men wouldn't follow, and if he and the Zuni climbed back up the sheer face beneath the rimrock, there would likely be no way Jim could make it. When the Apaches finished the work they were engaged in down below and turned on the line of white men perched above him, they would reach him first.

"What are you waiting for?" Corey Lane asked the men above him. The wrath and contempt in his voice was sharper even than his dismissal of Granby Stafford's offer in his office. *Surely,* Jim thought, *that scalding voice will bring them to their feet, and then in willing leaps to the lawman's side.*

But no one moved.

"All right," Corey said, "die on your bellies, then, like snakes, instead of on your feet, like men." His eye swept along the ridge. "Bill Talley! Throw down your sidearm." The deputy's face flamed red as he reached back to his hip and tossed the revolver into the sheriff's outstretched hand. Lane turned then to the editor. By now Jim had struggled to a sitting position, the painful leg out in front of him.

"Thanks, editor," Corey said. "Let me have that rifle of yours. It's Sam Riordan's, isn't it? Long as you're going to be out of this fight, old Sam will be glad to know it killed a man or two." Without waiting for an answer, he stuck Talley's handgun in his belt and took the Winchester from Jim's grasp. He laid it and his own rifle on the ground and, reaching down, took hold of Jim under the arms and, as if the editor were a feather, pulled him behind a boulder five feet away. He picked up the two rifles and looked at Mike Calico.

"Cover me, Mike. Whenever I settle in to fire, you come down some, too. But don't get too close to me. If things don't go well, you'll have to take care of the editor here. Haul him back up on the ridge if you can—kill him if you can't. And then lead those cowards up there back to the horses in the *malpais*, if that's possible."

As through a white thin haze, Jim McPherson saw the Zuni nod. The harrowing shock of the words "kill him if you can't" went well beyond the bounds of human fear, but he knew with a nauseous certainty why Corey Lane had said them, and he knew as well that it was a great compliment that the sheriff would say them in front of him. Then it came to him how foolish he had been to think for even the shortest instant that this man would ever retreat, ever to the now dubious protection of the rimrock.

Then Corey Lane was walking. There was no more hurry in his gait than if he were crossing the square in Black Springs to arrest a drunk.

It was too much to hope that every Apache in the boiling fury down the slope was so heavily engaged that none had seen the three of them as they left the rimrock, and when Jim focused his eyes on the raging scene he saw a warrior beside Victorio pointing toward the descending figure of Corey Lane. The Apache chieftain turned, fixed his gaze again on his enemy, and with a quick sweep of his hand detached four men from the advancing line. They began firing even before they managed to gain the cover of still another line of rocks, and Jim could hear the whine of their ricochets. Lane made no reply, just kept walking steadily, the rifles in his two swinging hands sliding back and forth like silent Johnson bars on a locomotive.

Mike Calico had gone down the hill a little, too. He was kneeling now, firing steadily, the barrel of his rifle jumping out of his mangled hand with each report. After three or four shots he would rise and run, grotesquely, his twisted little legs jabbing at the stony hillside. Jim couldn't see that his support of Corey was having any effect at all, but he reasoned it must be, the way the tall figure moved so confidently toward the enemy.

Behind him, he could hear gasps from the men on the ridge, gasps which echoed his own sense of wonderment and awe. Like him, they must be waiting with unspoken dread for the inevitable moment when the giant moving so resolutely toward his death would meet it.

Then he saw Corey Lane take his first Apache bullet. He

didn't stagger, but there was a noticeable break in stride. Jim thought the hit must have been high on the right shoulder. A second later another reached him, and this time Jim could see the gout of blood from the left thigh—but still the lawman kept on walking, undeterred; and still he hadn't fired or attempted to.

Calico moved along perhaps a hundred yards behind him, on his stomach now, slithering from rock to rock like some sun-blackened lizard, firing every time he found a rock big enough to hide him while he took his time in aiming. He was close enough now that his shooting could become effective, and the four warriors Victorio had assigned to bring down Corey Lane were rushing their shots, ducking quickly after each of them.

Now it became apparent to the editor that Corey wouldn't waste one round. There had to be a limit to the number of chances he would get once he reached whatever he was headed for, and he was going to make the most of every one of them before he fell. If this mountainside with its natural cover, the boulders and gullies, the scrub oak and cedar, made it ideal for the defense Victorio had planned, it now worked against this Apache. But why didn't Corey Lane break his terrible walk and take advantage of these safe hiding-places?

Then Jim knew why. Corey couldn't take time to stop, not even for a moment. Above the rifle pits and to the right of them was a long curled slab of stone which even Jim could see would be an ideal breastwork, and this, obviously, was Corey Lane's objective. Once in its shadow, he could bring his guns to bear on the warriors in the pits and the advancing line as well. Victorio had seen it, too. With another wave of his hand five more warriors broke off the attack on the major and his men and began to climb toward the slab in an effort to cut the lawman off before he reached it. Lane did halt then. He laid one of the rifles at his feet, brought the other to that wounded shoulder, fired, levered another cartridge into the chamber of the Winchester, and fired again. Two Apaches dropped like stones. Two more turned and scrambled down the route they had just come up. The fifth, frantic in his climb, moved up the far side of the shelter that the sheriff, moving again as deliberately as before, was heading for. When the Indian disappeared, Corey broke into a limping

but lightning run, and Jim knew that the slow steady walk to
that point had been a carefully calculated plan. The warrior
would come across the top of Corey's destination confident
the sheriff was still many yards away. Under the shadow of
the rock Lane knelt. When the black hair tied by the headband rose above the rock, he fired. The top of the Apache's
head exploded into bloody fragments of meat and bone.

In a moment Corey was snugged in behind the protection of the slab, firing across the body of the man he had just
killed, the barrel of his Winchester (or Sam's—Jim couldn't
tell) actually laid across the dead man's back, the other gun
propped beside him. Blood was streaming down his pants leg
from the wound in his thigh, but there was no sign he was
favoring it and certainly he wasn't favoring his shoulder, not
from the way the rifle stock was jammed against it, slamming
it brutally with every shot.

Mike Calico had taken advantage of the attention being
paid the lawman to move another fifty yards downhill, and
between him and Corey, their rapid fire was beginning to
tell. It wasn't that so many of the enemy were falling, but
almost all of Victorio's secondary attack force was pinned
down in shallow depressions just behind the rifle pits. Jim
could see the Apache leader standing on the lower side of one
of the countless outcroppings which studded the hillside. He
was looking upward at Corey Lane again.

Suddenly, inexplicably, all the firing stopped. Jim could
see Calico reloading, and he could see Corey settle back a
little. Neither of them would want to expend ammunition
now with their targets almost completely out of sight, but
the rest the two of them were taking couldn't account
for the silence from the rifle pits or among Major Lattner's
men. The Apaches who were still on horseback in the flats
seemed to have broken off their harassment of the few soldiers
and civilians guarding the horse herd—the pitiful remnants of
it—and even White Hair and Opera Hat had retired a little
distance from the militia's seemingly hopeless position.

Some signal had been flashed by Victorio, obviously, but
the editor hadn't seen it. Was this the quiet before the last
lethal storm? Jim wondered. Would the Apache chief soon
unleash every man in his command, send them screaming
and whooping into the major's crippled forces? The editor

tried not to think of the butchery he would witness—if he found the strength to watch.

Then, across the slope from him, at eye level and above the battle, he saw something else. Women and children were emerging from the rough brush huts he had seen from the rimrock. He wondered why he hadn't noticed their absence up till now.

They were gathering in groups on a sort of flat ledge overlooking the rifle pits, silently, or so it seemed—at least he saw no indication that any of them was talking. The women shooed the children in front of them to the very limit of the ledge, and soon there must have been fifty or sixty of them standing there, all gazing down on their fighting men, an audience as mute as the stones their feet were rooted in. There were infants in arms, toddlers whose hands were tucked into those of the women (these were girls; the ones Jim thought were boys were a pace closer to the edge, small brown statues with lean arms folded across thin bare chests), and women of every age and shape. Their faces, adult and child, were as blank as the mountain wall behind them.

McPherson looked down again to see if Victorio had taken notice of the silent throng above him, but he found the Apache leader still staring up at Corey Lane's redoubt.

Something had changed in the Indian's attitude. Jim wasn't sure just how he knew this, but he thought Victorio stood a bit straighter, stiffer than before—and taller, too. He seemed to be drawing breaths deeper than necessary for a man who hadn't been subjected to any great exertion. As Jim watched, fascinated by this man who was going to kill them all if he could (and it surely looked as if this was well within his power now), he saw a warrior crawling up toward Victorio from the rifle pits. Mike Calico's rifle barked twice, the reports so close together they almost made one sound, but the Indian crawled on until he was with his leader in the safe shade of Victorio's rock. The noise of the Zuni's rifle, coming after the lull, shocked McPherson even more than had the first volley fired from the ridge. Then he saw Victorio say something to the man, and the warrior's nod. The man crawled down again the way he had come, and Mike Calico fired at him and missed again, or if he did hit him, the man didn't stop.

Once the messenger had regained the rifle pits, things happened quickly. The riflemen in the pits turned away from the cattlemen and troopers they had besieged with such success and faced up the mountainside toward Corey Lane. Volley after volley suddenly outraged the silence, but even with all the fearsome noise echoing from the heights around him, the scene below Jim McPherson became dumbshow and pantomine.

Victorio's attack line was rising from the little gullies it had nestled in when Corey opened fire, but instead of moving to overrun Major Lattner, as the editor had expected, the Indians started up the slope toward Corey's rock, where the cloud from the lawman's busy Winchester was mushrooming above him as black as the *malpais* which seemed years and leagues away from them.

Corey's fire was deadly accurate, and so now was that of Mike Calico. The Zuni had been either forgotten or deliberately ignored by the score or more Apaches advancing so intently on Corey Lane. Five, six of them fell, stopped cleanly. They didn't move once they were knocked back by the fusillade coming from the slab of rock. The sheriff was taking a terrible toll, but if Corey and the half-breed killed most of them, there would still be too many left to stand against. It would soon be over.

Then, just as Jim was about to turn and begin the probably impossible struggle to get up the rockface behind him and save himself, he heard the thuds of booted feet hitting the ground around him. Will-Ed and Talley and the others were leaving the safety of the rimrock. My God! He had forgotten all about them.

Men landed running, racing past his rock on either side, shouts and cries rising even above the blasts of rifle and revolver fire. The lot who had cowered on the rimrock, even in the face of Corey Lane's scathing dismissal of them, were suddenly raging animals. Now the chaos and madness of battle Jim had expected to see when he first looked into the stronghold had become reality. It was as if a wild cyclonic wind were sweeping down the mountain. His heart doubled its beat in sudden hope, but it slowed immediately in the almost certain knowledge that this charge had come too late, perhaps not too late to save this bloody day, but too late to save the valiant man who had brought them here.

He looked down to Corey's personal battleground. The warriors mounting the slope had covered nearly half the

distance, and if there weren't as many as before, there were
enough. Victorio himself was with them. He didn't once turn
to face either Mike Calico or the cattlemen now joining the
little Zuni, joining him and then moving again as Calico
pressed closer to the awful thing about to happen at Corey's
rock. The Apaches were splitting now to flank the slab from
either side when they got that high, and Victorio stopped
between them. Corey was swinging his rifle from side to side,
firing rapidly. One rifle was dropped beside him and he
grasped the other one. No time for reloading now. Then the
second Winchester was empty, too, and lay at his feet as he
pulled Bill Talley's weapon from his belt and his own from
the holster on his hip.

The line of warriors was two lines now, only twenty feet
from the outer edges of the rock. A red blotch suddenly
flagged out on Corey's neck and McPherson knew the lawman had been hit again. Good Lord, the amount of blood he
must have lost.

Then the group farthest down the slope stopped. When
Jim looked past them, he could see the reason: Lattner's
men, like those on the rimrock, had poured out of the rocks
they had been cringing behind. They had reached the rifle
pits, and some of them were doing grisly efficient work with
sabers and sidearms; the rest were storming up the hill
toward Victorio and the men climbing with him. Only three
of the Apaches continued on toward Corey Lane. One fell to
the lawman's pistol as he rounded the downhill side of the
curved rock, the other two stopped for a moment above the
sheriff. One took careful aim, but before he fired, someone,
most likely Calico, had him in his sights. His body jerked
convulsively, but he staggered forward and fell at Corey's
feet. Corey raised his sidearm and killed the other one—and
then he fell, too. He struggled to a sitting position and
dropped his head on his chest.

The end came swiftly for the rest of the Apache army.
The men left alive in the rifle pits threw down their guns and
sat crosslegged, their hands raised above their heads. A few
of the men farther up, the ones who had walked toward
Corey Lane with Victorio, had begun to run toward the
saddle, but most of them surrendered, too. The women and
children had already started upward for the ridge line, but

only a few made it to the other side before the soldiers reached them.

Victorio wasn't among the ones who were herded together in the unreal hour that followed the last echo of the last gun fired.

"Jesus Christ, *no*, we ain't going to bury them!" Will-Ed Martin said. "We've hardly got time to get our own people underground before we move over the saddle for the night. And we *got* to get out of here. This place is going to smell to high heaven pretty quick."

It had been a miserable sickening hour for Jim McPherson, and not because of the aching knee Matt Hendry had bound tightly in Jim's neckerchief and his own. About the only decent moment Jim could remember was when he had hobbled with the aid of the stick Matt had cut for him from a dead ocotillo to where Horace Lattner and the sergeant who acted as medic for the militia bent over the prostrate body of Corey Lane. When he saw the man breathing easily, and saw him flick the blue eyes in his direction, his heart had leaped with heady relief.

The sheriff tried to say something, but Jim shook his head. "Don't talk, Sheriff Lane. Save your strength."

The major was shaking his head, too, but when he walked off with the editor, Jim found it was for a different reason.

"I can't quite believe everything I saw today, McPherson," Horace Lattner said. "Oh, I'd heard all about the affair at Apache Pass, but I'd always taken it with a grain of salt. Never did put too much credence in folk-hero stories. I'm willing to think about it now. Incredible! I've never even *heard* of a one-man army like that man was today."

Jim swelled with pride as though he had done it all himself, or at least had forecast it.

"Don't mistake me, though," Lattner went on, "I'm still not sure I'd want to serve with him again. He took me over the road about my charge—just before he passed out for a while. Chastised me as if I was a truant schoolboy."

"You did make your charge then, major?"

"Such as it was, McPherson, such as it was." Lattner walked off toward his officers, shaking his head again.

Jim looked for Will-Ed. He wanted to be with someone

who would have no reservations at all about the special worth of Corey Lane.

It was clouding up for a late-afternoon storm, but the prospect couldn't dull Jim's spirits now, not even with all the dead around him, nor could the chance that a bad rain might wash out the promise of a campfire to cheer him, and hot food and drink for the first night in four.

He found Will-Ed standing guard over a group of captives near the temporary wicki-ups. The men sat on the ground, hands tied behind their backs, legs remaining free until the victors and vanquished would walk over the saddle above the encampment to the new campground by the spring Mike Calico had reported. The women and children stood in a half-circle behind their men. They didn't look down at them, nor did the defeated warriors turn and look at *them*. To Jim it seemed they didn't look at anything, any of them. Their empty black eyes stared straight ahead into the sky above the silent rifle pits, where a few wisps of powdersmoke still hovered in the air. They didn't lower those vacant eyes to the pits, either, where fifteen or twenty Apache bodies sprawled. The dead or wounded white men had already been gathered up and carried over the ridge, the wounded to be tended as well as possible, the sixteen dead troopers and eleven fallen ranchers to be buried "in the piñon," Will-Ed said, "where the ground ain't as hard as a Chihuahua *puta*'s heart."

One of the last litters moved up the hill carried Bill Talley, his face a white, drained, smiling mask above a midsection which looked as if it had been sloshed with a bucket of thick red paint.

Will-Ed stopped the two men carrying the boy. "How's it going, deputy?"

"Not bad, Will-Ed. It don't hurt near as much as I would have thought. Well, you old bastard, I guess you beat me into this here fight. But only because Sheriff Lane kept me back. You own my horse now, I reckon."

"Don't worry, Bill. I'll rent him to you free, for the rest of your born life."

When the litter-bearers had hauled Talley far enough up the slope to be out of earshot, Will-Ed turned to the editor. "Wasn't much to promise. He's gut-shot so bad he won't last an hour."

Jim fought back tears, and then looked around at the slope again for something, anything, to change the subject. There were more Indian bodies scattered on the approaches to the stone slab where Corey Lane had made his stand, and coming down through them he saw Mike Calico. The Zuni stopped by each of the bodies, stared down at it intently, and then moved on. Once in a while he bent over and grasped an Apache by the shoulder and did something Jim couldn't quite make out.

"Will-Ed," the editor asked, "what the devil is Calico up to? He's not robbing those poor devils, is he? What could they possibly have of any value to him?"

"Hell, no!" Will-Ed chuckled. "Mike ain't no thief. Look a little closer, Jim."

The Zuni was standing over an Apache nearer to them, as he had stood over all the others on his way down the hill, his face impassive as always, his eyes, dull black beads, fixed on the dead man at his feet. Then Jim saw the slight rise and fall of the Apache's chest, and realized the man wasn't dead after all. When the wrangler bent over the limp form, Jim saw a skinning-knife. Calico grasped the warrior's shoulder with his withered left hand as he had the others, and rolled him onto his back. The Apache's eyes were staring straight up at the Zuni. They didn't waver or turn away, nor did the man make the smallest struggle when Calico leaned over, placed the point of his blade under the left ear, and sharply, but calmly, plunged it to the hilt. It was done with such precision there was hardly any blood. Then the Zuni walked away without a backward look and headed for the rifle pits. He looked like a man who had just finished fixing a roof or mending a length of fence.

The horror in Jim's bowels left him too weak for words. Choking, he reached out and clutched at Martin's sleeve. When the rancher turned to him, he pointed to the Zuni, who was now repeating the terrible process on a figure in the rifle pits.

"Oh, that? Well, yeah." Will-Ed shrugged. "Well, they was going to die anyway. This is better, really." He turned away, tucked the rifle he'd been holding on the captives under his arm, brought a briar pipe from his hip pocket, and began to load it.

Jim looked around him in desperation. Looked for what,

help? What he saw seemed even worse than the neat unhurried executions Mike Calico was performing as he moved from pit to pit.

Five or six of the soldiers and as many Ojos Negros men, Will-Ed Martin's guard detail, were lounging near him, joking, laughing, two of them eating something. Calico and his ghastly surgery were in clear view, but none of them was looking.

The tied Apache prisoners and their expressionless women and children weren't looking, either.

The storm didn't break. It moved over and past them, way down the piñon- and yucca-dotted trail the fleeing Victorio and his few warriors (no more than six or seven, Will-Ed had estimated) must have taken, together with the squaws and children who had escaped the militia-rancher dragnet.

Jim McPherson huddled near one of the dozen campfires blazing in the piñon groves. Even the bright flames couldn't chase the shadows from his mind, and he thought ruefully that the only blessing he could count was the fact that he felt so depressed in every other way he no longer noticed the pain in his damaged knee. Well, there was also the near-miraculous revival of Corey Lane, but that wasn't as much heartening as it was astonishing. The sheriff had taken a full and commanding part in the post-battle decisions—assigning captured Indian ponies to the men whose mounts had been killed, selecting a small determined force to hunt down the remnants of White Hair's band. He'd had to be carried up the hill with the other wounded, but after mess he'd actually walked around for a little while, alone, not even Mike Calico by his side.

If the editor hadn't felt bad enough already, it was worse for him to look at the blood-soaked bandages wrapping a third of the sheriff's body. He remembered with shame his asinine promise to Virgie Lane to look after her husband. The flickering light from the campfires turned Corey's rigid features to bronze as he made his way, stately, silent. McPherson could understand Virgie's feelings for her husband. But—he felt a tremendous surge of some unknown feeling here—she *couldn't* love him with an ordinary mortal woman's love. It wouldn't do for this Olympian paragon. But there must be a torrent of very *human* passion raging in her—which he had sensed and which had brought him so perilously close to humiliation in the store that day. Why, a man could dare to . . . The folly of the hope he had been about to permit himself overwhelmed him then, and he sank even deeper in his well of gloom.

It didn't make it easier to realize that he would probably see Corey's wife before Corey did himself.

At mess Major Lattner had voiced his plans to take the Apache captives into the agency at Fort Stanton, and had asked Corey about routes and the possibilities of provisions along the way.

"Don't worry yourself about the details for a moment, major," Corey had said. "I'm going with you. Will-Ed can boss the Ojos Negros show back to Black Springs!"

"Good Heavens, man! In the shape you're in?"

"I'm going, major. Settle your mind on that point once and for all."

That was when the sheriff had stood up for the first time since he'd been carried up from the battleground. Half a dozen of the men around the fire leaped to aid him, but he brushed them aside impatiently.

"I can't chance any more of them getting away," Corey said, "like Victorio did!"

He'd turned then and walked out of the reach of the fire's light, as if he'd gotten up from a fitful sleep.

Bill Talley lasted only a little longer than the hour Will-Ed Martin had given him. The burial detail had broken for the supper hour, and the boy's stiffening body was tucked under a juniper tree until they came back to it. Jim had leaned on his stick, hat in hand, looking down at the young deputy. Nobody was saying any "words" over any of the fallen. "We'll wagon out with their kinfolk and a preacher and do it proper," Matt Hendry had said. "Ain't none of us could do it. Unless *you* want to, Jim."

McPherson hurried off, hobbling, to find Will-Ed again.

He found the rancher back on duty as a guard once more. There was so much Jim wanted to ask the more experienced man, so much he wanted to get sorted out about everything he'd seen during the course of the long frightening day. Perhaps Will-Ed would explain just why he and the others, not cowards (Good Lord, not cowards!), had hung back when the sheriff, the Zuni, and, yes, *he*, the petrified dude Easterner, had made that wild leap into the Apache camp back in that other century—and what had made Will-Ed, who after all should have had more faith than any other man in Corey's magic, wait so long to risk it. Of course, Jim *couldn't* ask, but he could listen, and to the things unsaid as well as those the Ojos Negros man might voice.

He didn't get any answers to his unspoken questions.

Will-Ed was seated with his rifle across his knees, puffing on his pipe. The pipe, which had come out at the close of battle, hadn't been out of his mouth since, except at mess. Jim wished he had the pipe habit. It might even be better if he chewed. Perhaps the strong tobacco would get rid of the awful taste of vomit he'd had since he'd witnessed Mike Calico's gory chores of the afternoon. Even food hadn't driven it away.

"Howdy, Jim," the rancher said as the editor sank down beside him.

The Apache men were bound hand and foot for the night, and a few of the cattlemen were herding the women and children away from them into a clearing in the piñon which gleamed silver under a full moon.

"Glad you don't have to tie *them*, Will-Ed," Jim said.

"Yeah. All we got to do is keep them from releasing any of the braves. They sure as hell wouldn't run without them."

There were a few clouds left in the sky from the storm which had missed the camp, fast-moving spectral clouds with dark centers and glowing edges. They would slide across the moon and then uncover it, and when they did, it seemed as if someone had stalked across the landscape with a giant ghost lantern. Suddenly Jim was exhausted, but, to his surprise, not unpleasantly so. Perhaps, instead of opening any deep talk with Will-Ed, it would be better just to sit here while the older man smoked, and let the beauty of the night effect whatever cure it could for him.

The warriors close to Jim were all asleep, or seemed to be. It was hard to believe now that the peaceful harmless heaps he looked at had been, but a few hours earlier, hellions on the verge of killing him. He was glad he wouldn't see them much past daybreak, when they would begin the long brutal walk to Stanton.

His eyes, beginning to glaze with the need for sleep, wandered to the clearing, but they focused sharply when he saw some of the guard detail—cowmen, from the look of their outfits—standing by the lumpy forms of the Apache women and children. His newfound ease and restfulness turned to mild disgust when he saw that two of the men, without having bothered to move away from their sleeping prisoners, were urinating, the streams bright insulting platinum arches in the moonlight. The faint sound of laughter drifted up to him, and raucous voices, too.

When the two men had finished, they and the others, five of them all told, began wandering through the huddled bodies. One by one they leaned over the women, shook them by the shoulders—one of them grasping a sleeper by her long black hair—and then stood back as the women rose.

"What are they up to, Will-Ed?" he said, his voice an echo of the afternoon's when he'd asked the rancher about Mike Calico's deadly journey across the battleground. "They're not going to . . ."

"Hell, no, Jim!" The cattleman erupted with laughter. "Just watch for a second." The men were moving off toward the scrub on the edge of the clearing, each of them followed by a woman. "See," Will-Ed said, "they're just taking them off in the bush for a little fun."

For a moment Jim couldn't find his voice. It was as if an unseen pair of hands were choking him. Will-Ed went on, "You could join them, if your tastes run that way. Apache women are pretty clean, not all clapped up like squaws from the tribes that swarm around the towns. Myself, I'm willing to wait for white meat, but I mind me when—"

Jim found his voice, strangled as it sounded. "But, Will-Ed —it's rape!"

"Hey! Just one God-damned second!" There was a nasty, steely, cutting edge to the rancher's voice. "It ain't rape!" Then, more softly, and slowly, as if he were explaining something to a child, "It ain't rape. Get that out of your mind once and for all. You don't see them putting up a struggle, do you? It's just what's *done*, Jim. Bear one thing in mind: they lost." He tapped the pipe on the heel of his hand. "Maybe you'd better find your bedroll and get some shuteye. We'll be riding hard for Black Springs tomorrow morning."

Jim got to his feet painfully. The nausea he'd been sure he'd finally escaped was coming back. The men and the captive women had disappeared. Will-Ed was right. He'd

better find his bedroll. He didn't want to stay a second longer
and chance hearing anything.

"I should think," Will-Ed Martin said, "that you'd be
singing and dancing, Jim. Leastways as much as that bunged-up
knee would let you. God damn it, we won a hell of a victory
today. And you—you were a regular fourteen-carat hero,
jumping in with Corey and Calico the way you did."

Jim started up toward the campfires. There was nothing
he could say.

Will-Ed's voice followed him. "Jesus—I keep forgetting
how much you still got to learn."

". . . I thought to crush him in an equal force,
True sword to sword . . ."

VIII

Victorio reined his pony to a halt near a thick stand of
storm-drenched mesquite and greasewood. He hadn't wanted
to lead the headlong rush down the trail; he would have
preferred to herd his people along gently, but they wouldn't
have done nearly this well if he hadn't been out in front. In
truth, it made little difference either way.

They could rest here while Nariz Roto died. There was
almost no chance the soldiers and the other white men were
following them. They had their own wounded and all their
captives to look after, and it would take them some time to
round up the horses he had released and scattered when he
found he wouldn't have time to kill them. It was too bad he
couldn't take long enough to ruin the water after he and his
tiny group had topped the ridge during the last confusion of
the battle, but the whites' pursuit had still been hot then.

He was now well past the shame he had felt when Nariz
and Long Hand pulled him away from the men attacking the
white chief Lane behind the rock. No matter that it would
have been a thousand times better to die there; he knew now
that it was wisest to run one more time like this. Nariz and
Long Hand couldn't lead even a band as small as this one.
Still, there would have been no way for them to get him over
the saddle and onto this trail if he had known that the woman
hadn't been among the few who made it.

Poor foolish Nariz. He wouldn't be dying now with that
terrible stinking hole in his chest if he hadn't paused on the
crest of the ridge to shout one more insult at the troopers

doing such deadly work on the other Mimbreños and their
wives and children. Foolish Nariz? No more fool than he,
Victorio.

No, not nearly so big a fool.

To break off the attack on the soldiers beneath the rifle
pits when victory was in his grasp and turn toward Lane was
the worst kind of stupidity. That they would soon have run
out of ammunition was only half a reason. He would have
done it anyway: it was as sure as the stones themselves from
the moment he saw Lane standing on the rimrock. When he
shook his rifle at the figure looming against the sky, the thing
was decided. It didn't matter that he had moved farther down
the slope as though disregarding the white man's challenge.
He had known then there was only one thing he would
do—and Lane must have known it, too. Of course he knew it.

If *Lane* ever made a mistake, this would be the very kind
he would make, but this time, as at the pass, he made none.

Twice he had fought this man. Twice he had been defeated. He knew now that he would always lose to him. Gone
was the wild dream of honorable face-to-face combat with the
fearsome yellow-haired white giant. Now it came down to
trickey and cunning, things he despised as much as he despised himself for thinking of them. Somehow he would have
to bring about the death of this man before death found *him*,
even if Lane was a guest in a Mimbreño wicki-up. He would
have to put his own pride behind him until he found a way.
His pride was as great as his enemy's, or was it? Would Lane
stop to think of what would happen to *his* people in the
course of any fight? He doubted it. And if his doubts were
sound, it was all the more reason to admire this white warrior
while hating him.

But now what? There weren't enough of them left to
even make small raids well. And there was the woman in his
mind, too. He must see her one more time at least before he
set his pony's feet on the trail which had no end.

The soldiers would take their Mimbreño prisoners up to
Mescalero, to Fort Stanton and Agent Russell, he was sure of
it. They had been badly mauled, as badly as Victorio's people, and would have little stomach for any march other than
the shortest one. Something hurt inside when he thought of
the woman walking, roped like a mule, across the desert
badlands with the others. She would live, though. She would

live if every other member of the band shriveled up and
died. She would live until he came to her one more time.

And he would come to her. He would seek out Agent
Russell and convince him he would stay as tame as the
Mescalero cousins. Russell didn't like him very much, but he
was fair and good, so far as agents went, no thief like the one
at Selden. He would want to believe that Victorio was ready
to call it quits at last. It would mean lying, but lying only
done to get at the larger truth.

The Mimbreños were all dead men now. All that remained was to find the final grave and, with one last echoing
battle cry, leap gladly into it with no hope of getting out.

He would spend the summer at the agency—while the
water holes were dust and the cattle on the *estancias* were
thin and ragged—making *tiswin* beer, and he would spend
the fall and winter drinking it and growing fat on provision
corn and beef. Then, when spring came again . . .

Maybe he could drive the *gáh'n* from the minds of Loco
and good old Nana, chase away the spirits which had made
them as meek as the village Indians who rotted on the fringes
of the white man's world. Probably by now they had planted
another crop under the fatherly eye of the well-meaning
Stanton agent. Probably, too, they had forgotten all the crops
they had put in so many times before, crops they never
harvested because the soldiers always moved them before the
stalks had begun to bend. Once even he had thought there
might come a time when they would settle down and be the
kind of Indians the white masters wanted them to be, but
now that he was as old as the fingers on five sets of hands he
knew this could no longer be. All of the people—even the
newest child, even the unborn one in the belly of the girl on
the pony next to Long Hand there—were now as old as he
was, and could never change.

It would have been different if every white man were as
fearless as the tall man Lane. A few of them came close, but
it was not enough. As long as white men feared the Mimbres
and the Chiricahua and some of the other tribes, there would
always be someone to force them on the raid again. And with
more white men coming to the deserts and the mountains
every time the seasons changed, there was only the one way
for it all to end.

There was enough food and ammunition for a week or

two on the run, then he would have to go up the side of the peak with the two high summits and surrender. Lane should be gone by then, back to the town and ranch which were the center of his power. He, Victorio of the Mimbres Apaches, didn't want Lane there to hear the lies Victorio would tell the agent.

The storm crashed into the desert in a new burst of fury, gathering the clouds into one great black lowering curtain. When the Indians saw that Nariz Roto had breathed his last, the five warriors, seven women, and two young boys urged their horses to a walk and set off down the trail. Water ran in roiling dark rivers through the arroyos on either side of them.

PART
TWO

*"No more of this; it does offend my heart.
Pray now, no more."*

I

"What's Jacky heard, Jim?" Sam Riordan said, leaning against the Sacramento House bar, a glass of whiskey halfway to his lips.

"That scout who rode in this morning brought word that Corey and Major Lattner should reach town this afternoon, as planned," Jim McPherson said. "The militia's gone straight back to Santa Fe, but most of the officers will stay overnight here in Black Springs for the celebration."

"No trouble on the march?"

"Not a bit. They turned the Indians over to Russell without a hitch. I guess he was a little shocked to find out how few there were of them."

"Any sign of Victorio?"

"Not yet. Russell seems fairly certain that it's just a question of time, though. He recognized Victorio's wife among the captives. Says Victorio won't leave her there alone. The scout says the agent is a little disturbed at the prospect of playing jailer to the Mimbreños, but he'll try to keep them docile."

"What kind of shape is Corey in?"

"Good, I guess. It amazes me, Sam. He's still all wrapped in bandages, according to the scout, but he rode with the best of them all the way up the mountain, and believe me, Sam, he was all but shot to pieces."

"Told you, didn't I?" Sam said, a wide smug grin cracking his tanned old features. "Well, God damn! We're going to have a *fiesta* like Black Springs never saw before!" He looked

105

at the circle of other drinkers who had gathered around the two of them. "Don't hang back, you mavericks. Let's make a start on the party we'll have tonight. Belly up! The booze is on Sam Riordan."

Jim smiled—Sam had made a fair-to-middling start already—but the smile faded when he saw Granby Stafford at the edge of the crowd surging forward to get in on Riordan's hospitality. The merchant walked deliberately to the far end of the bar, all by himself.

"Let's drink to Corey, boys," Sam said, after the bartender had filled the glasses shoved at him. The old rancher's was already raised above his head when he saw Stafford, his head bowed over his own empty glass.

"Hey, Gran!" Sam shouted. "Ain't you going to get in on this? It sure ain't every day you can tap me for a drink."

The merchant mumbled something, but didn't turn his head.

"Come on, Gran," Sam pleaded, "don't be a sorehead. You could lift one to our next Territorial senator, couldn't you?"

Jim McPherson opened his eyes wide. He had forgotten the slight shadow cast over the jubilation in Black Springs when Will-Ed and his men had ridden into town three days ago with the news of Corey's victory. George Meadows, the octogenarian lawyer who had been a much loved fixture in Santa Fe while representing Chupadera County, had died in his sleep in Black Springs as the cattlemen were trooping back from the battle in the Oscuras. Wilson Blaine, Black Springs' restless—and mostly forgotten—mayor, disregarding any thought of the bad taste it showed to be in such a hurry, had appeared in Jim's office at eight in the morning of the editor's first day back to announce that he was standing for the vacant Senate seat in the special election sure to follow.

Fussy and obnoxious as Jim found Blaine, the idea made a certain amount of sense. The mayor had spent so much time in the capital he was bound to know his way through the tunnels of Territorial power better than anyone else the Ojos Negros district could send. Jim hadn't even thought of Corey— but now he wondered why. The idea excited him. The respect the sheriff would command, particularly after his triumph over the Apaches, would reach all the way into Governor Wallace's office and, through him, to Washington without a doubt. Yes, why not? He was wondering how Corey felt about it before he realized the lawman couldn't possibly know. This must be entirely Sam's idea. Well, it was a good one.

Granby had turned now to look at Riordan, and Jim could see the idea had come as a surprise to the merchant, too. He glared at Sam. Then almost angrily he motioned to the bartender, threw a wad of money on the bar, and shook his head when the man pointed to Sam. He tore the bottle from the bartender's hand.

"I'll take the whole damned thing, Joe," he said, adding, as he continued to look straight at Sam, "and, paying for it myself, I can drink to who I damned well please. Keep the change."

He tucked the bottle under his arm and strode toward the door. When he reached Sam, he turned to face the old rancher.

"You *are* one of the wolves, after all, aren't you, Sam?"

Sam smiled. "Come *on*, Gran. If you don't like the idea, you can say so when the vote comes. Don't spoil Corey's homecoming now."

Stafford cleared his throat and spat right at Riordan's feet. "That's what I think of your Corey and his homecoming!"

The men around Sam at the bar moved aside as if they had been pushed, and Jim's heart gave a wild thump. It was a second before he realized neither of the two men was armed, and that in any case they were both far too old for any really violent nonsense. Sam, whose blue eyes had been gleaming with the first twinkling hints of the mild good-humored drunkenness he regularly sought from Saturday morning until Sunday night, was suddenly cold tough sober, his lips pressed together like a clamp.

"God damn it, Granby Stafford." His voice was low, intense, but more thoughtful than menacing. "How come you're still so sore at Corey? Haven't things turned out exactly the way I said out there two weeks ago?" He pointed out the open door of the barroom toward the plaza. "The rains this past week have set Eloy and his people up for the whole summer. And didn't the other thing I tried to warn you of come about, too? And didn't Corey come through just like I said?"

"Look, Sam . . . I . . ." It sounded as if the merchant

were strangling. He finally got some control of himself, but when he went on, his voice still sputtered and crackled like the fuse train on a blasting charge. "Shooting Apaches ain't the same thing as legislating up at Santa Fe—and you can bet your sweet life I'm not alone in feeling the way I do."

Sam drew a breath. "No," he said, "no, I don't suppose you are. People like you could never be alone in anything. I guess the thing that really sticks in your craw is the thought of one man alone. You're so God-damned happy to band together like sheep, or little kids, you just plain can't understand a man like Corey Lane. It's got nothing to do with the facts of the matter at all, has it?"

Stafford didn't say anything, just stared at Riordan with a hate that seemed to fill the barroom. Poor Granby. Yes, Sam would have to allow that much. This was no bad man. Granby felt strongly about Black Springs and the Rio Concho people. He was just a bit confused by all that had happened the past two weeks.

It was a bad moment all the same, but Sam didn't seem to realize it. The rancher gestured to the crowd holding the glasses full of whiskey he had bought, and they closed around him, leaving Granby Stafford alone with his hate, alone in that very way Riordan had said so confidently that the merchant couldn't be.

Stafford turned without another word, took a tighter grip on the bottle, and left the barroom for the street. His shoulders sagged as he went through the door, revealing how thoroughly he had been beaten once again. It must have shocked him that everywhere he turned he saw the erosion of whatever power he had once possessed. The men gathering around Sam, shouting Corey's praises between gulps of Sam Riordan's whiskey, were only echoing the kind of thing heard this past week on every Black Springs corner.

Jim walked to the door and watched Stafford make his way down the boardwalk veranda of the Sacramento House. He saw him glance once at the welcoming banner stretched across Estancia Street before he disappeared in the crowd beginning to fill the Black Springs plaza.

It was explosively bright in the plaza. With the summer solstice less than three weeks off, the noon sun couldn't have been more than a few paltry degrees away from directly overhead, and the good rains which had pelted the town while he had been on the march with Corey had washed the dusty cottonwoods until their leaves, now fully out, sparkled as if they had been scrubbed and waxed. The noisy reds, whites, and blues of the bunting and crepe which had been appearing all morning long in the plaza like new spring growth shouted at him from every storefront and office around the square. Even the livery stable and his own drab *Chupadera County News* building leaped with color. And the people! How different from the crowd which had grown here like a tumor two short weeks ago. They were picnicking on the caliche now, prepared to wait for Corey, apparently, if it took the entire summer. Picnicking! Pity there wasn't a green blanket of grass to cradle them, as in the village square back in Puckett's Corners. By George, he could come out for that on the editorial page of the *News,* for that and for a bandstand, too, perhaps.

He winced. That would be a brave thing, wouldn't it, coming out foursquare for grass? Grass meant precious water, and that would be sure to raise the issue of the Sinuoso dam again—just when he might need all his editorial muscle to help hoist Corey Lane into the vacant seat in the Territorial Senate. Not that the sheriff would need him—this sudden adulation was apt to sweep Corey Lane to Santa Fe like a flash flood, but, oh, how Jim wanted to be part of such a wave. It occurred to him that he might have become part of it already with the article he had splashed across the gray, usually featureless front page of the *News,* describing the battle with Victorio. He was proud of the piece, and if it was a trifle purple, he certainly hadn't tried to heighten the color. The simple facts of the conflict and Corey's remarkable heroism came out so strongly there had been no way to weaken it.

"Hell's fire! Don't our town look pretty, Jim?" It was Sam, finally detached from his drinking buddies, at his elbow. "Wonder when Corey will get here."

Our town? Yes, he had begun to think of it that way himself, but it was gratifying to hear Sam include him.

"Hey!" Sam said. "Lookee there. Now that *she's* come to town, the shindig will be complete!"

Drawing to a stop on the hotel side of the Sacramento House was a buckboard, and next to the driver Jim saw Virgie Lane, her Spanish hat tilted well down in front to shield her eyes against the blinding sun. If the plaza had seemed bright before he set eyes on her, it was now a sea of hot color.

So she had come, after all, to join Alicia in her rooms at the Sacramento. The elder Mrs. Lane had been here during the whole time he had been on the march with Corey, and had remained to await her son's arrival from the Mescalero. Jim wondered when (certainly not *if*) Virgie would tell her of Jim's coming to the X-Bar-7 with the news of the fight against Victorio—and of Corey's wounds.

He had split away from the returning column of Ojos Negros men when they cleared the *malpais,* riding straight for the Lane ranch faster and better than he thought he could, streaking hard for that forbidding *palacio* in a way that belied the fear and trembling inside him, leaving Will-Ed astonished at the speed of his departure.

It was something he knew he had to do, something he had decided on long before they broke camp that last grim morning in the mountains when Corey had ridden off with the militia toward the Mescalero agency at Stanton. The memory of her voice saying "Make Corey take care, please do it" had awakened him when it was still dark that last night in camp, and he had forgotten the battle, Mike Calico, the men with the Apache women, everything. He only knew he had to carry the news of his delinquency to her in person. It didn't matter that he had known all along there could be no way he could have stopped the headlong courting of disaster which was meat and drink to her husband; he had nodded a promise— and he had failed.

As he whipped his horse across the rough hard ground, his mind tumbled wildly and his heart pounded in the confusion of mixed joy and fear. He wanted to see her again more than he had ever wanted anything, but he dreaded the moment her face would darken to contempt for him, when he told her of the new scars she would soon see on her husband's body.

It didn't turn out the way he thought it would.

"He's alive, Mr. McPherson—that's all that matters."

He refused her first invitation for supper, but she insisted so eagerly that he allowed himself, finally, to be persuaded. He had told her of Corey's wounds, but they didn't talk of the battle itself until María had cleared the table. When Virgie ushered him into the sitting room for a brandy, his bad knee, which he had completely disregarded at the sight of her, and which had stiffened as they sat at opposite ends of the long dining-table, buckled under him and he staggered, almost falling. She rushed to his side, and he felt her slim arm around his waist, steadying him with unexpected strength for a moment. Then her touch almost brought him down more surely than the collapsing knee.

"Mr. McPherson! You're hurt! A bullet wound?"

It pained him even more to confess it wasn't. When he could look at her face again, it seemed she was far more concerned with him than she had been when he described the savage agonies Corey had suffered. Maybe it was the soft uneven light of the oil lamp María had left for them with the brandy, but it looked as if a hundred different emotions were moving her fine features.

It couldn't have been the one small glass of brandy which had loosened his tongue until it seemed it would wag itself free, he thought, as he babbled away, powerless to stop himself. He spilled out every last detail of the march, the fight, the near-disaster when Major Lattner had charged into Victorio's trap—and how Corey, single-handed, had saved them all. He omitted nothing except Mike Calico's killing of the wounded and the heartless manhandling of the Indian women. And, of course, every other sentence began with "Corey." He told her everything, so caught up in the narrative he could scarcely believe he had really seen it all. Then, at the end, he slipped.

"—and even after the fight was over, I still thought Corey was sure to die." My God, why had he said that? She hadn't seen her husband yet. She must be frightened half to death, and he, so astute with words, was guilty of the basest kind of boorishness.

To his surprise, no trace of anguish, not the tiniest hint of it, appeared on her face.

"No, Mr. McPherson," she said, "Corey wouldn't die, not then."

Could it be that she didn't care? Then he saw the odd light in her eyes, something glowing with an almost holy ardor.

"No, death won't come for Corey Lane that way," she

said. "Never *after* a battle. And never when he isn't seeking it."

Perhaps it was her odd use of both her husband's names that gave him the feeling, but it almost seemed she wasn't discussing a *man* at all, but a concept, something devoid of flesh and blood. Suddenly he felt as though he had stepped into quicksand, and he searched for some way to get out of it.

"Please call me Jim, Mrs. Lane," he said, the words awkward-sounding, contrived.

"Only if you remember my name is Virgie."

They were both silent then, and he thought that he should take his leave. Just as he was about to say so, though, she spoke again.

"Did you find it thrilling, Jim—the battle?"

He searched for words.

"No," he said at last, "I was terrified—every minute." The look on her face told him he had been right to be honest with her. "I guess *now* I think it's thrilling, now that it's over and I'm still alive, but not then. When it was going on, I was half-convinced I was dead already, and that someone would come along and bury me if and when they got to it."

She smiled. He looked for scorn at his admitted weakness, but that wasn't what he found. Then the smile faded. "That's when Corey *lives*, I'm afraid," she said.

When he rode from the X-Bar-7 into Black Springs, under a floating moon which seemed to cover half the sky, he found the night had turned cold, but it didn't chill him. His waist, where her arm had gone around it, was girdled with a band of flame.

"Let's give Virgie's man a hand with that luggage, Jim," Sam said. "Looks like she's fixing to stay a week."

Jim lagged behind the cowman a few feet as they both moved toward the buckboard. Virgie was getting down, her dark skirt swirling like a flower against the clay-white caliche. His first instinct—and it nearly did take charge of him—was to leap ahead of Sam and offer his hand to her, but the memory of her arm around his waist was too strong. The actual touch of her might spill his feelings into the sunlight, in plain sight of watchful, curious old Sam.

"Howdy, Virgie," Sam said. Jim just nodded, and as he did, another voice cut through his thoughts.

"Good to see you, Virgilia. I'm glad you decided to come, after all."

Jim turned and saw Alicia Lane standing on the Sacramento House veranda. She was looking hard at the woman descending from the buckboard, and one white hand was tapping her hip with the riding-crop she always carried. There was an edge to her voice—nothing alarming, but something cutting all the same, a slight hardness that seemed to warn that Virgie shouldn't waste much time with the likes of the rancher and the editor. But if Jim thought this signaled a quick dismissal of the two of them, he was wrong.

"Sam," Alicia Lane said, "if you can pull yourself away from the saloon long enough, I want you to have lunch with us." Jim was sure she hadn't even noticed him until, without looking in his direction, she said, "You, too, Mr. McPherson."

A close thing! If he had feared a betrayal of himself in front of Sam Riordan, oh, how much more damaging it would have been to take Virgie's hand in his and let the heat of the touch flare in front of this haughty old female eagle.

He busied himself by grabbing and hauling a large trunk, almost wresting it away from Virgie's driver.

"Well, Sam," Alicia said, after they had finished one of the Sacramento's pedestrian luncheons, even more tasteless than usual to Jim with Virgie Lane across the table from him. "Did you wet a finger in something besides whiskey and lift it to the wind the way I asked you to?"

"Sure did, Alicia," Sam said, smothering a small belch in his napkin.

"And . . . ?"

"If we held the election I told them about tomorrow, Corey would breeze in with no more than a handful of votes against him. And when he rides in today, they'll get even wilder to have him up in Santa Fe."

So the trial balloon Sam had sent aloft in the bar an hour ago had actually been inflated by the sheriff's mother. It didn't surprise Jim much. It was of a pattern with the other things he had learned about Alicia in the past few weeks. How did Virgie feel about this, though? He searched her face for a clue, but found none. If anything, she looked less curious, as she glanced from her mother-in-law to Sam, than he must himself, the look as detached and unrevealing as if it were someone else's husband they were discussing.

"Sam Riordan, you blockhead!" Alicia's voice was loud enough to turn the heads of the few diners at the other tables. "I guess I should have taken care of it myself," she went on, her voice subdued in volume somewhat but not one whit in intensity. "Of all people, *you* should know that *my son* shouldn't have to go through anything as vulgar as an election. Corey Lane grubbing for votes? That post is his by *right*. Chupadera County shouldn't have to be told that, either."

"But, damn it, Mrs. . . . *Alicia*—" Sam said. He had almost whimpered "Mrs. Lane" and it was only some forced truculence that finally got the "Alicia" out. Jim couldn't quite suppress a smile, and when he looked across the table and saw Virgie smiling, too, he felt more comfortable than he had during the entire meal.

"Damn it, Alicia," Sam began again, "if you want him in Santa Fe, he just plain *has* to stand for election. This Territory's a democracy, whether it squares with your notions or not. And it ain't like he had any chance of losing. As I see it, an election is pure formality."

"And as *I* see it, it's common, base, degrading," Alicia said, "and totally unnecessary. If you would take the trouble, Sam Riordan, as *I* have, to read the Territorial Charter, you'd find that Lew Wallace has the authority to *appoint* a new senator in a case like this. He can call for an election if he chooses, but he's not required to. Isn't that correct, Mr. McPherson?"

Jim almost dropped his coffee cup. He had supposed she had forgotten about him being there. All he could do for an answer was nod—weakly. He didn't know whether Alicia's presumption was correct or not, but he did know that he wouldn't bet against her. He knew, too, that even if his nod was closer to lying than he wanted to come in front of Sam and Virgie, there *were* times when discretion was indeed the "better part of valor" and this was one.

"Alicia," Sam said, "if you knew all this, why did you even bother to have me test out folks' opinion?"

"I wanted you to smoke out any opposition—but I most certainly didn't want you talking *election*."

"Maybe they'll forget I mentioned voting."

"*Was* there any objection to Corey, Sam?"

"Only the one man you might expect—Stafford."

Alicia looked thoughtful. "Well," she said, "Granby is mostly talk—but a talker might be dangerous now. This settles it. Sam, you get yourself ready to go to Santa Fe. See if Will-Ed Martin will go with you. And take Mr. McPherson here. If Lew Wallace sees Corey has the support of the ranchers and the *Chupadera County News*, he'll appoint Corey to the Senate without a peep."

Jim felt he should be outraged. Alicia hadn't even asked if he *wanted* to endorse her son. The fact that he had already made up his mind was still his secret. He should be boiling at being taken for granted, but the confidence of the elder Mrs. Lane was so overpowering—and then so suddenly contagious—he felt almost as if the entire scheme had been of his own devising.

"All that's left, then," Alicia said, "is to talk Corey into accepting."

Jim thought he saw a cloud pass over Virgie's face.

Sam laughed. "He won't stand no chance at all against you, Alicia."

As they left the table, Virgie turned to Alicia.

"I have to go to Mrs. Spletter's, mother, and pick up little Corey—shouldn't be gone more than ten or fifteen minutes."

"Mind you don't linger, Virgie. It wouldn't do for you not to be here when Corey rides in. Why don't you take Mr. McPherson with you, to carry the boy's things?"

Neither of the women seemed to consider Jim for an answer. How alike they were in this one small regard, at least. They were used to having things their way without question, but what a different expectation showed on the two faces. Demand was written in a large bold hand across the features of Alicia, while in the face of Virgie he saw only the warmth of grateful acceptance. But perhaps his prejudice was filtering and transforming what his eyes observed.

They walked down Estancia Street together and made the turn onto Frontera toward Meg Spletter's without a word, and if the silence was total, there was nothing uncomfortable about it, not so far as Jim McPherson was concerned. The sun seemed no longer so unbearably hot, only soft and soothing on his back, and the untidy streets and caliche yards of Black Springs suddenly became Elysian Fields they were traveling through. He was thinking how content he would be to stroll on this way forever when they arrived at the Spletters' rickety front gate. Corey Jr. was sitting on the steps of the porch, holding a butterfly net in his small hands.

When the blond youngster flew to his mother and buried himself in her outstretched arms, and when Jim saw the look in Virgie's eyes as she clasped the son she hadn't seen for more than ten days, Jim realized that the cone of silence which had covered Virgie and him on the walk from the Sacramento House hadn't been a shared thing after all. Her deep quiet had only been in anticipation of this meeting. Most likely she hadn't been truly aware that he had come along.

He stayed outside the gate until the young mother and her child had absorbed enough of each other for the moment, not entering the Spletters' yard until Virgie turned and beckoned to him. It was a tiny solace, but it was something, that she hadn't forgotten him entirely.

"I'll just be a minute, Jim. I want to pick up his things and thank Meg." She disappeared inside the front door and he could hear her calling to Meg Spletter.

He leaned back against a porch post, suddenly tired, and looked down at the son of Corey and Virgie Lane. In an idle glance, there was little of Virgie in the boy; physically, he was all Corey—and, by extraction, Alicia. The father's hair swept across the father's fine forehead and blue eyes, and the well-shaped head of Corey Lane in miniature rested on shoulders which promised to display someday every inch of the same breadth. But behind the eyes and the smooth, only slightly immature face and in the board-flat chest of the young boy were a heart and a mind quite different from those of the father and grandmother. Those vital organs were Virgie's legacy to her son. How Jim knew this he couldn't have said for certain, but he knew it.

"You were with my pa at the war in the mountains, weren't you, mister?" the boy said.

"Yes."

"Did you kill Apaches, too?"

"No—at least, I don't think I did." The youngster was

looking at him so intently Jim wondered if he had lost ground with him even before he gained it.

"I don't care much for killing things," Corey Jr. said. "I *have* to kill my butterflies, I guess. No other way to keep them. But I don't much like it. My pa says I'm squea . . . squea . . ."

"Squeamish?"

"Yes, sir, I guess that's the word. Don't know what it means, but I don't think it's good. Mike—Mike Calico—he works for pa—just laughs."

The small face tilted up to him was so earnest and had so many questions in it that Jim McPherson stopped feeling sorry for himself. There was a hard trail ahead for this yellow-haired boy with the bright blue eyes. Growing up as the son of Corey Lane and the grandson of the dowager empress plotting still more conquests back at the Sacramento House would be difficult—impossible without the sustaining patient strength Jim was sure, after his supper with her, that Virgie Lane possessed. It was none of his business. All the same, he was already forming a vow to help her somehow, when she appeared on the porch again, sweet-faced old Meg Spletter at her side. Virgie was carrying a saddlebag and a bundle of soiled clothing. Jim took them from her, and although he tried, this time there seemed to be no way to keep their hands from touching, and the heat—all his, he knew—seemed great enough to fuse them.

"Yes," she said, "well, I suppose we ought to hurry on back to the Sacramento." She wasn't flustered, but she couldn't have missed the look of consternation he was sure was written across his features, a declaration in letters larger than the biggest typeface in the cases in the press room of the *News*. He turned away quickly so Meg Spletter wouldn't see.

As they walked the length of Frontera Street with the boy trotting in front of them, they saw the traffic quickening on Estancia, moving like a river toward the plaza.

"Good Lord," Jim said, "Corey—Sheriff Lane—must have gotten here!"

He expected a hurried change in the gait of the woman walking with him, but it didn't come. She moved along at the same steady pace, and when he looked at her, he saw no urgency.

"You run on ahead, please, Corey," she said, her voice

calm and even. "See if your father has reached the plaza yet."
The boy sprinted away from them, the butterfly net billowing
back over his shoulder like a guidon as he ran.

"You know, Jim," she said, and the sound of her voice,
directed now at him, jolted him. He had thought the rest of
the walk would be made in the same rich satisfying silence as
the one to the Spletters'; not to say that this conversation
couldn't be, in its own way, immeasurably better. "You know,"
she began again, "I really and truly don't know why Alicia is
so insistent on my being here. Corey's my husband, of course,
but when she's with him at something like this, I'm purely
decoration." He listened for an echo of hurt or bitterness, but
heard none. Instead, there came bright peals of full-throated
laughter, a cascade of liquid warmth. "Oh, Jim, how con-
ceited that must have sounded. *Decoration!* I'm sorry." She
laughed again. Then, as quickly as it had burst forth, the
laughter stopped. "Please don't misunderstand me, Jim. What
I just said wasn't meant to be critical of Alicia in any way. I
suppose it might look like she's the typical possessive mother-
in-law, the kind who resents the son's wife, but she isn't. She
has been of more help to me in my marriage than anyone
could possibly imagine. But sometimes . . ." She broke off
abruptly, and Jim saw a flush on her face. She shook her
head. "I really don't know why I'm burdening you with this,
Jim. It's just that you're the easiest person to talk to I know in
Black Springs."

The throngs they had seen on Estancia Street, rushing
toward the plaza, had, it turned out, been drawn there by a
partly false alarm. Tom Hendry, Matt's gangling black-haired
son, had posted himself on the hill southeast of Black Springs,
the best approach to town from the Mescalero, and when
he'd spotted Corey Lane, Major Lattner, and the officers
with them, he had ridden like fury for the crowded plaza with
the news. When he galloped in shouting, people had suddenly jammed every corner of the square.

"Ten more minutes," Alicia murmured as they sat in the
easy chairs hauled out to the veranda from the lobby of the
hotel.

"You'd better brace yourself, Alicia," Sam Riordan said.
"From what Will-Ed and Jim here have told me, he's going
to look a sight. Three bad wounds, you know."

"Hah!" The cry came from Alicia like a detonation. "If he was wrapped from head to toe like an Egyptian mummy, it couldn't suit me better! Every inch of bandage on his body is worth a hundred votes in that ridiculous election you talked about—and which we're not going to have, if I get my way."

Jim wasn't sure, but he thought he heard a small plaintive moan come from Virgie.

"He can't be any worse off than he was after Apache Pass," Alicia said. "What are death wounds for most men are only scratches on that son of mine."

Across the plaza, a big farm wagon had been drawn across the entrance to the livery stable. A huge flag, the ensign of the Territory, Jim guessed, was draped across the side of it, and in the wagon bed, as erect and rigid as figures on a wedding cake, stood the short round figures of Mayor Wilson Blaine and his hoopskirted wife, Louisa May. Mrs. Blaine held an outsized parasol over her bonneted head and that of the mayor, whose bald pate was hidden by a tall hat which made Jim think of the last Apache in the line that had ridden with White Hair at the battle. In the wagon bed with them, looking, in their crisp shirts and shiny black bowties, like starched puppets, were the Blaines' ten-year-old twin boys, whose names Jim could never remember. Around the neck of one of the boys hung a drum no bigger than a toy, and in the hands of the other Jim could see the shining brass bell and silver valves of a fine cornet. Smug-looking little monsters they seemed to the editor.

For heaven's sake, Jim thought, as he surveyed the comical group in the wagon, Corey Lane would smash Blaine to splinters like a hurricane if it came to an election. Then it dawned on him just how wise fierce old Alicia was. Standing on the hustings and asking for votes against an absurd nonentity like Wilson Blaine would be the deepest kind of insult, not only to Corey Lane but to the Chupadera electorate as well.

Excitement and tension were rising in the plaza. Except that this time there were women and children, dozens of them, the crowd had much the same make-up as the mob of two weeks ago. There were even some of the Rio Concho *campesinos* standing stiffly in their immaculate Saturday homespun.

Once again Black Springs was waiting for the arrival of Corey Lane.

Then Jim heard the first cry of "Here he comes!" It began far down on Estancia Street, out of sight, and the shouted words were passed along into the plaza like buckets of water in a fire line, except that instead of quenching the flames of greeting they only caused them to leap even higher. People pressed into the opening of Estancia Street, jamming the intersection, massing there until Jim thought there would be no way for Corey and the other riders to make their way. Glad yells of "Welcome home, Corey!" and "Long live Sheriff Lane!" mingled with choruses of "Hip! Hip! Hurrah!" until all the individual words were lost and screams of wild pleasure blended into one long, swiftly rising crescendo. Across from him, Jim could see that the stiff little drummer and his trumpeter twin were readying themselves to do their best—or worst—under the beaming eyes of His Honor Mayor Blaine. Mrs. Blaine patted her hair and squirmed her nervousness as the rat-a-tat-tat of the tiny drum barked weakly into the mighty reverberations echoing through the plaza. When the cornet was tilted to the other Blaine twin's lips and the first squawking notes blared out, Jim McPherson winced. Whatever it was the red-faced puffy-cheeked youngster was trying to play—Jim couldn't make up his mind whether it was "The Battle Hymn of the Republic" or the Kermesse Waltz from Gounod's *Faust*—he was blowing the tune so badly it came as blessed relief when it was drowned out by someone starting the crowd on "For He's a Jolly Good Fellow." With all this going on while Corey and the other riders were still making their way unseen up Estancia Street, the editor wondered what peak the noise would reach when those in the plaza caught sight of them.

Then the cordon of greeters at the plaza entrance parted, and there he was.

There was a huge one-voiced gasp from the crowd in the plaza—and then a hush.

Corey Lane looked like Alicia's "mummy," sure enough. The doctors at Fort Stanton had replaced the crude dressings the militia medic had applied to the sheriff's wounds in the camp in the piñon grove, and the professional white wrappings on neck and thigh and the sling which held the supple gun-arm so securely looked, here in the bright sunlight of the

Black Springs plaza, somehow strangely more grim and limiting than the dark bloody rags Jim had seen in the campfire's light on the back slope of Victorio's mountain. In the brief moment before the cheering began again, Virgie Lane sobbed into the silence.

Now the noise grew deafening. Hats were tossed in the air and their shadows fell on the plaza as if a flock of birds were circling overhead. *Oh, how we love heroes,* Jim McPherson thought—*and how we need them.* Detached and objective as he might try to be, the thumping in his chest told him his own emotions were no more proof against the giddying intoxication of the moment than were those of the wide-eyed children who raced alongside Corey and the other mounted men.

Then, about fifty feet north of the veranda, near the sheriff's office, he saw two men who were far from caught in the exhilaration.

Eloy Montoya looked as placid as always, smiling a little and curious, but not swept up by the noise and color or the vortex of movement in front of him. At his side, clutching his bottle—a third empty now—his knuckles so white from the tightness of his grip Jim thought he might actually crush the neck to powdered glass, was Granby Stafford. If the man's usually round ruddy face had looked drained and ravaged by defeat two hours earlier in the bar of the Sacramento House, now it sagged with the unhealthy look of a carved pumpkin three days past Halloween. What supreme lust for self-punishment would keep the merchant here to watch this triumph?

Corey, Major Lattner, and the half-dozen other officers of the militia companies had moved up the plaza and now were between the mayor's wagon and the hotel veranda. Out of the corner of his eye Jim could see Alicia and Sam Riordan on their feet, the cattleman applauding, forgetting he had his hat in his hand, crushing it to a shapeless wad as he beat his two hands together, the lawman's mother holding her riding-crop aloft like a scepter.

In the wagon the mayor was waving his arms above his head in an attempt to quiet the crowd. One hand held a giant wooden key, painted gold, with a yard of red ribbon trailing from it. The mass of people moving with the horses ignored

him, and so, too, did the eight riders. Jim McPherson looked
carefully at Corey Lane.

The look he saw on the lawman's face was one he had
seen before—that day when he sat with Will-Ed and the two
other men on the ride out to face Victorio. An almost erotic
rapture was suffusing Corey's features. Like a revelation it
came to Jim that he knew, as sure as death, what was coming
next.

The small cavalcade rode on past the mayor's wagon,
past the veranda and on by Eloy Montoya and Granby Stafford, and turned at last toward the door to the sheriff's office.

Jacky Jameson, an adoring grin on his young face, stepped
forward as Jim had seen him do once before and caught the
reins Corey Lane flipped to him in the same sure but casual
motion. The big man slid from his horse, not minding, apparently, that his wounded right arm bumped heavily against the
saddle.

"Glad to see you, Sheriff Lane," Jacky said.

"Thank you, Jacky," Corey said. "Everything in good
shape in the office?"

"Yes, sir. There ain't been nothing I couldn't handle."

Corey nodded. Then he turned to face the crowd which
had followed the horses. The ecstatic look Jim had seen
during the short ride across the plaza was gone now. The
rugged features had set hard. The mouth was a straight,
rigid, uncompromising line under the blond mustache, and
above Corey's eyes, narrowed until none of the blue came
through, the strong brows seemed almost to bristle.

"What the hell is all this?" The voice was as cold as a
winter wind. "You people ought to know by now that I can't
abide this kind of nonsense."

My God, Corey! Jim McPherson thought. *Have you the
least notion of what you might at this moment have thrown
away?*

The crowd around Corey had turned deathly silent. It
was as if someone had held out to each of them a long-sought
prize and then snatched it back the very moment it brushed
their hands. He didn't examine every stunned frozen face,
but he stared through eyes which had become quickly salt
with tears at the hurt foolish look on Wilson Blaine's. The
mayor had clambered down from the wagon and pushed his
way through the mob around the lawman, thrusting the golden

key to Black Springs at the tall man with both hands as if it
were some sacred object. Corey didn't even look at him. He
turned and walked the fifty feet to the hotel veranda. When
he mounted the three wooden steps, Alicia had already moved
directly into his path.

"Corey."

"Hello, Alicia."

Her two hands reached out and touched his bandages
with caresses as sensous as strokes of passion, loving touches
reflecting a smile so ardent Jim felt he was an eavesdropper
at a scene far better played in private.

"Badges," she said. "Truly, it lifts my heart to see them.
I'm proud of every one of them—and you."

"Alicia . . ." Corey was smiling, too, the smile turning
his face so boyish Jim could nearly have mistaken him for the
youngster standing so quietly with the sheriff's wife. "Alicia
. . . I think you'd really be happiest of all if they brought me
home in a long pine box." There wasn't a trace of mockery in
the words.

Then the spell was broken. Alicia turned and reached
back for Virgie and the boy. "Here's your wife and son,
Corey. Welcome home."

Jim McPherson felt his stomach churn. It was as if Alicia
were pushing the other woman and the boy at her son just as
Wilson Blaine had held out the gilded key. The editor turned
away, afraid to see Corey spurn this reward as well, and
afraid, too, to see the looks on the faces of the spoils if they
were accepted.

At the side of the veranda, through the railings, he saw
Granby Stafford and the thoughtful man from the Rio Concho.
The merchant wasn't smiling, but there was a look of shrewd
satisfaction on a face that had miraculously recovered much of
its old stubborn vigor. Jim turned back again.

"By Jesus, Jim." It was Sam Riordan at his elbow. "Election or appointment, it don't make the slightest bit of difference anyway. Corey will be the greatest senator the Territory's
ever seen!"

"Let me o'erleap that custom; for I cannot
Put on the gown, stand naked and entreat them. . . ."

II

As Sam predicted, Corey Lane didn't "stand no chance at all" against Alicia. Jim listened to his acceptance with mixed feelings.

It came after Riordan was prompted again by the sheriff's mother ("Damn it, Alicia—*yes*," the old rancher had whispered in exasperation as the three of them walked into the Sacramento dining room for supper, just before Corey, Virgie, and the boy came down from their room, "I'll *mention* it. But *you* may have to roll out the big guns. The way Corey acted this afternoon I ain't so sure he'll agree"). He dutifully brought the subject up at dinner, when Will-Ed and Val Martin joined them.

"Well, Corey," Sam said as coffee was served, "how about it? *Will* you be our senator?"

The sheriff's look said "No" in no uncertain terms, but his firm mouth didn't even open. He leaned back in his chair and fished in the inside pocket of his coat with his left hand, bringing out a silver cigar-case. It was an awkward process for him, working the case open with just one hand, but no one offered to help, any more than they had when he cut his food during the meal, savaging his meat into bites with the edge of his fork. This took even longer. He spirited a penknife, a silver one that matched the case, from his waistcoat and with precise surgery snipped the end from a long, thin, jet-black cigar, Mexican by the look of it. With the cigar at last between his teeth, he leaned forward and lit it with the flame from the chimney lamp in the center of the table. The pungent smoke curled around his head like the clouds which had swirled there just before he leaped from the rimrock at the battle.

"Sam," he said finally, "what you simply won't face up to is that I'm not nearly so popular in Black Springs—or the rest of Chupadera County—as I am with you and Will-Ed there."

"What are you talking about, Corey? Were you deaf to all that hullabaloo when you rode in today? They love you!" Was it possible that Sam had been looking some other way this afternoon when the lawman cooled the crowd with his display first of irritation, then indifference? Jim couldn't help shaking his head in wonder and hoped no one had noticed, but then he caught sight of Virgie watching him. He wiped his mouth with his napkin, flustered, mopping rather more of his face than necessary in an effort to hide his embarrassment from the young woman's discerning eyes.

"Hell of a lot of difference it makes," Will-Ed put in. "You'd be good for them, even if it took a spell for them to realize it. God-damned riffraff don't really know what they want anyway." The Sinuoso man was clear-eyed, at any rate; he had watched the thoughtless disregard of Black Springs, too.

The way the conversation was going, Jim was sure it had been Alicia who had first broached the subject to her son, most likely during the afternoon when Corey was reported to be "resting." Even the superb control of this man smoking so contentedly wouldn't have stood against these questions if he hadn't had some preparation. Jim looked at her.

At first glance he thought she wasn't giving anything away, but on closer inspection he could see faint signs of worry on her face. It was while he was examining her carved but expressive features that Corey surprised him, jolting him out of any coherent thought for a moment.

"What's your opinion in all this, editor?" he asked.

When the first mild shock passed, the surprise that whatever Jim might say could be of any value to Corey Lane made him feel as he'd felt earlier when Sam had said "our town." But this was stronger beyond measure—this inclusion.

"I think," he said, wishing he had a drink of something to ease the tightness of his throat, "I think you should accept, Sheriff Lane."

"That's not what I meant, editor—and you know it."

Jim looked at the others at the table and found mouths open with expectancy. He had gained a tremendous amount of currency, he saw, from the very fact of Corey having turned to him, new interest coming even from the lawman's family. Alicia, thin-lipped and still fierce, nonetheless seemed just then to view him with something like respect, and there was a warm, if disconcerting, curiosity in Virgie's luminous brown eyes; it took no second sight to know that it was a rare day when Corey Lane sought any opinion but his own. There was no way Jim could lie to Lane, no more than he could have that night in camp before they came to grips with Victorio. And the full truth could be brutal, and risky. It wasn't any wrath he might stir up in the sheriff which worried him; it was the displeasure, even enmity, he might provoke in the other hero-worshipers at the table. Unlike Corey, who, when the editor did see him, seemed an alien dropped from a distant planet, remote and unapproachable, Will-Ed and Val, Sam, even Alicia and her daughter-in-law were people he had to face from day to day, or, in the case of the two Lane women, at least from month to month.

"Sir," he said finally, his voice echoing in his head as through a mile-long tunnel, "I think you should accept, because I believe there is no one else who could speak for the Ojos Negros in Santa Fe with anything like your wisdom and authority. And I think the acceptance should come without delay. Any show of coyness could be fatal." Good grief! Had he dared mention Corey Lane and coyness in the same breath? He plunged ahead. "Waiting for an election might be the end of it. If a vote had come about this morning, before you rode into Black Springs, it would have been a landslide in your favor, very near acclamation, but now . . ." He didn't go on. He knew the rest of what he might say was as clear as a Chupadera sky to Lane; what the others thought, he no longer cared.

"Thank you, editor," Corey said.

There was an awkward silence. Lane drew deeply and deliberately on his smoke, and when he exhaled, another cloud drifted in front of his face and Jim was spared any reaction which might have appeared there. As if begging punishment, he sought Alicia's eyes. She was looking at him, but if he expected her anger, he didn't find it.

"Splendid advice, Mr. McPherson," she said. "Corey, it certainly should be apparent that you've got to say yes, and the quicker the better. I know how it goes against your grain to ask anybody for anything, but in this case you don't have to lift a finger—just nod your head. Sam and Will-Ed and Mr. McPherson here have agreed to go to Santa Fe and see General Wallace." She waited while the lawman sat as unreadable as a block of stone. "From Santa Fe"—a new tone, not sinister or secret, but just as surely one which wasn't meant for any ears but Corey's, had come into her voice— "from Santa Fe you could lead the people of this territory as effectively as that Apache demon leads his."

Her son looked at her sharply. Unless the editor was imagining things, Corey quivered, almost imperceptibly.

The long ride up the valley of the Rio Grande was apparently old-hat to the two cattlemen, but to Jim McPherson it was a revelation. When he'd come to Black Springs last winter he'd crossed the Llano Estacado in a stage which had bounced and jolted so much he had seen little of anything except the swells of grassland which rolled away for countless miles like a frozen lonely sea, in gray desiccated billows which did little to lift the anxiety he felt as he moved toward the newspaper he had bought sight unseen in New York. The grinding rattle of the coach wheels had seemed to croak, "Pig in a poke, pig in a poke" ceaselessly as the other three infuriatingly silent passengers dozed, yawned, or tried to stretch in their tiny mobile prison.

Now, traveling with Will-Ed and Sam, his eyes opened wide to see still another kind of New Mexico. The *bosques* along the river were hedged about by small neat farms with new growth puffing above fields whose soil, if not the deep black loam of New York State, was reminiscent of it. To soften the picture even more there were still a few blossoms left in the orchards stretching away from the occasional clusters of adobe houses and outbuildings. The *bosques* were more densely populated than the Ojos Negros or even the Rio Concho, and the fields were thick with workers.

"God-damned clodbusters!" Will-Ed snorted. "Oh, I reckon they got *some* right to live—so long as they don't spread out down our way—but, Jesus! They breed like jack-rabbits."

Despite the rancher's scorn, Jim took pleasure in the sight, and he let his eyes feast on the civilized gentleness of the scenes they passed, not looking at the lofty wild mountain ridge on the east of their line of march or the desolate hills which encroached on the river to the west. Even the sprawling, unkempt, smoky panorama of the Indian pueblo just before they reached Albuquerque seemed restful compared to the remembered savagery of the Ojos Negros far behind them. It was a paradox: the valley they rode through was by any reckoning something new, a landscape freshly shaped by the hand of man and the mute plodding diligence of his animals, while the one that cradled Black Springs in its vastness was much the same in appearance as it must have been ten times ten thousand years ago when its first floods and fires tempered it. Strange that the Ojos Negros should look so new, so raw, so . . . unfinished . . . as if the Creator on His seventh day hadn't merely rested, but abandoned His cataclysmic work entirely, perhaps in awe at His own handiwork.

As they pressed on north, with Sam even more silent than Will-Ed, Jim tried to picture Corey Lane making the same ride when the Legislature was in session, and to divine (ridiculously before the fact) what thoughts might come to *Senator* Lane as he looked at the changes being wrought on this wide land. Would Lane be able to make the accommodations demanded by those changes? Jim wondered, and he wondered, too, not for the first time, just what had made him enlist so readily in the cause of Corey Lane.

The sheriff, like the Apache he had defeated in that savage blood-letting in the Oscura Mountains, was a mastodon, a creature extinct, or heading irreversibly for extinction. That Englishman Darwin had the right of it. What was it he called the process—natural selection? Even in blasé New York the church types had been incensed when the eccentric Britisher's book had crossed the Atlantic. Aside from the obvious charge that "he makes us all descended from monkeys," the religious crowd was terrified at the picture the scientist painted of a world formed and reformed on the theory of "survival of the fittest." They took Darwin's meaning to be the victory of the strongest over the weakest, in tooth-and-nail jungle bestiality. It frightened them out of their soft-headed wits. It seemed to Jim they missed the point entirely, else how could Darwin or anyone else explain a globe not completely overrun by hairy mammoths and saber-toothed tigers? The key word, if he read it right, was "survival," not triumph.

And so the Corey Lanes and Victorios were doomed to go, in their time, and if the time wasn't now, it surely was at hand. It gave Jim McPherson a queer turn to realize that on this very mission he was flying in the face of history—and nature.

Why was he? It had nothing to do with any innate desire to impress Corey Lane, even if that were possible. He could come to no conclusion.

They holed up overnight twice on the way up to Santa Fe. Jim supposed there must be coaching-inns or hostelries of some crude kind on the Las Vegas road or on the other side of the river where a good trail spurted north from Socorro, but, traveling as they did, hugging the low-lying riverbanks, they were forced to seek shelter from the small farmers whose adobe crofts they'd passed all day. The one they stayed at the first night was so small and poor they had to bed down in an open-sided stable with their horses. Supper, offered timidly by the farmer's slight brown shadow of a wife, was beans spiced to hellfire by the Furies themselves and fatback pork sufficiently greasy to soothe away most of the searing burn. In the morning they bathed in the turgid water of an irrigation ditch, and for a while, until the sun rolled their sweat down from their scalps in rivulets, washing them again with their own salt moisture, Jim thought he might smell dank and rotten for the entire trip.

The second night, in a gathering of buildings almost large enough to be called a village, they were quartered more grandly, if not exactly luxuriously. The Mexican farmer here was prosperous, at least by the standards Jim could use for comparison, and the big kitchen with the monstrous beehive fireplace where they were invited to spread their bedrolls was redolent of rich food, animals (the family's entire menagerie of livestock seemed to be penned up in the adjoining room), and close-packed humanity—and warm with generosity.

Here his two companions surprised him pleasantly. On both days' rides they had sniffed their contempt for the denizens of these patchy green plots of earth, criticizing at length and with frequent maddening obscenity the husbandry of these "greasers," the architecture and construction of the huts and houses which Jim found peculiarly appealing, and the noisy freedom of the half-clad frolicking youngsters whose unfettered aspect Will-Ed and Sam patly called "neglect." Face to face with their host, a magnificently mustachioed, friendly man, and his swarming, grinning family, the two rough cattlemen turned suddenly not only civil and decent but downright neighborly, particularly—and it stunned the editor—Will-Ed. After an evening meal of very nearly Lucullan splendor, for which the farm wife wouldn't accept a penny, the farmer mentioned a listless ox whose apparent malaise was costing him hours of precious water-drawing time, and the Sinuoso rancher swelled with ill-concealed importance, allowing that "while I ain't what you might call a vet, an ox's miseries can't be too all-fired different from a cow's. I'll have a look-see." The cattleman and the grateful farmer were in the other room for an hour, figuring out the problem, while Sam sat at the table, surrounded by wide-eyed tots, making shadow figures by the light of the oil lamp with his tough old hands. Jim, enjoying himself, wished wistfully that they could stay longer than one night. The cloud of euphoria parted only once—when he wondered what the demeanor of Corey Lane would be if by chance *he* would ever stop at this very farm on one of the trips he would make as he helped shape the business of the Territory.

An hour before sundown on the third day they crested the redrock rise of "La Bajada" hill ("Means 'descent,'" Sam said, "but since we've just come *up*, the moniker won't be right until we come back this way") and saw Santa Fe snugged in its cup of tufted hills, softened by the haze of the evening's first cooking-fires, behind it the high delight of the peaks of the Sangre de Cristo, on a few of which the last shimmering snowfields had not yet been burned away by the summer sun.

The hotel a block west of the capital's central plaza was a real surprise. While not luxurious, it was clean and obviously well run, with an excellent dining-room and a modest but well-appointed lobby boasting easy chairs of almost indecent softness. After a steaming bath in the room the three travelers shared, Jim felt human. He would have liked to walk the town, but the lateness of the hour was beginning to tell on him by the time he had pulled his best suit from his saddle-bag and brushed it out for the call on the governor in the morning. Besides, his two roommates, who had been full of plans for the evening as the three of them sat at dinner, had collapsed summarily while he had gone about his chores, and resonant snores were rising from the double bed they shared. He sank into the cot which had been placed in the room while they had eaten, grateful for the luck of the draw which had let him sleep alone.

He dreamed about a tall man and a dark woman, both of whom seemed to be beseeching him for something.

"This way, *señores, por favor.*"

The Mexican clerk led the way through alabaster hallways to the rear of the Palacio de los Gobernadores, where a door opened onto a patio sparkling in the morning sun. Everything was so quiet, so well ordered, that the clicks of their boots, first on the parquet floors and then on the mirror-smooth stones of the patio, seemed blasphemies of clattering noise.

They found Lew Wallace seated on a campstool near a sprightly tinkling fountain, a large drawing-board braced in his lap. A young Indian, flat-featured and expressionless, leaned against a mulberry tree. The most notable thing about the model was the outrageously large turquoise pendant hanging around his neck. A difficult subject to bring to life, Jim thought. He had a great urge to step forward and examine the charcoal sketch the governor was working on—see if the old boy was actually any good. He'd heard he was.

"That will be all for now, Juan," General Wallace said, waving the boy off with a hand smudged black by the crayon it held. He turned to the three Black Springs men. "Ah, yes. The deputation from Chupadera County. Refreshments, gentlemen?" He pointed to a low tiled table which held a pitcher and glasses. Jim could almost feel Sam Riordan wince at the sight of nothing on the table but lemonade.

The governor presented an odd appearance for a man whose greatness went far beyond even the bounds of the huge Territory under his mandate. The gold epaulets on the faded uniform tunic were tinged green with age, but a forelock stuck out almost boyishly from under a floppy straw sombrero. It was difficult to make out the hero of the Mexican and Civil wars in the face above the full beard and mustache, but Jim could easily detect the shrewd eyes of the longtime lawyer behind the gold-rimmed elliptical spectacles, and even more easily see the novelist said to be working on a truly mammoth book.

"Now, gentlemen," the governor said, wiping his charcoal-blackened hands on a cloth and looking from one to another of them, "what may I do for you?"

Jim waited for either Sam or Will-Ed to speak up, but neither of them did, and he realized with a start, and with considerable trepidation, that he, McPherson, had suddenly become the spokesman for the trio. He might have known. Since they had arrived in the city last night the two cowmen had alternated bumpkin jesting with wide-eyed open-mouthed awe. Surely the two of them had been to town to "see the elephant" before, but you couldn't tell from the way they acted. Jim had even had to order dinner for them; the menu could have been in Greek for all the sense they'd made of it.

"Your Excellency—" he began. The governor looked amused at the formality of the opening, and Jim himself was surprised at the cool correct sound of his voice. It didn't betray even the tiniest part of the nervousness he felt—nervousness prompted either by the commanding look of the old warrior he faced or the presence of his two silent companions. "You are aware, sir," he went on, "that the senator from Chupadera County, the Honorable George Meadows, passed away three weeks ago today."

"Yes, Mr.—uh—" the governor consulted a slip of paper on the low table "—McPherson. Tragic. He was a fine man and a splendid public servant. Yes, tragic—but not unexpected. He was no longer young, was he?"

"No, sir."

"And you three gentlemen are here, I take it, to submit a name for consideration as his replacement?"

"Exactly, sir,"

"And that would be . . . ?"

Jim looked at Will-Ed and Sam. By rights, one of Corey Lane's longtime friends should speak now—offer his name, at least. It was hopeless. They looked as tongue-tied as backward schoolboys. He looked back at the governor.

"The sheriff of Chupadera County—Corey Lane." The name had come readily enough, he hadn't hesitated or stumbled over it, but somewhere in the back of his mind there rang a tiny bell of doubt. Could the others possibly have heard it, too?

"Hmm—" Wallace put his fingertips together and looked at Jim over the rims of his spectacles. "Hmm—"

Will-Ed or Sam, one of them, coughed. Jim didn't look to see which.

"Mr. McPherson," the governor said next, "can you come up with one good reason why I shouldn't call an election—let your people pick the man, not I?"

"Well, sir . . ." Jim had tried to prepare himself for this question, but it suddenly demanded more than mere readiness. He felt exactly as he had on the rimrock in the split second after Corey's leap. As then, he was propelled forward willy-nilly, with no more time for thought. "Well, sir . . . it comes down to the office seeking the man. Although Sheriff Lane is clearly the best choice the citizens of Chupadera County could possibly make, it's doubtful in the extreme that he could be persuaded to stand for election."

Lew Wallace smiled. "In my experience, young man, and purely as a practical matter, I've often found that if the best men don't step forward, they may not be the best men after all. That's conjecture, though. I know your Corey Lane, but only by reputation. Tell me more about him."

In for a dime, in for a dollar, Jim thought. He began talking, relating the story of the battle with Victorio, swelling a little self-importantly, he feared, as he made certain the governor realized it was a first-hand account. He described the peculiar excellence of the Chupadera sheriff's department, the fine training Corey had given his deputies, the respect for law and order Corey had inculcated in the Ojos Negros, as evidenced by the way he had prevented bloodshed in the squabble over the Sinuoso dam, and he didn't even blush or blink as he attributed to Corey an interest in the well-being of the meanest citizen he wasn't totally convinced the lawman had. Well, damn it, this was politics. And, by God, he *was* being eloquent!

Wallace nodded pleasantly once or twice during the peroration, and then Jim played his biggest trump.

"We've never had the kind of trouble in our locality that

they're having over Lincoln County way—thanks to Corey Lane."

The governor fixed him in his gaze so firmly Jim was terrified that he might have overplayed his hand with that last remark. He stopped talking. Silence could be eloquent, too.

Wallace leaned back and gazed out over the roof of the *palacio*. It seemed an age before he lowered his eyes again.

"You're a worthy advocate, Mr. McPherson. Sheriff Lane is a fortunate man indeed to have a friend like you. If you're remaining overnight in Santa Fe, I'll give you my decision in the morning. Pleasure to have met you gentlemen."

They were dismissed, but as they reached the door to the hallway, the governor called out to them.

"Forgive me, I almost forgot. It will interest you to know that Victorio and twelve other Mimbres Apaches came into the agency at Fort Stanton two days ago, peaceably. Your Sheriff Lane will get the lion's share of credit for that good news, too, I'm sure."

Will-Ed and Sam's bucolic silence was broken at a rambunctious festive lunchtime celebration, with Riordan even rousing himself to order champagne, "The best in the house!"

"It's a sure-fire cinch. Corey's in!" Martin said. "Ain't no way in God's green earth Wallace won't see things our way. You were an absolute spellbinder, Jim. Them big words really popped the old boy's eyes. God damn it, if we couldn't have Corey, well, the Ojos Negros could do a lot worse than have *you* up here talking for us."

"Wait until we tell Corey how you spoke up for him, Jim," Sam said. "Yes, sir. Like Will-Ed says, you were really something."

Pleased as he was at the approval of his two friends, Jim wasn't sure he wanted Corey to know about his championing of him. He didn't know why he felt this reluctance, but he did, and it took the edge off the little party for him.

Sam and Will-Ed staggered away from the table at two o'clock and headed arm-in-arm for the staircase leading to their second-floor room, Sam announcing, "Time to get a little shuteye—get ready for tonight." Will-Ed turned and shouted back, "Do *you* good, too, Jim. Perk you right up for Señora Gabaldon's fancy women."

"No, thanks, Will-Ed." Jim smiled. "I'm going to poke around the government offices—see if I can dig up some items for the *News.*" It was only partly his intention. After the ride up the valley and the close quarters of the room they shared, he craved solitude.

There was little doing, and even less to be discovered, in the seats of the Territorial authority he was fortunate enough to find, and he wound up by walking all the way up the Alameda, the cottonwood-shaded street that ran beside the little river which bubbled its way frantically into the heart of town. He liked the look of the capital. The ancient adobe dwellings, half-hidden behind their concealing walls, the tiny crooked *calles* running off at curious angles, the whole snug foreign scene reminded him somehow of a Europe which, if he hadn't visited it, was real to him from all the books he'd read and all the stereopticon slides he'd gazed at in wonder.

Suddenly he thought of Will-Ed's remark. Yes, it would be good to live and work up here, and maybe he could indeed "do the talking" for the Ojos Negros.

A strong feeling of disloyalty chased him all the way back to the hotel, where he sat in the lobby and waited for his friends to finish their restoring nap.

The *casa* of Estrellita Gabaldon was brocaded and perfumed, a caricature of all the luxury brothels Jim had ever heard or read about. It was all there: the sumptuous furniture, the heavy tasseled drapery, the crystal chandelier, even the mahogany bar crowded with well-dressed men, the whole gaudy, extravagant paraphernalia of cash-on-the-barrelhead indulgence—but all in miniature. The rooms were tiny, and made even more so by a bewildering collection of bric-a-brac. Señora Gabaldon herself was a bulky but well-proportioned woman nudging the half-century mark, with a towering pile of ink-black hair sweeping up from a face which glowed like hand-rubbed, rich, dark wood. Her décolleté revealed most of a bosom so vast and pillowed Jim felt sure a man could easily get lost in it. Actually, her girls looked pale and insignificant in her shadow. There was an air of massive dignity about her, even when she let out a bellow of delight at the sight of Sam Riordan.

"*Rojo!*" she cried. "*Rojo* Riordan! It must be ten years,

amigo." Well, Jim thought, Sam *could* have been a redhead once.

"It's been *fifteen* years, Lita," Sam said, embracing her.

"Oh, no, *caro.* Not that much time could have passed. Not the way you look."

"Thanks, old friend," Sam said, "but you'll realize how *many* years have come and gone when I tell you that all I'm looking for tonight is a poker game—and whiskey."

The madam looked genuinely saddened, and Sam said quickly, "Yep, Lita, when you retired, I did, too," the pathos of distance in his words. "You can fix my friends up, though. This here's Will-Ed Martin, but I think you've already met. The young good-looking buck is Jim McPherson, the new editor of our paper. Watch him. He'll probably pump you hard for all the dirt you got on the high muck-a-mucks here in Santa Fe."

Señora Gabaldon turned a pair of gigantic black eyes on Jim, and he almost wilted under the frankness of her stare. It looked as though she was making up her mind right then and there just how he might compare with all the other men she must have known, and it was disturbing for a moment, until he forced himself to remember that her look meant only business.

"Do you speak Spanish, Señor McPherson?"

"Very little, *señora,* I'm ashamed to say." He discovered as he said it that he *was* ashamed.

"*Bueno.* I think our Juanita will be right for you, then. *She* has almost no English—so she can't give away the secrets we gather here." She laughed loudly, warmly, and in spite of his nervousness, Jim laughed, too.

She turned to Will-Ed. "And your pleasure, Señor Martin?"

"Well, now," Will-Ed said. He looked to Jim as if he was salivating. "Since it ain't likely it can be you, *señora,* I reckon I'll have to settle for second best."

"*Muchas gracias, señor.* You are too kind." Her look clearly showed she was weary to the bone with all the times she had heard that particular gambit. "But first, *caballeros,* let us have a drink together." She moved to the bar, and the drinkers shifted aside to make room for the four of them.

Jim had at first said no to Sam and Will-Ed when they reaffirmed their intention of coming here. It wasn't prudery. He'd had a few adventures with prostitutes even as long ago as college, and there had been no scars or second thoughts, not when enough time had passed that there had been no further worry about disease. But that had been back in the great lonely anonymity of New York: To go to a whore in the company of the two Black Springs men was almost as unsettling as the idea of doing it in Puckett's Corners. So he had shaken his head with determination until he realized that in some subtle way he might risk his inclusion in "our town" if he didn't join the escapade. Now he was glad he had agreed. It had indeed been a long, long time.

His thoughts were interrupted by Estrellita Gabaldon handing him a snifter glass awash with brandy. He took it and murmured his thanks, only to find she wasn't looking at him.

"*Caro*," she said to Sam, "how is that fine blond giant you brought here once?"

"Corey? Corey Lane?"

"*Sí*, that one. El Soberano, I called him; he *was* a prince —just a boy he was, but all man. *Mucho hombre!*" She seemed to shiver, a delicious sensuous shudder making her full figure tremble like an aspen leaf. Jim looked quickly at Sam, expecting embarrassment perhaps, but the leathery old face was wreathed in smiles.

"Yeah. I remember. He sure had you and the rest of the *señoritas* in a hell of a lather."

She laughed. "I didn't think it was funny then, *caro*." Her eyes flamed briefly. "I thought it was me, but he wouldn't go with La Gatilla either. And she was even younger and prettier than I was then." The dark eyes turned dreamy. "In all my years in the *casa*, he is the only one who—" She stopped, her face suddenly reddening under the dark complexion. Jim knew what she had been about to say, and when he saw Sam's smile widen even further, he knew that Riordan had understood her, too. "Sometimes," she began again, "we think someone like that is, you know, not quite a man, but it wasn't like that with him. He was too good for us, too proud." Now it seemed she was talking to herself. "But that would have made no difference to me." She snorted then, her nostrils flaring. "Nor to La Gatilla either."

The girl Juanita was good, very good.

She drained the reluctance out of him which had almost made him say no again, reluctance which had swept over him

at the *señora's* memories of Corey Lane, and which had come
on still more strongly at the look of the young whore's room,
bare and white, stark after the fussy splendor of the rest of
the Gabaldon establishment, with only an iron bed, a straight-
backed wooden chair, and a stand with the inevitable washba-
sin and a neat stack of towels. It seemed more hospital room
than chamber of assignation.

Yes, Juanita was good. She used no tricks, no artifices in
her ministrations; her embraces and caresses seemed sponta-
neous, and if he knew her passion to be feigned, he willingly
let himself become steeped in the belief. He went to her
fiercely, surprised at the overwhelming force of his need. He
was glad he had come to Señora Gabaldon's—but later, back
at the hotel, and deep in the sleep of his double exhaustion,
he dreamed again of the tall fair-haired man and the dark
woman with the Spanish hat.

The man was smiling, the smile thin, wintry, and sar-
donic, almost cynical. The woman had turned her back to him.

The desk clerk had two letters from Governor Wallace.
One, on the stationery of the governor's office with the Great
Seal of the Territory emblazoned at the top, was a certified
and sworn copy of the letter appointing Corey Lane to the
Senate to complete the term of George Meadows, deceased.
The other, on the personal vellum of the general, was ad-
dressed to Jim. He walked away from the yips of glee of
Will-Ed and Sam, and sank into the depths of one of the
lobby easy chairs before he read it.

July 2, 1879

Mr. James McPherson, Editor
The Chupadera County News

Dear Mr. McPherson;
    Please accept my personal congratulations on
the way in which you conducted your mission yes-
terday. As you can see from the letter of appoint-
ment accompanying this, it was a complete success.
    However, I would be less than fair, both to
myself and to you, if I didn't make clear that my
decision was not reached without a modicum of
misgiving. Your skill and fervor in your presenta-

tion of the case of Sheriff Lane was such that I totally forgot to ask the question uppermost in my mind when you arrived, and which I would ordinarily consider paramount and overriding.

Is your Sheriff Lane a popular choice for this important post?

Please believe me when I assure you that I do not ask this idly, nor out of narrow political considerations. You struck me as a man who believes in the fundamentals of democracy. To you, like me, it must be a sacred thing to discover what the people think. I am certain you have asked the question I pose now for yourself, and found the answer satisfactory. It is too late, of course, to give me an answer, and in any event, I require none.

It is with some embarrassment that I tell you also that this letter is admittedly a touch self-serving. I didn't want you to think that I was such an easy mark as to endorse your man without careful thought to the above and other vital matters. My first inclination, and some small fear still lurks that I should have followed it, was to deny your request and call for a special election. It is, of course, the most right and proper course in a case like this. However, with the Territory in its present parlous state, due to the depredations of the Indians in the South, the swelling flood of immigrants and their attendant problems, the incipient schisms in an area populated by peoples of different tongues and colors, and, the point on which you were most telling and effective, the troubles which the Press has lamentably chosen to call the Lincoln County War; all these things combined to convince me that I could not pass up enlisting the services of a man with the uncommon strengths you so convincingly attributed to Corey Lane. I pray you may be right. Certainly we need strength and purpose now even more than popularity. I hope the Territory has been fortunate in securing both with this appointment.

Please—never come to the Capital without

paying a call on me. Until then, I shall watch developments in Chupadera County with the keenest interest and affection.

Yr. Obt. Svt.
Lew Wallace

Jim didn't show the governor's letter to Will-Ed and Sam, and it seemed they had forgotten it. They asked no questions.

*"Why in this wolvish toge should I stand here
To beg of Tom and Dick, that does appear,
Their needless vouches?"*

III

"Mr. McPherson, what on earth *is* that thing?" young Tom Hendry asked. "Looks like something you'd make bob wire with."

"That, Tom," Jim said, trying not to laugh at the boy's open mouth, "is a typewriting machine." He ran a sheet of bond into his new possession and slowly pecked out the youngster's name.

"Sure looks nice," Tom said, "but it ain't half as fast as *writing* writing, is it?"

"Oh, I imagine it will be when I get the hang of it."

He would have to practice, that was sure. Tom was right. Actually, it did seem he could throw seven-point type into the compositor's stick faster than he could hammer out words on the new machine, but he remembered the girl in the office of the publisher of the *Sun*. Her fingers traveled the keyboard in a blur of motion. Well, even if he couldn't reach her dazzling professional speed, he would have to get fast enough to impress Matt Hendry's bright-eyed son, since the boy was working for him full-time now that school was out.

He gloried in his new contraption, not so much because of the mechanism itself as because in a way it represented the calmer steadier course he wanted his life to take for a little while at least. Marauding Indians; ranchers and farmers ready to kill for water; his own surprising involvement in the political future of Corey Lane—he wanted all that behind him while he pushed his roots deeper and more firmly into the resisting caliche of the Ojos Negros. When he pried open the crate in which the typewriter had been freighted to the office of the *News* and when he smelled the delicate machine oil and marveled over the rows of keys and the great snug fan of letter-strikers, he had suddenly remembered his thoughts as he had gripped Sam Riordan's Winchester with such wary fascination the day they'd fought Victorio. Perhaps he had been wrong then in thinking that the ultimate flowering of man's creative seed could be seen in his engines of destruction. No weapon had ever been fashioned with greater love or with more meticulous attention to precision than this superb instrument had. It was pure hard-finished beauty. It didn't escape him either that the brass plate above the keyboard read *Remington Firearms Co., Ilion, New York*. Talk of "swords into ploughshares"—perhaps this was an omen of a better time for man and an end to war and weaponry; brighter days here in Black Springs, too.

There were plenty of other signs if he could rely on them, and Lord knew he wanted to.

Victorio was up on the Mescalero, a model ward, apparently, from all the gossip which had rolled down the mountainside since the editor and Will-Ed and Sam had returned from Santa Fe. The suddenly wet spring had been followed by a midsummer rainy season of more than satisfactory storms across the length and breadth of the Ojos Negros grazinglands and in the stony valley of the Rio Concho, too; there had been no more fuss about the Sinuoso dam, and it didn't appear there was going to be. He hadn't caught sight of Granby Stafford or Eloy Montoya since he came back to Black Springs after the session with the governor, but he hadn't heard the faintest rumble of discontent at Corey Lane's appointment.

As far as Jim knew, neither Alicia nor Virgie had come to town. Secretly, he was glad he hadn't set eyes on the younger woman—completely irrationally, he had been plagued with guilt about his adventure at Señora Gabaldon's—but with admitted selfishness he wanted to see Alicia and bask in whatever praise she might heap on him for his work on behalf of Corey. She knew about it: Sam Riordan had ridden straight for the X-Bar-7 with the letter of appointment directly after the three of them had returned from the capital. Jim, anxious to miss no more editions of the *News* after the battle in the Oscuras, had declined to accompany him. That was when he made the discovery that he didn't want to see Virgie—yet.

He saw Corey—almost every day. He had wondered how he might best turn aside the tall lawman's thanks, how he might mix modesty and a decent pride of accomplishment in the face of the gratitude the sheriff was bound to show. It didn't come to that. Corey didn't so much as mention the trip or say "Welcome home." It hurt, there was no point in denying that; but it solved the problem of his response.

Beyond these minor twinges which were in truth only surface lacerations, life was good. He threw himself into his work with a fervor that surprised him. He almost doubled the paid advertising in the paper in the first ten days, glad to see that among the merchants of Black Springs his stock had risen like a Roman candle since he'd been in on the kill with Horace Lattner, Will-Ed, and all the others in Corey Lane's supporting cast. The fact that he hadn't really *fought* didn't trouble anyone, and it didn't trouble him. He had risked his life. He'd been shot at and missed, just as much as any of the other unscarred veterans of the short campaign. It *was* his town, too.

After the Fourth of July, with its pleasant, only slightly laughable parade and the truly comic oratory of Wilson Blaine —who apparently wasn't inclined to fuss about Lew Wallace's decision—McPherson had put to bed his twenty-seventh issue of the *Chupadera County News*, the one containing the story of the trip to Santa Fe, and left Black Springs on a little jaunt of his own.

The ride from the town of Tularosa, much more Spanish and somnolently picturesque than Black Springs, was a strange one. The trail to the Mescalero wound up out of the high desert into heavy stands of ponderosa, and while the sight of the stately great trees was welcome to eyes now strained a bit from gazing half a year at the unrelieved corroded sweeps of the Ojos Negros, it brought some disquieting thoughts. The way the trail closed in as he traversed the mountainside and spun his horse about on the countless switchbacks wasn't nearly as comforting as he had expected. He couldn't help thinking of the feelings of the remnants of Victorio's people as they were driven up this same forlorn path by Horace Lattner and Corey Lane while he and Will-Ed and the ranchers had been going back to town. He wondered, too, about the thoughts of the war chief himself when he had ridden up here voluntarily just last week. How many times had the Mimbres war chief wanted to turn around and bolt back to the open desert country?

The idea of going to the agency and asking Agent Russell for permission to interview Victorio had come to McPherson on the trip down from Santa Fe. When he had discovered how well Tom Hendry had taken care of the shop during his absence, he had decided to do it. As far as he knew, nothing had ever been written about this particular Apache leader, nothing which had appeared back East anyway, and there was every chance that an accurate word-sketch of Victorio, together with the account of Corey's defeat of the Indians he was working on in his room at Addie's almost every night, might get some kind of syndicated circulation. At least his old editor on the *New York Sun* would run the piece. It should fetch a fairly decent price, perhaps enough to buy the new font of type he wanted and make the repairs his rundown flat-bed press needed. He had allowed himself to get excited at the notion—until now.

Indian Agent Samuel Russell was a decent friendly man, but there were deep worry lines etched into his high domed forehead. Jim suspected that they came from far more than the big stack of paperwork on the agent's desk in the board-and-batten shack which served as headquarters for the Mescalero agency.

"It's all right with me, Mr. McPherson. I'll want to check it out first with Victorio, though. I'm sure you understand."

"Of course, sir." Jim said. The last thing he wanted was for the Apache to feel he was in a zoo, fair game for any curious reporter.

Russell offered McPherson a spare room in his own quarters. At this high altitude it grew cold quickly after the sun went down behind the western mountains, and the agent had a young Indian start a fire in the huge stone fireplace which covered most of one end of his cabin. After a good meal of roast venison ("Gift from my Mescaleros. Probably came from off the reservation, illegally," Russell said, "but I don't look too particular close when I'm the beneficiary") they moved in front of the fireplace with a bottle of pretty good corn liquor. "I keep this stuff locked up a lot tighter than I do the guns and ammunition," Russell chuckled.

They traded gossip idly for a while. Russell expressed mild interest in Corey's being appointed senator for Chupadera County. "Impressive man. Actually, he's not the worst friend my Apaches have ever had." The words "my Apaches," like "my Mescaleros," were said simply, even lightly, but Jim sensed warmth and affection in them, not possessiveness. The man pulling carefully on his pipe in front of the fire and drinking sparingly seemed so open and honest it made Jim bold.

"Mr. Russell," he said, "I've heard that you, personally, don't get along too well with Victorio. Is that true?"

For a moment the agent didn't answer, just stared into the flames. Then he leaned forward and knocked the ash out of his pipe on the stone hearth. When he settled back into his chair, he laughed uncertainly.

"Can't rightly give you an easy yes or no to that question, Mr. McPherson. 'Getting along' hasn't much to do with it—and, believe me, I don't dislike him, far from it. The truth of it is that when I'm with Victorio, I feel insignificant. I spoke of Corey Lane as being impressive? It's the same with this Mimbreño." He took out a small knife and began to scrape the cake from his pipe. "To begin with, I don't believe in what I'm doing here. Does that shock you?"

"I don't exactly understand."

"Let me put it to you straight. I'm up here at this agency with orders to turn the Apache into farmers. My reason tells me my government is right, but actually I don't really want to change these people. Well, I'm not doing such a hell of a good job—with the Mescaleros, at least. I probably won't with the Mimbres Apaches either. And it disturbs me that I'll be trying to do it with Victorio watching." He fell silent then, and it became obvious to Jim that the man didn't want to talk about this any more. The fire was burning low.

"I think we'd best turn in," Russell said abruptly. "We've got a fair ride out to the Mimbres section tomorrow, and we'll have to make an early start."

Jim's excitement was back full-force and growing keener every mile they rode through the cold thin mountain air toward Victorio's new *ranchería*. Something of the same feeling which had troubled him on the ride out a month ago was enveloping him again, but, of course, the physical fear he had felt on that harrowing journey was missing this time. The prospect of the singular story he hoped he was going to be able to write as a result of this meeting danced and shimmered in front of him. Russell wasn't talking, and Jim was grateful. He was too full of himself and what was about to transpire to want conversation.

They rode through long corridors of dark trees, and once in a while they caught sight of the twin summits of Sierra Blanca.

Then they broke out into a wide clearing, an open space fully a mile across and very nearly that in length. The quick passage from shadow into sunlight left Jim blinking, and it was several seconds before he could focus properly on the scene. A creek split the meadow at its lowest point, and on the far side he could see the grouped wicki-ups looking far more sturdy and permanent than the ones which had housed the Mimbreños in the Oscuras. Smoke was rising from a score of fires, and a tribe of dogs yapped at the heels of men, women, and children apparently marching out to work in the fields.

The editor liked what he saw and was sure that Agent Russell, despite his disclaimers of the night before, was looking with pride at the success of the experiment under his stewardship. Instead, the man's first words as they came nearer the small village were, "It breaks my heart, Jim, and that's a fact. I'm supposed to teach farming in this rockpile." It was said with such sharpness that the editor recoiled.

Jim took a harder, closer look. No farmer, he didn't have to be one to know what was plaguing the government man. The meadow they were moving through, so pleasing to the eye at first, was more tundra than tillable soil, with rocks of all sizes scattered through the alpine flora, and closer to the huts the garden plots were pitiful. Squash vines (green, yes, but with the appearance of dried leathery tentacles) lay on the hard ground as though they had given up the struggle, and in the cultivated patches stunted cornstalks, looking as tough and metallic as Spanish Bayonet, poked their tops no more than a foot above the caked dry furrows.

"The Mescaleros planted that stuff," Russell said, "but

they gave up and moved closer in to the agency compound. They'll live on provision beef and beans from here on out. I'm going by the book with the Mimbres, but it's just a question of time before they quit, too."

As the two men walked their horses toward the little village of huts, the yelping dogs they had seen from a distance barked at their heels—more, it seemed, out of duty than enthusiasm. They were an emaciated lot—ribs outlined sharply through thin mangy coats. Russell laughed bitterly, "Probably the only Indian dogs in history that will live long enough to starve to death. If it weren't for the fact that Apaches don't eat dog, they would have been in the cooking-pots by now."

In one of the corn patches they passed, a half-dozen men and women were working, their hoes ringing on the rocky ground like hammers striking anvils. None of them looked up as the editor and the agent rode by, and it gave Jim a good chance to study them.

On backs bent nearly double—by defeat as much as toil, he was sure—their ragged clothing hung in tatters, flapping in the fresh morning breeze like apologetic flags of poverty and pain. The Mimbreños struggling with this unpromising counterfeit of a garden were actually dressed no more wretchedly than when he had seen them last, through the smoke of battle—but what a difference. There, in the heat of war, with the proud invisible cloak of freedom still wrapped around them, even if only for the moment, they had seemed as well turned out as any fine regiment of guards.

"There he is." Russell reined his mount to a halt, and Jim drew up beside him. "Let me go on ahead and have a few words with him. I'll wave you in if he agrees to talk."

Victorio was standing by one of the brush-covered huts, a three-pronged spading-fork slanted across his strong right shoulder. He had his eye fixed on the two of them, and as Russell moved toward him, he shifted his gaze to the agent for a second and then back again to Jim, and the editor could feel it on his face across the hundred yards or so between them like the heat from the fire he and Russell had shared the night before.

He was grateful when the agent dismounted and the Apache chief turned to face him. The Indian and the government man talked for a moment, or rather Russell did the talking while his listener looked at him with a face frozen and immobile. Then Victorio turned and looked at Jim again as Russell motioned to him.

He urged his horse into a walk, and as he moved toward the two men waiting for him, it seemed to Jim that he was on a long slide and was powerless to stop. Suddenly the face of Corey Lane came into his mind. For a moment he was struck by the idea that these two men with whom he had become so intimately, so mystically, involved (even if they didn't recognize the involvement) were interchangeable.

"Victorio says he'll decide how much he'll tell you about himself as you go along and he hears your questions," Russell said when they were all seated in front of the wicki-up. "I'll be your interpreter, Jim. He understands English, but he doesn't always feel comfortable speaking it. Ask him what you want to know. If you put your questions to me, this interview may well end before it's fairly started."

Something told Jim it wouldn't do to rush this talk, and something else told him it would have to be done without taking notes. He stuffed his writing-pad back inside his coat and used the time to collect his thoughts. Victorio didn't look much as Jim thought an Indian would look, but then he hadn't the faintest notion of how an Indian was supposed to look— and this was *Victorio*, not "an Indian."

"Victorio—" he said, then paused and swallowed. "I don't have any questions. I want you to tell me only the things you think I have a right to know—about your life, about your people, your hopes and plans for them"—he swallowed again, then plunged ahead—"about your wars. . . ."

Was he wrong, or did the man actually allow a tiny smile to bend his mouth? Victorio said something, obviously in his own tongue but with a Spanish word intruding now and then, and Jim picked up *guerra, Oscuras, muerte,* and several others in the soft torrent of alien sounds. The Apache looked at Jim steadily while he talked, turning to Russell only when he finished.

"He says you already know everything there is to know about his wars. They were all alike. He remembers you from the fight with Lane," the agent said. "He says war is simply death, and one death is like another, no matter how it looks."

Victorio had laid the spading-fork across his knee when the three of them sat down before the wicki-up. Now he grasped it and held it straight up beside him, the tines pointed at the sky, the haft planted firmly on the ground. The gesture had been a smooth powerful one, and Jim was so mesmerized, it wouldn't have caused the smallest wonder inside him if the commonplace garden tool had suddenly become a lance. Victorio thrust his free hand out in front of him, palm down, the fingers held tightly together. If anything, the still, empty hand seemed more dangerous than the imagined weapon would have been.

"Jim," Russell whispered, "don't be distracted. Look him in the eye or there won't be one more word."

For half a minute there was a silence. Suddenly Victorio's face darkened, and until the editor realized that a small cloud had covered the sun, he was convinced it was an act of will on the part of the remarkable human being who sat across from him. When the cloud passed, Victorio began to speak again and Jim found himself witnessing a performance unlike anything he had ever experienced.

The Apache's lids drooped so that the obsidian eyes were scarcely visible, and if his dark face had been a mask before, now it was indeed as stiff as wood—mahogany. His lips were barely parted, unmoving, but a stream of strange sounds began coming from them while he swayed back and forth almost imperceptibly. The sounds were words, but Jim wondered if they could have been understood even by someone born and raised in the Apache language. Somehow it didn't seem human speech.

It began in singsong, rising then until it became the keening wail of secret winds moving through long-needled pines, falling back on itself to brutish grunts, animal sounds sharp and explosive. Jim wanted to look at Russell and see how the agent was taking all of this, but he knew he couldn't. Nothing could draw his eyes away until Victorio was done.

The chant went on. Victorio's right hand, the one he had held rigidly in front of him, began to rise and fall, just an inch or two at first, then finally beating down on his knee, drumming out a dull muffled counterpoint to the high-pitched inflections hovering in the air about him.

Now something even stranger happened. Jim McPherson began to understand.

He knew instinctively and immediately it was nothing he could ever put in words. Grotesque shapes and half-remembered gods and demons fought each other to gain entrance to his mind. He and the song and the singer were linked to these creatures of atavistic blood-memory by chains forged long before time was measured.

Then, suddenly, Victorio stopped.

Jim felt emptiness he could find no way to justify, deprived, bereft.

But now a real wind had begun to move through real long-needled pines. Jim looked at Russell, wondering, hoping against it, whether the agent would attempt an interpretation of what they both had heard. He saw that he needn't worry. Russell wouldn't, couldn't, spoil the moment. He was as silent as the high rocks overhanging the edges of the meadow.

When Jim turned back to Victorio, whose eyes were once again wide open and finding his, he saw that a woman had come out of the wicki-up and was standing behind the Apache chieftain. From the way she looked at the man Jim faced, he knew at once that this was the wife whose presence among the captives Sam Russell had been so confident would bring the Apache leader "in." She was a sturdy woman of middle years, her face enough like Victorio's for her to be his twin, except for the softness, a softness Jim could now see was washed with sorrow as her look rested on her husband.

The editor watched through eyes still partly glazed from the effect of the Indian's performance, and he was jolted when Russell spoke.

"I think we are finished here, Jim."

Jim stood up slowly. Should he offer his hand? What was the protocol when taking leave of a legend? He stood there mute for a moment, then finally gave a little nod and turned toward the horses, content that he must have acted with correctness when he saw that Russell was almost in the saddle.

"Wait." It was Victorio.

Jim turned back. "Yes, sir?"

"Agent Russell says you are a man who knows the tracks of many words. Is this true?"

"Tracks of words? Yes, Victorio. I have a newspaper. You know what that is?"

The Apache nodded. "Strong medicine, words," he said. "Will you use this medicine against Victorio?"

Jim shook his head. "No, Victorio. The only things I

could write truly of will have to stay with you." He hadn't
realized until he heard it himself that he had reached any
such decision. He prayed Victorio couldn't read his thoughts
and think him patronizing; he only knew he could never tell
the world of this Mimbres giant's disgrace and poverty. Defeat in battle, yes, but *this*—never.

"You were with the soldiers in the mountain fight."

"Yes, Victorio."

"You jumped into battle with the white chief Lane. You
are brave, a mighty warrior."

"No, Victorio, I'm not. I was terrified . . . afraid."

"You leaped to battle. You are brave. Fear is always with
the brave."

Jim was dazed.

"Tell the white chief Lane I think of him," Victorio said.

Jim nodded and mounted, and before he turned his
horse to follow Russell, he looked once more to where Victorio
sat, but then his eyes were drawn toward the woman. She
was looking at her husband as he had once seen another
woman staring at a coffin.

Halfway down the mountain Jim stopped where a small
stream made a sudden wild spilling dip over some high rocks
into a sparkling pool. He tethered his horse and knelt at the
water's edge, parted a thick growth of Parry primrose leaning
far over to calm his still-fevered face in the clear cold water.
His head felt swollen and congested with the memory of
everything he had seen in Victorio's demeaning *ranchería*,
and his ears buzzed with things he was no longer sure he had
really heard.

He wondered if he'd been hoodwinked. Even if he had,
there was no gainsaying the fact that the wily old savage who
had sat cross-legged in front of the wicki-up had extraordinary
powers. He had conjured up ghostly visions, dim memories
of a time Jim had no conscious knowledge of, a time when
men were warriors in a world where absolute freedom cas-
caded down all the mountainsides and flooded every stretch
of every plain. Could such a time . . . ?

He shook his head. No! A thinking man couldn't wallow
in such a romantic swamp today. This was the nineteenth
century. James Watt's mighty engines were shrinking the
land masses of the earth to minute parishes and reducing the

seas to puddles; de Lesseps had already sliced the sands
joining Africa and the Holy Land; and men like Pasteur and
Lister were conquering the dread plagues which had ravaged
humankind since long before the timeless time in the Apache's
chant. Faced squarely, the world today had little use, and
less desire, for men like Victorio—or Corey Lane. Well, to
give that noble devil back there in the Mescalero his honest
due, he knew it. Running all through the haunting song he'd
sung was a strong lament for things long gone which could
never come again. Small wonder the man had smiled when
Jim had asked about the hopes and plans he had for his
Mimbreños. There were none. Hopes were fled, chased from
all the Victorios still struggling in this wasteland, driven away
by the telegraph and the railroad, the Gatling gun, banished
even more surely by the *Chupadera County News* and vacci-
nations and schools and churches and all the other trivia of
progress. Plans? They were no longer in Victorio's hands.
Death was the only plan that meant a thing, and Victorio
knew that, too. So did the woman who had looked at him.
Had Jim heard more than mere acceptance of this death?
Perhaps. There had been some chanted promise of a going
out to meet it. It was over for the Mimbreños and their
leader. When it came was of small concern.

Yes, Victorio knew his destination, and his destiny.

Then the real, the ultimate question came to Jim: Did
Corey Lane know his? . . . No—no chance. The lawman was
impervious to such considerations.

Whose was the greater tragedy? he wondered.

Damn it. This dark bloody mountain is bewitched.

He climbed back into the saddle and dug his spurs into
his horse's flanks forcefully. The horse bolted forward, and
the descent Jim had begun so gradually when he had left
Agent Russell's cabin became a pell-mell plunging dive, a
rock-scattering gallop which brought laughing satisfaction at
how much better his horsemanship had become in just the
few weeks since the battle.

By the time he broke out into the last high rocky place
overlooking the Ojos Negros Basin, the wild ride had jarred
him into something resembling a return to common sense.
He could put to rest that fanciful, Lo-the-Noble-Redskin-
induced hokum about the inevitability of Victorio's death and

the arrant nonsense of "a going out to meet it." Agent Sam
Russell, clear-eyed and matter-of-fact, had the right of it.

"I don't really think Victorio will go out again," he had
said when they parted at the cabin. "We may have seen the
last of the Apache wars." The man knew what he was talking
about, without a doubt.

And as for Corey—how could Jim see the victor of the
mountain battle as any kind of tragic figure? The sheriff
would soon depart for Santa Fe and the seat in the Territorial
Senate which might even lead to greater things. That he,
Jim, had been in some small way instrumental in Corey's
going was nothing to brood about.

When Jim reached Black Springs, well past dark, all he
felt was a normal, peaceful, mundane, far-from-unpleasant
weariness.

"Gee, Mr. McPherson, am I ever glad you're back. All
hell is busting loose." Tom Hendry was so excited he could
hardly get it out.

The editor had meant to go right to his room at Addie
Hepburn's, but the sight of the crowd milling in front of the
Sacramento House had turned him from Estancia Street into
the plaza, and when he saw the lights ablaze in the *Chupadera
County News* he had ridden straight for the office, mystified.

"It all began this morning," Tom said, still spluttering.
"Mr. Stafford is taking a pe . . . petition around town to get
folks to ask Lew Wallace to set aside his appointment of
Sheriff Lane for an election." The boy drew a deep breath.

"The sheriff's locked up five of the people helping Mr.
Stafford—and he's got Jacky Jameson out with a warrant for
Granby's arrest right now."

PART
THREE

"Behold, these are the tribunes of the people,
The tongues o' th' common mouth. I do despise them. . . ."

I

He was reading Lew Wallace's letter for the fourth time next morning when his office door opened and Eloy Montoya entered.

The Rio Concho man stood quietly by the high customer counter waiting for Jim to finish. He had removed his sombrero and his face was fully visible in the sunlight streaming through the window. It gave away nothing more than it ever did, but something about Eloy's silence said he wasn't there to pay his paper bill.

Jim knew he might have expected a visit like this, but he wished it hadn't come as he was rereading, "To you, like me, it must be a sacred thing to discover what the people think."

He finished reading the letter before he looked up and acknowledged Eloy's presence.

"Señor McPherson," the Mexican said, "I have just come from the office of Mayor Blaine." He shrugged as though shedding something from his good shoulders. "He will do nothing, of course, as I feared." Jim nodded. It was gratifying that Montoya wasn't given to long-winded explanatory complications to get a point across. Quick and perceptive himself, he seemed to extend to others the courtesy of assuming they were, too. *"En verdad,"* Eloy went on, "I didn't think *el alcalde* would do other than turn aside, but, *por forma,* it seemed the thing to do. Now I am here."

Jim nodded again, and this time it was a far more than perfunctory nod. He knew that he had just been quietly

157

challenged by the Rio Concho man, and he knew that the nod had been his acceptance.

"I'll ride to the X-Bar-7 this afternoon, Eloy. You have my word on it."

"I will go with you if you wish, *señor*."

"No, thank you, Eloy. I think I want to do this by myself —although I'll confess I'm not entirely sure."

"*Gracias, señor*." Eloy headed for the door. When he reached it, he turned and faced the editor again.

"You will know what to say to him, Señor McPherson— but, forgive me, *por favor:* there is something Sheriff Lane should know above all other men, and yet I fear he does not. It is a strange foolish thing—but even poor men will fight more fiercely for *los principios* than for *las panzas,* much harder for their beliefs than for their bellies. This can be a more certain road to blood than Señor Martin's dam."

He was gone before Jim could make a comment—which was just as well. There was nothing to be said.

His only real regret (regrets being something other than misgivings, of which he had far more than enough) was that his promise to ride to the X-Bar-7 this afternoon meant that he wouldn't be able to get more than the briefest hour's sleep. Facing Corey Lane and telling him the home truths he was going to have to tell him would have been difficult fully rested. Now, with his strength drained by his sleepless night in the office and at the jail, the task was formidable.

When young Tom Hendry had unloaded his news last night, Jim's first ridiculous thought had been that Corey Lane had panicked, but the boy's voice hadn't even died away before the realization came that the proud master of the X-Bar-7 and of the lives and fates of so many people in Chupadera County would never just let go, that nothing Jim could think of in his wildest imaginings would ever cause the lawman to lose one small fragment of that strong hard-willed control he had shown in every crisis since the editor had known him. No, this was no mistake. Error in judgment, perhaps, but a reasoned one. But why? Surely Corey, isolated in his private tower of arrogance as he might be, must have known or guessed how Black Springs would react to this raw high-handed display of naked strength and belittling scorn.

McPherson hadn't come to even the beginnings of a conclusion when he crossed the plaza to the sheriff's office.

As he reached the porch steps, Jacky Jameson, on horseback, entered the corner of the square with Granby Stafford, also mounted, behind him. Jim peered into the half-darkness anxiously and was relieved to find that the deputy hadn't bound or secured his prisoner in any way. He stepped inside the lighted office to wait for Granby and his captor, a hollow feeling in his chest. Remembering the way the man had sagged in the confrontation in the plaza, and again during all the fuss the townspeople had made over Corey in the welcoming celebration, he was sure Granby would appear ready for the grave—or just pulled out of it.

Joe Harris, the jack-of-all-trades cowhand and former deputy Corey had talked out of retirement to take the place of dead Bill Talley, was cleaning a rifle at the sheriff's desk. He looked up smiling as Jim came it. "Howdy, Jim. Come to take a look at our menagerie back there?" He motioned over his shoulder to the open door which led to the cells. "Can't remember this big a crowd in the lock-up since before the war."

"Let me talk to Corey, Joe," Jim said.

"Ain't here. Lit out for the ranch right after he gave Jameson and me our orders. Be back on Monday."

Jim was staggered. The least Corey could have done was to stay on the scene of this travesty. "Has anybody tried to free these men?"

"You mean bust them out of here? Naw. Even without the sheriff here they wouldn't stand a chance."

"I mean legally. With a writ."

Joe laughed. "That's what was so slick about the whole deal. Judge Timmons left for Santa Fe on the noon coach. It was right after that Lane said nab them. They'll cool their righteous heels in our hotel until the judge gets back some time next week, I reckon."

Jim looked at the open door. Apparently noticing his glance, Harris spoke again. "Want to go back and see them?"

The editor shuddered. In his days on the *Sun* he'd talked to a dozen poor devils locked up in the Tombs, and even if this small jail held only a minute fraction of the miles of cells in that dark forbidding monument to inhumanity, the difference would be only one of degree and not of kind. As it was, it seemed that some dank evil vapor was oozing out through

the open door as he gazed at it, and he hated to think that
Granby Stafford would soon be herded into that black maw.
Lord knew he didn't hold any particular brief for the aging
merchant. The man was a troublemaker, small-minded and
petty beyond reason—but in the name of ordinary human
decency it was wrong to lock him up like a drunk or a thief.
Doubly so: in the first place, Jim was sure Stafford had
violated no law (certainly the right of petition extended to the
Territory), but beyond that, it was criminal to subject any old
man to such indignity. He wished now he hadn't left his office.

"Everything quiet, Joe?" It was Jacky entering the door
behind him. "Good evening, Mr. McPherson." Jim didn't
want to turn, but he forced himself. Granby Stafford was at
the deputy's side.

The "beaten merchant" hadn't looked this hale and hearty
since Jim McPherson had come to Black Springs.

The man was smiling, actually smiling. There was high
color in his cheeks, and he held himself as straight as any
young man could.

"Well, well," he said, his voice affable—friendly. "Mr.
McPherson. The Fourth Estate. And what do you think now
of that hero you've covered with so much glorified ink? I
don't believe even the *Chupadera County News* can fill the
hole he's dug for himself this time." Granby laughed as Jacky
Jameson directed him through the door leading to the cells.

Back at the desk in his darkened office Jim stared into
the blackness.

The one big puzzle remained: why had Corey risked this
final rupture of the fragile membrane connecting him to the
people of the Ojos Negros? But the solution, such as it was,
seemed at hand, if only half-revealed. When first considered,
the arrest of the petitioners was like a drowning man grasping
at a straw—but that would only hold true for someone who
had desperately *wanted* the post in Santa Fe, and Jim had
never been convinced that Corey really had. Hadn't they all
had to talk him into accepting to begin with? Certainly the
man had held fast to his reluctance right up until the moment
Alicia had made her plea. Jim had been sure he was accepting it more for her than for himself. If such were the case,
though, why this fatal fuss now? Why not let an election
happen? Corey could sit it out at the X-Bar-7, doing his job as

sheriff when and as it suited him; there would be no need to expose himself to the supposed indignities of even a short campaign. And in spite of his cavalier dismissal of Black Springs' adoration at the homecoming celebration, he could still be supremely confident of winning—against *any* likely candidate. Wilson Blaine? If the mayor *did* have the guileless effrontery to announce against the sheriff, his bid would be laughed out of the polling-place. The man had a tiny following, but real strength? Nonsense. He might drum up some kind of support in the town, but he couldn't count on a single vote among the ranchers, and even if there was a residue of bitter gall left in the valley from the Sinuoso dam affair, the farmers of the Concho would only sit the election out, unless . . unless Eloy Montoya took a hand. Now, after this autocratic blunder, he might.

Didn't Corey Lane know all this?

The man was far too intelligent not to. The peerless strategist who could "think for this Apache," as Will-Ed Martin had pointed out, surely had the brains to dope this out for himself, particularly if the situation was as transparent as it seemed to the editor, with his mere half-year's knowledge of Chupadera County and its people.

So, again—why? Corey hadn't seemed to care about the appointment, hadn't shown the slightest sign of satisfaction, hadn't even (Jim felt small to think of this, but it was true nonetheless) thanked the editor for his successful trip to see the governor. True enough, there hadn't been any show of overbearing triumph; he had merely accepted Lew Wallace's naming him senator as his due—something belonging to him all along and at last acknowledged, something rendered unto Caesar.

That was it.

What a fool Jim felt not to have seen it sooner. Those petitioners in the jail across the plaza were trying to take from Corey Lane something that he considered his by right, and Jim, who had been so smugly sure, after his pilgrimage to Victorio in the Mescalero, that he knew the man "at last," had failed again to reckon with that pride he had watched ever since he came to Black Springs. The only thing the editor could summon to his own defense was that this pride was of such colossal scope he had been unable to see the forest for the trees. It was a pride so great, so vast, it had no need to show itself. It hovered above, and lurked below, every action the sheriff took, and in every thought, or if not consciously in every thought, behind it.

The worst of it was: Corey Lane, quick and lively as his mind might be, hadn't the least awareness of the dread burden he labored under. Formless, unseen, intangible to all natural reach and touch, his pride was beyond the control of the man himself. Unlike his great ability and the matchless courage which made it work, this force was something Corey didn't own. It owned him. He was mere receptacle and agent for it.

What was it Eloy Montoya had said to Granby Stafford in the plaza that dark Saturday afternoon before the dust had blown away and Jim had seen Corey staring at the Oscuras— gilded, splendorous, and powerful? "Pride, señor. This Lane has enough of it to fill the Ojos Negros five times over. It will bring him low someday."

At that moment, with the coming adventure against the Apache marauders still to be accomplished, and with the singular dominance of Corey Lane over the angry crowd still fresh in mind, Jim had put the statement down to venom generated by defeat. Now, with that special hindsight made possible by all that had happened since, he heard the Mexican's voice again, and this time, if the dark here in the office wasn't playing underhanded tricks with his sense of recall, he heard the genuine sorrow in Eloy's words.

Where did all this leave the editor of the *Chupadera County News?* Alicia Lane had been right. Though the old empress didn't want Corey standing for election on the narrow grounds that it might leave the statue she in large part had sculpted covered with pigeon droppings, Jim now knew the even greater danger. A defeat could send the statue toppling, crushing everything around it. It was a case of damned if you do, double-damned if you don't.

Clearly, he knew the Corey Lane he looked at now shouldn't go to Santa Fe. Not so clearly, but with an uncanny certainty, he saw the shadow of doom falling on everyone around the man if he *didn't* go. By "everyone"—no point in hiding from it—the editor meant Virgie.

He had been the "worthy advocate" who had brought about the governor's appointment. If he was going to be of any earthly use to "everyone," he had flanks to guard.

That was when he lit the oil lamp on his desk and took Lew Wallace's letter from the drawer.

He ripped the sheet of paper from the typewriter and crumpled it, smiling, but muttering a curse under his breath. Damn it, he *was* too slow with the confounded new machine. The things he wanted to write should be said fast and in white heat, hammered into print quickly before he changed his mind. He would have scratched them out in longhand, but it seemed more fitting to have them close to the look of type from the very outset, the hard strokes and serifs giving his words a weight he wasn't sure he could grant them with his feeble pen. He knew the notion for the flimsy conceit it was, probably brought on by the fact that he was tottering on the edge of absolute exhaustion from the long grueling night in the office coming on the heels of his ride down from the Mescalero. Well, conceit or not, that's the way it was going to be.

He went to the case and looked it over, finally deciding on the Caslon ten-point, one of the two fonts he'd brought with him from New York, the only ones in the shop numbered in the new fashion. All the type he'd bought with the *News* still carried the old-style size names. The Caslon was sharp as a razor and could carry cleanly the heavy ink load he meant to give it.

Slapping the metal type into the stick felt good. It certainly *was* a good deal faster than the typewriter, and he could apply more force composing this way than with the delicate machine. Stick by stick, he transferred his sentences to the galley in the small proof-press, slugging them out with quick care, but not bothering much with justifying the line ends; he was in too much of a hurry for that.

When he finished, he clamped the type into the frame-bed, tapped it carefully into level with the rubber mallet, and gave it one last wipe with a cleaning rag.

Then, after he had smeared a spatula full of ink on the round plate, he pulled the little hand press through half a dozen cycles, and when he was satisfied he would get good clean impressions down the entire length of the galley, he fed the paper in.

His hand shook a little when he stripped the first sheet off and held it up to the lamp. He swallowed the constriction in his throat and read the whole piece over. There were only two small typos, inconsequential things, a comma spaced too far to the right of one clause ending, and a black mark where a spacing-slug had unaccountably popped up despite his care. He could tap the slug into place later. The comma didn't matter. All in all, he was pleased—pleased enough to be a little terrified for a moment.

When he had pulled ten copies and laid them out to dry on the cutting-bench, he became aware of a gradual lightening of the lamplit press room. The sun must be coming up.

Suddenly he realized he was hungry, ravenous. His late arrival in town the night before and then the excitement, of course, had meant no supper. He hadn't given a thought to food till now.

To his surprise, he wasn't the first early-morning diner in the Sacramento House. Noah Strasberg, who owned the mercantile establishment on Frontera Street, was seated by himself at the big round table in front of the fireplace, the table Jim had shared with the Martins, Sam, and the four Lanes the night after Corey had come down from Fort Stanton and the Mescalero. Jim didn't join him, just nodded when Noah looked up from the stack of paperwork in front of him. He didn't know Strasberg very well. The man was constantly traveling, covering a huge territory, leaving the management of the home store to his wife and son.

Apparently it was too early for any of the waitresses to have come to work. The Chinese cook, Kim or Kee something, the other name a long line of fractured syllables, was bringing a steaming tray of breakfast out of the kitchen.

Jim began laughing softly. As Tom Hendry had said the night before, all hell was busting loose in Black Springs, but, ironically, the only people who seemed to be awake were three outsiders.

He ate deliberately and slowly, consuming far more breakfast than he had in years. There was plenty of time before he had to get back to the *News* and leave a message for Tom about the day's work. His bed back at Addie's was going to feel like the ultimate in luxury and indulgence.

After Eloy Montoya left, and before Tom showed up for work, Jim decided to forgo sleep entirely. If he went back to Addie's and did more than just bathe and change, it would be past noon before he could start for the X-Bar-7. That would put him at the ranch at suppertime. He couldn't break bread there today.

He inverted a couple of empty stationery boxes over the galley in the proof-press, with a note which read, "Tom— please don't tear this down. Leave type set." Then he gathered the copies he had pulled by the first light of dawn and stuffed them into an envelope. He didn't bother to read his work again.

When he left Addie's, shaved and scrubbed and freshly dressed, he went to Kelly's Livery to hire a horse for the ride to the X-Bar-7. Two months ago it would have been a buggy. He reflected that he must have spent more time on horseback since coming to Black Springs than he had during his entire life, even if he counted the long summers at his Uncle Seth's Herkimer County farm, with his skinny young legs stretched across the broad back of Ned, the plowhorse. If life was to go on like this, it would pay him to buy his own animal outright, rather than hire from old Kelly as he was doing now and had done for the trip up to the Mescalero, and the one before that, to Santa Fe.

When the liveryman had trotted out a fine easy-standing saddle horse for him, he mounted and headed toward Estancia Street. He was still tired, and the huge breakfast hadn't completely filled the hollowness which had been with him all through the night. It would now be necessary to draw on whatever reserves he had; he couldn't permit himself to fall apart for a few more hours yet.

He patted the side pocket of his coat, where the envelope with the "Open Letter to the Voters of Chupadera County" was stuffed, and when it gave beneath his hand he felt a small tremor, as if the newly printed message had moved under his fingertips.

At the Estancia corner he suddenly reined the horse around. There was one more thing to do. He urged his mount toward the sheriff's office.

Jacky had just come on duty. The young deputy certainly hadn't spent the kind of night Jim had. He looked bright-eyed and rested.

"Jacky," McPherson said, "what happened to the petitions your prisoners were getting signed?"

"They're in the safe, Mr. McPherson. I guess they'll be evidence, most likely."

"May I see them?"

The boy looked doubtful. Jim could almost hear him say, *What would Sheriff Lane want me to do?*

"Freedom of the press, Jacky," Jim said. He could see the loyalty to Corey crumbling under the assault of words Jacky must have heard in school a thousand times.

"Well . . . I guess your just looking at them won't hurt none."

When the young lawman had dug the carton with the papers out of the deep recesses of the black strongbox (Jim noticed he didn't have to unlock it), the editor gazed at the oddest collection of signatures he'd ever seen. There were at least as many Xs, with the words "His Mark" subtended under printed names, as there were whole recognizable signatures. A certain "Socorro" Simpson had signed three times— and on adjacent pages. No more than half the names had anything like an address after the crude scrawls. The laws of the Territory would have to be a good deal more flexible than the ones in New York State for this pathetic document to carry any weight. Still, there was a brave sincerity coming from the lists.

"Jacky," he said, "I want to take these with me."

"Holy Crow, Mr. McPherson. I can't allow that!"

"I'm riding out to the X-Bar-7, Jacky. I'll deliver them to Sheriff Lane in person. No one else will see them until he says so."

Jacky Jameson looked as if he was beginning to sweat.

"No, sir," he said at last. "Those things are my responsibility. I don't mean no disrespect, Mr. McPherson, but Sheriff Lane would have my—"

"These are *public* records, Jacky."

"Now don't give me none of that stuff, sir . . . please. And don't start that 'Freedom of the Press' business again, either."

Jim thought for a moment.

"All right, Jacky. But please consider these two things. One—I *know* Sheriff Lane would want me to bring them to him. Two—it's legal. I give you my word on both scores."

As he left Black Springs behind him, Jim McPherson realized that in his own fashion he was going armed. He hoped his weapons were stout enough.

*"I prithee now, my son,
Go to them, with this bonnet in thy hand. . . ."*

II

"Come in, Jim," Virgie Lane said. "He'll be coming into
the house in just a minute. He's been down in the corral with
Mike. Little Corey's having a riding lesson."

He had seen them as he rode into the compound of the
X-Bar-7, the three so different figures, two fair and one as
twisted dark as the black thorny branches on the mesquite-
covered slope rising behind the piñon-post enclosure. The
corral was too far from where he dismounted, at the hitchrail
in front of the massive carved door, for him to see the face of
the small boy on the big chestnut with the white star blaze.
Probably nothing unfortunate would be showing on that serious little countenance anyway. From the few moments Jim
had watched as he came in, the boy seemed to ride very well,
but, remembering the short talk he'd had with the youngster—
and his own thoughts afterward—Jim wondered. But he'd
better concentrate on the things he was here to say and do.
He would have enough trouble keeping the face of this woman
out of his mind's eye while he did his business.

"How are you, Virgie—and how have you been?" He
knew there was far more in his voice than just the ordinary
polite social question. He could hear it—and he didn't care.

He followed her into the sitting room he had first entered in awe what seemed a century ago. As she led the way,
he watched the gentle, lovely sway of her body. Unabashed
desire swept over him and he had to remind himself of the
purpose of this visit.

"Please sit down, Jim. Corey probably saw you arrive, but I'll go and call him just the same." She smiled.

She left and he looked around him. Where was Alicia?

He wondered if he was up to tackling the sheriff and his mother together. Well, it probably made little difference. He would have to face them both on this issue sooner or later. Sitting in this austere room by himself, he felt as if unseen eyes were on him—not that Alicia would ever stoop to peering from behind an archway or a door. She was too forthright and too bold for secrecy. It was more likely that she might see through walls than peep around them.

"Well, editor. I expected *someone*." It was Corey. "I guess I'm not surprised it's you."

The sheriff had seemed to appear from nowhere. The man didn't ever just arrive, he materialized. Corey went to a dark wood sideboard, poured half a glass of whiskey, and then held the bottle out toward Jim. The editor shook his head. He could have used a drink, but he decided to forgo any such crutch for his courage. If he couldn't do what he came to do on his own, perhaps it shouldn't be done at all. He watched Corey while he drank. As big as the cool room was, the man filled it.

Yes, the room was cool. The thick adobe walls were soaking up the hot sun on the outside, but their inner surfaces were still holding their nighttime coolness. Marvelous invention, adobe. Jim smiled to himself that he could think something so trivial at a time like this. It seemed to him that it was clammy in the big white room—either that or it was cold sweat which made his face feel damp.

Corey motioned Jim to a seat, but the lawman remained standing—by the fireplace, with the shield and the crossed lance just off his left shoulder. The scabbed rust on the point of the lance looked even more like dried blood than when Jim had first examined it.

"I've taken the liberty of asking Alicia and my wife to join us," Corey said. "It will save me the trouble of relaying what you've had to say, once you're gone."

Virgie! That was what was troubling McPherson most. He didn't want Virgie as a witness to this confrontation. He had made the ride out from town thinking he was utterly confident of the motive which had brought him here, but had he been honest with himself? How much of his determination to bring Corey Lane face-to-face with the reality of the damage he had done himself in Black Springs had been prompted by a legitimate concern over the politics of the situation, and how much by the feelings Jim had for the sheriff's wife?

All he could be sure of was that in this present pass he dreaded the thought of criticizing Virgie's husband in front of her. But with a sinking feeling he realized he had no choice. Corey Lane wanted his wife and mother there and that was that. He had indeed taken "the liberty"—it wasn't a question of asking the editor's permission or approval, but this was all beside the point. The two women were entering the sitting-room.

"Alicia . . . Virgie," Corey said, "come on in and protect me from the editor. Got a hunch he's going to come down on me like a rock slide." He laughed, but there was something forced about the laughter. If the bantering tone of the sheriff's remarks was meant to put Jim at his ease, it didn't. Corey Lane wasn't good at small talk, and Jim wished he wouldn't try it. This was serious business Jim had come on, and now that he'd summoned up enough courage to beard the lion in his den, he didn't want the lion to try to joke about it.

"Well, editor," Corey said when the two women had taken places on the long sofa opposite the fireplace, "let's have it."

Jim looked at the two silent women. He wished Virgie had chosen some other place to sit. He was going to have to check Alicia's reaction to everything he said, and when he did there would be no way to avoid seeing how Virgie took it. He looked back at Corey.

"Sheriff Lane," he said, pointing to the wrapped parcel he had placed beside his chair, "those are the petitions Mr. Stafford and his people got signed before you issued your order stopping them."

"So?"

"I want you to look at them . . . but only if I have your promise that they'll be safe."

Corey's blue eyes flared, but he said nothing. He looked at Jim over the rim of his glass as he took another drink. When he did speak, Jim wondered why the whiskey hadn't sizzled as it passed the straight hard lips, there was so much hot threat in the words.

"And if I want to simply *take* them from you? Will you fight me for them, editor?"

Jim swallowed. He was more than a fool not to have
anticipated this—but maybe he had, unconsciously. He must
have known all along that he was in a high-stakes game, even
if the color and the value of the chips were but dimly seen.
Now the whole gamble suddenly took on an unreal air, as he
remembered that he'd actually seen men killed here in the
Ojos Negros. He swallowed again. Was he beaten before he'd
even started?

"Yes, sir," he said, "I *would* fight you. I'd lose, I know
—but I'd fight you. All the way."

Somewhere in the house a clock chimed the single stroke
of the half-hour. It sounded like the blow of a battle-ax. He
kept his eyes steadily on those of Corey Lane. There was no
other place to look, until he heard Alicia.

"Hah!" The cry was involuntary, and if there was scorn
in it, there was something else as well—not necessarily respect but surprise, perhaps. Maybe to prove something to
himself, but more likely willy-nilly, he kept his eyes fixed for
a second longer on the terrible blue ones of the man standing
by the fireplace before he turned them on Alicia.

The hawk face was a study, but he didn't linger for more
than a passing moment on it. It was Virgie who claimed his
most searching gaze.

For some reason fear had drawn that fine face into an
almost ghostly mask. What had frightened her so?

"Fair enough, editor," Corey said coldly. "They're safe.
You have my promise. Now let's see them."

Jim picked up the parcel, untied it, and handed the
loose pile of papers to him. The relief he felt wasn't triumph
by a wide margin, but he did allow himself a small feeling of
satisfaction.

"Go right on talking, editor," Corey said as he took the
petitions in his mammoth hand. "I can listen while I read."

That's right. There was still a great deal more to be said.
"Sheriff," Jim continued, "as you most certainly know, I've
thought all along that you're the right man to go to Santa Fe
for Chupadera County. I think I proved that when I went to
the capital with Will-Ed and Sam." While Jim talked, Corey
alternated looking at the lists he was reading and dropping at
his feet with quick flicks of his eyes to the speaker. "But what
you did—arresting honest citizens exercising a legal right—
appalled me," Jim went on. "Now I'm forced to confess to a

considerable amount of doubt. Besides the obvious high-handedness of your action, and the fact that under law you had absolutely no right to take it, it was deplorable strategy. It calls your judgment into question."

Apparently Corey had given the petitions all the time he was going to. He barely glanced at the last few pages, letting them slip from his fingers and drift down to where the others lay about his feet. If he moved he would trample them beneath his boots, and it almost panicked Jim to think of the promise the lawman had made so firmly just a few moments earlier, but then he calmed himself, or tried to. Corey Lane wouldn't break his word.

"Am I to take it, then," Corey said as the last of the signed lists settled with a whisper, "that you're withdrawing the support of the *Chupadera County News?* You're pulling out?"

Jim heard Alicia gasp. He didn't want to look in her direction, but he had to. She was staring at her son. Was he wrong, or was there just the faintest hint of disappointment in her face? He wanted to study her, see if an attack was going to come from her direction when he gave his answer, but his eyes turned again to Virgie as if they had been pulled. She was looking at *him.* The fear was gone, and he was grateful. In its place was a look he couldn't fathom. He turned again to Corey.

"Not necessarily, sir. But there is a proviso."

"A proviso?" The voice, in spite of its level tone, was a cudgel. "Do you mean you're laying down conditions? For *me?*"

"I'm afraid so, sir."

"And they are . . . ?"

Jim reached inside his coat pocket for the envelope. "I think it says it all right here, sheriff."

Corey took the envelope and pulled the proof letter from it. His eyes raced across the heading and then they turned on Jim. Without taking them from the editor's face, he took one giant step toward the couch and dropped the galley sheet in his mother's lap.

"Read it aloud, Alicia," he said. "We should all hear it together—even the man who wrote it."

The older woman picked up the paper in one of those delicately tough hands. The other hand lifted a tortoise-shell pince-nez dangling from a ribbon. Jim was struck by the thought that a lorgnette would have suited her even better. She glanced at him sharply just once, then settled in to read.

" 'An Open Letter to the Voters of Chupadera County.' "

Jim looked at Alicia. He didn't have to turn to Corey to know where those blue eyes were riveted. He could feel them—hot, intense.

" 'Three weeks ago,' " Alicia was reading, " 'the editor of the *Chupadera County News* and two other citizens of the district traveled to Santa Fe to persuade Governor Lew Wallace to appoint Sheriff Corey Lane to the vacant Senate seat in the Territorial Legislature. Past issues of the *News* have reported the success of that mission. What the stories and editorials did not stress was the fact that the delegation which met with Governor Wallace was a self-appointed one, without a legitimate portfolio or any legal standing. The whole venture, it must be admitted, was ill-advised.

" 'It would be self-serving in the extreme to hide behind the excuse that the editor and his fellow pleaders honestly believed that Sheriff Lane was the best man available for the job—although that is so. There still remains the undeniable arrogance, particularly on the part of the editor, of thinking that a small group knows the people's wants and needs better than they do themselves. All that can be done now is to make to the voters of this county the most contrite apology the *News* can offer. This would have been of paramount importance even if the sad events of recent days here in Black Springs had not made it necessary.' " Alicia, for all that her voice was strong enough, read all this in a dull monotone, like the slow measured beat of a metronome. There were people, Jim knew, who could read aloud without the message registering on their inner ear, and he wondered if she was one of them. He would know soon enough. The shocking part of the message was coming up in the next paragraph.

He hadn't looked back at Corey, and he wouldn't until the whole load had been spilled in front of him. Once he did look at Virgie. The fear which had ebbed was coming back.

" 'The easiest—perhaps the wisest—course of action for the *Chupadera County News* at this present juncture would be to abandon the cause of Corey Lane completely. But in the editor's judgment this would not only constitute rank cowardice, but would in the long run be cutting off the district's nose to spite its face. Nothing alters the fact that—despite his rash imprudence in the matter of the petitioners—Sheriff Lane, taken *in toto* as lawman, citizen, and protector of the lives and property of the people of the Ojos Negros Basin, remains what he has been all along, the best man for the job. He has now agreed to put this matter to the test in the polling-place.

" 'The *News* is pleased to announce that Sheriff Lane has released Mr. Granby Stafford and the other citizens so wrongly detained, without charge or prejudice. He has written Governor Wallace declining His Excellency's appointment and urging a special election for Territorial Senator from Chupadera County. He has asked this newspaper to announce that he will be a candidate.

" 'Most importantly, in order to allay any fear of interference with the efforts of any other would-be candidate, Corey Lane is tendering his resignation as Sheriff of Chupadera County, effective immediately.

" 'By these actions he has earned the unqualified support of this newspaper.' "

When Alicia finished, the silence was heavy—something concrete and touchable. It settled on Jim McPherson like a great weight. When he had set the word "resignation" in cold type in the eerie nighttime quiet of his office, the sharp metal letters had clicked into the stick with a neat rhythmic finality, as if the whole thing were over and done with. Now, even in Alicia's emotionless crisp intonation, the word held all the threat of the opening salvo of a heavier set of guns than any he had ever heard. It was only a beginning, not an end.

He could see the effect the one word had on Alicia, too. He had expected to see the hard red lines of wrath on her face when she finished, had braced himself for the withering look he was sure would be sent his way, but she took the pince-nez away from her sharp blade of a nose and lifted her eyes to her son with a look Jim could characterize no other way than imploring. Virgie was looking at Corey, too, and her face now was full of the fear he had seen before. Then he looked at Corey.

What he saw there filled Jim with fear, too.

It was as if the rock-hard features were about to break apart, disintegrate under some strange and violent pressure. A softer, more malleable face might ease the terrible force out slowly through the eyes and mouth, but Corey's stone mask seemed to be resisting the stress behind it.

"No!"

The report of no rifle in the battle in the Oscuras had cracked as savagely in Jim McPherson's ears. The vicious sound of it shook him, and shook him again as it echoed off the bare white walls. Incredulous, he found that when the blast had died away, his fear was gone. It was as if the very strength of the eruption had scorched all the weakness from him. An odd calmness took hold of him, a feeling almost of detachment, as if he were floating above this scene as serenely as the lone puffy cloud he could see drifting across the Chupadera sky through the high slit window across from him.

Things hidden from him before were now clear. Now he could understand why so many men in the Ojos Negros Basin worshiped this lonely forbidding giant and his crippling pride.

"I'm sorry, sheriff," Jim said at last, "I'm sorry you can't see the wisdom of what I'm suggesting. This Territory needs you, and I'm afraid there will be no other way. The people of this district will insist upon their say." To his mild surprise—and considerable relief—the editor found that he meant every word about the Territory needing Corey, despite all the doubts he'd had. If he'd been mesmerized again, so be it. He could take some comfort in the words of Governor Wallace: "certainly we need strength and purpose now."

But none of this meant a thing if the man in front of him was not convinced, and the fury and grinding anger showing in the monolithic face had not diminished in the slightest.

"No," Corey said, his voice not quite as loud as before, but still pulsing with a rage which filled every corner of the room.

"I will be sheriff until *I* decide to go. Until then, whoever wants my badge will have to kill me for it."

Melodramatic as the words sounded, Jim knew he could never scoff at them, or at the man who uttered them. Corey Lane meant exactly what he said. It was a vow. That badge was just one more of those "things which are Caesar's."

The unseen clock chimed the hour: four. For the second day in a row Jim would ride back into Black Springs after dark, and for the second time in as many days he would return after leaving a ruined giant. That one had been brought low by circumstance while the other was clearly the instrument of his own entirely needless, pathetically needless, destruction was of little consequence compared to the one great attribute they shared: their anachronistic but still lofty magnificence.

Something not quite despair—something like weary resignation touched Jim McPherson. He had been ready, in spite of all doubts his reason sent his way, to go the entire distance with Corey Lane. Now it no longer mattered. The sheriff had dug his own grave with his intransigence.

He wondered how Alicia was taking the shattering of the dream image which was as much of her making as anyone's. He looked at her.

The two extremes he might have expected didn't reveal themselves. There was neither the sag of defeat nor the white-hot rigidity of anger showing in her face. Instead—and at the sight of it his wary respect for the woman turned suddenly to admiration—he saw the fine subtle touch of some new determination, nothing grim, but the unmistakable look of purpose which can only come to one who won't recognize defeat.

"Corey," she said. "Corey, sit down and do some listening."

Corey moved to the big armchair Jim had occupied on his first visit. The huge muscular body hadn't lost any of its threat or tension, but it moved quickly, as if controlled by reflexes quite outside it. When he sat down and faced them, though, Jim could see there had been no quenching of the fire which raged inside the man.

"It seems to me," Alicia said through tight lips, "that you could have waited until you got this post before you threw it away, Corey. Bend a little. It's a whole lot better than breaking."

"Bend?" The fire roared again. "Bend, you say? I would as *soon* break as bend to the people in Black Springs."

"Corey Lane! God knows I realize how much of me there is in you. I'll admit to the ambition, the stubbornness, even *most* of the pride—but not all of it. No, not all of it by a long shot. I'd certainly never let it stand in the way of my ambition—and I'd never let it stand in the way of something I owed myself . . . and my friends."

Corey drew a breath which threatened to collapse the room before he spoke.

"Do you have the faintest idea of what you're asking me to do? Kowtowing to those shopkeepers and farmers would be cheating. It wouldn't be Corey Lane. My friends—if there are any—would see it, too. They'd be disgusted, and I wouldn't blame them. No—Chupadera County can have me as I am or not at all."

With that Corey got to his feet and walked to the high windows and stood gazing out toward the mountains McPherson couldn't see. His back was as rigid as the lance across the shield. Again Jim was sure that everything had been said, but as he readied himself to rise and say goodbye, Alicia spoke again. There was something even more strident in her voice, something that lent it the urgency of a trumpet.

"All right. You want to be Corey Lane and play it absolutely straight, with no deception. That's just fine—for peacetime. What you can't seem to see is that this is war! It's war just as much as if Granby Stafford and the rest of them were Apaches or Confederates. Can't you get that through your head?"

At the word "war" Corey had whirled about.

"Supposing it is," he said. " A war has to be fought with honor, too. None of this changes the fact that I would have to pretend to be something I'm not. No prize is worth lying for."

Alicia's eyes had narrowed, but not enough to hide the shrewd calculating gleam.

"Corey—" Now her voice was hardly more than a whisper. Suddenly Jim understood. Alicia went on, "Corey, have you never used deception in a battle? Do you always let the enemy know exactly where you are and how your forces are disposed? Are there no feints? No shams? Did you strike Victorio head-on at Apache Pass? Or in the Oscuras?"

Something had happened to the man standing by the window. He looked as if he'd been taken unaware and clubbed almost insensible.

"Virgie," Alicia said, her voice still as soft and gentle as a feather, "please take Mr. McPherson into the kitchen and have María fix him something. Corey and I have plans to make."

They didn't talk while María busied herself at the huge woodstove. Perhaps they had pulled the freighted air of the sitting-room after them. Maybe, too, in some odd way their leaving had cleared the air where Alicia and her son still faced each other.

Two or three times Virgie seemed about to speak, but each time she shook her head, and her face wore a look so quizzical Jim was reminded of the night they had dined together after his mad ride away from Will-Ed and the Ojos Negros column. He could find nothing to say, either.

From time to time their eyes met, though, and on the first of these occasions his had dipped swiftly to the plate of food María brought him. But from that moment on, each time he looked up she was looking at him. It was during one of these times, when their eyes were locked across the heavy block table, that Alicia entered the kitchen. Corey wasn't with her. In her arms was the bundle of petitions, once more neatly stacked and tied as they had been before Jim had presented them to Corey.

"It's settled, Mr. McPherson," she said. "Corey has agreed to everything." She put the bundle beside his plate, then one by one she dropped other papers beside the bundle. "Here's the order to Jacky to release Granby and those other rabble-rousers—and here's my son's resignation." Her face turned briefly dark at this, and then she hurried on. "I would appreciate it, Mr. McPherson, if you would see that this letter to Governor Wallace gets posted as soon as you possibly can."

It all had been said as if she were making an announcement to an unseen audience. Then her eyes settled on the two of them and she looked from one to the other searchingly. Jim knew a moment of panic, a tiny throb of guilt his reason assured him was totally unwarranted. Alicia shook her head. It wasn't an involuntary movement, but deliberate, as if in answer to a definite spoken question.

"I think you'd better go now, Mr. McPherson," she said. "I realize it's poor hospitality to send you from our table before you're finished, but I don't think Corey should see *anyone* for a while. You'll have to accept his thanks through me. He and I will come to town in a day or two. If you'll alert Sam and Will-Ed and a few of the others who would be most apt to help, we can map out our campaign then."

She turned to leave the kitchen, turned back.

"Please see Mr. McPherson out, will you, Virgilia?"

*   *   *

"Goodbye, Jim," Virgie said. "I don't think I'll be seeing you until the election's over. This is another time I would only be 'decoration.' " He looked hard for signs of pain, but found none. This woman was as baffling as she was beautiful.

Suddenly she leaned over and kissed his cheek, a movement with all the darting speed of a hummingbird, and the lightness, too. Had it been anyone else, he wouldn't have been sure it had happened, but the feather touch of her warm lips seared him like a branding iron.

"Thanks for coming, Jim. I think I have some idea of what it must have taken."

"What is the matter
That being passed for consul with full voice,
I am so dishonored that the very hour
You take it off again?"

III

Corey Lane's campaign was scarcely a day old, and the special-election commissioner sent down from Santa Fe by Lew Wallace to oversee the voting hadn't yet arrived, when two more hopefuls filed their petitions for candidacy. That one of them was Wilson Blaine made Jim McPherson smile, a smile quickly washed away by pity when he saw the desperate attempts at confidence the little man made as he marched into the Chupadera County courthouse with his filing statement. Even foolish ineffectual Wilson didn't deserve the defeat looming for him.

"I'll be over to see you about some printing, McPherson," the mayor said expansively as he turned from the clerk's desk. "I'll be needing cards, posters, circulars, and the like—and I expect there'll be a nice piece of change for the advertising I'll want to run in that *great* journalistic enterprise of yours." For a moment Jim feared the man was going to make a plea for his editorial support, but perhaps he had taken to heart the pieces that had appeared in the issue Jim and Tom had rushed out the day after Jim's conference with Corey at the X-Bar-7.

"We'll be glad to accommodate you, mayor," Jim said. He was eager to get away from Blaine, even if he was supposed to be covering the filings for his next lead story. As he hurried toward the courthouse door, he almost ran into Granby Stafford.

The merchant was carrying a stack of documents much like the ones Wilson Blaine had handed the clerk only moments earlier.

"Are you filing, too, Mr. Stafford?" Jim said.

"No, McPherson. Not that I don't think I could beat our sheriff—our *ex*-sheriff—if it came right down to it." Granby was smiling broadly, as he had that night on his way to the lock-up, and Jim couldn't help but wonder again what had happened to the whipped man he had seen slink out of the plaza the day of the Sinuoso row. "No," the merchant said, "it's not me—but I've got a candidate."

Just then Eloy Montoya came in from the sunlight, his slim figure limned against it, and Jim knew in an instant who Granby's candidate was. He was aghast at his own stupidity. Of course! His commitment to Corey notwithstanding, the thoughtful intelligent farmer from the Rio Concho was the perfect man for the Senate seat in Santa Fe. Jim felt a pang of remorse that he was so far down the road with the sheriff (the *ex*-sheriff, as Granby had pointed out) that there was no turning back—not even any chance to seek another fork.

"*Buendos dias*, Señor McPherson," Eloy said. There was a shy smile on his face.

"You're going to make the run for the Senate, Eloy?" Jim asked.

Montoya nodded.

"You *bet* he is!" Granby broke in. "And he'll win, too."

"Good luck, Eloy," Jim said. He meant it. "I sure thought it would be you, Granby—if you weren't going to support Wilson Blaine."

"No," Stafford said, "I reckon I'm too old—but not too old to hit the hustings for Eloy here. As for falling in behind Wilson"—he laughed—"I'd almost as soon go with Hero Lane. *Almost*, mind you." He laughed again, and this time there was something mocking in his voice, mocking and, in a way Jim couldn't pin down, wicked. "I got a little something else in store for Corey Lane, something a mite worse than an election defeat."

Eloy Montoya suddenly looked puzzled—and uncomfortable.

"We're going to start Eloy's ball rolling up in the Concho, and by the time we reach Black Springs it'll be going too fast for anybody to stop it," Granby said.

"What did you mean when you said 'worse than an election defeat,' Granby?" Jim asked.

"You'll see," the merchant said. "First things first. We're going to whip him good first in the polls, and then you'll see."

Jim looked at Eloy for some clue to what Granby was hinting at, but the farmer's face was so blank it was obvious that he had no knowledge of what Granby was talking about. It was obvious, too, that Montoya was a little embarrassed at Stafford's loud endorsement of him. The poor man probably couldn't figure out how to escape the merchant's support without offending him and perhaps hurting his chance of making a respectable showing when the votes were counted. He surely realized he couldn't win. Nothing in the sniffing around town Jim had done in the past few days had altered his conviction that Corey would outdistance *any* rival.

The ranchers led by Will-Ed Martin would be behind Lane to a man, as would many of the other old-timers like Sam Riordan. Eloy would strip away any Rio Concho votes Wilson Blaine might have gotten in the unlikely chance that the Mexicans of the valley above Black Springs would bother to cast their ballots. Checking the few records the editor could find in the courthouse revealed that only a scattering of votes from up the river had ever been registered in the one or two elections and referenda held in Chupadera County.

Feelings for and against the man of the X-Bar-7 ran high, though. The barroom of the Sacramento House echoed with fierce argument whenever more than two drinkers gathered there. If Jim was elated when someone sang Corey's praises as the hero of the Oscuras and Apache Pass, or as the tough but fair lawman he had been for seven years in the Ojos Negros, he was just as depressed when someone in the anti-Lane faction complained about some of the things Corey had done to them while sheriff, real or—as was often the case—imagined. That the events related by the complainers were trivial for the most part didn't seem to matter, and again the editor thought that the snarls of the men in Black Springs who opposed Corey were prompted more by what he was than by anything he'd done.

One man in Black Springs seemed outwardly aloof, impartial, and above the battle. Jacky Jameson, acting sheriff since Corey's resignation, and running unopposed for the office in the same election where the three others were contesting the Senate seat, parried every question as to how he was going to cast his vote.

"I'm a public servant," he would say, his grin turning his young face even brighter than the silver star fastened over his left breast pocket. "It wouldn't be seemly for me to take sides. I'm for whoever the people choose."

Of course he fooled no one. Jacky's worship of Corey, plain enough when the editor had arrived in town, was even more highly visible now that he sported the badge which had graced the broad chest of the former sheriff. He began to walk like Corey and even tipped his hat down over his eyes in exactly the way Corey wore his. A new maturity not unlike Corey's, except that the proud isolation was missing, covered Jacky like a tailored garment.

Jim had been in the sheriff's office when Corey came in to clean out his desk and pack up his personal belongings. There hadn't been any conversation until after the big man had filled a wooden box with his things. When he'd finished he turned to the deputy.

"You'll be needing this, Jacky." He began unfastening the Chupadera County Sheriff star. The powerful fingers seemed to have turned to putty and he had a terrible time separating the star from the fabric of his shirt. Jim felt embarrassed watching, but he couldn't turn away. At last the star was loose, and Corey held it in the palm of his hand and stared down at it for at least a minute before he spoke.

"Mind if *I* pin it on you, Jacky? Not sure I could stand to have someone else do it. Don't suppose you have a legal right to wear it until Judge Timmons swears you in, so I guess you should take it off again—but not until I leave. All right?"

"Sure, I'd be proud, Sheriff Lane."

"*Mister* Lane, Jacky."

Jim wished fervently he were somewhere else.

"Yes, sir," Jacky said. "But I won't take it off until I'm forced to."

Corey moved to the boy. The putty fingers were tough and rigid again for an instant, but as the badge neared Jacky's pocket they began to tremble. The editor feared Corey might back off at the last minute, but finally the emblem was in place. Lane stepped back.

"One more thing, Jacky," he said. "I want you to have this, too."

His hand went suddenly to his hip, and when it came up again, in less time that it takes a man to blink, the Peacemaker Special was in it, the bone handle toward the deputy. Jim couldn't even begin to register in his mind how the draw and flip of the weapon had been managed, the motion was so rapid.

"Holy Crow! Not your *gun*, Sheriff Lane."

"*Mister* Lane!" It was a sharp command this time, not a plea.

"I'm sorry, sir." Jacky shook his head.

"It's yours, Jacky. I wanted you to have it. But some advice goes with it." He placed the revolver on the desk.

"Yes, sir."

"Never draw that old beauty unless you mean it. I want your promise on that."

"You've got it, Sher—Mister Lane."

"The only other thing I've got to say is old-hat by now. We've gone over it all during the years we've been together, but it's important enough to bear repeating. Some of the people in this county are going to want you to *interpret* the law. Don't do it. Just enforce it—by the book and by the letter, right down to the last crossed T and the last dotted I. Read it to them, and if they don't listen, draw that gun and show you mean it. If you lose once, you'll lose forever."

Then Corey picked up his wooden box, turned, and left the office without another word.

Later, at the Sacramento House bar with Sam Riordan, Jim had told the old rancher about what he'd seen, feeling a little as if he was telling tales out of school, but shrugging off any pangs of guilt at passing gossip along, in the hope that Sam could shed light on a scene which still had funny little shadows in it. The way Corey had looked and acted with Jacky was completely different from the way Jim had seen him with any other human being, a fact he had to consider again at Sam's first words.

"I guess Jacky Jameson is about the only soul in the world Corey's ever felt close to, if you don't count Virgie and young Corey—and Alicia, of course. Started out kind of like a father-and-son thing. Jacky signed on with Corey about the time Virgie was carrying." Sam laughed. "I always figured

Corey was practicing how to be a daddy for when little Corey
came along. Jacky had been a wild kid. Drinking a lot and
running with a tough crowd down Tularosa way, a bunch of
nasty young gunslingers all locked up now, or dead. Corey
straightened him out in no time at all, and the result is a fine
young *hombre*. Gradually the father-son business turned into
older brother–younger brother. It's natural. They ain't all that
far apart in age."

That was it—close. It was the closeness Corey showed
with Jacky which had cast those peculiar shadows, but even
recognizing this didn't drive them off. The editor remembered too vividly how Corey, while insisting that Jacky stop
calling him "sheriff," had still insisted on the formality of
"Mister Lane." Formal closeness? On first consideration it
seemed a contradiction, but when he thought about it, it
wasn't so out of character.

"Speaking of Acting Sheriff Jacky Jameson, it seems the
young bucko's been having supper a couple or three times a
week with Mary Ellen Talley and those two cute kids Bill left
behind when he died fighting Victorio. Wouldn't be a bit
surprised if things got cozy there as soon as enough time's
gone by for it to look decent."

"Aren't you being a kind of wishful matchmaker, Sam?"
Jim said. "After all, Jacky and Bill worked together. It's only
natural he'd want to look out for his pal's widow and her
children."

"Well, maybe. Maybe I *am* wishing things. But it would
tidy things up. I've seen how a good-looking young widow
can upset a town like Black Springs. Ain't really any eligible
single fellows good enough for a gal like Mary Ellen. Hey!
Sonny Jim. How about *you?*"

"Now, Sam—"

"Just spoofing, Jim." Sam was smiling, but Jim detected
something a little sad around the old blue eyes. "I know how
things stand with you."

Jim didn't feel the quiet panic he would have felt two
months or even a month before. That Sam knew how "things"
stood with him no longer mattered. The two other people
most involved surely didn't. Though perhaps Alicia did. Certainly her keen eyes had picked up something. Somehow,
though, he was positive she would never breathe a word to
either Virgie or her son and it wouldn't make a particle of

difference in Alicia's attitude toward Jim. He had been in her grudging good graces only because he was useful to her, and likely would seem so for a good while longer. Besides, her ego would never admit that the royal enclave of her studious fashioning could ever be breached.

"Thanks, Sam," he said.

"Yeah . . . well . . ." The old boy shrugged. "Getting back to the interesting situation between Jacky and Mary Ellen. When Bill Talley went off to get himself killed in the Oscuras, he didn't have a pot to piss in beyond the few bucks a month the county paid him as Corey's second deputy. Ain't it peculiar that his widow ain't asked for a cent of credit from either Noah Strasberg or Granby Stafford or anybody else in town? And ain't it even more peculiar she hasn't looked for work or took in washing or sewing like any other woman in her circumstances would? Now, I got me a pretty strong hunch that our handsome young sheriff-to-be is helping to put the groceries on that table he's tucking himself in to so often. Sounds promising, don't it?"

"Sam Riordan, you're the damnedest old woman in this town. You've got a back-fence telegraph that would put the Reuters news agency to shame."

"Well, Sonny Jim"—Sam's laugh was loud—"I've lived a long time in this Territory. I'd hate like hell to think I left it without learning everything about it there was to learn. Matter of fact, when the time comes all I can do is push up daisies, I'd appreciate it mightily if you'd visit my last sod from time to time. Pour a little redeye on the mound and bring me up to date."

"I promise, Sam, but that will be years yet."

"Yep, I truly expect it will."

Watching him toss back two more tumblers of the Sacramento's deplorable whiskey, Jim was sure of it.

Even if his fine-tuned impartiality was only on the surface, Jacky Jameson carried out his duties with remarkable evenhandedness in the weeks before the election. If he locked up a Wilson Blaine supporter he caught tearing down Corey's and Eloy's posters, he was just as tough on a bunch of riders who came down the mountain from the Sinuoso with mischief in mind. He let them ride up and down Estancia Street and across the plaza mingling cries of "Corey Lane for Senator!"

with their trail-herd yips to their hearts' content, but when
they began to harass members of the other two factions in the
Sacramento bar, he ran them across the square to the jail
coolly, disarming them and locking their guns away until they
were ready to ride on out of town.

It was after one such incident that he met with the
commissioner from Santa Fe and the two of them decided
everybody coming into Black Springs between then and when
the polls finally closed would have to check their weapons at
the sheriff's office. There was a considerable amount of grous-
ing from everybody except the Concho people, but the word
went out that the young sheriff meant business.

Generally, the electioneering for Corey went as Jim
hoped it would, quietly, and with the candidate himself doing
very little. The editor couldn't help but think wistfully of how
easy and acceptable it all would have been if Alicia hadn't
insisted on Lew Wallace *appointing* Corey . . . and if Corey
hadn't blundered. Well, things had simmered down now, and
if Corey didn't do or say something rash, there should be no
more impediments to his march to Santa Fe. Why, then, did
Jim feel vaguely troubled? And why did he think he saw
trouble in the ordinarily steady eyes of Alicia Lane when they
met with Sam, Will-Ed, Matt Hendry, or any of the others in
the Lane camp? If their attempt to cram Corey down the
throat of the electorate and the man's behavior when he rode
back into town with Horace Lattner had trimmed his majority
some, it should still be a piece of cake—even if it wasn't
layered quite as high or wasn't quite as splendidly frosted as
it might have been.

At the first strategy session, held in Jim's office at the
Chupadera County News, he had swallowed hard and faced
Alicia directly. "Mrs. Lane," he said, "I hope you won't get
the wrong idea from what I'm going to say, but I don't think
it would be wise for Corey to take a real active part in the
campaign. Running on his record and letting others beat the
drum for him should do it nicely."

"Good of you to put it that way, Mr. McPherson," Alicia
said, following the remark with her rare laugh which always
surprised him. "What you really mean is that my son shouldn't
be allowed to put his foot in his mouth. I agree with you. I'll
keep Corey under cover as best I can. The only official public

appearance he should have to make is at the rally, and I'll have him so well rehearsed for that we shouldn't have to worry."

The "rally" was the one thing in the campaign Jim was truly looking forward to, the big meeting in the plaza the night before the election. It was much like the way he had always anticipated the town meetings in Puckett's Corners even when he was a child. If Corey didn't lose his head and estrange too many voters at it, he should "breeze in" the way Sam and Will-Ed were predicting.

Then one fine Saturday morning the southbound stage dropped a party of four men off in front of the Sacramento House. Because of them, and before the day was out, Jim felt even more certain of Corey's election.

One of them was an executive of the southwestern division of the railroad, and his three companions were an advance surveying crew. After they settled into their rooms, the leader of the contingent crossed the plaza to the *News* office and asked how he could get in touch with Corey Lane.

"The folks in Santa Fe said he's the one man in Chupadera County to talk with if we want to get things done."

Jim sent Tom Hendry tearing for the X-Bar-7 with the news and set up a dinner with Corey, Alicia, and the railroad men for that evening.

Corey was superb. He conversed easily and comfortably with the visitors and demonstrated amazing knowledge of railroad operations, pointing out—with surprising tact—some flaws in the route the professionals wanted to lay out for their iron horses. In the dining room with its customary Saturday-night crowd, nothing in the talk was hidden from people at the other tables, and Jim was gratified that Noah Strasberg and other merchants seated nearby were privy to everything being said. By the time dinner was over, plans had been made to run a telegraph line into Black Springs before two months' time had gone by. Actual rails might come within two years. Jim could scarcely contain his excitement. This would serve as his lead story in the last issue of the *News* to come out before the rally and the election. Without stretching the truth one bit, he could play heavily on the respect these important visitors had for Corey. The scowl on the face of Granby Stafford, two tables away but within earshot, was satisfactorily canceled out by the shining pleasure on Alicia's.

The troubled look she had worn during their recent meetings was gone.

Jim's only regret was that Virgie hadn't come to town with her husband and mother-in-law. Something in him had changed in that regard. Perhaps it was the feeling that his work on behalf of Corey's political career was the accomplishment of some duty he owed her, but he knew suddenly that he would never again want to avoid seeing her.

If the election hadn't been so imminent, the quite different news which hit town on the Monday of the rally would have been electrifying. Now, with so much excitement already in the air, it was only a minor shock, despite the look of grave concern on the face of Indian Agent Russell as he sat next to Jim's desk in the office of the *News*.

"Governor Wallace wants a first-hand report," Russell said. "I'm not going to enjoy making it."

"Does it mean war again?" Jim asked.

"Can't be sure. If it does, it will be the worst one ever. Victorio will never come in again—*alive*."

"When did he go out?"

"Day before yesterday. I tried to follow and reason with him, but his trail petered out five miles from the reservation. I doubled back to Stanton and wired the commissioner in Washington, the governor, and the Army's district commandant. Wallace ordered me to Santa Fe, or, rather, asked me. I'm on my way there now."

"But why did he go out *now?*" Jim said. "Summer's more than half gone. I would have thought he'd stay put until after harvest time at least."

Russell looked pained—more than pained, tortured.

"It would have surprised me, too, up until about three weeks ago," Russell said. "He had me about convinced he was off the warpath for good. Yes, I really think he meant it. Anyway, I did a lot of missionary work up and down the Ruidoso and in the Hondo Valley, calming the ranchers and farmers there. More little scattered parties of Mimbreños came in to the Mescalero, and I reckon I must have had nearly a hundred and fifty of them in the agency. Things looked settled. Then, on the thirtieth of July, maybe the thirty-first, I got word that the authorities in Grant County had brought in indictments against Victorio for horse-stealing and murder and were sending arresting officers to bring him in. Now, I've got no doubt Victorio may be guilty of a lot of things, but in this particular case he was hiding out in the badlands, trying to get away from your man Lane, when all this is supposed to have happened."

"Can't he prove that?"

"I don't believe Victorio thinks he can get a fair shake in a white man's court. Not at all sure he can myself."

"How did he find out they were coming for him?"

Agent Russell looked miserable. It troubled Jim to see the weathered features drawn, the honest face contorted.

"Blamed if I know, Jim. Maybe I let the cat out of the bag myself. Don't think I did—but I did pay a lot of extra attention to him after I got the word. At first I thought he'd just plain guessed something was wrong, but it wasn't any guess. He *knew.* Knew *exactly.* An old squaw, one of only three Mimbreños he left behind, gave me chapter and verse on how *much* he knew. I don't cotton to that second-sight stuff, but if anybody has it, that Apache does."

"Surely you're not blaming yourself?"

"No. Not rightly. Not for anything I've said or done, leastways. But I've sure been ripped up by some funny thoughts. Part of me says track him down and bring him in for trial. In the long run it's the only way for him and his people to escape tragedy. But another part, maybe the biggest, says let him go."

Jim thought about the possible effect of this on the rally and the election. "Do you think we're in danger here?"

Russell took his time in answering. "No. If my guess is right, he'll head across the river for one of his old hideouts in the Black Range, somewhere within rifle-shot of the Ojo Caliente country he loves so well. Either that or he'll strike out south, out of the Territory entirely and into Mexico. He might raid a little in the Ojos Negros on the way, for food and a few more horses, but sooner or later he's got to reach a place where he can trade for guns. No, I think you're safe here—basically. Of course, eventually it does mean war, and, like I said before, it will be the bloodiest we've seen. He's got all his Mimbreños, two damned good fighting chiefs in Loco and old Nana, and a couple of dozen Mescaleros he talked into going with him. Formidable band. And—he left a message."

"Oh?"

"Remember that spading-fork he was toting when we talked with him that day?"

"Yes."

"It was lying on the porch of the agency office, the handle busted to smithereens . . . splintered into matchsticks. That took a bit of doing."

The news spread through town like wildfire, but a wildfire with weak flames and no heat. To Jim's amazement, Russell's news was only a twenty-minute wonder, lost in the frenzy of the fast-approaching rally, and by suppertime what little talk there was about Victorio ran parallel to the thoughts expressed by the Indian agent. Black Springs wasn't threatened by the breakout, nor was Chupadera County or the Ojos Negros Basin. Victorio was streaking for other hunting-grounds. Let the people there worry. "We got us a senator to elect."

By the time the beer kegs had been rolled out of the barroom to the veranda of the Sacramento House, and by the time the four big bonfires had been built at the corners of the plaza for lighting when darkness fell, all speculation about the need for doing anything about Victorio had vanished.

And by the time Corey Lane and his wife and mother arrived from the X-Bar-7 (Alicia for once sedate and prim in the buckboard with her son and daughter-in-law instead of on the back of the prancing horse) only one man in Black Springs even thought of telling the former sheriff—and he chose not to.

Later Jim McPherson would wonder why he hadn't. It might have made some difference.

To Jim's great joy, it was a happy-go-lucky crowd, good-natured and friendly. He smiled, thinking that perhaps he would feel that way even if he had suddenly been plumped down among all the congregated imps of Hell—providing that, as now, Virgie Lane was there,

She greeted him warmly, extending her slim hand for his, and he wouldn't have shied from her touch this time even if Alicia and Corey hadn't been just as generous in the warmth of their greetings.

"Sometimes I've been a trifle remiss in my manners," Corey said, while Alicia nodded her approval, "but I want you to know I'm deeply appreciative of all you've done on my behalf, editor."

The three Lanes had left the ranch without supper, and although Jim declined on the grounds that he'd already eaten, they insisted he join them for a late meal at the Sacramento House. "Let's have them set a table for us on the veranda," Alicia said, "where we won't miss anything going on." Jim had some doubts, wondering how she might react to the men lurching past to get at the free beer the hotel was contributing to the evening festivities, but he hadn't reckoned on what a consummate politician Alicia Lane could be. People she had snubbed almost dutifully in the past she now treated to affable greetings and gracious smiles, but with nothing overdone, all of it managed with enough apparent sincerity to convert the most suspicious Doubting Thomas.

Corey, too, was an agreeable figure as the crowds surged past the veranda. His arrogance was so completely checked that Jim whistled to himself at how well Alicia had prepared him for this evening. Jim's admiration leaped even higher when she showed him the notes she had made for Corey's speech later on.

Will-Ed and Val joined them, and then Sam and the Hendrys, father and son, and Tom's pleasant quiet mother. The talk was small but sprightly, bubbling with understated but confident assurances of Corey's victory tomorrow.

And Virgie. Jim thought, with only a touch of rue, that no one could cast a vote against any man this radiant woman had chosen for a husband. He looked at her more often than he knew was wise. Always beautiful, that evening her rich dark skin glowed in the amber dusk of the plaza.

Through the Estancia Street opening to the square he could see that the dying sun had made a russet smear over the tops of the far Oscuras. Even with all the bustle of the crowd beginning to gather in front of the bandstand built for this event, he found himself thinking of Victorio. How far across those dark red sweeps had the Apache ridden by now, and what was he thinking of? Jim turned to tell Corey of Russell's news, but found him with his head bent toward Will-Ed Martin, and by the time the ex-lawman straightened up, Jim had changed his mind. To introduce this into the evening's proceedings might look like some cheap trick to the straightforward men and women gathered here. Better to go

right ahead on the strength of the work he and Alicia had
done so far. Truth to tell, it was looking better to him with
every passing moment.

"Damned crying shame," Val Martin was saying, "that us
womenfolk ain't allowed to vote. Don't get upset, Virgie, but
I'd bet we could get a vote for Corey out of every petticoat in
the Territory."

Virgie smiled.

Alicia snorted. "Having the vote doesn't interest me a
bit, Valerie," she said, "just as long as we can have our way
about who wins and loses. You don't need a vote for that."

It was nearly full dark now. The plaza was filling up. Jim
could see Wilson Blaine near the bandstand, his buxom wife
by his side, and the twins (the editor breathed more easily
when he saw they weren't carrying the cornet and drum)
trailing in behind their parents. He saw Jacky Jameson moving through the crowd checking holsters, it seemed, smiling
and nodding to ranchers and townsfolk alike, refusing an
offered mug of beer. The youngster's hand rested on the
bone handle of the Peacemaker Special strapped to his thigh.

The men and some of the women and children from the
Rio Concho were beginning to enter the square. With the
crowd promising to dwarf even the one at Corey's homecoming from the Mescalero, the river farmers had evidently
parked their wagons out of sight on Estancia Street. Consid-
erate people. Pity their candidate had so little chance, particularly now that by their numbers Jim could see they were
taking an interest in the election. In a small group of them he
spotted Eloy Montoya.

For once Eloy wasn't dressed in the homespun of the
men around him. He was wearing a well-cut black suit and a
string tie knotted at a crisp gleaming collar. The suit made
him look taller and slimmer—impressive. As Jim watched, he
wondered if Granby Stafford could be far from his candidate,
and even as the thought came to mind he saw the merchant
edge into the group. The two of them bent their heads
together, with Eloy doing the talking. Granby lifted his after
a second and looked straight toward Corey Lane on the
veranda. In the last dying light Jim could see the face redden, and Granby began to shake his head almost violently.

Eloy broke away and began walking toward the veranda,

his stride firm and purposeful. When he reached it, he stopped
directly in front of Corey.

"*Señoras,*" he said, bowing slightly to each of the Lane
women. Then he looked directly at the ex-sheriff. "*Bueno
suerte,* Señor Lane." His smile was dazzling.

"Good luck to you, too, Eloy," Corey said. Both of them
sounded like they meant it, and Jim's heart warmed.

"If you win tomorrow, *señor,*" Eloy said, "—and even if
it is not good politics to say so, I admit it looks as if you will—
the people of the Rio Concho wish you well. You will be our
senator just as if I had won myself. I promise."

"Thank you, Eloy."

Montoya bowed the same slight graceful bow once more
and was gone.

"Jim, psst!" It was Sam Riordan. "Too damned bad, ain't
it?" he whispered. "You know, if by some disaster Corey
didn't make it, I sure wouldn't feel too bad about Montoya
sitting up there in Santa Fe. Sure ought to be some way they
both could go."

"You're a pretty big man, Sam Riordan," Jim said. The
old rancher's words had helped—a little.

Someone was lighting the lanterns on the brand-new
bandstand, and the crowd, sensing that things were about to
begin, began surging toward it, a tide of ranchers, townspeople, *campesinos,* cowhands, mostly men but with an occasional courageous woman elbowing her way through them.
Boys were putting torches to the bonfires at the far corners of
the plaza, and as the fires blazed up, sending gyrating shadows whirling over the fronts of the buildings across the way,
Jim saw Lew Wallace's special-election commissioner mount
the bandstand and step to a small lectern set on an upturned
flour barrel.

The man, in spite of the fact that Jim had met with him
half a dozen times, still had for the editor the drab anonymity
of most minor officialdom. He wondered if these types consciously developed this protective coloration.

In flat tones he announced the two offices to be filled in
the next day's election, named the candidates, outlined the
rules of voting and the tallying process, and faded into the background just as Jacky Jameson climbed the stairs to face the
people of Chupadera County. Good-natured boos and whistles
greeted the young lawman until he held up his arms for silence.

"I ain't running for sheriff on account of there being a great public outcry for me to do so," he said, his smile streaming over all his listeners, "but because I need the job!" A cascade of laughter drowned his next words, and he had to begin again. "Seriously, folks. You know me, and you know my work. I'm truly sorry there ain't another candidate so's you could have a *choice,* but if some write-in don't beat me tomorrow, I promise I'll do the best job I can." He looked as if there might be something more he wanted to say. He was staring straight at Corey Lane, and for a moment Jim knew a small tickle of alarm. If Jacky should praise Corey now, it could trigger a bad reaction in the acting sheriff's former boss. He needn't have feared. Jacky certainly knew Lane as well as anyone. His smile widened, and he tossed a neat salute to the man seated on the veranda and left the bandstand.

The applause was still thundering in the plaza as Eloy Montoya mounted the platform, and the Concho man had to wait a long time for things to settle down. That he did so with simple unaffected dignity came as no surprise, but it did cause Jim's eyes to burn.

When Eloy began to speak at last, Jim found it hard to follow everything the man was saying. His own thoughts competed so strenuously with the calm reasoned words that he was lucky to absorb anything from a speech nearly as brief as Jacky Jameson's. In the back of his mind, though, he registered that Eloy was covering a lot of important ground in his few words, and covering it well. When he finished, or seemed to have finished, he began again abruptly, this time in Spanish. It was obvious to Jim that the man was too astute to let his own people think even for an instant that he was taking them for granted. There were a few almost apologetic cheers in that soft musical language, but more than that, Jim could feel the warmth coming from the Concho farmers clustered nearest the bandstand. At last Eloy was done, and with that same small inoffensive bow, he left the platform.

There was a general scattering of applause, the clapping not wild but respectful. Besides the men and women of the Concho a number of anglos—even some of the Sinuoso ranchers—were applauding gently, thoughtfully.

Then Wilson Blaine was at the lectern, his beaming face just barely visible above its top. The sight seemed symbolic of all the reasons why the mayor couldn't be the one to go to the seat of power in the capital. He simply wasn't big enough in any way. Jim felt embarrassed for him.

Blaine made a great show of clearing his throat and looking from side to side out over the heads of the crowd. There was a ripple of good-humored laughter from the waiting audience, but the ones with better manners shushed those nearest them.

"Voters of Chupadera County!" Blaine began, then paused. "I stand before you tonight . . ." Again there was a pause, a longer one. *Get on with it, man,* Jim thought. "I stand before you tonight to announce . . . that I am withdrawing the candidacy urged on me by my multitudes of friends and supporters!"

In the dead silence following the mayor's ringing words Jim's first thought was that the silly little bastard was still beaming, beaming like a man claiming victory.

"I want to thank the good folk who have worked so long and hard on my behalf," Blaine went on, "and I sincerely hope they will find surcease from their keen disappointment by falling in behind my worthy opponent . . ." He stopped again, waited, clearly savoring the suspense he was trying to build. ". . . the next senator from Chupadera County . . ." Another wait. *"Mr. Eloy Montoya!"*

Now Jim could feel the stirring in the people around him, the hard-core backers of Corey Lane. He looked at the candidate himself and found exactly what he expected—nothing. The big man was as unperturbed as if he weren't involved in any way. The editor turned and looked into the crowd, finally finding the serious dark face of Eloy Montoya. Clearly, the Concho man was as surprised as anyone in the plaza.

The man standing beside him wasn't, though. Granby Stafford was looking hard at Corey Lane. The merchant had obviously had a hand in this, had engineered it. Promise or payment—*something*— had been made to the little fusspot now shaking every hand thrust at him as he left the bandstand, the look of a solid winner on his round moon of a face.

"That snugs the cinch a whole hell of a lot tighter than it ought to be," Sam Riordan said in McPherson's ear.

It did. Some lightning arithmetic told Jim that Corey would have to get at least one in four of Blaine's people to make dead sure. It wasn't a wild hope, but it wasn't going to

be easy, either. The other people on the veranda didn't seem
to have grasped the significance of the mayor's sudden with-
drawal, not from the look of their smug faces. Perhaps Alicia
had. Her old look of fighting determination had returned.
Virgie just looked thoughtful.

"Guess the little sonofabitch couldn't face the licking he
was sure to take tomorrow," Will-Ed Martin said. There were
echoes of agreement from the other Lane people on the
porch.

Then Jim felt, more than saw, Corey Lane rise from his
chair. His eyes went to the tall man when he stopped for a
moment at the top of the veranda stairs. It seemed every face
in the bonfire-lit plaza was turned toward him.

As he stood there, Jim wondered if this gathering on the
veranda might not have been a serious tactical blunder. It
made Corey's friends, already a privileged elite of sorts,
separate from the crowd, and the few feet the veranda loomed
above the caliche in the square could seem an Olympian
height to the people looking at him.

Then Corey was down in the mass of people, walking
with those giant strides toward the bandstand. Twice before
Jim had seen the man take command on almost this exact
patch of earth. He would have to do it differently this time.
Could he? Was there any bend in the man?

McPherson watched Corey shuffle the notes Alicia had
given him, watched as though he were a complete stranger to
the man—and to Black Springs, too. *Convince me, Corey,* he
pleaded to himself as Lane began to speak.

Even as Corey began, his voice clear and bright as a
trumpet, something strange was happening, something incredibly gratifying. If the man at the rostrum bore any resem-
blance to any of the Corey Lanes Jim had come to know in
the past, it was to the one he had seen pinning the badge on
Jacky Jameson in the office that day. It wasn't that he was
condescending or less sure of himself; he was firm enough.
But the firmness had no insulting heat in it. It took a clear
and well-directed eye to see the effort he was making for this
performance. It was worth it. He was winning them over one
by one.

Less specific on the issues facing Chupadera County
than Eloy had been, still he did come down hard on a few
things: the coming of the railroad; the bonds which tied every

man and woman of the Ojos Negros to every other; the need
for strength and courage in the face of future change—and
the great history of that same strength and courage in the
past. *Alicia has coached him well,* Jim thought, and then he
thought that it was small of him to take one jot of credit away
from the man standing so confidently at the lectern. If most
of the things he uttered in that strong voice were platitudes,
that meant no diminution of their importance. Jim began to
remember just why he had enlisted so readily, so totally, in
the cause of Corey Lane. The man from the X-Bar-7, towering above the rapt crowd, bronzed by the light of the lanterns
and the fires in much the same way he had been that night
after the battle, was as glorious as any human being the
editor could remember. The only tiny flaw in the whole
display (Jim was sure no one who remembered it would fault
Corey for it anyway) was that he looked exactly as he had
standing on the rimrock in the Oscuras, a touch too precipi-
tate and ready to leap. A small worry here? Perhaps.

"—and nothing—" *(He must be nearing the finish now.)*
"—nothing can shake my abiding faith in the citizens of Black
Springs and Chupadera County."

There were a full five counts of breathless silence before
applause and cheering rolled across the plaza. He had won
them—every man of them.

At last the reverberating hurrahs died to echoes, and the
speaker, smiling, stepped from the lectern.

"Wait a minute, please!" It was Granby Stafford, twenty
feet or so from the bandstand stairs. "Will the candidate
answer a question or two?"

Corey stopped, looked down at the merchant, and nodded. The men who had been pressing forward, hands outstretched for Corey's, backed away, leaving a passage through
which the two men stared at one another.

Jim McPherson's heart grew cold.

"*Mister* Lane," Granby said. His voice on the "*Mister*"
was grating, derisive, bantering, all at once, and an ominous
sigh moved through the crowd. "Mister Lane. That 'abiding
faith' in the people here was a mighty warming thing to
hear—but I want to ask if you've *always* felt that way."

Corey was silent. He gave no sign of any change in
attitude or manner, but Jim was sure he could feel the rising
heat filling the man.

"Did you feel that way, *Mister* Lane, when the Sinuoso ranchers caused this town to nearly die of thirst?"

Corey started to speak, but Granby was on him again like a hawk. "Did you feel that way when the Apaches broke out of their lawful reservation that selfsame day?

Now the heat in Corey's face must be visible to any pair of eyes in the gathering.

"Cast your mind back to that day if you please, *Mister* Lane." Granby's taunting banter now was just a thin fabric over the razor edge in his voice. "Do you remember when you told a bunch of us about Victorio's breakout—without taking the people you've blessed with this new 'abiding faith' into your confidence? Do you remember my offering the help of the men of Black Springs and the Rio Concho?" There was some muttering in the men near the platform and Granby waited for it to stop. "*Do* you, Mister Lane? I want your answer, please."

Corey nodded.

"And do you, Mister Lane, remember what you said when this help was offered? The truth, *Mister* Lane. It shouldn't be difficult for you—you're famous for it."

When Corey Lane spoke, it was like the first sound of the cracking of a dam.

"I said I didn't think they could stand like fighting men against Apache warriors."

"Ah, yes, Mister Lane, but what you really meant to say was we were cowards! Isn't that the truth?"

The dam broke apart completely.

"*Yes,*" and then again, "YES!"

There would be no need to count the votes. Jim couldn't look at Corey. His eyes found Eloy Montoya, and when they did they rested on a man as stricken as if he'd been dealt a mortal blow. Jim's heart went out to the Concho man. Eloy's victory tomorrow, which would come about as surely as the sun would rise, hadn't been brought to pass by anything that fine decent man had done. Nor could Corey's coming defeat be laid at Jim McPherson's door. Why, then, did he feel this sense of guilt?

He looked at Virgie Lane and he knew. Everything he'd done he'd done for her, and there was no longer any point in disguising it.

Virgie was looking at him with eyes clouded with confusion—and dark with sorrow.

*"You common cry of curs, whose breath I hate
As reek o' th' rotten fens, whose loves I prize
As the dead carcasses of unburied men
That do corrupt my air, I banish you!"*

IV

"Does Corey know about this yet, Sam?" Jim said.

"I expect not. No, of course not. Hell, he ain't even been in town since he lost the election, and nobody's been out to the X-Bar-7 since Granby walked in and dropped this sorry crap on Judge Harry Timmons' bench a week ago."

"Has anybody talked with Granby?"

"He won't *see* nobody. He's letting the clerks run the feed store while he's holed up in that backroom office of his. Been there ever since he went to the courthouse and filed that 'criminal information,' or whatever it is, document of his. Jesus, Jim, I think he must be *sleeping* there. The door's locked from the inside and there's a note on it says he ain't going to show his face until Corey comes to court to face his charges. Don't blame him. I think Corey might kill him when he hears. Jim, what the hell is 'misfeasance' anyway?"

"Criminal misuse of lawful authority or position."

"Serious?"

"Well . . . yes. It's a felony. Conviction would bar Corey from ever seeking office even if he wanted to now—and a lot of other things."

"What's the penalty if he's found guilty?"

"Depends on the judge," Jim said. "Timmons has a certain amount of leeway. But the disgrace of it, even if sentence is suspended . . ." The editor shook his head.

"God damn it!" Sam's hand was clenched so tightly on

his glass Jim feared he might break it. Never had he seen the old rancher so white with bitterness and anger. "It's like back-shooting. Come on, Jim, let's get the hell out of here. This whiskey is starting to taste like piss." Sam left the bar, his stumpy legs unsteady, but not from drink this time.

Outside in the plaza he started in again.

"What beats the hell out of me is *why?* I know Corey has stuck in Granby's craw for years, but I sure would of thought Eloy's trimming him in the election would have been enough."

The merchant's new attack had shocked but not surprised Jim McPherson. Perhaps Sam had lived so long in the crossfire of enmities like Granby Stafford's for Corey Lane that he no longer payed attention to them. Or more likely Sam was just so fundamentally decent he couldn't understand rancor like the merchant's.

"One thing," Sam said, "it sure blew all kinds of holes in my theory about who was looking after Mary Ellen Talley and her kids."

"You think Granby's charges are true, then?"

"Hell, yes. No doubt about it. I just plain don't see anything wrong with what Corey did."

"But why did Corey have to use the fine money and the other sheriff's-office cash? The town would have rallied around Mary Ellen."

"Sure they would. But that's just the point. Of all the Ojos Negros men who died in the Oscuras, Bill Talley was the only one who wasn't pretty damned well heeled. If we'd passed the hat, Mary Ellen would have been taking charity all by her lonesome. She would have stuck out like a sore thumb. Corey apparently couldn't abide the thought of *that.*"

Yes, that indeed was the crux of it. Injury to the pride of his dead deputy's widow would be something Corey would understand very well.

"Another thing that pulls my cork," Sam was saying now, "is that Granby waited until Eloy was nicely up in Santa Fe, meeting the governor and all, before he made his move. I think Eloy might have been able to stop him, and I'm damned sure he would have tried. At that, Granby must have been in a real sweat. The new senator had to get out of town while Harry Timmons' circuit still had enough time left to hold a hearing and maybe put Corey on trial. Two more weeks and the judge would have packed up this term and headed for some other part of the district. Be a year maybe before he's back here in Chupadera County again."

"Corey could pay back the money," Jim said. "But that won't alter the fact that he used it in the first place."

"I guess I feel as sorry for Jacky Jameson as I do for anybody. If Corey won't come in for the hearing next Tuesday on his own, Jacky will have to go out and get him," Sam said.

Jim felt sorry for Jim. He dreaded having to write the story he would run in the Thursday paper, no matter how the hearing went. It wouldn't do to bother Sam with his troubles, though, particularly since the old rancher suddenly seemed to brighten. "Corey will understand what Jacky has to do," Sam said. "Well, Sonny Jim—I got me one consolation about this whole thing. I was sure right about Jacky and Mary Ellen. She was so upset about people finding out Corey had been helping her, Jacky decided the best thing was to announce their plans so the town would have no doubt who'd be taking care of her from now on out."

Jim's mind ran back to what Sam had said just before. "You don't think Corey will balk at coming in voluntarily, do you, Sam?"

"Oh, I reckon not. He's got too much affection for Jacky to put him through any trouble. Besides, you know how much respect Corey's got for the law."

Sam was silent then. He moved his booted toe in circles through the caliche dust. His face was grave, worried-looking. "I'm only concerned about what Corey might do to Granby when he sees him."

"What gets me, Sam, is the fact that everybody and his brother knows now that Stafford bribed Wilson out of the race by telling him Eloy would get him a job in Santa Fe. Too bad we've got no proof to throw at Granby. Maybe that would get him to withdraw his charges."

"Well, Wilson will never admit to it. Be like self-incrimination, I guess. Thank God Eloy don't feel bound by promises Granby made." The old man drifted off again. Finally he shook his shaggy head. "Oh, God, Jim! I got a real bad feeling about things. Way worse than this ridiculous fuss over a few bucks nobody will ever miss would warrant. Guess I'm too old to stand the idea of a great man like Corey being brought down by a pick-nose like Granby Stafford—that and

what it's apt to do to the other people at the X-Bar-7." He
looked straight into Jim's eyes then. "Yeah," he said, "I can
see something like that has already occurred to you."

It wasn't surprising, that last remark. Jim had given up
trying to hide anything from Sam Riordan. Somehow the
admission that he no longer cared if his friend knew how
much he grieved for Virgie and her situation made it a little
easier to bear. Misery loves company? Perhaps.

Company or not, he had known enough misery since the
night two weeks before when Corey Lane had stalked away
from the bandstand, taken his two women in tow, and left
immediately for the X-Bar-7, abandoning the plan to remain
overnight at the Sacramento House and lead a triumphal
march to the polling-place in the courthouse in the morning.
The Lane exodus had been so swift, so final, that Jim had had
the paralyzing feeling that he was seeing Virgie for the last
time. It was bad enough to feel this way at all, worse to think
that this last sight, the one which might remain forever in his
mind's eye, would be of her loved face ravaged by the grief of
this awful moment. In what he could only in fairness call
cowardice, he had wrenched his eyes away from her and
fastened them on the other two.

Alicia and Corey had presented an incredible sight. Walking across the plaza toward Kelly's Livery, with Virgie half a
pace behind them, they didn't check their movement for the
crowd in front of them, didn't wait to see if it would part.
They just walked, and the throngs moved aside as if an
unseen plow were making a wide furrow through them. As
the trio reached the other side of the plaza, Virgie must have
turned. Out of the corner of his eye Jim saw her dark face
suddenly lighter, paler, in the dying glow of the bonfires. He
hadn't looked at her—he couldn't. And he couldn't ever
forgive himself for not looking.

"Sonny Jim," Sam said, his voice coming through the
editor's blue fog of thought like a steam whistle, "when Harry
Timmons clears up all this nonsense for Corey, why don't you
and me mosey up to Santa Fe? We could check and see how
Eloy is settling in, let him know he ain't been forgotten—and
then we could pay a call on Lita Gabaldon's establishment.
Might be just the thing you need."

God bless you, Sam Riordan. The fact that the prospect
of visiting the whorehouse now was absolutely sickening didn't

take anything away from the old rancher's kindly concern for him.

"I don't think so, Sam. Thanks anyway," he said. "If Corey comes through this all right, I don't think we'll need that kind of diversion, and if he doesn't, I don't think we'll feel up to it."

Except for news of some horses stolen at Three Rivers, not one more word had come down the mountain from Russell about Victorio, nor had anything been heard from Santa Fe or Washington, as far as McPherson could discover. As the agent had surmised, the Apache chief must have raced his band of escapees clear across the Jornada del Muerto into the Black Range, or else headed south and out of American jurisdiction. Either way, he must be lying low, gathering recruits and arms. It was too much to expect that this silent substitute for peace would last forever, but it was a blessing no depredations were taking place. With Corey under attack by Granby (and, through the merchant, the law), who in the Ojos Negros could rally a defense? Jacky Jameson had all he could do trying to put the sheriff's department back in shape. He needed a new deputy right away, and in the long run Joe Harris—not, by all indications, the most reliable of lawmen—wouldn't do, so that made two additions the new sheriff would have to look for.

Will-Ed and the ranchers on the Sinuoso, and Matt Hendry, Dan Stone, and the rest of the basin stockmen would have their hands full for the next month bringing their herds down from the high summer pastures, grazing lands spread over a thousand square miles of Chupadera mountainside. Most would be branding, gathering shipments for the trail herds which would push through the passes to the north and east to connect with the Goodnight-Loving and the Chisholm. They couldn't be counted on until their big workseason ended.

To make matters worse, a good many of the Regular Army units normally assigned to the Territory were being transferred to the Dakotas and Montana. The flight of the Cheyennes the year before had left the military highly nervous in the northern districts, and now the unlawful detention of Big Snake and the Fort Reno Poncas had made the Plains tribes edgy and, in the opinion of some of the agents, ready for another widespread war.

The whole "parlous state" of things, as Lew Wallace had called it, was made to order for Victorio if he tumbled to it, and with the Mimbres leader's uncommon genius for gathering intelligence, there was no reason to believe he wouldn't.

Jim could only pray that Victorio and the Mimbreño and Mescalero fugitives with him had gone to ground so deeply in some remote mountain fastness they couldn't make their way out of it again, that or had fled to some safe barren district of Chihuahua. As things were, the Ojos Negros lay open to rape and pillage like a maiden in a restless sleep, a sleep only a Corey Lane could wake it from. How much longer the man of the X-Bar-7 would hold that power was now as uncertain as the Apaches' whereabouts.

The editor didn't hide from himself the fact that he didn't wish Victorio far away solely because of the danger he presented to Chupadera County while on the loose. He wanted that remarkable man free—forever. This hope wasn't something he could say out loud in Black Springs, not even to tolerant understanding Sam.

It would be well if Corey and Victorio never met again. That they were fated to, though, was a feeling Jim couldn't drive away.

On the Saturday before the hearing Jim saw Jacky mount up and ride out of town, heading for the south trace and the X-Bar-7 to serve the summons of Judge Harry Timmons' Circuit Court on Corey Lane. The editor sat like a rock at his desk, unable to work, hearing over and over again Sam's mournful voice saying, "Oh, God, Jim! I got a real bad feeling about things." He knew exactly how Sam felt.

He stared at the new sign which had gone up on the *vigas* of the office across the plaza two days after the election: J.J. JAMESON—SHERIFF. The paint was still shining white and the letters were as sharp and black as Corey's lettering had faded away to fuzziness. Jim wondered idly what had happened to Corey's sign. Nothing official was left of the former sheriff in Black Springs now, unless the old sign was still languishing on some rubbish heap to which the torch had not as yet been put. He smiled bitterly at how well the tinder-dry weatherbeaten board would blaze up if that hadn't already happened.

After a disconsolate lunch at the Sacramento House,

where he deliberately avoided even peeking into the bar for Sam, he returned to his desk and resumed staring across at the sheriff's office. He jumped as each horseman rode by his window, in spite of knowing Jacky couldn't possibly have made it back in so short a time.

It was dusk when he saw the young sheriff rein to a halt at the office hitchrail. Jim sprinted across the caliche, his tension leaving him breathless. When he reached the porch, Jacky had already gone inside, but Jim found he wasn't alone at the office door. He very nearly collided with Sam. The old rancher must have been watching from the Sacramento in an identical nervous state. Once inside, they both tried to talk at once, until a grinning Jacky cut them short.

"Hey! Hold on there. I ain't going to keep things from you."

"How *was* Corey about it?" Sam got the words out first.

"Nice as pie. Didn't even seem too surprised."

"He'll come in on Tuesday? No argument about it?"

"Not a bit."

Jim wanted to ask about Virgie. He thought he had better not.

"You know," Jacky said, "I'll admit I sure didn't cotton to this little chore. Ain't real certain I got the sand to have faced Corey down if he'd been the least bit ornery." He smiled. "If I'm lucky, I'll never know for sure." He unbuckled his gunbelt and hung it on a gun-rack peg behind him. The Peacemaker Special looked innocent in its holster. "Now, gentlemen," the sheriff said, "if you'll excuse me, I got to scrape off some of this beard and skedaddle over to Mary Ellen's."

Jim wondered if Sam's "real bad feeling" had subsided. He didn't quite know whether his had or not.

"Hear ye! Hear ye! The Circuit Court for the Third Judicial District of the United States Territory of New Mexico, the Honorable Harry O. Timmons presiding, is now in session. All rise!"

During the morning's fussing with papers, frequent trips to the bench by the part-time prosecutor from Mesilla, and all the comings and goings of the hangers-on in the dingy crowded courtroom, Jim had remained as unimpressed by the quality of Territorial law and justice as he had been from his reading in back issues of the *News* and his rummaging through the courthouse records. He had seen as much formality (and a good deal more juridical sophistication) in New York City police courts in his apprentice days on the *Sun*. The judge's horse-sense and personal sense of fairness would count as much here as precedent. He hoped it would be enough.

Actually, he had a hunch that the loose weave in the fabric of the law here might work to Corey Lane's advantage. If Harry Timmons applied the test of reasonableness to the man's actions while sheriff, he might find it difficult to bind him over for trial on Granby's charges. Sam, sitting next to him behind the defendant's table, was in full agreement when he whispered his opinion. Then the editor's hunch, if not entirely shattered, took a blow as he saw Judge Timmons bite his lip in ill-concealed displeasure when Corey announced he would defend himself.

"No one speaks for me," Lane said, his voice flat and low, but with unmistakable overtones of defiance in it.

"Are you sure that's wise, Mr. Lane?" the judge asked. His voice was sharp.

"Doesn't matter if it's wise or not. It's the way it's going to be."

"Mr. Lane! While this is just a hearing, it could result in a trial. I advise you not to take the matter of the people's charges too lightly, sir."

"I'm giving them all the weight they deserve." Corey's contempt for the proceedings, and the men running them, couldn't have been more plain if he had worn a sign proclaiming it.

Corey, Corey! Jim thought. *Can't you at least say "Your Honor" when you address the court?* He wished Alicia had come to town for the hearing, but he pushed the thought away when he realized that would have meant leaving Virgie alone at the X-Bar-7 to wait it out. And he wouldn't wish *her* here—just in case. It posed the question, though.

"Wonder why Alicia and Virgie aren't here, Sam," he said while Corey, the Mesilla lawyer, and the judge were huddled together on some minor matter.

"Corey wouldn't *let* them come, I expect. He faces trouble alone." It made sense. As a matter of fact, as far as Jim knew, Corey hadn't so much as spoken or nodded to a soul other than Harry Timmons since he'd ridden into the plaza on the chestnut just before court convened, not even to Jacky

Jameson when he turned his gunbelt over to him at the long table just inside the door.

Corey's words to Timmons had been the first break in a strange kind of silence, something akin to a cold boredom, which puzzled Jim. He couldn't believe all the heat had gone out of Corey, but except for the one brief flurry with the judge the only signs of life in the man from the X-Bar-7 came when he would from time to time glance quickly at the door at the rear of the courtroom. They were midway through the short morning session when Jim figured it out. Granby Stafford wasn't here. It was the merchant Lane was looking for. He wanted his enemy at hand.

The thought must have struck Sam, too. "Wonder where he is—the louse who started all this itch," Riordan said. His voice was heavy with bitterness and loud enough for several other people to hear and to begin muttering until Timmons gaveled them into silence. If Corey heard, he didn't turn around.

"Suppose he's afraid to show his face, Sam?" Jim asked when a sufficient length of time seemed to have gone by so that he wouldn't risk the judge's wrath.

"Well . . . Granby ain't the bravest man in Black Springs, but . . . no, I don't think he's *that* yellow. Besides, if his case has any chance at all, he won't want to miss the fun."

Granby wasn't missing any "fun" as yet. As in all the trials and hearings Jim had reported on, nothing much happened in the next hour but procedural discussions and a lecture from Timmons on the rules of evidence. Things wouldn't likely liven up until the afternoon, when the prosecution promised a "parade of witnesses, Your Honor." Jim almost laughed out loud as it suddenly struck him how close Corey Lane and the glacier speed of this frontier court came to Hamlet's "the proud man's contumely, the law's delay."

At last the judge recessed the court for the noon meal with the admonishment that the principals for both sides had "better get your tails back in those chairs at one o'clock sharp and be ready to go at it. This court gets riled mighty easy if it's kept waiting." Perhaps things would move more speedily then.

Corey rose and moved swiftly toward the door. As he passed the row Sam and Jim were in, the editor started to slide toward the aisle to talk with him, but the rancher's hand caught him at the shoulder. "No, Jim. I don't think so, not now."

As the crowd trooped out, making a small jam at the single door, Jim found himself standing at the table where Jacky had piled the weapons checked at the opening of court. The young sheriff had left with the first of the spectators, and now Jim smiled at the limp security of the small arsenal. No one was guarding the pistols and rifles on the table. Sam Riordan's ancient never-loaded Navy Colt was snuggled next to Corey's gunbelt, from the holster of which protruded the bone handle of a Peacemaker Special almost the twin of the one Lane had given Jameson.

Outside, when he had blinked away the first glare of the bright noon sun, Jim saw that Corey Lane had walked to the stairs of the bandstand and was looking up to where the lectern had been the night of the election rally. But he hadn't even had time to reflect on this when Sam said, "Well, I'll be . . ." and Jim turned to find the rancher pointing to a slim man in a dark suit hurrying toward them from Estancia Street.

"*Señores!*" Eloy Montoya said when he reached them, out of breath. "I rode down from Santa Fe after I received this terrible news just two days ago. All this morning I have been trying to get Señor Stafford to withdraw these foolish charges. He will not listen. *Verdad*, I am sorry. . . ." His voice trailed off.

"Don't fret, Eloy," Sam said. "Ain't a soul in town but what knows you'd never have stood still for this, any more than we would. Unfortunately, it ain't up to us, *amigo*."

Jim looked to the bandstand again, but Corey was gone.

After a glum lunch (Sam took his solely from a bottle) during which they didn't talk at all about the hearing, they found their seats in the courtroom, this time with Eloy beside them.

"You can call your first witness, Mr. Telford," Harry Timmons said to the lawyer for the prosecution. The Mesilla man nodded to the clerk.

"Mrs. William Talley."

Corey Lane didn't turn his head to watch the young woman as she walked to the witness stand, but when she finished taking the oath and looked directly to where he sat alone at the defendant's table, there was a noticeable stiffening of the ex-sheriff's back. The fire wasn't out by any means.

The lawyer from Mesilla was good, very good. He elicited Mary Ellen's testimony swiftly and easily, and Jim couldn't help but admire his adroitness as he turned her fear-tinged admissions that "Yes, sir. I got money regular-like from Sheriff Lane" into something resembling guilt. But he never once bullied her. His patient courteous style of questioning would have a powerful effect on a jury if a trial was ordered. When he finished, he thanked her with a kindly bow and returned to his seat.

"Hold it, please, Mrs. Talley," the judge said as Mary Ellen started to leave the stand. "You got any questions of this witness, Mr. Lane?"

"No!" Corey's back rippled with impatience.

Sam leaned toward Jim. "Where do we stand?" he whispered.

"He's only established that Mary Ellen got the money. Now he has to bring out that it wasn't Corey's. The next witness will be the one that counts."

Timmons requested the next call, but before the clerk could read the name, the door at the rear of the courtroom creaked on its tired hinges. A buzz of voices at the back turned every head. Granby Stafford was just inside the door.

There was some fear in the face Jim saw, but the pleased flush of anticipated triumph kept it almost out of sight. Granby must have enjoyed the effect his appearance had made on the crowd, for he stood stock still, not even looking for an empty seat. He might have stood there forever had not Harry Timmons barked, "Will the late arrival at the back of the room find a place to park, *pronto?*"

Half a dozen conversations broke out across the room, but Jim didn't even try to gauge the tenor of them. He did catch Sam's *"There's* our next witness, the sonofabitch!" as he turned back to the man at the defendant's table.

Corey was looking at Granby with eyes filled with what seemed more like revulsion than hate or anger. If he could only hold this cool disdain and not erupt as he had at the rally, there was every chance he could destroy the merchant in cross-examination and perhaps prevail. There was no way to refute the "evidence," of course, but if he could reduce Granby to a stuttering, inconsequential cipher as he had that

May day in the plaza, the evidence wouldn't count for much. Even as irascible as Timmons was, and as ill-disposed toward Corey as he had seemed at the beginning, the man surely was astute enough to see Granby's charges for what they were—the obvious results of a spiteful lust for petty revenge. A mere warning for Corey, a mild slap on the wrist, and this ridiculous business could end right here.

The noise had been swelling, and now the judge was pounding his gavel on the bench with angry vigor. "One more outburst like that," he shouted when the room finally got quiet, "and the back of this courtroom will look as empty as Bronco Canyon! Mr. Clerk, let's get on with it."

Corey turned back to face the bench, and Jim heard Sam chuckle. The old rancher must have reached something like Jim's conclusions.

The clerk stood, cleared his voice, and rustled the paper in his hand a couple of times before he began to read.

"The people call as their next witness," he declaimed, "Sheriff J. J. Jameson!"

The silence which greeted the words seemed even more thunderous than the outbreak Timmons had pounded to death a moment earlier.

"Oh, my God!" Sam Riordan groaned. "Jacky? For the *prosecution?*"

Now Jim realized the full extent of the Mesilla lawyer's shrewdness. Calling Jameson as an unfriendly witness for his side was the smartest thing he could have done. If he drew anything damaging from the youngster, no cross-examination by Corey could counteract it. And again Sam ratified his thinking. "The way Corey's brought that boy up, there ain't a chance in Hell he even *knows* how to lie any more, even if he had a mind to."

Jim could hear Jacky's boots clicking down the aisle as he left the table with the guns, but he didn't look. There would be time to search the young sheriff's face when he was on the stand. It was the broad back of Corey Lane which claimed his whole attention once again. The man's huge, preposterously delicate hands were gripping the table on either side of him as if he was about to spring. Delicate? No, not now. Now there was nothing but brute strength showing. Then, as if from a great distance, Jim heard the clerk swearing Jacky in.

" . . . and nothing but the truth, so help you God?"

"I do."

Then the editor did pull his eyes away from the defendant to look at the man on the witness stand, but it wasn't a
man he saw there, it was a boy, a frightened boy. The fresh
clean grin was only a shadow of the exuberant thing Jim had
known most of his days in Black Springs, and the usually firm
square shoulders were rounded, hunched forward tightly, as
if their owner knew a lash was coming. He was looking
straight at the prosecutor, but like a blind man.

The lawyer moved to the attack, and even though Mc-
Pherson had a revealing vision that it was all as good as over,
he felt sickened at the cool, deadly control of the prosecutor
as he posed his first question.

"Sheriff Jameson, are you acquainted with the defendant, Mr. Corey Lane?" It was a quiet, harmless question; no
danger here at all, but . . .

Jacky made the one mistake Jim knew instinctively would
tear everything to pieces. He looked at Corey. He looked at
Corey with wide eyes that threatened to fill with tears. His
mouth opened and he seemed about to speak, but no sound
came. He licked his dry lips. Wordlessly he implored the big
man, and it was indeed as if he had spoken: *Help me, Corey.
Get me out of this—please.*

"The witness will answer the question," Harry Timmons
said. Jacky worked his mouth, and at last words seemed
about to come, but before they could, Corey Lane erupted
from his chair, sending it flying, clattering against the wooden
rail behind him.

"Enough!"

It was like the gunshot that long-ago day in May, but
more frightening, more vicious—more compelling. The silence which settled on the court made prisoners of them all,
even Harry Timmons with his gavel arrested in the air above
the bench as if an invisible hand had gripped his wrist.

"I've had enough of this," Corey said. "I've decided not
to grant you people the right to sit in judgment on me."

Judge Timmons was beginning to stir.

Corey went on, "At first I thought I might go along with
this charade, but I know now that humoring you will only
lend you an importance you can never rightly have." He
turned and faced the back of the courtroom. "This is all over
with," he said. "You might as well go home." Jim McPherson

didn't turn, but he wondered if Corey was looking at Granby Stafford.

Timmons found his voice. The words were strong enough, but there was no sustaining force behind them. "Mr. Lane, sit down!" Corey ignored him. "*Mr. Lane!* If you don't sit down, I will have to order restraints for you!"

Corey turned and stared at him. "Restraints?" he said. "Restraints? Do you seriously think there's a thing, Harry, or a man, or a dozen, who could restrain *me* if I set my mind against it?"

And then he began to laugh.

It was a wild black laugh, terrible to hear. It rang through the courtroom, and Jim knew his wasn't the only heart to shrink from it. As it echoed off the walls, a strange thought came to the editor. The things he heard in the laugh weren't totally unknown to him. He had heard some of them in the eerie chant of Victorio that day in the Mescalero, except—except this was the dark mad side of the message the Apache's voice had carried.

When the laugh had subsided, Corey turned and faced the crowd again. "I'll be going now." These words were soft but final.

He pushed through the gate of the railing as if it weren't there and moved with those big strides up the aisle. As he passed the table with the guns, his arm snaked out and his big hand swept his gunbelt up as if it had been a piece of string.

It was a long minute before Harry Timmons broke the spell. "I want that man brought back—now," he said, his voice grim. Then, to Jim's horror, he turned to the forgotten man on the witness stand. "Sheriff Jameson," he said, "go out and get him. And when you return, remember you're still under oath. Now, move!"

Suddenly it was a different Jacky Jameson from the cringing pleading creature who had looked to Corey Lane for help. The shoulders were square again as he hurried up the aisle, and the jaw was set. As Corey had, he swept his gunbelt from the table and was wrapping it around his slender waist as he reached the door. He stopped there, bent over and tied the holster off above the knee, and disappeared from sight.

Like ducks rising from a pond, the crowd broke from their seats and jammed against the big windows facing the plaza. Timmons was pounding and shouting for order like a man possessed, but it had no more effect than if the people in the courtroom were indeed wild birds. Jim felt Sam leave. He followed, and in a second the two of them were pushing their way up an aisle choked with jostling bodies. It took the better part of a minute to fight through to the door, but at last they reached it and were quickly out in a sun which blazed only a little less brightly than it had at noon. Jim saw that Eloy Montoya had made the effort, too.

Across the plaza, in front of the Sacramento House, they could see Corey Lane already in the saddle. Jacky stood in front of him, his left hand raised in the air in an odd mirror image of the way he had looked when the clerk had sworn him in. His right hand was curled just above the bone handle of the revolver strapped to his hip.

"Please, Corey," he was saying. "It's the job you taught me. *Don't make me draw on you.*"

"Get out of my way, Jacky. No one holds me here now. *No one!* Understand?"

"I've got to stop you, Corey. I've *got* to. You know that."

"I sure hope you won't make the try, Jacky. Now stand aside." He dug his spurs into the chestnut's sides, and the big animal moved forward.

Jacky Jameson's hand went to his gun. The move seemed fast enough, but the hand never got there. He was dead before his body crumpled to the caliche dust.

"He'll come back by himself. Nobody will have to go and get him," Sam said. His voice was weak and plaintive. "You'll see. He's got too much regard for law and order to go on the dodge. Corey Lane would *never* run."

"Oh, Sam, you poor deluded fool," Jim said. "Don't make any more guesses now, old friend. The man who rode out of here wasn't the Corey Lane you knew. Maybe he never was."

PART
FOUR

> *"though I go alone,*
> *Like to a lonely dragon, that his fen*
> *Makes feared and talked of more than seen . . ."*

I

The man on the chestnut horse with the white star blaze knew he had to make a decision soon. He rubbed his hand across a three-day growth of beard and stared hard at the mountains blotting out the last yellow ribbon of sunset sky. The big river was behind him at last, but there still remained more than a hard day's ride through desert country. If there was going to be a moon tonight, the choice would be a simple one: make the ride now. If he didn't get the horse to grassland soon, the old brute's once strong legs would collapse beneath it, no matter how much heart it had. No moon. The dark now creeping from the eastern rim behind him would quickly flood the sky. Even at that it wouldn't be too difficult to find decent going through the yucca if he could count on stars, but if it clouded up again, as it had shortly after sunset both evenings since he left the ranch, there was too much risk the horse would break a leg. He had water enough to make the rest of the distance mounted—on foot the margin would be too thin to measure. There was still too much deadly power left in the September sun for the water in his canteen to see him aross the miles of wasteland ahead of him.

There was no fear of pursuit—not now. If the spineless nothings in the town had summoned up the will or courage to form a posse and come after him, they would have reached the ranch during the two days he had raged about the house and compound in the mind-storming time before the knowledge came to him that he had to go. He had *wanted* them to

come, hungered for them. Once he had seen riders on the
rise between the Concho and Bronco run-outs, and the eager
hope that they would come at him and have it out had leaped
wildly for a moment, but they had turned back and been lost
to sight, and in a spasm of bitter gall he had known how
foolish it was to think even for a second that they would want
him badly enough to overcome their cowardice. The only
man in town who would have had guts enough to make a real
show of it had died facedown in his blood in the bone-white
clay of the plaza.

Of all the times he had killed, that was the strangest.
The boy had gone for his gun knowing he would die, *wanting*
to die. He had begged to be killed the moment he came from
the courthouse into the full sun of the plaza. It had been
necessary to oblige him, even if the hollow people watching
didn't understand. That was why he felt no sorrow over the
killing now—and of course he had felt none then. What he
had felt was passion, a surge of lust such as he had never felt
for a woman, not even for the dark creature he had left
behind, who had stirred him more than any woman ever
had—once. Besides the passion there had been love, too,
when he had killed the boy, as much love nearly as for the
other woman at the ranch he had ridden from three days ago.

The boy had gone for the gun he had given him, a plea
in his eyes, *Kill me, do it, do it now.* And he had done it, and
the plea had died in the heat and dust. All the boy's eyes had
held then was surprise. That was what was so especially
strange about that killing—the surprise. It must have been
there every other time, but he had never noticed it before.
Now he would wager that if a man fell into a canyon so deep
it took him an hour to smash against the bottom, and with all
that time falling to ready himself for the certainty of death,
that man would, in that last heart-stopping fractured second,
be surprised. It always came as an ambusher, death, no
matter how much it was expected.

He remembered how his father had gone, more than a
score of years ago. Through a long winter the disease had
chewed remorselessly on Jason's entrails until even that brave
man couldn't choke the screams to silence, and then the
Ambusher had come, and the blue eyes had swelled as big
and round as the Chiricahua shield hanging now in the sitting

room. Jason's son hadn't recognized it then, the surprise, but he would now.

The sunset now was no more than a jaundiced sliver resting on the black shoulders of the mountains. To the north and west the clouds were rolling in, the build-up so thick and viscous-looking he knew the decision had been made for him. He wouldn't waste a great deal of time picking a campsite here in the desert; one was like another as long as he stayed out of any depression which might flood in the unlikely chance the gathering cloudbank brought a storm. The overcasts of the last two nights hadn't let down even a gentle mist.

After tethering the horse to a yucca in the lee of a rock ledge which loomed a few yards above the otherwise featureless level sands, he gathered dead ocotillo branches for a fire. He built a small one, Indian fashion, not one of the great wasteful bonfires most white men set ablaze. It wasn't that he feared it being seen. He didn't care. Heat enough for coffee was all he wanted. He had no need for the companionship other men sought in flames and glowing coals. He probably wouldn't even look at the fire again after the pot had boiled.

Still, as the evening wore on and the darkness settled around him like a smothering blanket, he found himself feeding the little fire again and staring intently into the circle of stones holding the burning wood. It did jog his memory, and it did make him think.

There was no doubt about it, the flickering light winked some kind of magic at him. He could see the faces of the two women when he told them he was leaving, could hear the small tortured cry from the dark young one and the even louder stubborn silence of the older. Her mute questions, the ones she was too wise to put in words, were the worst of it. They were bad, but only because he couldn't answer them. *Where are you going, my son?* He didn't know. *What will you do when you get there?* Again, he didn't know. *Will you come back to us?* He knew that least of all.

It hadn't been a real choice he had made. His decision, if his it was, had come gradually. He couldn't even remember the exact moment when the knowledge came to him that he had to go. All he remembered was the terrible familiar heat rising in him as he stalked through the house and around the compound, trying to shake the thing which possessed him

whenever he'd had too much of other people, too much of
the silly sickly men and the simpering women who filled his
world, crowding it with their disgusting weaknesses, sullying
the cool majestic solitude he wanted, needed, had to have.

Whatever the thing was, it never let him go for long.
Maybe now he could know it for what it was. Maybe it was
the Ambusher himself, trying as always for surprise. More
likely, though, the thing was merely the Judas goat loosed in
his path to lead him to where the Ambusher lay waiting. That
seemed more in keeping with the kind of guile the old
schemer would need to employ to keep his record clean.
Well, he would ride carefully, eyes open.

He would have to close them soon now, though. The
gentle persistent heat from the small fire had made his eyelids heavy. No danger in letting them drop. In all his time in
the field nothing had taken him unaware in sleep. One ripple
in the placid pattern of the night sounds of the desert and he
would spring to full alertness. He heard an owl somewhere in
the middle distance, its night-hunt cry sharper and more
shrill than the mournful hooting earlier when the bird was
resting. Farther away a coyote yapped weakly, as if in disappointment at the moonless starless sky; near him a cricket
fiddled manically, its falsetto tune reminding him that the
desert hadn't known a freeze yet this season and surely
wouldn't tonight, with the overcast packing the day's heat
against the ground.

At the ranch the two women should be sleeping now,
and the boy as well. The reliable Zuni would be prowling the
compound, on the lookout, unseen silent knife in hand, ready
to slash the windpipe of any intruder who came in the night
with mischief on his mind. It would take five armed and very
determined men to break through the twisted little wrangler's guard, and by the time they did, the rest of the hands
would be out of the bunkhouse with their weapons. If the
Zuni had been one of the men in town, *he* could have
brought the Ambusher and it might all be over. But with the
merchant and farmer curs leaderless and cringing . . .

Wait. To be fair, they weren't *all* quite that craven.
Even at his advanced age, the old rancher who had been such
a staunch friend of Jason's could probably be someone to
reckon with one more time, but no power on earth would put
him in the saddle with any posse which rode against Jason's

son. And, too, there was the courteous quiet Mexican who had beaten him in that ridiculous election. *He* would have come if the others would have followed him, but there was little chance of that. Coming alone wouldn't have held more than momentary terror for that dark *hombre*, either, if he'd judged him right, but he would have dismissed the idea quickly when he saw the others didn't care enough.

There was only one other to be reckoned with—the editor. That one was an enigma. On the rimrock during the fight in the Oscuras the fright of the man had been as easy to read as the print in the newspaper he ran, but he had jumped into the thick of it when all the others, those tough scarred veterans of other bloody wars, had skulked behind the protecting rock until his own march to victory had flushed them out. Yes, the editor was a puzzle.

Strange that when he thought of the two women sleeping he had thought about the boy. He thought about him very seldom. The boy was an even larger mystery than was the editor. Sometimes as soft and gentle as his dark young mother, still there were moments when his blue eyes seemed to hold the same engulfing fire he felt consuming *him*. So much remained to be done with the boy before he would be ready for the world.

There was no more sound from the owl. It must have caught its prey. Yes, as if there had been an unmistakable signal from some secret trumpet, the crawling things of the desert were on the move again. Their turn wouldn't come tonight.

Sleep came. It was a drugged, deep, dreamless sleep, but an oddly conscious one.

He was awake and on his feet before the echo of the horse's first terrified whinny died away. *Lion!* Only a lion brought this kind of fear. As he sniffed for it in the thick impenetrable blackness, he wondered what a big cat might be doing down in these desert flats so far from its usual high-rock range. Game must be scarce in the mountain heights, either that or the lion must be old or sick or both to give it the desperate need to come this close to a camp where the scent of man hung heavy in the air. He had better get to the horse quickly and calm it. Bending over in a movement more of instinct than intelligence, he pulled the Winchester from

the saddle boot in the gear lying close to the spot still warm
from his sleeping head.

With his very next breath he cursed himself when he
realized the cost of that brief second's delay in moving to the
horse. It was then the lion, crouched somewhere on the rock
ledge above his head, coughed a wet hot cough—and the
chestnut reared, ripping loose the tether on the yucca, and
went bounding off into the blackness at a frenzied gallop.

Trying not to compound his error, he started after the
fleeing animal swiftly, racing through the darkness and feeling the thorny undergrowth tearing at his face. After a dozen
running steps he would stop and listen, and each time he
could hear the hoofbeats of the horse more distant, fainter.
Finally there was no sound at all. He was annoyed, but he
felt no panic. Although it was doubtful, the horse *could* come
back of its own accord when the big cat left. If it didn't, it
would be bad, walking the rest of the way to the black
mountains, but it could be done—if he was careful with his
water. It was time now, though, to find his camp again and
think about the lion.

He laughed. *If you're with the cat, Ambusher, I've over-
estimated you. You're not ready for me yet.*

The chances of the lion presenting any problems were
remote. For all the talk he had heard about the big cats down
through the years he had hunted and warred across this land,
he knew that was what it mostly was—talk. Attacks on humans were even rarer than the rare glimpses anyone ever got
of these shadowy creatures, and those attacks were only on
the very young or crippled. He was neither. Still, it wouldn't
pay to take any foolish chances. He began gathering more
dead ocotillo to rebuild his little fire, and this time he would
let it flare up as big as any tenderfoot's until morning came or
the watcher on the ledge wearied.

It was when his arms were filled with the rifle and the
fuel that he thought he heard the horse again, and when
he began running toward the sound, his foot struck against
the unseen root of a pitifully small desert bush. Even
as he cartwheeled through the black night, knowing himself
helpless to prevent it, he understood what was about to
happen. He heard the report of the rifle and felt the pain
in his leg all at once, and then he heard the echoes from
the shot bouncing off the nearby rocks.

It wasn't a bad wound, but bad enough. By morning he wouldn't be able to walk. Now he would need his firewood for another and more pressing reason. He reached around him and began to retrieve the scattered ocotillo; when he had secured as much as he could find, and when the rifle was safely in his grip again, he began the slow crawl back to his camp and the dying embers of his little fire.

When he had built the fire to a great roaring light, he sat up as best he could, facing the ledge. With his blood-smell reeking in the air, the odds against the lion coming down were reduced a little, but as long as the fire lasted he should be safe. Now it was time to begin the surgery. He cut his pants leg away and then twisted the knife in the heart of the flames. His left boot was awash with blood and it gurgled as he moved. On the ledge behind him the lion snuffled and coughed again.

Twice he almost let himself be claimed by unconsciousness, and both times he fought hard against this easy exit, until at last he had reached and removed the chunk of lead lodged against the bone. When the wound was bound in his neckerchief and battened even tighter with strips cut from his leather vest, he rested, weak from pain and effort. He thought he could hear the lion sighing with him as he finished.

Perhaps he had spoken too soon. Perhaps the Ambusher could make it with the cat. It would take some doing.

The fire lasted only a little more than an hour, but it was long enough. The first gray streaks of dawn had reached the campsite when the lion made its move.

He shot it cleanly, needing only a single round, and the sleek tawny body fell in a heap across the ashes from him. Then he let himself sink into earned oblivion, but he had time for one more thought: the horse would never come back now, not with that carcass lying there.

The cloud cover had burned away by the time the sun climbed a quarter of the way through the sky. In the full glare, which he couldn't escape because the rock wall under the ledge he had struggled so painfully to reach faced south, the leg had begun to swell and throb badly. It was too much to hope that he had escaped all infection with the knifework done by firelight. He should know by nightfall.

Once he had moved to the wall, the buzzards which had

circled overhead since dawn had settled on the lion, picking at the soft tissues of the eyes and belly first, but finally ripping at the furry back and legs. He had thrown stones at them several times—they shouldn't have things all their own way—but he gave that up when it made him hot and tired and too much in need of the water remaining in his canteen.

Off in the mesquite and greasewood scrub of the desert he could see at least two coyotes reconnoitering the scene. He wondered if it was fear of him or the birds which kept them at a respectful distance. As the day wore on he decided it must be the ugly busy birds. The rest of the crawling life around him seemed to have no fear of him. Horned toads, pocket mice, a myriad beetles came and went as they pleased, and even a good-sized bullsnake glided almost within reach. There was no sign of the horse. He didn't allow himself really to hope for it, but looking for the chestnut across the wastes kept him occupied.

The bullsnake made him think about rattlers, but he shook his head. The Ambusher wouldn't be that blunt—or in that much of a hurry.

He was going to die here. That, of course, was the unalterable fact. The only thing not certain was how long the process would take. If the wound didn't do it quickly, thirst would, in its own sweet time. It was now ironic that there wasn't a posse after him. Well, there wasn't. It would be far too much to expect that men without the courage to come and kill him would have enough courage to follow him and save his life.

He slept some in the scorching afternoon, short fitful naps which didn't rest him. Each time he awoke he knew the fever had mounted a little higher. Each time he took another tiny sip of water, sips so small they did no more than wet the lips his tongue told him were cracking badly. Once he awakened with his head ringing as if someone were beating it like a gong, and he found that his hat had slipped off. The sun was coming through his eyelids to cook his brain as if there were nothing at all to stop it. He didn't move much. He did crawl to his saddlebags near the end of the afternoon. If he was going to string this out as long as possible, he would have to eat, but when he tried to chew on a piece of jerky, he found he was too weak to work his jaws.

It was an idle thought, but he wondered if the buzzards

would gorge themselves on the carcass of the lion to the point that when his turn came they would have no hunger left for his parched raddled flesh. Not that it mattered. There were hordes of other greedy gluttonous things above and below the ground to nibble him to nothing when the Ambusher had gone his way. He thought of wrapping himself in his slicker if he could manage to get it out; it would make them earn their keep. Too much bother.

Neither the pain in his leg nor the fever was constant. Both, separately and sometimes together, would well up to the point where he thought they could go no higher, then they would slide down to where they were but mild annoyances, only to shoot to an even higher peak in the surge that followed. He did think of suicide—and seriously—several times. He felt it could not be considered the "coward's way out," as he had heard it called. Putting the Peacemaker down as often as he picked it up was prompted by something else. He had to play it strictly on the up-and-up with the Ambusher, even if that grinning devil had no intention of being fair with him. There could be no cheating on the last test he would ever face.

And killing himself to escape the pain would soon become unimportant. Before many hours went by, the fever would have taken care of that. When the delirium began, the pain would stop. He had often seen this happen in other men.

The only thing he feared now was the torment to come when the half-full canteen surrendered its last half-drop.

Time began playing tricks. The sun seemed to take longer to go down than it had the night before, but when it finally did and the rose glow disappeared, he couldn't believe the day had fled in such a hurry. He waited for the same clouds which had blanked away the stars the last three nights, but this time they didn't come.

The buzzards had retreated from the remains of the carcass they had rammed their bloody beaks into all day long. He could see some of them perched in the brush in the dim light from the stars, and one of them had settled over his head, on the rock ledge the lion had come down from.

The pain subsided, and he knew the fever's hold on him was now so great a hot frenzy would soon make his brain run like molten lava. The sneak attack of the Ambusher could come at any moment after that. There was one more thing he could do while his mind was still clear. He could not allow himself to be tyrannized by the thought of what was left in the canteen nestled against his useless leg. He unscrewed the top of the canvas-covered flask and drained off the rest of his water in three swift greedy gulps. Finished, he threw the canteen as far as his weakened arm could manage. When it clattered against the stones beyond the now dead fire, the birds rose from their perches as if a shot had scattered them. As they fluttered down again, he thought for an instant he heard the horse whinnying somewhere close at hand, but when he listened for the sound to come again, there was nothing, not even a breeze moving through the scrub. He laughed. It was only a question of time now and not much at that. The delirium had him in its grip.

They came down from the nighttime sky. It was ridiculous, absurd. The Ambusher had reached deep into his bag of tricks to transport these people across the empty miles in such a quick wink of his shifty eye. It almost seemed as if he had flown pieces of the town itself into the starlit desert. He couldn't see the Ambusher yet, but he could hear his laugh behind each of the ghostly faces which advanced on him, floating through the fog which had suddenly settled everywhere. Ghostly? No. They were real enough, those faces. He would have to take hold of himself and not be fooled. Some of them would have to be killed over and over, many times, but he must play the game. While he was dropping them to the death they all deserved, he must always be ready for the laughing Ambusher to show *his* face.

There was the merchant now, coming at him with more daring than he would have dreamed the man possessed, a daring forced on him by the Ambusher, without a doubt. The quiet Mexican was by his side. He fired and their faces disappeared, dissolving into the night like images in a pool when a stone is tossed into it and its mirror surface fractured. In their places came the editor and the fat fraudulent little mayor, and they went, too, blown away in the smoke and fire just as speedily. On the right, trying to take him on the flank, was the deputy, with the judge and the lightning-tongued lawyer at his side. They pretended they were only talking, but they didn't fool him for a second. They had to die—and he fired rapidly and they puffed away in wispy whirling fragments. The laughter didn't stop, and he knew how right he was about the Ambusher.

And of course they all came again, and he was ready for them. What kind of a fool did the Ambusher take him for? There they were—merchant and editor and Mexican—lawyer, judge, and mayor, and then deputy, Mexican, judge, lawyer, editor, merchant—as fast as he could send them scattering, they came again, their faces forming and reforming like the same images in the same pool when the last ripple dies against the sides. The Peacemaker had long since been emptied, and now it was the rifle shattering the night.

And all the while he fired, he heard the wild, crazy, mocking laughter. At first it was only irritating, but soon it became something else. He looked for the Ambusher everywhere, but his was the one face which wouldn't show. The laughter began to pierce his eardrums like a white-hot glowing needle—and for the first time in his life he knew the real touch of fear. It wasn't any fear of death. It was fear of that laughter, fear of the high sickening insanity of it.

Death would be easy when the laughter stopped, if it ever did.

He awoke clear-headed when the mounted warriors were still half a mile away from him. As they walked their horses warily toward his camp, he checked his weapons, knowing that he would find them empty, and that all his spare ammunition would be gone as well when he looked for it. He was dimly aware that he had done a powerful amount of shooting in the night, but when or at what wouldn't come to him. Now he would have to face the approaching Apaches with just his knife, next to worthless with him stretched out on his back like this. His leg, which had stopped hurting when the fever had filled his brain with red fog the night before, was torturing him again, but it wasn't going to trouble him for very long. These warriors looked intent on business. They would finish him quickly and be on their way. He saw one of them pointing at the dead buzzards lying in the sand like heaps of black oily rags.

Then he recognized the warrior in the center of the band of horsemen, plainly the leader of this party. This was the Mimbreño he remembered from so many other places, the

one he had sought through the smoky heat of battle at Apache
Pass and again at the fight in the Oscuras.

This is crude, Ambusher, he thought. *I win. I am not
surprised*.

Then he began to laugh. Once he began, he found he
couldn't control the laugh at all. It spilled a fountain of
frenzied wildness from his throat. It was a laugh he had heard
not long ago, but he couldn't remember where.

*"This is a happier and more comely time
Than when these fellows ran about the streets,
Crying confusion."*

II

"Nobody's heard a word for the better part of a month,"
Sam said, "not even Virgie and Alicia. He's just disappeared
like he was wiped right off the face of the earth."

"But, Sam," Jim said, "he must have let slip something
about where he was going—to somebody."

"Not so far as anybody at the X-Bar-7 knows. There's
nothing, not a clue—unless he told Mike Calico. That's the
same thing as nothing. You could tear Mike in two before
he'd let anything out Corey wanted secret."

Black Springs was quiet, had been quiet for almost three
uneventful weeks. Jim, who had once longed for just such a
time of peace, found he was uncommonly restless, even
jumpy. Nothing quite suited him. He was nervous, but without the heightened sense of living such nervousness should
bring. He had fallen victim to a strange mix of lethargy and
apprehension, and nothing altered it, not even the ceremony
presided over by Wilson Blaine when the last telegraph pole
in the long line marching down from the north was planted
next to the office shack hurriedly thrown up for the survey
crew. The fact that wire wouldn't be strung for a while,
possibly not until winter had come and gone, hadn't deterred
Wilson. He vowed importantly that he would be delighted to
hold another, bigger celebration on the "auspicious day Black
Springs is linked with that great world out there." The editor
knew that he, of all people, should be at least as excited at
the prospect as the mayor, but he couldn't feel so much as a

tingle. The tall stark poles, looked at singly, seemed more gallows trees than sentinels of communication.

If there was no word of the whereabouts of Corey Lane, there was little more of Victorio. As Russell had speculated, the Apache had made some small raids—like the Three Rivers one—on his way out of the Mescalero agency, but nothing serious or bloody yet. The signs of the Mimbreño passage pointed to a clear flight from the Ojos Negros Basin far across the river and into Black Range country (or south to Mexico, Jim hoped), and it seemed almost certain any fear in Chupadera County would be only that of lingering recollection. There had been some muttering at first to the effect that "the Army ought to finish up that nonsense in the Dakotas and get back down here before old Victorio gets his dander up," but by now nearly everyone in the town seemed to have forgotten there ever had been an Apache war.

Indeed, with both the Indian and the tall man gone from the basin (just an assumption where Corey was concerned; no one *knew*) it did seem a real peace had come at last, but it was a perplexing peace. It brought no satisfaction, and little of the relief it should have. The town seemed to Jim as it might have in the aftermath of a fire, or in the wake of a deadly silent epidemic. The unfailing Ojos Negros sun lit a scene of pathetic listlessness. That it was the pathos of guilt, not tragedy—despite the shocking death of Jacky Jameson— was obvious. Tragedy, oddly enough, would have been easier to bear.

Harry Timmons' issuing of the murder warrant for Corey Lane caused no more than half a dozen comments in the plaza or the barroom of the Sacramento. The noncommittal shrugs which greeted the news seemed to ask the question in most Black Springs minds: Who was going to serve it? Joe Harris tried to deputize some of the men in town, but sighed with relief when he found no takers. If there was to be any attempt to apprehend the fugitive, it would clearly have to wait for instructions to come down from Santa Fe. That the Territorial authorities expected their hands would soon be too full of things like the Mimbreño exodus (quiet as things seemed) to be chasing one lone killer was all too plain. Eloy Montoya was called back to the capital for a special session of the Legislature, and although Jim was sure he would send word, nothing came. Black Springs, which he'd been grateful was such a backwater, suddenly seemed even more out of touch with the world and reality. Business seemed to be conducted in a vacuum of casual indifference. If the *campesinos* of the Rio Concho still made their Saturday trips to market, they didn't linger, and the ranchers, still busy with the fall cattle drives, didn't show up at all. Except for the ribbon-cutting at the installation of the last of the telegraph poles, Mayor Blaine didn't put foot outside his office. Doubtless the man was bitter because Eloy didn't feel obliged to honor whatever pledges Granby had given him for his part in Montoya's election victory, but of course he didn't dare breathe a word of his disappointment, as Sam had said.

Jim's heart was heavy when he considered how Sam Riordan had aged since the horrifying killing in the plaza. He could seldom be tempted into a game of chess, and when he could, his erratic play was an embarrassing revelation that his mind was ten days' ride away. The old rancher didn't seem to realize this. He still spent his days in the Sacramento barroom, but his assaults on the bottle seemed made more from habit than desire; the zestful glee with which he had tippled his weekends away seemed to have departed when the tall man had ridden out of the plaza that awful day. But the clearest indication that something damaging had happened inside Sam's tough old hide came when he and Jim saw Granby Stafford for the first time since Corey's hearing.

"I wouldn't be Granby Stafford for nothing in this world or the next," Sam had said. McPherson had braced himself for some dire prophecy about what Corey would do to the merchant when he returned. "Poor bastard," Sam went on, "I feel sorry for him, I genuinely do. What he did was plenty wrong, but nobody ought to suffer the way he's suffering." The Sam Riordan of Jim's first acquaintance would still have been spitting flame.

What he'd said about Granby was surely true enough. All the petulant irascibility which had marked the merchant in the time the editor had known him seemed to have sloughed away. He walked the streets of Black Springs very rarely, and when he did, his chin was sunk on his chest and he ignored in silence even the most cheerful nod. Strangely—perhaps Sam's failure to predict danger for the merchant at Corey's hands was based on sound intuition—fear had nothing to do with Granby's manner. What ate at him was something far more soul-corroding than fear could ever be. Even if Stafford's cruel predicament hadn't been alluded to by Sam, Jim would have seen it for himself the day that Mary Ellen Talley, her two youngsters in tow, bumped into the merchant while coming out of the dry-goods store. When Stafford saw who had run into him, his face first turned beet-red, then drained into white shock. He put his hand to his chest in such a dramatic gesture of heart-attack it seemed almost comic. His ravaged face, though, wasn't funny, nor was the way he set off at a wobbly trot which threatened to leave him staggering before many steps.

Nothing in Mary Ellen's sweet sad smile and certainly nothing in her bright eyes—yes, bright, no matter that they must have been washed by tears a thousand times since Jacky's death—revealed that she knew she had become the conscience of Granby Stafford and, by extension, of Black Springs. Her double loss weighed on everyone. Jim couldn't look at her without feeling sharp pain.

He couldn't look at her without feeling and thinking other things as well.

When he had watched Virgie disappear across the plaza the night of the election rally, he had had the absurd notion that he was seeing her for the last time, but as early as the next morning he had shrugged such nonsense off. Corey's defeat surely wouldn't keep her and Alicia out of town, and even if he missed her time and again, the moment was sure to come when she would reappear. Now, though, with so many weeks gone by and still no sight of her or word that she had been in Black Springs, he began to wonder if his first despondent notion had been right.

It took very little effort to persuade himself that he had some kind of duty to see how the Lane women were in Corey's alarming absence.

The year was dancing sedately into the first day of bright blue October as Jim rode into the compound of the X-Bar-7.

Down in the corral Mike Calico was currying a frisky paint pony. The pony's lead was wrapped around the stump left hand of the Zuni, wound tightly like the tape on a boxer's ungloved fist, while the hand holding the brush stroked across the animal's flank in busy sweeps. The wrangler seemed intent on his work, but as McPherson neared the hitchrail at the ranch-house door Calico stopped and looked straight at him. There was no sign of recognition from the little man, no nod, no wave. He just looked at Jim out of that dark face, and if the editor couldn't see the eyes at that distance—fifty yards or more—he knew there was no more life in them than he would find in a slab of *malpais* rock. Sam was right. Nothing could be pried out of Corey's man.

By the time Jim dismounted, tied off the reins, and dusted himelf with his hat, the Zuni and the pony had disappeared.

María answered the call of the knocker. The lines of strain on her face shocked him. What would show on Virgie's face?

She was on the couch in the sitting room, reading to her son.

"Why, Jim! It's so good to see you." Her face was beautiful, as always, and bright, but the darkness *had* been there. "I was sure you must have forgotten us by now—or tried to."

"Lord, no, Virgie! No chance of that. Ever!" He felt dizzy, light-headed, when he heard the breathy passion with which he had invested the last word, and he reddened at the thought that the boy had heard it, too. "Hello, young man," he said. How he had managed the greeting without a stammer seemed a small miracle.

"Howdy, Mr. McPherson," Corey Jr. said. What a grave child this boy was. "Will you excuse me, please, sir? I got to practice on this some before Grandma gets back next week."

Alicia not here? It jolted him. For all the times he had wished that shrewd, too perceptive, woman somewhere else, now that it had happened it distressed him. Where was she? When the youngster disappeared into the hallway, he asked.

"In Santa Fe, Jim," Virgie said. "She has an appointment with Governor Wallace. There's a good chance he'll pardon Corey. Eloy Montoya has already talked with him about it."

He was about to tell her, as gently as he could, how little hope there could be for a pardon for a crime like Corey's, but she spoke again. "You know," she said, "Lew Wallace has been *trying* to pardon Billy Bonney ever since the war in Lincoln County started. If that young killer can be forgiven, why not a man who's done as much for the Territory as Corey has? Besides . . ." She stopped, and it seemed to Jim she blushed an apology before going on. "Besides, it's not as though the Lanes were lacking in influence in Santa Fe. Anyway, Eloy says that it's as good as done. When Corey comes back to face the law, of course." Jim thought it odd that Virgie had said *the* Lanes. Why not *we?*

"And Eloy is lending Alicia his support?" Jim asked.

"Yes. Chupadera County is lucky to have such a man in Santa Fe. Certainly he holds no brief for Corey, but he apparently bears him no ill will, either. And he says the only way he can be sure of peace with the ranchers in his district is for the whole unfortunate thing to be forgotten."

Yes, Eloy, though not afraid of Will-Ed and the others for himself, would know that he had to come to terms with them. It made sense. The new senator would soon have many problems to face as big as the one presented by Corey Lane. As for the governor, doubtless he viewed the whole affair as just another one of the Territory's growing pains. He was, after all, an eminently practical politician.

But if Corey was to be the beneficiary of Lew Wallace's practicality, there was still one mammoth consideration.

"Have you heard from Corey, Virgie?"

"Not a word."

"Did he say where he was going? Or when he would come back again?"

"Nothing."

He looked at her. There was pain in her face, all right, but the strangest kind of pain he had ever seen. She was looking at him, too, the huge eyes steady and clear. If they had known the salt of tears in the weeks since Corey rode away, not a trace was left. There was strength and courage there.

"I don't think he knew, Jim," she said. "When he left here he was obsessed, driven, but I'm as certain as I can be that he didn't know what was in his mind himself." She fell silent, looking down at the slim hands folded in her lap. Then she suddenly looked up at him, her face again all smiles and brightness. "You'll stay for supper, won't you, Jim? It *has* been lonely here."

Of course he would. He would stay despite the fact that he felt danger to his heart more keenly than at any time since he had first met her. My God, that seemed so long ago.

Corey Jr. ate with them, his blond head bent earnestly over his plate halfway down the long polished table which separated the two adults. Jim, fearing to look at the mother, studied the boy. Even if he hadn't belonged to *her*, Jim was certain he would have judged him to be a remarkable lad. His table manners were good, proper without being fussy or prim. He looked at the speaker whenever he was spoken to, and his soft politeness seemed natural. But there was a suggestion of toughness under the soft exterior. Jim could see a day when people might underestimate the strength of this boy as they might that of the mother he drew it from. Yes, he *was* a fine boy. It would, or should, be a source of joy to be a father to such a child.

"Ma," Corey Jr. said when they had finished the *natillas* María brought them for dessert, "if I can be excused from table, please, I'll go down to the bunkhouse and see how Ernesto is."

Virgie nodded. The boy slid from his seat with a smile at the editor and was gone.

"Somebody sick?" Jim said. He really didn't care, but it seemed a way to begin the conversation again without too much awkwardness. To his surprise, Virgie didn't answer. Her face, which had been warmly placid in the candlelight all through the meal, seemed troubled, and she wasn't looking at him. Suddenly, without knowing why, Jim was terrified for her. "Virgie!" he said, "something's wrong. What is it?"

She looked at him then. "Oh, Jim! I wasn't going to bother anybody with it—you least of all. But we had some trouble here the other night. It was right after Alicia left for Santa Fe."

"Trouble?"

"Night riders. Actually, they've come twice before since Corey left, but the first two times they just rode the mesa and fired off their guns. The other night, though, they came right into the compound. Mike and the other hands drove them off, but Ernesto Gallegos took a bullet in his forearm. It shattered the bone."

"Virgie! I don't like that. Look, don't you think you'd better move to town when little Corey goes back to school on Monday?"

She shook her head. "No. You know I won't leave the X-Bar-7 until he comes back."

He hadn't known he could feel the anger he felt then, and he wasn't sure whether it was directed more at the cowards who had come in the dark of night or the man whose leaving had exposed her to this peril. And there was so little he could do. He didn't even have the right to give advice.

He followed her to the sitting room as María cleared the table. The last time he had made this little trip he had stumbled, almost fallen. Now he felt even more unsteady, and the memory of her arm about his waist that other time only increased the tremors in his legs.

A fire had been laid, and she knelt at the hearth and put a match to it. There was a strange cloud in the air too thick for idle words to penetrate. The snapping and crackling of the fire was the only sound until María called goodnight to her mistress, and again when the boy came in.

"Ernesto's coming along just fine, ma. He says to tell you *muchas gracias* and that you're a *muy bueno* lady doctor." He came to where Jim sat and shook hands very formally for one so young, and then crossed to the couch for his mother's goodnight kiss.

I should leave. It was torment sitting so close to her (and yet seven leagues away), but—departure would be worse.

She offered him brandy, silently, by holding up the decanter. He refused with thanks just as wordless.

Was it hours they sat quietly together or only minutes? Even if he counted heartbeats against the time, he knew these moments to be measureless. He could stay with her here like this forever. It was truly out of time—eternal. It was joyous, and yet it was heartache.

The fire burned low. He should build it up again so he could see her face—if he dared to look at it. Somehow he couldn't bring himself to move.

Then she did. She rose from the couch and went to the stack of logs alongside the fireplace as if she had read his thoughts. When she knelt beside it, her full skirt puffed out around her like a fragile cloud. Suddenly she looked small and helpless, and if this tiny mundane chore was the only need she would ever have for him, he knew he would have to make the most of it. He left his chair, and in two steps he would never remember making he was at her side. His hands took the log she was lifting, and he turned and placed it on the andirons. It was a well-dried piece of wood, and the flames leaped around it as if they had been waiting a long time.

When he turned from the fire, she was standing beside him still, her face upturned to his. He took her in his arms before the first thought came.

You're a fool, Jim McPherson. You've smothered whatever spark might have passed between you. She'll pull away, and all will fall to ruin.

She didn't.

Her body came against his, the whole warm graceful length of it, everything touching all up and down, and if at first he could distinguish the firm but gentle pressure of her breasts, and if he could feel her hips seeking his with an insistence which astonished him and stopped his breath, all that ceased when he found her lips. In the heat of the kiss all definition of separate parts was gone. There was no his or hers or he or she—only theirs and them.

"Oh, Jim . . . Jim!" she cried when at last they broke apart, and then again, "Jim . . . Jim . . . Jim." His name in her clear voice was like the tapping of a silver spoon on crystal.

"I love you, Virgie."

"I know."

"I have for a long, long time."

"I know that, too."

"And you?"

"Oh, yes, yes, *yes!*"

He smiled. "Well, I *didn't* know."

"I tried so hard not to let it show, Jim." Then she placed her hands in the center of his chest. "Please sit down, Jim. We've got to talk."

He nodded dumbly. There would be no surprise in what she would say to him. "Forgive me," she said, "there can't be any more for us until Corey comes back again and I tell him. You know that, don't you?" He nodded again. Yes, he knew it. There was no surprise. She couldn't have lived as long as she had in this ridiculous temple of honor and sacred pride without some of the former at least rubbing off on her. It angered him—and at the same time shamed him. He wouldn't want it any other way himself. The two of them must never live a lie together. But it did seem a touch too much at this moment, with their love so new and so freshly declared, and with his desire burning brighter than the fire. He was here and so was she, and that was all that mattered.

"I love you, Virgie, but I *want* you, too. I want you *now*."

"Oh, God, Jim. And I want *you*. I'm not at all shy about that part of it, believe me. But as long as Corey doesn't know, I could never be free with you that way."

He fought against the heat rising in him. Whether it was a heat of anger and frustration or of desire made little difference; for her sake it must be checked. There could be no comfortable way for him to be noble about this, but he would try. She had much more to consider than he did. She, not he, would have to live with the effect of this discovery on little Corey, and on Alicia. Well, he would have to live with that, too, a little anyway. Corey himself suddenly didn't matter. Or *did* he? Was all the doubtful hero-worship of the past completely vanished? And if everything now beginning between Virgie Lane and Jim McPherson did work out, would it be possible for them to work it out here in the Ojos Negros? How important was this place to her? and to him? Well, that last didn't matter. Their future would have to be marked out along lines which were best for *her*. This wasn't selflessness, it was the only way to happiness for *him*.

"We'll come at what we've found tonight by any road you want to travel, Virgie," he said.

"Thank you, Jim. I knew I wouldn't have to expect less from you. I *do* love you. Keep that with you, no matter what . . ."

He felt relieved and content, but something else worried him.

For all his strong love of her, he knew so little about her. From the first time he had seen her in the dry-goods store and had learned that she was the wife of Corey Lane, he had fought against learning too much about her. The one paramount question was: Why Corey? At last he could ask it—now.

"Corey?" she said. "He came into my life suddenly and gradually, Jim. I know that sounds odd, but it's true."

She told him she had come to the X-Bar-7 as a girl of eight, sent out to live with her second cousin Alicia Lane when her parents had died in the flames which had destroyed their Kansas City home. "Corey was fifteen then, and I idolized him, although I didn't see a great deal of him that first year. I saw him even less after that, but when he came back from the wars, he slipped inside the picture Alicia had made of him so easily that it seemed right and natural.

"Alicia was my teacher—in everything. Oh, she was tough, but underneath that rawhide she was the soul of kindness, in every way. I felt a lot of love for her, and gratitude, of course. Still do. I realize now that I absorbed *her* love for Corey as my own. I honestly don't think either of us knew it, but all the years that I was growing up Alicia was packaging me for Corey. It never occurred to me to question what was happening. And it never occurred to me to object when I turned eighteen and Alicia tied me up in ribbon and gave me to him. It seemed the way things were meant to be.

"I wish I could tell you I've been unhappy with him, but I haven't, Jim. Not even after I came to know how much *you* would mean to me. There was little Corey, and an Alicia the people in Black Springs don't know. And Corey has always been wonderful to me—in his way." She laughed. There was more wonder in the laugh than bitterness. "Once in a while, of course, I wondered. There had to be something more than the things I felt for him. I always took myself to task when I thought that way, though. Other women would have thought me out of my mind. Corey was handsome, rich, brave—and faithful. Jim, I honestly don't believe there ever was another woman, not even *before* me." She laughed again. "God knows there was little enough of me. Oh, I don't mean there was anything wrong with him that way. He just couldn't give himself completely. Somehow I think that great pride got in the way. Anyway, for a long time the easiest thing was to blame myself. In a way, I always will." She looked at him with something beseeching in her eyes. "It won't be long for you and me after he gets back. I promise."

She saw him out the door. He turned to her and smiled. "Virgie," he said, "I don't think we'd be putting ourselves in the way of too much temptation now if—"

She buried herself in him.

In the saddle he tipped his hat to her and turned the horse toward the gate. He looked back over his shoulder as he rode. She waved and closed the door. Everything was dark except for a shaft of light coming from the high window next to it.

At the gate he saw another glint of light, only a tiny flicker this time, and as he rode through he saw what caused it. It was a reflection from the barrel of the rifle cradled in

the arms of Mike Calico, who must have seen the kiss. He
must, too, have intended that Jim see *him*. If the Zuni hadn't
wanted to be seen, he wouldn't have been but one more
shadow in the shadows. As Jim rode into the darkness beyond
the gate, he knew he should be alarmed at Calico's certain
discovery, but he wasn't. The intoxication he felt was too
great to permit the intrusion of any other feeling.

An express rider coming through from the Mescalero to
Santa Fe dropped off a letter from Agent Russell.

Dear Jim—

*You asked me to keep you posted about our
friend Victorio.*

*He seems to be breaking loose. After lying
quiet for almost a month he attacked Ojo Caliente
where Ambrose Hooker and his E Company of the
9th are bivouacked. He ran off more than 60 horses
and mules and killed the entire guard—8 men.*

*Then, near as I can figure the date from the
sketchy report I got it must have been on or about
20 September, Major Morrow at Fort Bayard signaled there was another run-in south of Hillsboro,
at the ranch of one McEvert or McEvers, something
like that. Ten soldiers killed and a lot of wounded.*

*Hooker says Victorio had 40 warriors with him
at the warm springs fight, which squares with my
records. There were 43 fighting age Mimbreños
and Mescaleros in the 154 with him when he left the
agency in August. What troubles me is Morrow's
account. Says they fought for five hours against
"more than 100 hostiles." Morrow's not given to
exaggeration, so all I can figure is Victorio had
recruited allies from the disaffected Chiricahuas
who left San Carlos over the past year. I'll confess I
don't much like the look of things, particularly now
with most of the Regulars out of the Territory.*

*One more thing, and I wouldn't even mention
it, except that Payson Morrow isn't the kind of
officer who dreams things up: he swears there was
a white man in the attacking force of Apaches, a big*

fellow. *This "white man" rode right next to Victorio. Looked like he was helping direct the action.*

Anyway, I guess what we ought to do right now is pray for a quick, hard winter. That might slow Victorio down until the Army can regroup next spring.

Regards—
S. E. Russell

Jim stared at the letter for half an hour. When he finally put it down, he realized the time he had spent with Russell's message were the first waking moments in three days—since he had been at the X-Bar-7, actually—that Virgie Lane had left his mind.

September 20! That was nearly a month ago. He thought bitterly of the gaunt naked telegraph poles whose line ended at the shack across the alley in back of the east side of the plaza. The isolation of Chupadera County, which had seemed such a blessing when he first came here, now brought icy fear. The whole Territory could be in flames, for all the Ojos Negros knew. There was no Harry Jackson to send messages across the river from Fort Craig—and no Corey Lane to act on them if there were.

Well, the least he could do was to get Russell's letter to Joe Harris and Mayor Blaine—fast. He wondered if it would do any earthly good. He was through his office door, thinking of ways to convince the mayor and the acting sheriff that they had better call in Will-Ed and the ranchers (if they were back from their cattle drives), when he saw Sam Riordan alighting at the hitchrail of the Sacramento. He hailed the old rancher and beckoned for him to come across the plaza. The barroom was no place to reveal this kind of news.

He watched Sam's face as he read the letter. His lips moved as he read, and Jim knew where he was in Russell's good legible script at every instant, but when he reached "he swears there was a white man in the attacking force of Apaches, a big fellow," the lips stopped making words, lost all their tough firmness, and began to tremble. If Sam Riordan had aged after the killing of Jacky Jameson, he now seemed close to death. When he finished reading, he looked at Jim, and the eyes the editor had seen sparkle with humor even when red from whiskey were as lifeless as if they had been empty sockets.

"Jim . . ." he began. He didn't talk. He babbled, stuttering in and out of coherence, his leathery face sagging to wet caliche, and graying to the color of it, too. Jim McPherson watched a man begin the final slide into senility, and his love for that man was almost overpowering. How many people would Corey bring to grief before he left this world? Jim wondered as he began to hate.

"No, Jim . . ." Sam was trying to talk again, but the words only came out as bleats and whimpers. "No, Jim . . . not Corey . . . Corey Lane a *renegade?* No, Jim . . . not Corey . . . never . . ." And then one last drawn-out hollow groan, "No-o-o-o . . ."

"Your soldiers use him as the grace 'fore meat,
Their talk at table, and their thanks at end. . . ."

III

Victorio's eyes were fixed so hard on the tall white man eating with the warriors who had come in yesterday from San Carlos that the woman had to push his food at him three times before he took it.

These new White Mountain recruits were good fighting men—young, strong, well tested in many raids if not in larger battles—but who would they fight for, the white chief or Victorio? It no longer made a difference, but there had been many times in recent days when he had thought how much wiser it would have been if he had let his men kill the yellow-hair when they found him in the desert. He had been close enough to death then. But no, the *gáh'n* had told him to let the man live. There had been no difficulty convincing his Mimbreños that Lane was crazy and under the special protection of the spirits who watch over the feeble-minded and the raving. And, truly, there were times when the man *had* seemed insane, even to Victorio, who was seldom fooled about these things.

The sun had risen twenty times since they had found him, hot with fever and wild-eyed, out of water and ammunition, lying in that bad camp with the dead buzzards and the picked-clean carcass of the lion, the stench of death heavy as that from a day-old battleground. Twenty times the sun had set on the same unanswered question: Why was this enemy of the people still alive and in Victorio's *ranchería?* Was it important that Victorio (if he didn't count the woman) was the only one who asked this now?

243

What had happened to the vow he had made after the defeat in the Oscuras? He had sworn then that he would take this white chief any way he could, by trickery and lies, *without honor*, even (hadn't he promised it?) were the man a guest in a Mimbreño wicki-up. Luck had smiled on him. He had made the oath in silence. The white man was lucky, too, that the woman hadn't been with Victorio when he made it. She would have known of the vow in that way of hers—and he would have had to kill this white man.

But his first sight of the giant, lying in the rocks of that death camp with the stink of his festering leg fouling the air, had convinced Victorio that for some strange reason he must let his enemy live a good while longer.

It hadn't been easy to bring him here to the *ranchería*. There had been no sound horse to throw him across, and Victorio had had to send a warrior to the hills to cut poles for the pony-drag he'd hitched behind his own mount.

When they had made their entrance into the encampment of the people, the woman had looked at Victorio and he had nodded. She had gone to work at once, coating the swollen leg with her secret ointments, wrapping the huge naked body—so surprisingly pale, for all its consuming heat—in the wet healing skins. That night she had made the sick man drink the brewed herbs she had forced on Victorio so many times when he had wounds, and Victorio had smiled a little, remembering how bitter her concoctions tasted. He had smiled, too, to see that Lane showed no more inclination to struggle against her ministrations than he ever had.

For three days and as many nights the tall man had drifted into deathlike sleep, only to burst raging from it when least expected. Victorio, lying next to him through the silences and storms of the long nights, had slept even less than the white man. The woman had built the wicki-up for only two. It was crowded, and finally Victorio had offered to take shelter with the unmarried boys, but she had made him stay. She was wise, as always. Little by little, the rages of the wounded man had made sense. He learned things.

Now Victorio would never have to ask this man what had brought him alone to the far desert to flirt and dance with death. Of course, the people in the town at the foot of Cuchillo Peak might have a different tale to tell, but if the facts resembled the wild rantings in the fetid air of the wicki-up, then the whites were even further beyond Victorio's understanding than he had thought they were. To turn a great warrior out the way this man's people had was something beyond his or any other Apache's capacity for reasoning, but it did tell him why Lane had some right to share his meat and smoke—for a while, a little while.

The man's powers of recovery were magical. He had begun to walk after only a week, barely limping on the leg which had been so swollen the woman had had to cut and peel away what was left of his pants. Once he was permanently on his feet, she'd herded him into a sweat lodge and kept him there from sunrise until long past dark. When he'd emerged, even the scar on his leg and the much older ones on the powerful white body hadn't prevented him from looking whole and completely fit again.

It was then, with Lane now dressed in Mimbreño clothing reworked by the woman to fit his towering frame, that Victorio and Lane had had their first talk. He'd made a strange Apache in the kirtle and thong-tied leggings, his chest draped with a buckskin vest of Victorio's which he couldn't fasten, cornsilk hair tied back from the white face with a scarf as sky-blue as his eyes. The strong chin was covered with yellow stubble, promising a heavy beard in another week if it wasn't scraped away. Somewhere in the contraband from one of last week's raids there was a razor. If asked, Victorio would tell him of it; he would *offer* nothing.

First he had had to find out if the man was going to stay. It had jolted him when he'd thought this. It was his, Victorio's, place to decide whether the white man would stay or not, not Lane's. It had troubled the Indian when he'd realized that he *would* let the white man choose.

Well, if he was indeed intent on remaining in the Mimbreño *ranchería*, there were things to be decided immediately. He could have his horse back, of course, the saddleless chestnut they had found wandering thirst-crazed in the desert, and whose tracks they had followed back to where the white chief lay near death. Yes, he could have his horse again, even though Victorio coveted the splendid animal himself now that rest and grain and water had restored it to soundness. And he could have his weapons, too: the Winchester and the finely balanced sidearm with the handle made of bone.

If he chose to stay, he would have to be provided with a woman. It mattered little whether he wanted one or not, he would have to have one.

"No, *viejo*—no woman. I have no need," Lane had said.

Victorio was not surprised, but he said, "There are women without warriors in my camp. Until you take one of them, it makes for trouble. You *will* take one." It was strange. Clearly, the decision that Lane would stay had already been made —without either of them bringing it into words.

When Lane was paired with Nah-kee-Ah, the woman whose man was one of those the white chief had slain from behind his fortress rock at the battle in the spring, he didn't argue. What he would do with the woman in the night, if anything, was up to him. Victorio left him strictly alone for the next two days, only watching from a distance as Nah-kee-Ah built the new wicki-up and cooked the white man's food. Then he went to him again.

"And now . . . ?" he said.

"Now," Lane said, "I wish to ride with you.

Victorio looked at him and thought hard, very hard. It wasn't a matter of whether this man with the yellow hair could be trusted. It was just that with those few words the heat of the man, which had seemed to disappear when the fever left him during his recovery, had come back with even more intensity, reaching a height Victorio could scarcely credit even while looking straight at it and feeling it on his face. Such a heat, no matter how well contained or carefully directed, could char to a crisp friend and foe alike.

"You would ride against your own people?" Victorio asked.

"I have no people."

Nothing more was said then, and Victorio left him alone for three more days. The Apache chief mounted up all the warriors and made a raid on the bluecoats at Ojo Caliente, leaving Lane as the only man in the *rancheria* with the women and children. Throughout the fight the thought of the man he had left sitting in the dust in front of his wicki-up made the chief even more warlike and daring than usual. He pressed his attack on the guard long after the Indians had secured all the horses and mules they could possibly drive back into the mountains, killing every soldier, almost as many as the fingers on both hands. It was rash, and he knew it. The heat of the white chief Lane must be contagious.

When they returned to camp the next afternoon, driving the spoils of their victory in a thundering stampede through the shouting joyous *ranchería*, Lane was sitting in front of his hut exactly as they had left him. He didn't look up, didn't seem to hear the boasting of the warriors, didn't look at Victorio. It was as if the triumph was of no consequence.

He is keener than the hawk, Victorio thought, *and wiser than the bear. He waits.*

He thought this again that night when Loco and Nana asked to share his fire for a while.

"Perhaps Victorio will let him ride with us," Nana said.

"He knows the ways of the white men in a fight," Loco said.

"Perhaps Victorio will take him on a *little* raid," Nana said, "one where no Mimbreño dies if he betrays us."

"I will consider it," Victorio said.

He hardly slept that night, thrashing about in the wicki-up until the woman asked him sourly if he wanted her to build a larger dwelling in the morning. After the day's first meal he went to Lane again.

"We have food now, much food, and more horses and mules than we can use. It will be a moon before we raid again. When we do, you can ride with us. *Ride,* not fight." The white man nodded. There was no other talk.

The next day the first group of Southern Chiricahuas came straggling into camp. There were more, many more, every day for the following five. Soon there was no longer food to fill the stomachs of the entire *ranchería*, and while the raid on Ojo Caliente had provided many horses, there were no longer enough for the luxury of a large reserve.

With dark misgivings, remembering his promise to the white man, Victorio gave orders for another foray. It couldn't be the "little" raid Nana had advised. Hunger would soon insist on entry to his camp. From the past he knew how swiftly its attack could come.

"We raid tomorrow," he told Lane. "You will ride."

They rode down the spine of the black mountains named for the Mimbres people. Lane rode somewhere in the back of the Apache column, and Victorio didn't see him—although he felt his pressure—all that day. The white man ate his

handful of cracked corn by himself when they camped that
night, and didn't join the council at Victorio's small fire.

Scouts had brought reports of the fat herds on an *estancia*
a day's ride south of the digging-place the whites called
Hillsboro. The herds were guarded by horse soldiers, the
"*black* white men" who were said to be such good fighters.
Nana had met such men in battle once, and he said that yes,
this was so, they were brave and hard. Loco didn't care. He
only worried that they might have moved since the scouts
had seen them. A warrior with eyes so keen they could see a
mouse in the talons of a hawk farther away than an arrow shot
from the strongest bow would come to earth was sent to
climb the last ridge separating them from the broad grazinglands leading to the great tawny river. When he returned, he
told of five watchfires in the valley, fires spaced twenty paces
or more apart. There would be many bluecoats, maybe more
than all of Victorio's Mimbreños, Mescaleros, and Chiricahuas
put together. Tight bellies would have to make every warrior
count for more than one.

In the morning, before first light, Victorio eased them
down the eastern slope, following a stream on whose banks
the ponderosa grew more thickly than on the ridges. He
didn't hurry them, not even when they left this cover and
reached the high tableland which overlooked the enemy tents
and the cattle and horses under guard. When they had rested
a little, while the sun broke clear of the mountains rimming
the eastern world, and while the food cooking on the soldiers'
breakfast fires drifted its smells up the slopes to them, he
looked for Lane.

He wasn't far away. It came to Victorio then that the
man on the chestnut horse had been moving up to the front
of the column little by little, but steadily, the closer they
came to what would be the battleground. He motioned the
white man to fall his horse in beside him, but he didn't talk to
him.

They were ready now. He looked up and down the lines
of warriors to make sure Loco and Nana were in their assigned places on the flanks. He raised the rifle in his right
hand directly above his head, and the warriors slid from their
ponies, handing the leads to the boys waiting in the ranks
behind them. After another look at Lane, and a glance down
the long arroyo-split slope to the soldiers' camp, Victorio let

the hand with the rifle fall, and his men slipped as silently as mountain cats into the gullies and brushy-banked creekbeds in front of them.

"You're sending them *all?*" Lane said. "You keep nothing in reserve?"

"What Mimbreño would be held back while others fight?"

Lane was silent for a moment. He studied the separate groups of men crawling through the defilades in front of them. "May I ask what your battle plan is, Victorio?" he asked at last.

The Apache nodded. "It is a simple plan. We bring the soldiers under fire before we clear the last of the broken land. After they come out to meet us and we push them back, the young men with the horses ride hard for the herds. The warriors in the fight slide toward them as they fight, and when the animals are ready to be driven, the fighting men join the herdsmen and the ponyholders and we are gone."

"You leave no rear guard?"

"We ride together, always."

The first shocking rifle shot echoed up the slope to where the Indian and the big white man sat their horses.

In no time at all the soldiers' camp was alive with motion. A heavy fusillade roared from the Apaches' almost unseen ranks, and very quickly the replies began to come. *Yes*, Victorio thought, *these black white men are splendid warriors. They do not surprise too easily.* The first notes of a trumpet call rose above the noise of the firing, but it died suddenly before the call was finished. One attacker's bullet had found its mark.

Victorio's heart should have leaped at this, but it didn't. Somehow the mighty surge he had always felt in his chest at the instant battle was joined hadn't come this time. He knew the reason and he suddenly despised himself. Why should he be bothered this way by the presence of the man beside him? His plan was good, simple, tested. Putting all his forces on an equal footing, no Mimbreño favored over any Mescalero or Chiricahua, was the only approach with any chance of success in a band of a hundred men with a dozen different clan and totem loyalties. If it wasn't the white man's way with war . . . He tried to shrug his way to indifference. It didn't work. Thoughts like these were not good medicine. Would the day go badly?

It was not disastrous, but it was hard. He had hoped to beat the enemy into retreat before the sun had climbed halfway up the eastern sky, but it was past noon before he could order the boys to make the planned run for the target herds. By that time he had lost almost twenty men, to perhaps a dozen for the bluecoats. It was a heavy price to pay to assuage a hunger which hadn't really arrived as yet. The black white men and their white officer chiefs were stubborn and resourceful. Instead of falling back in disarray, they even managed to mount a counterattack of sorts. To make things worse, the flanking party they sent around the right end of his line might have gone undetected until far too late, if it hadn't been for Lane. He had ridden a short way off in the direction from which the mounted soldiers came, as though he had expected them. He pointed out the movement of the enemy horsemen calmly, and smiled at Victorio.

Together they rode down the slope and split Loco's men away from the others to meet this threat, and the cavalrymen turned and fled, but in good order, from the fire from the Apaches' concealed positions.

At last the fight was over and they were on their way, driving a great herd of captured cows and horses ahead of them. Victorio should have felt the joy of victory then, but when he saw that the soldiers made no attempt to follow, he shrank under a wave of shame. With the courage the defenders had shown again and again through the long hot fight he knew how wrongly he had assessed their strength. He must have outnumbered *them* badly from the outset if they now made no pursuit. The wide spacing of the fires had been a clever trick. He must be getting old. Too old?

He didn't talk to Lane at all on the two-day ride back to the *ranchería*.

"You would not have made the attack the way I did," Victorio said.

Lane shrugged. He placed the revolver he had been cleaning back in its holster before he answered. "No."

It was good he was this direct, but Victorio hadn't expected him to be any other way. He would have to be every bit as forthright himself. "Perhaps I can learn from you. A man cannot remain a war leader very long when as many warriors die as in that last fight."

"I know," Lane said. *No*, Victorio thought, *he won't flatter or give me false assurances. The next time out the white man must be allowed to fight.* When he did, of course, he would have as much right as any other warrior to sit in council, as much right as any to speak and have his wisdom weighed. The danger was that it well might weigh as heavy as the bright yellow rock to the chiefs like Loco and Nana who had contested this man's power in the past. Well, he, Victorio, wouldn't try to talk away any counsel Lane might give. He would have to take the chance that it could rend the fabric of his leadership here, but he would do well to listen to Lane before the others did. At the council he could afford to show no surprise, no weakness, no anger. Sometimes, to lead, a chief must follow—without appearing to—for a time. If Lane did speak, and if Loco and Nana and enough of the others were impressed and wanted what Lane wanted, it might be necessary for Victorio to pretend the same desire—until he could bend them all quietly to his own will again. It was devious and cunning, but there was more to leading than riding recklessly into battle.

"Actually, Victorio," Lane said, "it wasn't the attack itself or how you made it that bothered me. Simple tactics generally are best. It was the idea I had, watching how well your warriors fought, that you will never get what you want for your people by means of these puny little raids. It's like going to market once a week and paying five times the price of goods. You irritate your enemy, but you really do little more than scare him into being ready for you. It's not big enough, or bloody enough, to stop the white man. It's not really war."

While Lane spoke, Victorio sensed a change in him—no, not a change, more an intensifying of the essential way he was, and had been. The heat which had reappeared as he had recovered from his wound was rising higher now. When Victorio had been but a boy, he remembered, the old ones had talked of a time now lost to every Mimbreño memory, a time when the black stone badlands beyond the river had flowed like a fiery golden stream. He'd only half-believed the tales. Now, looking at this white man, he could credit such a crazy thing.

"Not really *war?*" he said. "No, it's not war as the white man knows it. The Mimbreño makes war to feed himself and his women and children—or to get other women. We kill, but we do not crush our enemy. We need him too much for that."

Again Lane shrugged. " Have it your own way, Victorio. You command here. But if you don't fight the white man the way he fights you, there will be no more Mimbreños or Chiricahuas—or Victorios."

"What would you have us do?"

"Pick one place, a place where the whites feel safe, one big enough for them to feel the loss, but small enough so that when they lose they won't come again. Organize. Become an army. Cut this place you've chosen off completely from its sources of supply and help. Then—obliterate it! Leave nothing standing, not one stick of wood unburned—and not one soul alive, not one. Stay in the field until the job is done. Don't leave just because you can eat your belly full. Make war on this place—*totally.*"

"You know of such a place?" Victorio asked, his voice tense.

"I do—oh, yes, I do!"

For the next several days the Apache chief knew trouble in quite a different way from ever before.

No, he said to himself finally, *do not lie. It is not trouble, it is fear.*

In the hundred times he had faced death he had been sure that he had met fear in all its many forms, but this was fear with a different mask. No wonder it had taken him so long to recognize it. It was the fear which comes from hope.

He should have known it. How many times had he seen it over the years? A warrior dying of his wounds, knowing nothing could pull him back from the dark arroyo, would become suddenly stoic, calm, unafraid. Only the one who had some hope of living had the naked ugly look of fright, as if he were only carrion being ripped by crows. It was the same now with him, but in a larger sense than fear only for himself.

For years now he had known what the ultimate end must be for all the Apache people across this wide loved land. It made no difference whether they were hiding in the mountains and deserts as he was, raiding whenever the need or mood was on them, or if they were squatting in shame in an agency like Stanton or behind the stockade walls of a festering prison like San Carlos. They would all die, or if not all, then the living would surely be jealous of the dead. In the last iron grasp of such a fate, the only proper trail to follow was clearly marked: Fight. Run and hide and turn and fight, and run and hide and turn and fight again. Die. Die, but take enough of the enemy along that the rest would not forget you soon.

Now came the white chief Lane. He, too, said "fight" and there was a strong hint of "die" in his words as well, but there was another idea, too, one which no Mimbreño with half the sense of an unweaned bear cub would let invade his thinking. The one idea, the one word which Victorio had never been stupid enough to allow himself to think or say, this white man was now waving in front of him like a gaudy seductive banner. *Triumph!*

Certainly he had fought to win in all his raids and in the few larger battles like the one at the pass and the more recent one in the shadow mountains (both against this very man), but he had never fooled himself about how small the victories were or might have been. What Lane was suggesting was quite another thing. Against all reason, and counter to his own deep-seated instincts, so long trusted, the days since the talk with Lane had found him edging closer and closer to this foolish hope. That was why the fear had come, fear of failure. He could have lived very satisfactorily without this fear, and without this hope.

To be alone to think, he rode to where he could look out across the broad valley of the great river, the vast tan dish of a world which looked so empty. That the sight of such a universe of apparently uninhabited landscape was a misleading one brought a surge of bitter anger. All through the panorama which stretched in front of him the white man had fastened his greedy teeth. His *estancias* barred the way to every water hole with their cruel barbed fences. His towns blocked the mouth of almost every lovely valley. By great *Usén*, there should be enough room out there for his people and the whites; in all that limitless space they shouldn't even jostle one another. Enough! He would soon turn as crazy as the white chief Lane.

He smiled. What was it he had said to the young Man of Words when Agent Russell had brought him for the talk that day in the Mescalero? One war is like another.

*   *   *

"Victorio cannot eat?" the woman said.

He shook his head. "I will eat before we start on the trail tomorrow."

"If Victorio does not eat, he will not sleep."

"If I do not sleep, I will not dream," he said.

Tomorrow he would permit Lane to make his first fight as an Apache warrior. That it would only be another raid and not the mighty conflict the white chief lusted for mattered little. There would be an inevitable progression of events as certain as the sun rising in the sky each day or dropping under the high mountain wall behind them every night.

Lane would fight well, brilliantly. It was as sure as if it were etched in the solid rock walls of the *ranchería.* He would fight well, and these newly arrived Chiricahuas would see him do it, and so would the older ones and the Mescaleros and Mimbreños—and so would Loco and Nana. When they returned from the raid, the white man would speak in council. Then all the people would hear of the war for the glory of *Usén.*

Victorio had no use for sleep or the dreams it brought.

"We hear not of him, neither need we fear him. . . ."

IV

"Heard anything more, Jim?"

"Not a word, Sam. I'm sorry."

The old rancher had poked his head through the office door every morning for the past two weeks to ask the same pathetic question. Each time, after he had withdrawn, Mc-Pherson had gone to the door to watch him cross the plaza to the Sacramento House. He didn't really limp as he dragged his boots through the caliche dust, but he seemed to.

The first swelling rapturous tide of anger which had swept over Jim McPherson had ebbed somewhat, but he was still in the tight backwash of a deep determination that Corey Lane would be brought to account someday for what he had done to Sam, if for no other reason. Even though Jim hadn't printed the report of Major Morrow in the *News* (it was still hearsay, after all), it was evident the grim tale had made the rounds of Black Springs and found its way into every cranny of a suddenly stricken town. There was no mention of it at the Sacramento, no gossip in the stores or on the streets. Black Springs seemed to be pretending it hadn't heard, and this strange silence brought home to Jim more forcibly than any show of outrage might have the contempt and loathing in which this society would hold a proven renegade, any renegade. In this case the reaction (like Sam's) was one of pure, unadulterated, disbelieving horror. For the time being, the people in Black Springs were telling themselves that it simply wasn't true, and Jim knew what they (again like Sam, but perhaps for different reasons) *wanted* to believe they sooner or later would.

He tried to dig into his own thoughts on the matter. He felt, probably without sufficient reason, that he stood in a considerably different relationship with Victorio and the Mimbres Apaches than anyone he had yet met in the Territory save Agent Russell. Over the months his outlander's fear of the Indians had changed first to respect and then, after the trip to the agency, to a kind of mystic affection. That he had never voiced this affection to anyone except S. E. Russell— and then only elliptically—he had no trouble putting down to circumspection, not cowardice.

Even granting his newfound regard for the Apaches (at least Victorio's Apaches) he was shocked very nearly as deeply as anyone else in Black Springs by the apparent defection— yes, say it, treason—of Corey Lane. It was sobering to realize that although he had long assumed himself to be a true modern man, a product of the enlightenment the nineteenth century had brought, he was still in the grip of a powerful atavism, a tribal feeling. Try as he might, he couldn't escape the belief that it was innately evil for a man to leave his own kind, no matter how strong he thought his cause, no matter how wronged he might in fact be.

Gradually Jim found himself sinking into the same convenient vessel of delusion in which the rest of the town had submerged itself. Other, lesser men could turn renegade— not Corey Lane.

Turning his face from the truth served Jim passably— until Alicia alighted from the southbound stage on her way back to the X-Bar-7 from Santa Fe. She came straight to the office of the *News.*

"To answer your question, Mr. McPherson, yes, Lew Wallace is willing to pardon Corey."

Where was the elation? Her face was cold, absolutely glacial. Then he guessed the reason. Of course Morrow's report of the "white man" seen riding with the Apaches must have reached Santa Fe, and of course someone there must have told her. Had anyone in the capital identified the renegade as Corey? He didn't have to ask.

"The governor insists that Corey petition him in person. He thinks my son is still at the X-Bar-7. I didn't, I'll admit, disabuse His Excellency of the notion."

So they didn't know. Was it too late to put together the

broken pieces, get Corey back again before the word was out?

"Our new senator, Mr. Montoya," Alicia said without any of the bitterness he might have expected, "was the soul of kindness. I'm not sure I could have managed the audience with Governor Wallace without his help."

Jim doubted that. He almost smiled. Even supposing the woman seated across the desk from him was no longer the unyielding matriarch, there was still a skein of fiber in her tough enough to "manage" an audience with the Almighty.

"I wonder," she said next, "if Corey will ever come to realize just how his two new friends—men he didn't really know until a few short months ago—have rallied 'round him."

It stunned the editor to see her face suddenly turn soft and (this was surely one of the strangest thoughts he'd ever had) loving. He actually shook his head at the expression, but was shocked into immobility in the very next second when she reached across the desk and placed her delicate-looking hand on his and squeezed.

"Thank you for everything, Mr. McPherson. Lew Wallace showed me the letter you sent to him. All we can do now is pray that Corey comes to his senses and returns to us."

He'd almost forgotten the letter he'd written after getting home from the X-Bar-7. What would Alicia say if she knew the real reason he wished the way paved for Corey to come back again? Did it make him feel less guilty realizing that perhaps she soon *would* know? Maybe Mike Calico would tell her what he had seen from the shadows by the gate that night. No. For reasons Jim couldn't pin down, such a thing didn't seem likely. The Zuni might—face it, would—tell Corey if it were possible, but not the woman.

He scarcely heard Alicia say goodbye.

He hadn't moved when Tom Hendry came in with the mail packet which had arrived on the same stage with the departed visitor who still seemed to be sitting in the empty chair.

There was a big envelope, sealed with enough dark-red wax to mold a gross of candles, from Eloy Montoya. Jim opened it to find a sheaf of clippings from the newspaper in Santa Fe, perhaps half a dozen handmade copies of military dispatches, and a well-marked map of the Territory and an-

other of the northern districts of Chihuahua, Mexico. There
was a short note from the senator, too.

Amigo Jaime—

> *I leave it to you to say if it is wise to make a story
> in your paper from these things I send you. Maybe
> the friends of Señor Lane can make him see how*
> importante *it is for him to come home, and then
> to Santa Fe to see el Gobernador.*
> *It is not too late—yet.*

> Con mucho respeto
> E. Montoya

Well, that settled the matter of whether anybody in
Santa Fe knew. For the present at least, it seemed obvious
Eloy had told Alicia but no one else. Jim hoped that this good
man wouldn't have to pay too high a price for his forbearance
some fine day.

The other things in the envelope told an appalling story.
As he read, skipping from newspaper account to map to Army
report, he knew he would *have* to write and print the history
of the bloody depredations screaming at him from the fragments covering his desk. He was a newspaperman, and this
was news. And this time the sighting of the "white man"
would have to be set in type as well.

Victorio and his outlaw Mimbreños seemed to be everywhere at once. The indictment was complete, damning. There
was speculation that another well-known Apache chief called
Juh and a minor Southern Chiricahua terror named Geronimo might have joined him on his trail of killing and rapine.
To be fair, one writer *(God bless an honest, careful, workaday reporter,* Jim sighed) did raise some doubts about whether
all the pillaging and murder could be laid at the Mimbreños'
doorstep, since only a few scouts or soldiers had made anything like a positive identification of Victorio, but by all odds
most of the fires consuming the lands lying under the shadow
of the Black Range and all along both banks of the Rio
Grande had indeed been set by Agent Russell's runaway
wards. Russell himself was quoted in an uncharacteristic heated
denial that any great number of his Mescaleros were on the

warpath with Victorio, and the fact the charge had been made
pointed up for Jim how confused the civilian authorities in
Santa Fe and the military leaders in the scattered Army
commands still left in the Territory were. To his intense
surprise, he found a clipping from the *New York Sun*, and after
the first warm throb of affection for his old employers, he
remembered how he had thought—not so long ago—that he
had buried himself in an unnoticed inconsequential backwater, lost to Great Events and Time. Oh, Lord, how he wished
he had been right.

Whether all the outrages he pieced together were
Victorio's handiwork or not, the bulk of them, from the
evidence, most certainly were. No other chief of his stature
or with his genius and daring was out of any of the agencies at
present. Among the more knowledgeable observers, opinion
was unanimous that neither Juh nor Geronimo could hold
together the disparate marauding bands now fighting like a
determined, disciplined, and elusive army. More than one
hundred fifty soldiers and civilians had been killed in the
Territory during the three weeks covered by the clippings
Eloy had sent him, but the alarming total didn't register with
Jim half as frightfully as did the grisly details. The terse
military English of the Army reports couldn't gloss over the
bloody facts of death. A column of volunteers had caught up
with Victorio three miles south of old Fort Cummings, to
their sorrow. Six of them had died in an ambush which had
lasted no more than that many minutes before the Apaches
disappeared like phantoms. In another stroke of lightning the
Mimbreños had slaughtered all eleven teamsters in a wagon
train making its way imprudently through Magdalena Canyon. From there, marked easily by a string of lootings of
ranches and trading-posts, Victorio's trail led first to the
Mogollon Mountains and then back across the river to the
Caballos. In pursuit, his frustration too great to remain hidden in the stilted syntax of official soldiering language, was
that same Major Albert Payson Morrow (suddenly a colonel
despite no great success) who had made the first allusion to
the white man riding with the Indians. From the Caballos,
Jim could see as he checked the dispatches and news stories
against the maps, the raiders' bloodstained tracks led again to
the Mogollons and then to the Florida Mountains in a series
of bewildering zigzags which explained the bafflement of the

forces trying to corner them. He was cheered slightly when
he realized that, for all these mercurial twists and turns the
crafty terrain-wise Apache was making, he was drifting more
to the south with every move. Mexico! Maybe Jim's fervent
wish would be granted.

It was with joy almost unshadowed by any guilty shame
that he read the account of the double massacre at Tenaja de
la Candelaría below the border. Two separate commands of
Chihuahuan militia (one had come on a desperate forced
march to the support of the other) had been effectively butchered by a well-entrenched band of Apaches, and more than
thirty of them were dead. There was no question about it
being the work of Victorio this time. Certainly Jim felt sym-
pathy for those anonymous Mexicans who had died so horri-
bly (in his happiness he only briefly scanned the graphic
descriptions of the battle and the condition of the gory mutilated corpses left on the field), but there seemed a chance
Victorio might head now for the high distant safety of the
Sierra Madres. Maybe he and the tall white man with him
might disappear from the history of this plagued land.

The white man with him? That made all the difference.
Perhaps the day of reckoning Jim hoped was coming for him
and Virgie might not arrive, then. . . .

He chided himself for his selfishness. His and Virgie's
personal considerations couldn't be allowed to count when
assessed against the monumental danger facing the Territory.
He knew she would feel this way, too.

All of this suddenly became academic when he read one
of the most recent reports, dated long after the Chihuahuan
debacle. Victorio had been found again, well *north,* in the
San Mateos, tracked there and identified beyond all doubt by
the persistent if still frustrated Morrow. There went all Jim's
hopes that the Apache would retire quietly to northern Mexico, avoiding forever the showdown the editor feared.

As he went over and over all the material in Eloy's
packet, the enormity of the vengeful war Victorio was waging
began to dawn on him. While it was true that none of the
engagements—except for the defeat of the hapless Mexicans
at Tenaja de la Candelaría—could be called an out-and-out
catastrophe, the widely scattered violence threatened all of
New Mexico. Apache success was breeding more success;
Victorio's ranks were swelling with each victory. If this steady

recruitment went unchecked, he would soon be leading a
force larger than any under Indian command since the dangerous days when Cochise and Mangas Coloradas were at the
zenith of their power. Now Jim realized that the battle in the
Oscuras, cataclysmic as he might have viewed it through
his own uninitiated eyes, was a mere skirmish compared to what
might be coming.

There were, though, two consolations. So far Victorio
had confined his activity—except for the brief flurry in the
Caballo Mountains—to the other side of the Rio Grande.
Striking out of the timbered darkness of the Black Range as
he seemed intent on doing, it looked as if the Ojos Negros
Basin and Chupadera County had little to fear. The other
thing consoled Jim only because it promised time. In none of
the dispatches was there any mention of a white man riding
with the raiders. One soldier had spoken of a "giant" on a
chestnut horse, but the rider's color wasn't stipulated. "It is
not too late—yet," Eloy had written in his letter.

Alicia came to town the following week—with Virgie. At
his first sight of the young woman since his visit to the
X-Bar-7 Jim realized that neither of them had known of
Corey's probable whereabouts when they last had met. He
had an unpleasant feeling that it just might make some difference between the two of them, even if it shouldn't.

The two women, in town on Monday to shop for the
ranch and to fetch Corey Jr. from school for the Thanksgiving
holiday, spent three nights at the Sacramento House, and
although Jim saw them frequently and even took all three
evening meals with them, he began to despair of the chance
of having a single word alone with Virgie. Nobody so much as
mentioned Corey. That was just as well, but it was maddening for Jim to look at Virgie and not speak—not really speak.

Then the third day, Wednesday, she came to the office,
by herself. He had just sent Tom Hendry off with the last
deliveries of the *News,* off press a day early because of the
holiday. This issue carried the second installment of the long
feature he had put together from Eloy's material.

"Hello, Jim," she said. She stripped a pair of white
gloves from her slim hands and he raced across the office to
take them in his, forgetting his were still ink-stained from the
morning's printing. When he looked into the dark loving

shine in her eyes, he dismissed his earlier uneasy feeling.
Nothing fundamental could possibly go wrong between the
two of them—ever. All the same, he couldn't refrain from
asking.

"Have there been second thoughts, Virgie?"

"Good heavens, no, Jim! Or if there have been, they're
just stronger than the first ones. And you?"

He shook his head. "It's the way it is with you."

Then they came together. In the suddenness of it he
forgot that someone could come through the office door at
any second, and it wasn't until they broke apart for breath
that he remembered. His heart pounded. Nothing must be
allowed to happen to make trouble for her.

She took the chair at his desk, and, to his discomfort, he
couldn't rid his mind of the sight of Alicia in the same chair
the week before.

"I read the story in last week's *News*, Jim," she said. "It's
Corey, isn't it? The white man Major Morrow saw."

"I'm afraid so, Virgie." Hadn't she known before now?
Hadn't Alicia told her what she had learned from Eloy in
Santa Fe?

"If he doesn't come home soon," she said, "he will
destroy any chance he has to return at all." She didn't seem
to be talking directly to him. It was as if she was unaware that
she was speaking. The uneasy feeling had come back again.

"Will that make such a difference to us, Virgie?" he
asked. "Please don't misunderstand. I want him back, too, for
a lot of reasons. But what you and I mean to each other
should stand apart from the trouble Corey may be in." He
was astonished at how calmly he had said it.

"You're right, Jim, I *know* you're right," she said. Then
she shook her head in a way he knew was entirely involuntary. "But I couldn't live with you without his being told.
Worse, Jim," she went on, "is the fact that I wouldn't be able
to live with myself then, either. Not without you."

He raged inside. Why should telling Corey have become
such an impossible touchstone? Why should Corey have any
rights at all now that his actions had destroyed so many lives?
Jim should tell her this and free her from her straitjacket of
honor.

"I understand, Virgie," was all he said.

They talked of other things for a while—Victorio's bloody

peregrine wanderings, Alicia's half-promise of a pardon from the governor. He interrupted her in the middle of an account of how young Corey's schoolwork had suffered since his father had left.

"You're dead right, Virgie. He must be told."

Gratitude filled her eyes, and love, too.

When she left, he sat at his desk until it was dark outside. He didn't even stir when Tom Hendry came in to say goodnight. The boy must think him unhinged to be sitting there doing nothing but staring.

For the next two days he drifted from Addie's to work to meals like a man groping his way through a fog. He worked, but he wasn't conscious of it. The turkey dinner at the hotel— visually a work of art for the Sacramento's kitchen—seemed totally without taste or savor. He wasn't aware of it, but he avoided Sam. The Thanksgiving drink he had promised to buy the old rancher went unbought, and he didn't recollect catching so much as a glimpse of his friend by the time he laid a numb head on his pillow Friday night.

If he slept, he never remembered it, but he couldn't recall any particular wakefulness, either. What he did remember was that some time in the small hours of the morning the first glimmering of what he would have to do came to him—whether in sleep or not, he never would be sure.

Fear came with the decision.

He found Sam in the Sacramento bar, of course. He didn't even say hello to the forlorn old man until he had ordered a bottle from Joe and downed the biggest tumbler of whiskey anyone in Black Springs had ever seen him take. When he felt it hit his stomach, and even after he found that it did practically nothing to stop the fear still building there, he turned to Sam, amused even in his fright to see the surprise wiping the sadness from the seamed old face.

"Sam," he said, "how could we go about getting a message to Corey Lane?"

Sam was silent. "Well," he said finally, "Mike Calico could find him.

"Sam—" Jim started. He took another drink. "Sam, would you go to the X-Bar-7 with me and talk to him?"

"Why, sure, Jim." There was suddenly more life than Jim had seen in the tired eyes for a month or more.

"And, Sam—would you help me talk him into taking me along?"

His fear grew when he saw the next look on Riordan's face. The rancher took a long time before he answered.

"All right, Jim. It's a little like taking a man to his funeral before he's dead—but yes, I'll do it. If you're sure you want me to. God Almighty, Jim! Do you know what you might be walking into if you find Corey?"

PART
FIVE

"I think he'll hear me."

I

The badlands and the Jornada at last were far behind them, as was the river. With luck they would reach the dark-green pine-spiked pinnacles of the Black Range, or at least the soft bosom of the foothills this side of them, by nightfall and the next deathly quiet camp.

He stared at Mike Calico's back as it rocked back and forth in the easy somnolent rhythm which was as much an involuntary action to an old trail-rider like the Zuni as breath itself. For two days, ever since they had left the gate of the X-Bar-7 in the dark, Jim had kept his eyes fixed on that grease-stained buckskin-covered back. The editor had actually begun to wonder if Mike could speak at all and had decided that he couldn't, until he suddenly recalled seeing him deep in conversation with Corey before and after the battle in the Oscuras. Maybe it was only with Jim McPherson that he was as dumb as the black rock he resembled. Either way, he hadn't uttered a single word in the saddle, from his bedroll, or when they did their separate chores around the fire.

Well, at least by now Jim was more or less convinced that Calico didn't intend to murder him, although it had taken the better part of the two days to come to that conclusion. They must have ridden through a hundred desolate stretches of wasteland where getting rid of a body would have been child's play for a man of Mike's attainments. The Zuni could have dispatched him out of hand dozens of times, and then ridden back to the Ojos Negros with the report that hostiles had come down on the two of them. Who back there

would call Mike Calico a liar? Who, aside from Virgie and old
Sam, would care? God, but he'd felt alone and forgotten on
this ride.

At first he had felt so sure the man did mean to kill him
that he had ridden the whole first day bent over in a painful
crouch to keep his right hand near the stock of the Winchester in the saddle boot. It was nerve-racking, jerking himself
upright on the few occasions Mike turned to look at him with
those flat dead-black eyes. Then he'd given that up, dropping
back on the trail in the hope that the added distance might
just possibly bring a miss on his assailant's first try, and that
he might just possibly have a chance of surviving the duel
which would follow. Twice Mike had stopped and waited for
him, and more often only looked back at him, and while Jim
realized now that his guide was merely trying not to lose him,
he hadn't then. Strangely, in that whole harrowing first day
in the saddle he had never once thought forward to the easy
time the Zuni would have of it in camp that night if he was so
intent on lifting the editor's scalp and leaving his body for the
buzzards. When they did bed down that first night, he found
he was just too tired to worry about it any more, and he
closed his eyes with the perverse contentment that when the
end came he probably wouldn't feel a thing.

The second day he rode with the same jumpy wariness,
alternating the ploys he had tried the day before. He gave up
both dodges that afternoon when he saw Mike's rifle flash from
the saddle boot and erupt with smoke and flame so fast he
hadn't even started his own hand for his. Off in the mesquite—
when the blindness of shock left him—he saw a jack-rabbit
kick its last.

The Zuni skinned and cleaned the kill for supper. Jim
watched the deft handling of the knife as the rabbit was
stripped of its pelt and disemboweled, and he shuddered,
remembering this silent gnome's actions after the battle against
the Apaches. Mike hadn't shown a bit more emotion when he
finished off the wounded then than he did now with this
piece of meat.

Oddly, the killing of the rabbit ended his fears. If Mike
Calico was going to draw on him or gut him with that skillful
knife, there was absolutely nothing that he, Jim McPherson,
could do to stop him.

In all likelihood (and, for his peace of mind while on the

trail at least, how he wished to God he had thought of this a little sooner) Mike must be saving him for Corey's vengeance. The wrangler would certainly feel that honor had in no wise been served unless the wronged husband himself did the deed. It just postponed the worry, of course, until they found Corey Lane, but Jim could think about that then. He knew he very likely hadn't fooled Sam and Alicia about the terror he had felt at the prospect of chasing off into the wilderness to look for Corey, but he could hope he had fooled Virgie, although that was not likely, either.

What he could think about now were the things which had led to his being here in the desert with the deadly little man ahead of him, whose horse was reaching the first of the piñon on the long slant of green-dotted sand reaching for the foothills and the mountains.

Alicia had called Mike Calico into the sitting room at the X-Bar-7 when he and Sam told her the purpose of their visit. The Zuni had stood in the archway leading to the kitchen, through which he had apparently made his entry to the house. He hadn't removed his hat, spoken, bowed, nodded, or shown in any way that he even expected to be spoken to. Alicia had been deep into a recital of her audience with the governor, and she hadn't stopped when Calico came in. She went on for five more minutes, but Jim hardly heard a word she said. He was too busy looking at the Zuni.

The little wrangler didn't move a muscle. A braided leather quirt hung from the wrist above his good right hand, but, brutal as it looked, it didn't claim Jim's attention for more time than it took his eyes to shift to the ugly fascination of the half-claw curling from under the fringed left sleeve. Will-Ed's story of the catastrophe which had left the Zuni with those wicked-looking talons was never far from mind when he saw the man, but the actual sight of the ruined hand brought fresh shock each time. He'd felt a funny tremor in his spine and forced his eyes to Calico's.

"Mike," Alicia had said at last, and he'd welcomed her voice when Calico turned to look at her, "Mr. McPherson here wants somebody to take him to find Corey. Can you do it? Will you?"

There was no answer. The wrangler stood so completely motionless Jim couldn't even detect a sign of breathing. If he had been a corpse propped upright, he couldn't have looked more carved from lava rock than he did.

Then Virgie spoke. "Please, Mike," she said. The urgency in her voice made it seem like a barely controlled scream. "Please. It's the only chance he's got."

Jim was sure he saw the first tiny hint of softening in the stone eyes when they turned on Virgie.

The Zuni nodded.

On the way back to Black Springs after an early supper which had been pure torture for Jim (and for Virgie, too, from the look of her during the few glances he had trusted himself to give her in front of the other two) he began to curse himself silently for his folly. The course he was setting himself on was veering ominously close to suicide. But what earthly good did it do to stew about it? There was no way out.

"God damn it, Jim!" Sam had exploded as they neared the edge of town. "Won't you please consider what I said on the ride out? Let *me* go. I'm a sight more used to rough travel than any greenhorn."

"No."

"Then, for God's sake, let me go *with* you."

"No!"

If he had cursed in silence as they left the X-Bar-7, now he deluged himself with a cascade of unspoken blasphemies, partly because he had to admit to himself that Riordan's offer had tempted him. It was a short-lived temptation. A year ago Sam Riordan would indeed have been the man required by this desperate hour, but the creaky unsteady old shadow who rode beside him now would never make it. It had to be Jim McPherson who went. There simply wasn't anybody else.

Two days later, in line with the instructions he had gotten from Alicia after she'd had a private chat with the Zuni (he still hadn't talked to Mike himself), he arrived at the gate of the X-Bar-7 long before dawn, provisioned but unrested (he'd hardly slept a wink), riding his own horse (strange thought) and armed with his own Winchester (even stranger), not a borrowed one as in the ride to the Oscuras. He wasn't surprised to find Mike Calico mounted up and waiting.

He *was* surprised to hear Virgie call to him from the

doorway of the house. He started to ride to her, but she came running into the cold to meet him.

"Jim."

"Yes, Virgie?"

"There are two promises I must have or I'll not let you go."

He nodded. He would promise her anything.

"First," she said, "you're just to get Corey to come back. You're not to tell him about us. That's *my* job. Promise?"

He heard Mike's horse stirring. In spite of his love for her, he felt a moment's pique. Didn't she realize how she might be rekindling the Zuni's memory of the night he had watched them from the shadows? This might turn the man even more dangerous. But wait—she didn't know Mike had seen the two of them that night.

"I promise, Virgie." Reckless now that the cat was probably out of the bag yet another time, he reached down from the saddle and took her hand in his. "And the other thing?"

"Promise me you'll come back to me safe and sound. Don't laugh, Jim. You just might have a choice to make. Make it for me—for *us*."

He hadn't thought of laughing. The pressure of her hand turned fierce, and he knew if he didn't pull his away and go at once, he might never leave.

By the fourth day they were well into the thick forests just beneath the highest mountain ridges. On the northern and western slopes the early snows had piled up drifts they frequently had to go off-trail to avoid, if these narrow traces he could hardly see, but which the Zuni seemed to have no difficulty finding, indeed were trails. For the most part they headed west, right for the heart of the range; late in the afternoon, but still before sundown, Mike turned them south again, and the wind stopped biting at Jim's nose and cheeks, and by the time they settled into a campsite the heavier snows were far behind them.

Suddenly it occurred to him that there were still almost two hours of good light in the sky. He was mildly surprised that Mike had pulled them off the trail while they could still see. He hadn't the previous nights. It occurred to Jim, too, that they had made a highly circuitous ride to reach the valley they were in. Then the mild surprise gave way to wide-eyed astonishment when Mike Calico spoke the first words he had ever heard him utter.

"Big ride over. Short way to go now."

It was Jim himself who was now the mute of the two. He realized he would have to go back and try to recollect what it was the Zuni had said. The message was lost in the startling fact of the sound itself. Finally he got a question out. "Are we close to Corey, Mike?"

"Over there." Mike pointed in the general direction of a rocky limestone ridge across the narrow valley.

"How do you know?"

"Don't know. Mike make guess." Then, as if to add to Jim's confusion, the man grinned. "Make *good* guess, though."

Beyond the fact that the Zuni had spoken at all, Jim was amazed at how pleasantly warm, even musical, the voice was. He had unconsciously expected (in the improbable chance that the wrangler ever made a sound of any kind—words, actual words being out of the question entirely) that it would come out as some bestial grunt or growl. He shook his head. Mike was still grinning. The grin did something weird and wonderful to the dark wrinkled face.

"Mike," Jim asked, "can you find Corey—and the Apaches?"

"No find. Apache find *us*."

The grin vanished, and so did the lightness and strange pleasure of the moment. The tiny hairs on the back of Jim's neck quivered.

The morning sun seemed to hammer against the mountainside very quickly, considering that Jim was sure he hadn't slept at all. Mike hadn't made a fire for last night's supper, and none was burning now. The Zuni hadn't been idle, though. His horse was already saddled, and Jim hurried to pack his bedroll and make his own animal ready.

"No," Mike said, "you stay here. Mike go alone now, down to there." He pointed his claw hand to the bottom of the valley, and when Jim's eye followed he saw where the river curled around a small bald hill. "Apache find Mike there," the Zuni said.

"Why can't I go with you?" Jim asked. He heard the ring of alarm in his voice, and knew that the reason for it was that he wasn't at all sure he liked being left up here alone.

"Not sure how Apache act. They not like Zuni much. Maybe kill Mike. If they do—you leave. Back the way we come. Not too fast. When you reach snow again—ride like hell! No raise dust in snow." So that was why they had made that roundabout entrance to the valley. "If Mike fire three shots," the wrangler went on, "not at Apache but at sky, you come."

"Good Lord, man!" Jim said. "Maybe *you* could see where a man was shooting from this distance, but I sure can't. It must be two miles down to that hill."

Mike went to his horse. He reached into his saddlebag and drew out a fine-looking pair of military field glasses. "Belonged to major chief from Santa Fe," he said. "No lose. Please."

In another moment he was in the saddle, and in another two he was lost to sight in the trees. For a few minutes Jim could hear his horse picking its way down the rocky slope, and then the ensuing silence opened itself up to bird cries and brook sounds that he hadn't really been aware of before. He made a breakfast of hard biscuits and water, ravenous once the food and drink he hadn't even thought of until now reached his mouth—and then he settled himself to wait.

He used the binoculars impossibly early, and every ten minutes after that, but it was more than an hour before he saw Mike ride up the little hill, dismount, and tether his horse to what seemed to be the only shrubbery in sight. Some place on the ride down the Zuni must have cut a long pole from the mountain growth. To the top of it he had fixed a white square of cloth. He jammed the pole with its supplicant banner between two large boulders (getting it to stay upright took some time), went back to the horse and took his rifle from the boot, retraced his steps, and laid the gun against one of the big stones bulwarking the flag. Then he moved a dozen feet to what appeared in the distortion of the glasses to be the highest point of the little hill. He sat down cross-legged, facing the ridge opposite McPherson's vantage point, and folded his arms across his chest. With that last movement, and with the stillness which then settled on the tiny buckskin-clad figure, he almost seemed to vanish. Even knowing exactly were he was, Jim had to search for him every time he put the binoculars to his eyes. He would have kept the glasses of the "major chief" there constantly, but he found the pressure on the bridge of his nose and on the tops of his cheekbones too painful after just a few moments. Tension. He should have been able to hold them there more lightly, but he couldn't.

When he took even a short rest from his surveillance of the Zuni, he scanned the rest of the valley, searching up and down the river, up the far slopes with their heavy timber stands, and all across the ridge line knifing into a sky so intensely blue it needed but a star or two to be a midnight one. Every sound and movement in the far scene or close to him (there were an alarming number of these) screamed, "Apache!" but the splashes in the river turned out to be the settling of a flight of ducks and not the result of a hail of bullets, and the war cry which sent him half out of his shivering skin was only the squawking of a raven in a tree behind him.

Would they come today? There was surely no more guarantee than when they had all waited on the *malpais* for Victorio to show his hand to Corey and Major Lattner. How much scrutiny did the Apache give these hidden valleys? Even as watchful as they were supposed to be, they certainly wouldn't feel it necessary to post a sentinel on every peak looming over every forgotten canyon. No army large enough that they need fear it could make its way with sufficient stealth to take them by surprise in this lost savage country.

The penetrating cold of the high-country morning gave way to the weak warmth of noon. He was calmer now—for the most part. That he wasn't in total control of his emotions, though, came to him forcibly when he put the binoculars down and went to relieve himself, going behind a tree some distance away with the fastidiousness of long habit. He was in the middle of it when he suddenly panicked. *They've come!* He raced back and picked up the glasses again with sweat running down his forehead. When he got the hilltop in his field of vision there was nothing. Mike, he saw, hadn't moved.

The early afternoon stretched out interminably. It came to him once that he was more alone now than he had ever been, and the peculiar melancholy of total solitude weighed heavily on a spirit already badly overburdened.

Doing his few chores at short intervals, he gathered together what little was left of his and Calico's camp and saddled his horse, convincing himself against all probability that this activity might bring about the by no means sure result. If they did come and Mike did signal, he wanted to be under way before any second thought could stop him.

He returned always to his watching, sure each time something would have happened. Nothing had.

Then, incredibly, he grew sleepy. He struggled manfully against the sudden new weight of his eyelids for a while, but at last gave in.

How long he slept he had no way of knowing, but when he awoke with startled shame he grabbed the binoculars and jammed them fiercely to his eyes, positive he had let the Zuni down—betrayed him somehow. The feeling didn't leave him even when he got Mike clearly in sight and found him as before. Finally, satisfied only after long seconds of watching, he let out a great sigh of relief and decided he could take the field glasses from his face again.

Just before he did, he saw the first spurt of dust on the barren top of the little hill. It wasn't more than a yard from the feet of the cross-legged wrangler.

Two more splashes of kicked-up dirt even closer to the seated figure came before he heard the first of the distant shots. It was only when the angry sound reached his ears and he knew Mike had to have heard them seconds ago that he realized the Zuni hadn't even twitched. The wild thought that the man might already have met his death was more than half-formed when he saw Calico raise both arms above his head.

In the blink of an eye they were on the hilltop—six of them.

They were on foot, and Jim looked for horses, but couldn't find them. He looked for where the Apaches had been hidden, too, but his eyes told him nothing more than he had seen already. They circled Mike with rifles trained on him. Then the Zuni struggled to his feet and Jim could feel how stiff and sore he must be from holding that cruel position for so many hours.

Jim's heart began to beat again, feebly, when he realized that the miniatures on the hill had begun to talk. There was nodding and shaking of heads, and abandoned arm-waving from Mike.

Then the motion and gesturing stopped. When what must have been at least a minute had passed, with the seven

men standing as if in the arrested motion of a tintype, Mike
moved suddenly to where his rifle rested against the boulder.
He scarcely had it in his hands before the Apache nearest
him made a leap and wrested it from him with a violence Jim
could feel even from close to two miles away.

The Zuni and the Apache faced each other for still
another agonizing minute. Then the warrior with the rifle
raised it to the sky and fired rapidly. The dirty smudge from
one discharge blended with the one before it, and it wasn't
until the sound floated up the mountain to him that Jim knew
that, yes, there had indeed been three distinct and separate
reports.

Was it a trap? Mike hadn't done the firing. If Jim answered now, would he ride down there to certain death and
with no likelihood of rescuing Calico? He decided it didn't
matter. He had to chance it.

His legs were so weak it took him two attempts to
mount. He put the spurs to his horse and moved on down the
trail.

It was almost sundown when they rode into the *ranchería*
under the guns of their silent sullen guard.

The poisoned fog which had shrouded every thought
since the six Apaches had made him their prisoner on the
hilltop along with Mike had begun to lift a little, and he
looked around him with curiosity. This Apache camp had
none of the village aspect of the one he had ridden into with
Agent Russell up in the Mescalero. Even though there were
women and children and dogs aplenty, as in that scruffy
compound in the agency on the Ruidoso, and even though
they had passed small herds of cattle, mules, and horses
munching the thin mountain grass as they approached scores
of scattered wicki-ups, there was nothing settled about the
place, in looks or atmosphere. This was no mere hideout. It
was a war base as surely as the camp of Major Lattner and the
Ojos Negros ranchers had been the night before the battle in
May.

There was a clearly revealed sense of hostile energy on
every hand. Energy was too mild a word. Power. That's what
it was—power. It didn't come only from the number of
warrior men he saw (he had seen nearly this many in the
Oscuras) or from the rows of stacked repeating rifles which

made almost solid walls in front of the wicki-ups, or from the boxes of ammunition, some of which were piled dangerously near the cooking-fires. It was just there in the air. It was there in the faces which stared as the guard herded Jim and Mike between the huts and the fires and all the glistening instruments of death. And it lurked in the shadows cast by the dying sun.

My God! How was he to drag Corey Lane away from this? This was the very stuff which had sustained that pride of his all his life.

Where *was* Corey? Jim searched the brown faces of the warriors who pressed in on them as they were brought to a stop in front of a wicki-up set considerably apart from any of the others. He wasn't yet certain the tall man was to be found in this encampment, and he didn't even know if Mike Calico had discovered that much. Every time he or the Zuni had tried to speak on the long trip up through the narrow rocky defiles which led to the *ranchería* one of their captors had silenced them. Mike had persisted a time or two, but when the warrior who seemed to be in charge suddenly veered his pony over against the wrangler's and lashed him viciously across his dark face with the free end of his reins, it ended any more attempts Calico might have made. That had been the first inkling Jim had gotten of the deep hatred the Apaches harbored for his guide. Now, looking around after they had been commanded by gestures to dismount and squat in the dust in front of the lone wicki-up, he could see more of it.

A great many women had joined the ring of warriors surrounding them, and if the virulent loathing for the Zuni among the men was a silent thing, the women gave throat to theirs in an unceasing storm of jeers and taunts he didn't have to be an Indian to understand. Through it all, the Zuni sat with his arms folded, just as he had on the hilltop. That *he* understood well enough became apparent when, to Jim's astonishment, he actually smiled once or twice. The smiles might have lifted the editor's spirits, except that each one brought a louder shriller gush of invective from the women, and brought them in closer, too, well in front of the circle of silent men. Jim began to wonder when his turn would come, but the faces turned in his direction from time to time seemed to hold only an uncomplicated curiosity.

The women edged even closer now, and, to Jim's horror,

he saw that each one of them clutched a good-sized rock,
sometimes two. They turned the rocks over and over in their
hands nervously, eagerly. Then Mike spoke up in tones Jim
knew were deliberately calculated to provoke attack. "Funny,"
he said, "Apache think *Zuni* smell bad. Hah! Apache stink
like last moon's coyote shit." The women stopped their abuse
and leaned forward, and Mike spoke again (laughing!) and
this time in their own tongue . . . and the rocks came flying.

Most of them thudded sickeningly but harmlessly against
the wrangler's body, but one struck him high on his forehead,
alarmingly close to his right eye. Blood flowed, spurted, but
Calico didn't so much as put a hand to the wound, not the
good right one or the withered claw.

From under the voluminous skirts knives began to appear, and one old crone hopped to a nearby cooking-fire,
seized a burning chunk of wood, and advanced on the Zuni
with the flame from the brand reflected in her eyes. Mike
didn't even shrink as the glowing weapon neared his face.

"*Basta!*" The word, not loud but arresting, paralyzing,
came from the wicki-up behind them, and Jim turned to see
the face of Victorio.

Like magic, the crowd melted away, with even the six
men who had brought them in retiring several paces. One of
them said something to Victorio and he nodded. He hadn't
looked at Mike or Jim, only at his people while they moved
away, but now he turned toward them. Rather, he looked at
Jim and at Jim alone.

"Welcome to my *ranchería*, Man of Words," he said.
"What brings you to Victorio's fire?"

The question was pure formality. He knew well enough
what had brought them here, and yet, if it hadn't been for
the "Man of Words," Jim might have thought the Indian had
forgotten him. There wasn't the slightest sign of recognition
in the piercing eyes. And in spite of the fact that the Mimbreño
chief had just halted what would have been certain further
mayhem on Mike Calico, there wasn't the tiniest hint of
mercy or human kindness in those eyes, either—or, for that
matter, cruelty. It wasn't, Jim knew suddenly, that Victorio
stood above or below or apart from any of these things—this
was something else, a preoccupation he hadn't been burdened with (if burdened was the word) at the Mescalero
agency. War was everything now, the deep cold involvement

of the warrior king with his appointed purpose. If the Apache had been impressive in the demeaning squalor of the agency village, how would one describe him now?

This man was where the power McPherson felt around him came from. Granted this, how did Corey Lane react to it?

Corey Lane! Ah, yes . . . Corey.

"We come in peace, Victorio," Jim said. (Wasn't that the proper form to use?) "I wish to speak with the white chief Lane. Is he here?"

Did he detect a doubtful light in Victorio's eyes, or was it just some last flicker of the setting sun?

"No—he is not here."

Oh, my God! Have we come all this way and risked our lives for nothing?

Then Victorio went on. "He leads a raid today. If he lives, he will ride in tonight before the moon has set. You will speak with him tomorrow." He turned abruptly and strode to the opening of the wicki-up, turned toward them once again. "You will be fed, and my warriors will show you once where you can sleep. In the morning, after you have spoken with the white chief Lane—if he returns—you will leave, if Victorio has your word that you will lead no one to this place."

"You have my word, Victorio—and Mike's." He saw the Zuni's nod out of the corner of his eye.

"Good. I do not know how long Victorio can protect you. The hate of my people for such as him is great." He pointed at Mike while still looking straight at Jim. "Ride fast when you leave my *ranchería*".

Then he was gone, and Jim knew this was the last he would have to do with Victorio on this trip at least—or perhaps forever?

The same old woman who had advanced on Mike with the burning stick brought them their food. She was different now, friendly. Jim was bewildered to hear the white-haired Apache dowager and Mike clacking away together, laughing at some shared joke. My God, half an hour ago this dear old thing was willing to roast the Zuni's head like a chestnut.

The meat she plopped in front of them was dark and gristly, floating in a small sea of grease, and clinging stubbornly to the oddest-looking bones he had ever seen. Ravenous, he forced himself to overcome its bad smell, but when

he tried to take a bite, he found it tasted even worse. So
much for the kindly old lady standing there. It was a trick.
This Apache Lucretia Borgia was intent on poisoning them.
Oh, the hell with it. Better to die with his belly full of some
primitive toxin than to starve to death. He looked at Mike
and found the wrangler grinning and chewing at the same
time, the juices from this foul pretense for meat running
down his chin.

"Not bad mule," Mike said, "but Apache no cook as good
as Zuni." Revolted as Jim was, he went on eating. To his
surprise, the stuff began to taste more palatable and then
almost good. It had suddenly become flavored with the sauce
of the affection which had been developing within him for the
little Zuni. He had been impressed earlier by the wrangler's
toughness, stoicism, and courage, but the warmth he felt for
Calico now was something different. Certainly a large part of
the glow he felt had been prompted by the shared danger of
this trip, but there was something else, too. He couldn't pin
it down. The paradox of their relationship saddened him.
Mike Calico, even if he hadn't slipped his knife between
Jim's ribs, was still his enemy. When Corey got to them, Jim
could forget about the warmth of this moment.

Just before dawn the raiding party pounded into the
ranchería. Jim awoke startled and terrified once again, and
then, when he had calmed himself, bitterly upset to have
been snatched from his dream. Virgie had been with him.

As the riders cantered toward the corrals, he looked for
Corey, but in the half-light and early smoke of the camp it
was hard to pick out any single rider. He tried to go to sleep
again after the commotion of the arriving horsemen had died
away, but sleep—and the longed-for lost dream—wouldn't
come again.

He lay on his back staring into the bowl of the sky,
watching the last of the stars wink out, and hearing the first
real sounds of the awakening *ranchería.* Suddenly he knew
beyond all doubt that Corey *was* here. He didn't have to see
him. He could *feel* him. A change had come over the *ranchería,*
too.

"Editor."
"Hello, Corey."
It had been almost impossible to get the greeting out.

He knew, even before he tried, that the words would stick in his throat at first sight of the man. Corey Lane's appearance would have staggered even someone who hadn't known him. It was an appearance which touched a good deal more than just Jim's eyes. Everything Jim had ever known or felt about him, good and bad (there could never be mild indifference), was heightened. It had to be something more than the outlandish costume; he hadn't expected to find the same elegance he had seen back in the Ojos Negros anyway. Of course, the leggings and skirtlike breechclout must have had something to do with his first reaction, as did the buckskin vest straining across the vast chest and the scarf which gathered in the yellow curls. The bright new full beard gave the man even more of the Roman look Jim had remarked to himself when he had first seen him and which he felt was so much in keeping with the imperial manner.

But mostly—as it had always been—it was Corey's eyes. If the giant in front of him was indeed a Roman, he wasn't a Marcus Aurelius or Octavius but Nero or Caligula.

"Well, editor," Corey said, "have you come to me once more to tell me how abominably I've behaved?"

"No, Corey. In this matter I've no right to judge."

"What makes it different this time, editor?"

"This time it's clearly law, not politics. The law makes judgments of its own."

"But I'm beyond the law now, right?"

" 'Beyond' isn't exactly the word I would use."

"Oh?"

"Maybe at the border of it, Corey. It's not too late yet."

Corey smiled. It was a wintry smile. Suddenly all the hatred which had built up in Jim McPherson because of what this man had done to people Jim loved welled up until it nearly spilled. He would have to watch himself. If he wavered for even one moment from the reason he had come here, everything that meant a thing to him might be lost. Corey's return to the Ojos Negros must be brought about, at any cost.

"Corey," Jim said, "we want you back—all of us."

Lane kept right on smiling, but it wasn't an easy smile to look at.

"To hang me for killing Jacky, editor?" he asked.

"That wasn't what I meant."

"It's what it comes to, though, isn't it?"

"Not necessarily. You'd have to answer for that, of course."

Lane laughed. "Another day in court like the last one? I don't think I want to oblige you, editor." He stood up without warning and moved a few feet away from where Jim and Mike were sitting. "This is enough for now," he said, turning back for a moment. "We may talk again—but I doubt it. Everything was said back in Black Springs."

My God, Jim thought. *I've got to tell him, and now.*

"Corey, wait!" He fought to keep his voice level. "Does it make a difference that Alicia has seen Lew Wallace about a pardon?"

The big man looked blank.

The editor plunged ahead. "If you present your case to the governor in Santa Fe, it's an almost foregone conclusion that he'll grant a pardon, a full one. No strings attached. Eloy has been at him night and day, and the testimony he's prepared to give will thoroughly discredit Granby. And nobody in Santa Fe knows about your being here with—"

Lane had turned swiftly and started to stride away. There was no point in going on. As Jim had spoken he had seen the blank look grow even blanker. He watched the retreating figure of Corey Lane until the man was clear across the widest open space in the *ranchería*, realizing then that he was heading for Victorio's wicki-up. Just as he reached it the Apache leader emerged. The Indian and the white man talked together, both glancing at Mike and Jim from time to time.

For the briefest of moments hope flared in the editor that the big man was telling Victorio what Jim had told him, but the hope expired as he watched the Mimbreño and the renegade (yes, think it—face it—"renegade") as they bent their heads together. They were too far away for Jim to hear, but it was clear that they weren't taking leave of each other. These two were as linked as any two men Jim had ever seen, but linked in no ordinary comradeship. It was clear, too, that the conversation was a serious one. Finally Corey Lane shrugged like a man who knew his arguments would avail him nothing, and Victorio disappeared inside his wicki-up. Corey strode off toward the horse corrals at the edge of the *ranchería*. He didn't look back at Mike and Jim.

"Corey no listen," Mike Calico said. "No leave here, either."

Jim had almost forgotten the little Zuni. As the finality of the wrangler's words echoed in the editor's head, he realized he had given no thought at all to the news Mike must have wanted to pass along. It was but small consolation that Calico might never get *his* chance now.

"What happens now, Mike?" he asked.

"Mike not sure," the Zuni said. "Maybe Apache kill us now?"

Mike's remark brought Jim up short. What with trying to get Corey to return to Chupadera County, the editor hadn't concerned himself much with the dangers he and the wrangler still faced, though during the night and even in the early morning he had been conscious of the Apache guards a few yards from his bedroll. Now the guards were gone, and, thinking back, he remembered they had withdrawn right after Corey had ridden in with the raiding party.

Even if Mike was right and the Indians intended to kill them, the editor and the Zuni must now be on parole. It almost seemed that they had been granted the freedom of the *ranchería;* certainly no one was paying any attention to them. As much to take his mind off the other things troubling him as out of curiosity, he decided to test the situation. "Come on, Mike," he said, "let's look around." Mike grunted something, but struggled to his feet and trailed his stumpy little legs after Jim.

If it hadn't have been for the weapons and ammunition they saw in such profusion, the huge encampment wouldn't have seemed at all hostile. Mangy dogs sniffed around every wicki-up, as they had in the village in Russell's agency. Cooking was going on at a dozen places, even though the sun was nowhere near its noon zenith. Children, not as he had seen them during the battle in the Oscuras, but laughing, shouting, racing to and fro, played with some of the dogs or with a variety of makeshift toys. Now and then a horseman would ride by the editor and the wrangler, careful not to look directly at them. It was hard to take Mike's grim conjecture seriously.

The huts seemed to be grouped more closely in certain areas, and Jim guessed these must be clan or band divisions within the larger force, something which Mike more or less confirmed when he would point to a gathering of men or

women (seldom both) and say "Chiricahua" or "Juh's people"
or "Mescalero" and a few other words Jim didn't catch.

The *ranchería* was even bigger than Jim had thought it
when their captors had brought them in the night before. He
figured there must be more than a half a thousand people in
the camp. He almost smiled, thinking of how the newspaperman
in him was coming to the fore again. And that made him
think of something else: If there were indeed as many as five
hundred Apache here, more than two hundred of them could
be warriors. That would be a formidable fighting force by any
standard. That they would be well mounted if they went to
war was apparent. He could see at least a half-dozen corrals,
each of them bursting with riding-animals, and more tethered and penned-up mules than he had a way of counting.
Already he had been impressed by the huge stores of guns
and ammunition. The only things needed to make this a
full-scale military cantonment would be uniforms and an odd
piece or two of field artillery. It made Victorio's redoubt
in the Oscuras look small indeed.

As McPherson and Calico wandered unchecked—but not
unwatched, he was sure—a frightening thought came to the
editor's mind. Somehow he kept the thought from turning
into words until Mike spoke up again and did it for him.

"Mike right before. Apache kill us. Soon, Mike think."
There seemed no sound of guesswork in the Zuni's voice this
time. That there seemed no fear or alarm didn't help a bit
—Jim was sure he had enough of both for the two of them.
Mike went on, "Apache not let us see everything like this and
live."

"But, Mike," Jim said, "surely Corey wouldn't let them—"

"Mike think Corey not care much no more."

There was no time to explore this further. In the space
between two wicki-ups Jim saw something so disturbing it
drove his and Calico's predicament completely out of mind.
Several Apache women were badgering two young girls. The
youngsters, in tatters which might once have been dresses
like the ones Jim had seen on the young farm girls of the Rio
Concho and the big river *bosques,* looked Mexican and terrified. Captives.

"New here," Mike said. He had been listening intently
to the children's cackling tormentors. "Come in this morning
with Corey's raiders."

Jim didn't want to see any more of anything. He hurried Mike back to where they had left their packs and bedrolls.

When they were fed at noon—it looked and tasted like some kind of mushy cornmeal—he was still too sick to his stomach to eat. Mike finished both portions greedily when Jim shook his head.

Shortly afterward Corey came to them again—with Victorio.

"If you've anything more to say, editor, you'd better get it said. Victorio wants you out of his *ranchería* now."

Jim looked at Victorio. The Apache's impassive face didn't reveal a thing. Jim turned back to Corey.

"Corey," he said, "come back with us. I beg you."

Lane made an impatient gesture with his big hand. "When you're on the trail, move fast. That white flag you came in under will buy you a day—just one day! Victorio's warriors want your blood now. I'll be truthful with you: I advised him to let them have their way. They remember Mike from Apache Pass and the Oscuras, and you—well you're just another white man." The way that last was said staggered the editor. It was as if Corey himself were something else entirely. But Lane was still speaking. "One day— all Victorio's honor and power could get you is that one day. If I were you—well Mike knows, don't you, *viejo?*"

He had turned to Calico. Jim waited. Would the wrangler tell *his* tale now? It would be the last chance he'd have. When the editor looked at Mike, he found the Zuni had moved away from him and Corey and Victorio and was gathering his and Jim's gear.

"*You* got anything to say, Mike?" Corey asked.

It seemed to take forever for the Zuni to turn around and face Lane. Suddenly a broad smile lightened his dark features.

"Sure, Corey," Calico said. "*Adiós!*"

"*Adiós*, Mike," Corey said.

Then Jim saw that one of the warriors who had guarded them through the night was coming down the length of the compound leading the horses taken from him and Calico. Mike took the leads of the two animals and then made no effort to disguise his look when he checked his saddle boot for his rifle. It was there, and Jim saw his was, too.

There was an awkward silence while Mike packed the bedrolls and saddlebags on the horses. Jim couldn't bring

himself to look at Corey, and Victorio's face held no invitation
to conversation when he looked at the Apache.

Then Mike was in the saddle. "We go now, huh?" he
said to Jim. He was holding the reins of Jim's horse out to
him.

When Jim was mounted, he looked at Corey once again.
The editor stuck his hand out, but the big man ignored it,
deliberately, Jim was sure. It brought a sick feeling, made
more so because Victorio was seeing it, as were ten or twelve
other Apaches who had been pressing in on the small group
unnoticed by McPherson in the heaviness of the moment.

Jim turned his horse and urged him after Mike's. Calico
was looking back at him the way he had those two first days
after they had left the Ojos Negros. The wrangler's eyes
widened when he saw Jim jerk sharply on the reins and spin
his horse around until he faced Corey and the Indians once
again.

"Corey," Jim said. "Virgie and little Corey need you—
and Alicia!"

By God, the editor thought, that brought some reaction
—at least the sound of "Alicia" did. Corey Lane's hard face
showed *something*. And so, he saw, did Victorio's. The keen
Mimbreño eyes were on the white man now, and a questioning look had changed the impassive mask of the Apache just a
little.

Corey said nothing. He stared at McPherson as if he
didn't know him.

Then the editor felt something powerful happen inside
him. There was something else he had to say, no matter how
dangerous saying it could be.

"Well, Corey," he said, "if the pardon won't bring you
back, maybe this will. Virgie and I want to speak with you
together. We're in love!" He hadn't realized how his voice
was rising until he heard the last of this come out almost as a
shout.

Lane's face darkened, then twisted violently, and then . . .

Corey began to laugh. At the very first ordinary enough,
it became in an instant the same mad laugh Jim had heard in
Harry Timmons' courtroom. Back then the laugh had been
somewhat deadened in the crowded room. Here in the high
mountain air it winged its way to the lofty rocks buttressing

the *rancheria* and came back again with its wild force doubled and redoubled.

Surely, Jim thought (and he wondered at his calmness), Corey Lane would kill him now.

Then the laugh stopped, stopped as quickly and completely as if a candle had been snuffed. To Jim's surprise, Corey made no move toward the gun at his side which he had drawn so swiftly in the plaza. *When the move does come*, Jim thought without real feeling, *I most likely won't even see it.*

Then gradually McPherson realized Corey wouldn't draw. He would live today.

"You've got guts, editor," Corey said, "I'll give you that. Either that or you've got second sight. No, I guess you don't. That confession came out so easily and stupidly I know you didn't have time to remember you're still under Victorio's protection." He laughed again, the laugh this time an only slightly less insane echo of the first one. "So you and my wife are in love. And you think to take her from me? That's just fine. I don't think it will come to much, do you? Do you really think I would let you take what's mine?"

There was something odd about the questions in spite of the simple sound of them. Jim's mind struggled for a moment as he tried to pin it down. And then he knew.

For all the implied threat in Corey's words, for all that his voice throbbed with warning, the man didn't really care.

"Goodbye, Corey," Jim said. There was nothing more to say.

"One last thing, editor." Was Corey's smile now just the vestige of the laughter, or was there something else, something new? "One last thing," Lane went on, and now there was an even more dangerous undertone in the powerful voice than any the editor had ever heard before. "Your trip up here was unnecessary, you know. All that trouble for nothing. You see . . . it always *was* my plan to come back again. What you've just said may hurry it up a little, but I was coming anyway. Make no mistake, I will be back!"

As Jim turned his horse toward the trail and Mike again, he saw Victorio raise his arm in a salute.

They rode all the way to the snow line before Mike decided to make a camp. It surprised Jim when the Zuni built a fire, and he asked about it.

"Apache know which way we ride now. Anyway we had this one day free, remember? Big Apache present. *Hah!*"

Somehow Jim didn't feel inclined to explore the reason behind Mike's derisive "Hah!"

At this altitude, and with the nearby snowbanks draining away the last of the day's feeble warmth, there was no mistaking the fact that the season had passed over into winter. It grew bitter cold the moment the sun plunged behind the mountain wall. It was even cold in the bedroll in spite of Mike's defiant fire. Well, had it been blazing August, Jim would have been chilled this night. He thought it possible he never would be warm again.

He had felt bleak and frozen on the whole afternoon's ride, ever since Corey's promise that he "was coming anyway" and the vow "*I will be back.*"

Fording the river, climbing the tortuous mountain trail with only half an eye on Mike's rocking back, Jim had fought against the full implication of it. Improbable as was what he thought Corey had in mind, he couldn't really summon up doubt that the big man and his new allies could bring it off. The threat to him, McPherson, would have been difficult enough to face, but the more general vengeance he read in the hot blue eyes that last second horrified him. How much blame would he personally have to shoulder for the bloodshed which now seemed to him sure to come to Chupadera County?

He tossed and turned in his bedroll. He couldn't sleep, no matter how badly he needed sleep before the next day's ride. Finally he crawled from his blankets to sit by the fire. He threw another stick of pine on the coals and jumped when the fire, apparently seizing on a knot rich in gum, flared like a torch. Then he smiled, thinking of how he had kept himself so well under control in the genuine peril of the *ranchería*, only to start like a nervous boy in this safe camp Victorio's word of honor had granted them. Maybe he was deluding himself about the threat he was so sure Corey and the Apaches posed to the Ojos Negros too.

Across the fire from him, he saw Mike twist and turn.

"Mike," he said, "are you awake?" There was a mutter for an answer and then more stirring. The fire flared again and Jim could see the Zuni had propped himself on the elbow above the ravaged hand.

"They *will* come after us, won't they, Mike?"

"Yes."

"Tomorrow?"

"Yes."

"We'll have to ride fast tomorrow, then, won't we?"

"Not too fast. Save horses. Apache will have many fresh ones."

"Can we get away?"

"Mike not know. Think so."

It was almost laughable that he could be reassured by that, but he was.

"Mike," he said, "I've got to ask you something."

"Yes?"

"Were you going to tell Corey about Mrs. Lane and me?"

"Mike think about it."

"Why didn't you, then?"

If there was an answer, it was lost when the fire found another pine knot and cracked like a pistol shot.

"Why didn't you, Mike? You're Corey's man, aren't you?"

"Sure. Ride for Corey. Fight for Corey."

"And Mrs. Lane is Corey's woman, isn't she?"

There was more silence. Then—

"Not Corey's woman. She her own woman. Lady." The Zuni struggled out of the bedroll, fished in the saddlebag which had cradled his dark head, and brought out a plug of chewing-tobacco. By the light of the fire Jim watched the tough little jaws work the bite he had cut. Mike leaned toward the fire and spat a gob of the brown juice into it. The sizzle of it lasted several seconds. "Mike fight for Corey. Ride for Corey," he said, the words sounding a little like a protest. "Die for lady." He said it softly. Of course! Virgie would have the power to win him as she would anyone who knew her. That was why he had looked to her before he agreed to this expedition, risky enough for Jim—perilous for Mike Calico.

"Mike," Jim said, "you know what Corey has in mind for the Ojos Negros and the town, don't you?"

"Sure. Town has maybe ten days. No more."

"What will *you* do, Mike?"

Another squirt of tobacco juice hissed in the fire.

"Don't know. Mike not fight Corey. Not fight for Apache. Take you home first. Then make up mind." What must have been the last of the chew hit the fire and died there. "We sleep now. All right?" The Zuni crawled back into his bedroll and Jim got into his. After what must have been nearly five minutes Mike spoke again. "Go back to own people, maybe. If they take Mike back." The words didn't sound mournful when he said them, but when they echoed inside Jim Mc-Pherson's head they did.

Still, he was suddenly warmer, and sleep came easily.

What with the way Mike led them—doubling back on trails, splashing countless miles through ice-edged pebbled stream beds, seeking slickrock whenever he could find it so their trail would be faint and hard to follow—it was late afternoon of the fourth day before their pursuers reached them. They had almost crossed the Jornada and the *malpais* was no more than five minutes' ride away when the first shot plowed the desert at their horses' heels. More than a dozen Indians were in the hunt. The two men broke into a furious ride which left the animals in a dangerously heavy lather, and Jim blessed the Zuni's wisdom in husbanding their strength as he had the last three days.

Mike led the way into the lava beds, digging his spurs mercilessly into his pony's flanks. They climbed a slight rise to where two monoliths flanked a narrow trail thirty or forty feet above the point where they had made their frantic entry into the badlands. Even Jim's tyro eye could see that this was probably the only good place for miles around for them to make a stand. That they wouldn't be able to hold out for very long was just as clear. The Zuni had dismounted quickly, but when Jim started to do the same, he held up his claw of a hand.

"No." Mike said. "You take both horses and ride hard. Warn Ojos Negros. Mike stay."

"Good Lord, no, Mike! You'll die. You won't have a chance without me."

"Not much chance *with* you." The little man was grinning again. "No hurt feelings, huh?"

"I won't leave you, Mike."

The grin disappeared.

"Have to," the Zuni said. "You make two promises to lady, remember? Already you break one. Tell Corey. You go back safe to her. Other promise. Right?"

It was clear that argument would do no good. He would

have to return to her, or nothing, not even his death, would have meaning any more. Seeing her one more time, and warning Black Springs, too, came above everything, even above this decent little man. Before he could agree, Mike spoke again.

"No worry. Mike try not to die. Pretty sure dying no Goddam fun."

The reports of rifles went on behind him until McPherson had almost left the *malpais*. Then, just as the rolling grasslands of the Ojos Negros came in view, he couldn't hear them any longer. Was there a chance he was now too far away? No, he could have heard firing had it still been going on. Mike Calico would have no choices to make ever again. The little Zuni was dead and at long last truly a part of that grim black rock.

> *"I cannot help it now,*
> *Unless, by using means, I lame the foot*
> *Of our design."*

II

The last time Victorio had ridden to the cave was before the Battle of Apache Pass, eighteen years ago.

The lance had been safe then, resting on a dark ledge in its buckskin wrappings exactly where he had first placed it many summers before that battle. He had been little more than a boy when great Mangas had made him a present of it, and he had carried it joyously on raids, seven of them, before he took the rifle from a bluecoat he had killed.

Then, with the more deadly rifle now his, the lance seemed foolish, but he had kept it in his wicki-up until Mangas—who had little use for medicine or magic—had told him to break it in two and throw the pieces to the desert winds. It was too much to carry along every time they moved a *rancheria*, Mangas had said.

He had tried to break it, but the great strength of his arms suddenly left them, and anyway he wasn't wise enough, as Mangas was, to disregard the magic. Before the big raids which won for the Mimbreños all the Ojo Caliente country, he had gone to the mountains to make his battle medicine— alone—and he had found this cave.

When Cochise called for the Mimbreños to come and help the Chiricahuas in their fight at Apache Pass, he had gone again to the cave to get the lance, but he had left it there, shame burning his cheeks that he could so fear the *gáh'n* Mangas laughed at. Mangas would have laughed at him, too, if he had put his faith in anything but bullets to defeat the whites.

In the long bitter years since then he had often wondered if things would have gone better at the pass and afterward if he had taken the graceful weapon with him. Maybe not, but this time he wouldn't take the chance. Perhaps it was foolish. Perhaps he would never use it. Well, it would be no bother. The woman could care for it until he called for it.

The Mimbreños and their friends might need every bit of medicine and magic he could find when they fought the battle they were fast coming to, the one which was the dream of the white chief Lane—and which had now become the dream as well of Loco, Juh, Nana, and every Chiricahua, Mescalero, and Mimbreño warrior under his, Victorio's, command.

His command? No, it was unmanly to blind himself like that. Lane led now. He would lead until the town across the river and beyond the Jornada del Muerto and the *malpais* was taken and destroyed.

And how, truthfully, did Victorio feel about his loss of power? It didn't matter when he considered the hope Lane had raised in the hearts of the Mimbres people and their cousins, more hope than he had seen since Cochise and Mangas Coloradas had ruled the deserts and mountains almost twenty years ago. The white chief had proved himself on three hard raids, fighting valiantly, killing white men, every one he reached, as readily as he had killed Mimbreños and Chiricahuas in the past. It had given him the right to speak in council, and, in truth, Victorio himself had listened. Lane's plan was good. The new ways of fighting he was teaching Victorio's warriors were simple and effective. It was easy to see how the bluecoats and so many of the other whites could be so fearsome in a fight, even when they were outnumbered as the black white men had been during Victorio's raid on the *estancia* when Lane first rode with him. Yes, the white chief had earned the command for the attack on the town.

But there was this doubt Victorio could not utter. Some of it had been there all along, coming soon after they had found Lane crazy in the desert, and it was stronger now. Victorio had felt it most when he heard the second talk Lane

had had with the Man of Words, just before the Man of
Words and the Zuni left the *ranchería*. The other white man
had worked some powerful medicine on Lane with the word
Victorio had never heard, but which sounded like *Ah-li-sheh*.
The change which had come over Lane was a strange thing to
watch, but he had recovered quickly. Then, when the Man of
Words had told Lane that he would try to take Lane's woman,
Lane had made the bad mistake. Victorio could see on the
face of the Man of Words that he knew what Lane and
Victorio planned to do.

When Lane had said he was "coming back," the eyes of
the young Man of Words had opened wide. If he and the
Zuni made it back across the desert and the badlands, he
would alert the town. Not that there was much chance of
that. Ten of the swiftest Mimbreño riders had waited for the
one day's grace to pass like racers at the starting-pole. The
two fugitives would have little chance. Even with the skillful
Zuni leading them, they should be dead before the sun set
two more times.

Victorio felt something strange about that. He rather
liked the Man of Words—alone among all the white men he
had known. It might even have been like it was with Cochise
and Agent Jeffords. Too late. It was time for war, red war. All
enemies must die.

He dismounted below the cave and, some distance away
from it, tied his horse to a rock and stared at the black hole in
the mountainside.

When he neared the opening on foot, he knew at once
that no man had been inside it for many months. The old
smell of lion was so heavy in the thin air he knew more than
one generation of mountain cats had made it home. With
game so scarce in the high rocks, it was unlikely any animals
were crouched there now, but it wouldn't do to be mauled,
not with the battle beckoning. He returned to his horse and
got his rifle. When he came back near the cave again, he
positioned himself behind a boulder, picked up a stone, and
hurled it into the shadows behind the mouth. He did this two
more times, listening to the stones bounding and clattering
through the rocky tunnel. Then, satisfied, he went inside.

The lance was there all right, in its casing, precisely as
he had left it, but under more than a hand's thickness of
limestone dust. Was he imagining things? Did it move a little

when he touched it? There could be more magic in it than
wise old Mangas had ever dreamed. He took it, still in its
buckskin wrapping, out into the sun and laid his rifle against
the boulder. As he untied the thongs—still strong after all
these years—he smiled to see his hands trembling like aspen
leaves in the wind. Aha, old Mangas, you were right. It
wasn't the *gáh'n* which made the silent weapon jump. It was
Victorio's own nervous weakness.

There were a few spots of rust on the long hammered-
iron point, but the wood of the haft was without a crack or
splinter, whole and strong. True, the feathers were crushed
and shapeless, and the earth paint had faded and crumbled
until the colors had died, but the woman could make these
things right again. All in all, the splendor of it was almost
more than his heart could bear.

He looked from the lance to the rifle. It was a brand-new
Winchester, taken from the wagon train near Bayard. He
would take it back to the *ranchería* with him. Some warrior
cursing the jams of the old Henry he still carried would be
overjoyed to have it. He, Victorio, had no use for it any
longer.

He was sweating. He realized then how much fear had
been in him as he approached this moment. It was gone now.
The magic, or whatever Mangas would call it, was working.

His people would fight well under Lane, using Lane's
new ways of warfare, but it was important they always remember who they were. The lance would tell them; even
in—*particularly* in —the heat of battle. He looked down to
where the buckskin casing lay crumpled in the rocks. With a
swift movement of his foot he kicked it aside. As long as
Victorio lived, the lance would never hide in a sheath again.

He grasped the rifle in his left hand. It balanced poorly
compared to the slim lance in his right. When he reached his
horse, he stuffed the rifle into his holster almost with disdain
and leaped to the back of the startled animal. He chuckled. It
must be ten years since he had got astride a horse like that.
Suddenly a surge of gratitude passed down his whole strong
body. The white chief Lane! In fairness, he had that strange
man to thank for this. Without him this moment never would
have come.

He shook the lance in the air. His mouth opened, and
after he filled his lungs with a mighty draft of mountain air,

he loosed his war cry at the high, snow-covered peaks. The echo came back nearly as loudly as the cry itself, and his pony reared. He pulled the reins until the neck of the animal arched like a hunting-bow.

Victorio—chief of the Mimbres Apaches; lieutenant to great Mangas Coloradas; comrade-in-arms to mighty Cochise of the Chiricahuas; leader of Loco, Nana, Nariz Roto, Long Hand, and half a thousand splendid fighting men; enemy and killer of the cruel brave soldiers who had come unasked to his mountains and deserts—dug his heels into the sides of his pony and started down the trail to war.

"Can you think to blow out the intended fire your city is ready to flame in, with such weak breath as this?"

III

"Frankly," Wilson Blaine said, "I think you're crazy, McPherson. The idea of those savages making a real attack on Black Springs is preposterous." The mayor was puffed out with importance like a toad. "Why, our town is just a few people shy of being a city now. Even Victorio wouldn't have the bravado to put us under—"

"Wilson, shut up!" Jim said. "Are you going to make the proclamation or not?"

"No. It would be irresponsible of me, to say the least. Do you want me to cause a panic for nothing? I tell you, we've nothing to fear here in Chupadera County. Oh, I've no doubt there might be a few small raids. We've lived with them for years. But a full-scale siege? The idea!"

"Look, Wilson. Listen! This is a different Apache force than any you've ever seen or heard about. It's an army, man! Trained, disciplined, and armed and mounted damned near as well as the Regulars. Will you at least send a messenger to Santa Fe?"

"Of course I'll do that much. They'll be interested in what you *say* you've seen, and they'll want your report, for what it's worth."

"Are you doubting me, Wilson?" He'd had no idea he could sound that threatening.

"Certainly not, McPherson." The mayor was flustered. He took a handkerchief from his breast pocket and wiped the sweat from his forehead. "It's just that you're still a new-comer here. Doubtless you were very, uh—apprehensive when you were in the Apache camp. That sort of thing plays tricks on the best of men. No, McPherson, the hostiles haven't the will *or* skill to attempt what you're suggesting."

"Doesn't it make any difference in your thinking that it will be *Corey Lane* leading these 'savages'?"

There was no answer. He might have known. Nobody was ready to face that issue squarely.

Jim had ridden straight for the town offices after he cleared the *malpais* and, finding them closed, had sought the mayor out at his home. He could hear the twins practicing their musical atrocities on each other somewhere in the house now, and pots and pans rattled in the kitchen, where Mrs. Blaine must be fixing supper. The ordinary blandness of the scene in the Blaine home and the mayor's unwillingness to see the urgency was infuriating.

The mayor inspected his fingernails. "Well, McPherson," he said finally, "it's getting on for mealtime. I never like to keep Mrs. Blaine's culinary artistry waiting."

And Jim was outside the door without having been able to rouse any fears in Wilson Blaine's empty little head.

Then he realized it would be the same everywhere in town. The mayor and the rest of his fellow citizens simply weren't ready to admit that Corey had turned renegade. Even Sam, helping him enlist the aid of Mike, had always acted as if he believed Corey might be Victorio's captive, but nothing more. How would Sam take this news? Would *he* face the truth? Would Alicia? My God, would . . . ?

He felt helpless. When he had left the echoes of the shots dying on the *malpais* behind him and had seen the lights of Black Springs, some of the things he had seen at the *rancheria* were coming into sharper focus than when he actually witnessed them. What he had told Wilson about the high state of the organization of the Apache fighting force, for instance. Perhaps the little mayor did have something of the right of it when he suggested that Jim's "apprehension" had played havoc with his reporter's instincts. Thank God Mike had been with him. If Mike hadn't known, too, how deadly the threat was, he might have let the idea drift—as a lot of people in Black Springs were going to want him to.

It brought up another problem. How could Black Springs (even supposing he could jerk the ostrich's head from the sands of self-imposed ignorance) rally the strength to defend itself? Almost every leader the town could boast was gone. Corey had been such a pillar of strength for so many years that no other real one had developed, and the nominal holder of authority, Wilson Blaine, was a joke. Eloy was in Santa Fe. Even if the enemy granted more time than Jim thought he would, there surely wouldn't be enough time to get the Concho man back—and even if there were, would Black Springs follow him? Politics was one thing, war another. Joe Harris? No. The acting sheriff handled the routine minor chores of the office with only the barest competence. Sam Riordan, even if he hadn't fallen into the despondency of recent weeks, was just too old. Jacky Jameson and Bill Talley were dead. So was Mike Calico, but even had the tough little Zuni lived, he'd sworn he wouldn't fight Corey Lane.

The only hope remaining was that Will-Ed and the other ranchers were back in the Ojos Negros from their cattle drives. They had the strength and resourcefulness, and would be much better than the merchants and other townsfolk when it came to facing conflict, but would they leave their ranches and pasture-lands unprotected to help save the town?

The thought of the cattleman made him change his plans for the second time. When he had reached the high ground between the Concho and the Rio Bronco he had wanted to ride straight for the X-Bar-7 to see Virgie first of all, but he had shunted the longing for her aside in the knowledge that he had a duty to perform. His anger at Wilson's disregard of his warning had been made a good deal worse when he realized he hadn't gained a single second for the Ojos Negros Basin by the ridiculous conference with the mayor. Now he decided he had to see Will-Ed, if he could be found.

He left the Blaine front porch depressed. But instead of mounting, he led his horse back to the livery stable in the plaza. If he didn't look at the lights of the windows on Frontera and Estancia streets, Black Springs could have been a ghost town. The silence was peaceful enough, but it was a graveyard peace.

And he was tired. It wasn't only the long frenzied rides of the last three days, but the thought of Mike Calico out there in the lava bed which had drained him until he felt there was nothing more he could do that night. He decided to go to his room at Addie Hepburn's before he collapsed completely.

The next morning, early, Jim went to the sheriff's office
and told Joe Harris what he'd seen and heard in the Black
Range. His session with Wilson Blaine the night before had
prepared him for Joe's reaction—as apathetic as he'd expected
it to be. Then he stopped at the livery and hired a horse so
his own could rest, saw Noah Strasberg driving out in his
buckboard peddler's rig, affably beginning another business
trip. He wanted to scream at the merchant to make his way
north or east, stay away from the river towns at any cost, but
something—maybe the mayor's use of the word "panic"
—prevented him.

Then he walked across the plaza to the Sacramento House
to fortify himself with breakfast. Sam was in the bar, and he
almost turned and left, but the old rancher had spotted him.

"Jim!" Sam shouted even as he settled in to the table
with him. "When did you get back? Did you find Corey?"

The editor looked around him and was grateful to find
the dining room empty. He drew a breath and started in.
When he finished, he had to turn away from Sam's tears. Sam
was facing it, all right. Here was one man who recognized
that Jim hadn't been deluded.

"Oh, God, Jim," Sam said, "I wish you hadn't told me. I
know there was no way out of it, but I sure do wish you
hadn't told me."

Jim forced himself to eat. Damn it, he had to, even if it
looked as if he was unconcerned about the things he'd just
told his friend. There was a long day ahead of him, and with
the sole exception of seeing Virgie, not a moment of it promised to be any good.

"When do you think they'll come, Jim?" Sam said.

"Don't know, Sam. Soon. Look, I *could* be dead wrong
about the whole blasted thing. Joe Harris and the mayor
think I am. Wilson says I was so scared I couldn't see straight,
and Joe says that, man and boy, he's never heard of a real
town being attacked by Apaches except maybe down in Mexico. They may be more right than I am, Sam."

He walked Sam Riordan back into the barroom before he
left and had one drink with him. Sam took two and had
started on a third before Jim finished his. There was no fun in
the way Sam drank nowadays. Perhaps it was only the fact
that Jim wasn't used to whiskey this early in the morning, but
his own insides felt as though they might turn on him at any

moment. He paid, put his hand on Sam's shoulder, and hurried out.

It wasn't cold, but it was brisk with those first winter winds which warn of worse to come. The sun was hurrying across the sky as if ashamed of its poor pale showing. A clutch of tumbleweeds had lodged against the stairs of the bandstand where Jacky and Corey had addressed the crowd, and a group of little girls were jumping rope in front of the frame structure, already rickety. Nobody had taken a paint brush to the bandstand, and the new wood of summer had grayed out to the color of streaky driftwood.

Across the way he could see old Meg Spletter coming slowly through the front door of the dry-goods store, and at his own *Chupadera County News* building Matt Hendry had stopped by to chat with son Tom. The office was closed. Tom would be late for school if he didn't finish with his father soon.

Matt could be counted on when the nightmare turned to reality, but only as another willing gun. Jim's memory of the rancher from the affair in May convinced him the elder Hendry was brave enough, but his courage would only be brought to bear if someone else did the leading. It would be up to Will-Ed, or someone like Will-Ed, to furnish that. Hendry saw him and waved and Jim waved back. He hoped Matt wouldn't want to talk now. He wanted to get out of town before so much as one other soul pooh-poohed the notion that Black Springs was in danger. It was difficult enough to keep it in his mind when he looked at the peaceful dusty plaza. He broke into a run as he crossed the square to the livery stable.

When he turned his rented horse into the entrance of Estancia Street, he saw two people. A block away, Mary Ellen Talley, bundled against the wind, was walking toward him on the wooden sidewalk jutting from the stores on the west side of Estancia. Going in the same direction as Jim, and on the same side as Mary Ellen, were the unmistakable bent back and sagging shoulders of Granby Stafford. When he was fifty feet or so from the young woman and right in front of Jim, the old merchant suddenly moved off the walk with the quick sideways shuffle of a crab and crossed the street. The editor had to rein quickly to avoid running him down. Granby didn't seem to notice how close they'd come.

Jim touched the brim of his hat to Mary Ellen as he rode
by, and was answered by a smile so sweet he forgot the
chilling wind.

He didn't look back at Granby Stafford.

"Nothing will change your mind, Will-Ed?"

"Nope. That's the way it is, McPherson. Black Springs
has made its bed, and it's just God-damned well going to
have to lie in it."

"Do you realize how many innocent people could die in
that same bed?"

"Well, now—don't you think you might be overstating
the case a mite, McPherson? The hostiles might burn a few
people out, and they might even do a little killing—but my
view always has been that folk who can't look after their
scalps and property ain't got no legitimate business in the
Territory anyway."

There seemed little point in going over yet again everything he'd seen and heard in the stronghold in the Black
Range. Martin hadn't taken any exception to a thing he'd said
the first and second times he'd told him of his meeting with
Corey Lane.

"I don't like it, either," the rancher was saying now,
"that Corey's turned renegade, but the town ain't got nobody
but itself to blame, the way they tried to hang him out to dry.
One more thing: I could tell you that I was only looking out
for my own skin, that I had my own place to look after and
ten good hands I needed here, and that's partly true. Wouldn't
be altogether fair or truthful, though. I just plain won't stand
in Corey's way if he's bent on squaring things."

There would be no budging this man.

"Is there anyone else, Will-Ed? Will any of the Sinuoso
people come in and help us?"

"You could try, I suppose." Will-Ed's smile was thin. "I
think you'll find they feel exactly the way I do. Nope, I
believe you're on your own."

Jim stood up to leave.

"Jim—" Will-Ed said then, and the use of his first name
raised for just the fraction of a second a hope Jim knew he
couldn't trust. "Something else, Jim. I ain't going to sail
under any false colors with you, *amigo*. To say I wouldn't
relish the idea of going up against Corey Lane would be

putting it way too mild. The notion of fighting Corey scares me like to die."

It was only seven miles from Will-Ed Martin's to the X-Bar-7, but they seemed interminable. The wind was rising. If winter was here in truth, and if the weather turned foul and a norther screamed its blue freeze out of the mountains, if a genuine howler of a blizzard whipped in on the shifting winds—perhaps Corey couldn't move his Apaches. *His* Apaches? Why was Jim so sure that Victorio had abrogated all command? Maybe those two strong men had come to a parting of the ways and at this very moment all the Chiricahuas and Mescaleros and the other ragtag killers who had attached themselves to Victorio and his precious Mimbreños were on the trail for Mexico. No, he could convince himself of none of it. He looked out past the *malpais* to where the Oscuras blocked the Jornada, the river valley, and the faraway Black Range. That barrier would crumple like paper before the weapons of the man who was coming toward Jim McPherson's town.

When would he get here? Strangely, and in spite of the fact that Jim knew what the outcome would have to be, he found that he wanted it to happen soon. The waiting would be unendurable.

Perhaps even now Corey was advancing on the X-Bar-7 and would find him there and kill him. Would that square accounts so Black Springs could be spared? He knew it wouldn't. As important as he himself saw the wondrous thing between Virgie Lane and Jim McPherson, it was only one tiny stone in the edifice of hate Corey Lane had constructed.

An irony struck him then. He would likely be able to save himself if he stayed at the X-Bar-7 until the town had been reduced to ash. Then, when Corey had reached the *first* great orgasm of his revenge and turned toward home to claim the rest of the things which belonged to Caesar, there still might be time for Jim McPherson to run and hide.

He wondered how strong his will to live at any cost was. It wasn't strong enough for that. He knew he would have no will to live if life excluded Virgie Lane.

"Jim!"
She rushed into his outstretched arms, and they were

halfway through a kiss before he realized Alicia could be watching them from somewhere. He didn't care. They pressed against each other until they couldn't breathe.

He was still dazed when they finally broke apart and she led him toward the sitting-room. Alicia was on the couch, with her sewing. She looked smaller than he remembered her.

"Mr. McPherson," she said, "I'm glad you've come back safely."

"I had to, Mrs. Lane. I made someone a promise before I left."

"You saw my son?"

"Yes, I did."

"And . . . ?"

"He'll be back, Mrs. Lane, but in nothing like the way any of us expect . . . or want."

He told her then, sure at first that she would evidence the same disbelief as Wilson Blaine and cynical Joe Harris, but coupled also with anger. Neither appeared. She heard all his news without one tremor in that icy impassive face. Only near the end, when he recounted what had happened to Mike Calico, did she break her frozen silence, and then only by an almost inaudible gasp for breath.

When he finished, she stood up, said, "Thank you, Mr. McPherson," and left the room without a backward glance.

He looked at Virgie and saw her grief.

"I can't help it, Jim," she said. "You must remember I've lived with Corey for a lot of years. There's still a little something left, I'm afraid. It has nothing to do with us. You understand, don't you, Jim?"

"Yes, Virgie. I understand." He wondered if he did.

"When will he come, Jim?"

"I don't know, Virgie. Mike guessed ten days. Three are gone. When the warriors who killed Mike report back that I got away, they'll assume we've sent for help, and that might bring them in a hurry. It surely won't change Corey's mind."

"What are you going to do?"

He shrugged. Then he told her of the mayor's complacent idiocy and of Will-Ed's flat refusal to rally the ranchers to the rescue of the town and of his despair of finding anyone to lead in its defense.

"One thing you must do quickly, Virgie," he said. "You've

got to get little Corey out here with you. Surely Corey won't let them near the X-Bar-7."

She nodded. "But that doesn't answer my question about you."

"I'll stay in Black Springs. I've got to, Virgie."

There was panic in her eyes. "Must you, Jim? From what you've said, you've done more than enough for the people there. Why don't you come here with little Corey? Corey doesn't know about us yet. We can face that when we have to."

"Oh, but he *does* know, Virgie."

"What . . . ?"

"I told him. I *had* to. Suddenly there was just no way I could burden you with that."

Twice she tried to speak, but the words choked her. She shook her head violently and the rich black hair swung back and forth behind the graceful neck.

"Jim!" she said finally, her voice teetering on the edge of hysteria. "You promised. Don't you realize the risk you took? It's exactly what I didn't want."

"I think he took it well, Virgie."

"But he could have killed you!"

She stood up and walked to the fireplace. He couldn't see her face, but her head was tilted back so she could stare up at the crossed lance and shield. He wondered what she saw there. She stood that way, absolutely motionless, for no more than a minute, but it was a minute stretched out forever. When she turned to him, the fright and terror were gone. He wanted to go to her, take her in his arms as before, but something told him this was not the moment—he had better wait.

"Jim," she said, her voice so low he had to strain to hear it, "what I've loved about you—and still do—is the quietness of your courage. I've loved you because you didn't seem to have to prove your worth. God knows, I've had enough of heroes. I don't want a man who feels he has to slash at life with a naked sword.

"*I* wanted to be the one to tell Corey. I wanted not only to tell him about us, I wanted to tell him about him and me. Perhaps it's small of me, but I wanted a bit of my own back again. I know what you did you did for love of me, but I wanted to free *myself*." She walked to him then, bent over,

placed her hands on his cheeks, and kissed him. Then she
straightened up. "I don't suppose there's any way I can get
you out of Black Springs until this is over?"

If only he could bring himself to lie. "Look, I won't be a
hero if I can help it. I'll try *not* to be a hero. But I've got to
stay."

"Yes," she said, "I was afraid of that."

He was on his way back to town before he realized he
hadn't seen a sign of Alicia since she thanked him and left the
room. It hardly mattered. He had more than enough to
occupy him without considering the problems she now had.

Something, it seemed to him, had gone terribly wrong
between him and Virgie. That she still loved him seemed
more than certain. The embrace with which they'd parted
was as warmly and freely given as the one which had welcomed him. Her body had been as softly insistent as before,
and her lips had made even stronger promises than ever. But
the look in her eyes when they said goodbye had been an
enigma. He knew now that her cool gracious self-control was
a mask—to hide the pain. Over the years she must have
sustained wounds which had come close to killing her, and
only with the decision she had made for herself had they
begun to heal. And he—stupidly—had ripped them open
again with his self-serving rashness.

Was he begging the question if he chalked this up as one
more thing to lay at Corey's feet? Would it be only making
excuses for himself? Was it delusion to think the tall man had
some mystic power to induce foolhardiness in those who
stood against him?

He got out a special broadside telling the story of his and
Mike's journey to the Black Range, with his judgment of
Corey Lane's and Victorio's intentions. For a day arguments
laced with disbelieving laughter raged across the plaza, in the
stores, and, Jim imagined, in the homes of Black Springs.
People stared at him on the street, but no one asked him for
any further information, and, except for loyal Sam (who didn't
mention the subject), his occasional forays into the Sacramento bar found him drinking by himself, clearly and deliberately ostracized. Even young Tom Hendry, who had shown

something near worship for him in the months they had worked together, seemed uneasy with him.

Strangely enough, Addie Hepburn believed him, but perhaps that was only because of the affection she knew her brother Sam had for him. If she hadn't had such a grim determined look on her face, he would have laughed when on the second morning after his ride to Will-Ed Martin's and his visit at the X-Bar-7, she appeared in the kitchen with her late husband's gunbelt strapped beneath her apron. He smiled ruefully to think his only real allies were a doddering but fine old man and a widow lady of more than sixty years.

He wasn't idle. Before he'd said goodbye to Virgie he had dared indulge himself in one splurge of masculinity. Smiling but deadly serious, he had forbidden her to come to town for little Corey. "I'll bring him out or have Tom do it," he'd told her, and she had agreed without protest. He got the boy from Meg Spletter's himself, but, in what he readily admitted was abject cowardice, asked Tom to take him to the ranch. He didn't want questions from the youngster about his father.

A trip to two of the ranches in the Sinuoso country proved as abortive as the one to see Will-Ed, if for different reasons. The two cattlemen hadn't gotten home from their drives yet.

He put Addie to work discovering who in her memory, or by questioning among the men in Black Springs, had been in the Civil War either in the Territory or before coming to it, or anyone with any real fighting experience whatsoever. She found three who had been in uniform but had never heard a shot fired. Thinking bitterly that Puckett's Corners—no bigger than Black Springs—could boast a dozen veterans who'd seen action, he completely forgot that the conflict here had been a small one, and that the town had been but a quarter of its present size in the early Sixties.

And he was appalled when he found Wilson Blaine hadn't yet dispatched a messenger to Santa Fe.

"There will *be* no Apache attack on Black Springs, Mr. McPherson," Wilson said, smiling with uneasy condescension. "Consequently there will be no need to call for help—and make us a laughingstock."

Jim could have struck the fat-faced little jackass. But he did rant and rave until he extracted a grudging promise that

Wilson would send a guarded message of his own, and Jim's broadside, on the next stage north—the next day. As he left the mayor's office, he looked longingly up Frontera Street to where the gaunt naked telegraph poles made the start of their northward march. If only there had been wires draped across them, Corey would cut them without a doubt, but at least there might then be a chance that someone at the other end, hearing nothing, might divine the fact that something was amiss in Chupadera County. He wondered if there was such a thing as a heliograph in town . . . and someone with the skill to run it . . . and if it could be carried high enough on Cuchillo Peak to beam its signals . . . and if there would be anybody out there in all that empty vastness to *see* their pathetic blinking call for help.

Suddenly, and for the first time, he prayed that Wilson would be proved right. It wouldn't matter that he, McPherson, would look such a fool that Black Springs wouldn't tolerate him any more.

The northbound stage was back at its loading-place in front of the Sacramento House less than three hours after it left, the horses foaming and the passengers inside shaken, bruised, and terrified.

"*Apaches!*" Clinton Wade, the driver, shouted at the crowd which gathered around him as he hit the ground. Jim had sprinted across the plaza when he'd seen the coach's unexpected return. "Twenty or thirty of them!" Clinton said as soon as he caught his breath. "Perched like buzzards on the rocks at Stone Creek Pass. I sure thought it was all over with, but the only shooting they did was in the air. I turned my outfit around and whipped hell out of the team all the way back to Black Springs. They followed us for a while, at a distance, kind of like they was *herding* us. Can't explain it, but I got the idea they didn't want nothing happening to us. Like they wanted us back in town. They plain left us, disappeared, about three miles north."

"Clinton"—it was Wilson Blaine, who had reached the scene shortly after Jim—"if they weren't actually shooting at you, don't you suppose you could have made it through?"

"No, mayor, I sure don't!" Clinton sounded exasperated. "These bucks was stripped for fighting. They sure wasn't just looking for smokes or liquor. Anyway, I had passengers to think of, not to mention this old hide of mine. The company ain't about to issue me a new one."

"Well, of course, this is serious," Wilson said. He seemed to be avoiding a look at Jim. "But it doesn't necessarily mean war."

Jim could stand no more. "God damn it, Wilson! What's it going to take to wake you up? A massacre?"

In the knot of citizens surrounding the driver he saw half a dozen of the faces which had been turned away from him the past two days. By God, he'd gotten their attention—at last.

He didn't wait to hear any more. If Corey had been with the war party which had blocked Clinton's way, the stage-driver would have said so no later than his second word. That the Indians on the north road were indeed Victorio's, though, Jim was positive.

Joe Harris had left the crowd around Clinton and walked across the plaza to the sheriff's office, and Jim followed him.

"Well, Joe?"

"Yeah, I heard. Just one war-party, though—if it *is* a war-party."

"We can't get a message north, apparently."

"Any bright ideas, Jim?"

"How about Russell up on the Mescalero? Maybe *he* could alert Fort Stanton."

"I'll be in the saddle in fifteen minutes."

"No," Jim said, "better send somebody. You might be needed here. Soon."

"Makes sense."

"And, Joe—you'd better get started rounding up any man in town who's got a gun and knows anything about its use."

"Right."

Jim was back in his office before he realized he had actually been giving orders.

The first group of refugees arrived in Black Springs the next morning, half an hour after sunrise, and by noon three more bunches had straggled into town. The story was almost the same in every case.

The bedraggled people, still deep in shock, were all from small homesteads to the northwest or west of Black Springs.

In each attack the Apaches had howled in, driving off livestock and burning the home and outbuildings to the ground. They had dug the survivors out of root cellars and adobes suddenly turned to ovens, chased them into the cottonwood *bosques*, and then rounded them up like cattle. With wild gestures, and with rifle muzzles used like goads, they'd sent them all off on the roads leading into Black Springs.

Some of the older hands in town, who had lived through the wars with Cochise and Mangas Coloradas, shook their heads in amazement to find that, except for one farmer and his son who had exhibited stubborn courage and died in the flames of their pitiful mud shack while their women ran, the Indians hadn't harmed a soul.

Glad as he was that the nineteen men, women, and children were unscratched, Jim worried about Black Springs' reaction to this unexpected counterfeit mercy.

"Maybe they don't mean to raise a whole *lot* of hell," one man said.

"Sure," another spoke up. "Let them have the cattle and horses. We ought to gather in all the people in the county and just sit tight. The Army ought to be coming on the double anyway."

Jim just listened. No sense in telling the man that it would take the better part of another day before any troops could even make a start. He searched the sky to the west.

The brisk winds of the past two days had broken their promise and had blown themselves to nothing without bringing heavy weather. The sun was a brilliant disk in a sky of that same deep turquoise blue which had gladdened his heart so many times in the past long year. Now he hated it.

In the middle of the afternoon Joe Harris' man came galloping into the plaza with the news that the Apaches had covered all the trails leading up to Russell's agency.

"A rabbit might make it through their lookouts," he said, "but I ain't no rabbit. Not that I wasn't as scared as one."

Jim looked at Joe. The acting sheriff was worried now, and, sorry as he felt for him, Jim was gratified that he certainly wouldn't have to argue with Harris any longer about the seriousness of the situation.

"Did you get close to them?" he asked the exhausted rider.

"Sure did. About a dozen of them rode into the trail right where it fords the Rio Bronco. Came from nowhere.

Thought I was a goner, but all they did was sit their ponies, grinning like coyotes. Don't care much for Apaches anyhow, but *grinning*? Gave me the creeps, I'll tell you."

"Wonder what the hell they're up to?" Joe Harris seemed to be talking to himself. He turned to Jim. "Now, don't get excited, Jim," he said. "I ain't a doubter any more, but this sure ain't usual Apache carrying-on." He shook his head.

It *was* puzzling, on the surface. Jim was silent. In spite of the ready way he'd given orders to the acting sheriff the afternoon before, he didn't want to put his newfound credibility at risk by posing as an authority on the behavior of hostile Indians. But it wasn't really Indians he was thinking of. Of course their "carrying-on" wasn't usual. These aberrations bore the unmistakable imprint of Corey Lane. He felt they were only the first signals the renegade was sending in. That there would be more and deadlier messages soon, he had no doubt.

"Joe," he said quietly, "how about what we discussed yesterday? Have you started building a defense force?"

"Maybe I dragged my feet on that a little, Jim. I'll have them at the bandstand in the plaza by four o'clock."

"One more thing, Joe." Jim nodded at Harris' rider. "Maybe you'd better have Luke here go up and see Eloy Montoya's people on the Concho when he's had a little rest. I don't know if we could pry them away from their valley, but if we could, it would double the men we'd have here to make a fight of it."

Facing things squarely, he knew they didn't have any hope at all that Luke could make it up to the Rio Concho. Corey would have already blocked that route, too. But it had to be tried, in the event that Black Springs needed any more convincing.

He went to the Sacramento to look for Sam. The bleary blue eyes told him Sam must have spent the whole day leaning on the bar.

"Corey's out there somewhere, ain't he, Jim?"

"Yes, I think so, Sam." Hell, he *knew* so.

"He's coming in to get every last one of us, isn't he?"

"I don't know, Sam. I really don't." In the long run the lie wouldn't hurt a bit. Not with Sam. He would be more truthful with the others—when and if they asked.

"I realize I ain't worth much now," Sam was saying, "but

I'll be ready to fight when the time comes, Jim. It will break my heart—but I'll stand with these people here."

Jim bought Sam a bottle. When he checked his watch, he saw it was time for Joe Harris' meeting in the plaza.

Out in the slanting afternoon sunlight he saw that three more families of refugees had arrived in town. He recognized one of them, from a tiny cattle spread southwest of Black Springs, just a few miles beyond the Bronco run-out. He'd passed the place on his way in from the *malpais* when he'd left Mike Calico. He didn't have to listen to the conversation to know they had been driven in, herded, exactly as had all the others. Corey and his warriors (why couldn't he picture Victorio at the board in this macabre game?) had almost closed the ring.

At first glance, the display of weapons carried by the men assembling at the bandstand was encouraging, impressive, but on closer inspection he saw the same feeble armament which had greeted Corey the day of the Sinuoso row. His mind went back with despair to the stacks of rifles he had seen in the *ranchería*.

And it wasn't only the way they were armed. The resolute fire they had shown that day in May (at least until Corey had quenched it) was lamentably missing. Perhaps it was because it was Mayor Wilson Blaine standing in front of them and not tough Granby Stafford (the first Granby Stafford he had known, not the recent one) and likable but incapable Joe Harris instead of cool Eloy Montoya of the Rio Concho. What would make these men fight? Somebody would have to find the answer.

On the credit side, there were a lot of them. Going by fours, he totaled eighty before his counting became confused, and more were coming through the Estancia and Frontera entrances to the plaza. By scraping the barrel they could very nearly match in numbers if not in martial skill the hordes Corey led. It gave them a chance—if the will was there.

This time their women were with them, too. They lined the sides of the plaza as they had the night of the election rally. None of them pushed forward this time, though. His heart went out to the men who would have to do the fighting. Some few swaggered; all looked scared. Wilson mounted the bandstand, apparently about to speak. He didn't seem to be readying his usual histrionics. Calmer, steadier than Jim would have dreamed, he was about to begin any number of times, but new arrivals kept enlarging the throng and he waited patiently. Somehow he looked bigger than usual.

Then Jim saw him looking out over the heads of the crowd with an expression of pure horror on his face.

A man on horseback was coming into the plaza. He was leaning forward in the saddle with his arms dangling down the side of his horse's neck. On second look Jim could see they weren't actually dangling; they were tied beneath the animal's neck, as his feet were under the belly. He was hatless, and his hair and clothes were soaked dark with blood.

The crowd parted, making a pathway to the bandstand, and the horse slowly carried its burden to where Joe Harris stood by the steps. Wilson Blaine collapsed in a heap on the platform above the acting sheriff's head. Jim rushed from the veranda of the hotel and reached the foot of the bandstand stairs just as Joe was untying the man's hands and feet. He helped Harris ease the wounded man from the saddle. When the man was down and on his back in the caliche, Jim knew him as one of Will-Ed Martin's hands, one of the good fighters in the force Mike Calico and Corey had led through the *malpais* to take Victorio's stronghold on the flank in the Oscuras. He was breathing, barely. His chest was such a swamp of blood Jim could hardly make out the crude bandaging someone other than the man himself must have done. A canteen came out of the crowd, and Joe Harris took it and knelt beside the prostrate figure, cradling the gory head in the crook of an awkwardly gentle arm. He poured a few drops on lips caked with dried blood, and the man seemed to sense it. He opened his eyes and then his mouth. He drank surprisingly deeply for a man who looked so weak.

Wilson had made a recovery of sorts and was now down from the bandstand, at Jim's side in the group closest to Will-Ed's man.

Incredibly, the man on the ground began to recover, too. The gulps of water he had taken had produced a minor miracle. Amazed, Jim saw he wanted to talk. He knelt beside him. "Don't try now," he said. "We'll get the doctor right away."

"Can't wait. Doctor won't do no good nohow. Ain't in pain any more anyway."

"What happened, Nate?" Joe Harris asked.

"They came just before sun-up. Fifty, sixty, maybe more. We fought them hard till almost noon. Reckon we got a dozen or more of them. They got every one of us."

"Will-Ed?" Jim said.

"Yep. It was him they was really after. They did some crazy things trying to get Will-Ed in the early going. That's what made it so easy for us—for a while."

"And Mrs. Martin?"

"Her, too. And the Mex houseman, Porfirio . . . and the maid. Everybody. Only let me live to bring the word, I guess. Them red bastards wanted to kill me, too. Corey wouldn't let them."

"Corey?" Wilson Blaine asked. *"Corey Lane?"*

"Yeah. I didn't even know it was him until he wrapped me up like this—tied me on my horse. Looked like an Apache. Led me himself close to town. Tried to talk to him until I just passed out, but he wasn't having none of it."

Nate closed his eyes. He still breathed, but his shattered chest rose and fell more weakly every time he filled his lungs. It wouldn't take long now.

Jim McPherson realized that Corey had guessed how they would think. He knew someone would look to Will-Ed Martin for leadership. What he didn't know was that the rancher wouldn't give it. The bloody killings were as useless as they were tragic.

But now the savage knife was out, and even Wilson Blaine must know it.

Did this mean strikes at the other ranches, too? If the Sinuoso cattlemen and the others farther down in the basin had come in, their combined strength would have tipped things in Black Springs' favor. But now there was no longer a Will-Ed Martin to rally them, even if they still had time. Corey and Victorio could pick off each of the widely scattered ranches at their leisure.

The other ranches? Jim leaned over the dying man. He hated to disturb Nate again, whose eyes were closed and who seemed to be in the last restful moments—but he had to ask.

"Could you see how things were at the X-Bar-7 when you passed there, Nate?"

The eyes opened part way. "I thought maybe that's where Corey was taking me, but he didn't. They're fine there, far as I could tell."

* * *

The meeting after supper was in Wilson Blaine's office. Joe Harris reported that he had posted sentries selected by lot at all the entrances to town and on any high ground overlooking the approaches easiest to come through on horseback.

"Don't think they'll attack at night," Joe said. "Not that I hold entirely with the idea that Indians never do, but they don't know their way in and out of town."

"Corey does," Matt Hendry said.

"Sure, but one man can only lead a small bunch of them. We could deal with that."

There were other new faces at the meeting. Dan Stone, his family, and the three riders on his small ranch near Bronco Canyon had made it out just ahead of a whooping war-party. The brash young Stone was more subdued than Jim remembered him from the adventure in the Oscuras, quietly grateful he had been able to get his wife and infant son out of his log home before it became a torch.

If Dan was subdued, one other man, sitting alone in a corner, was a Sphinx. Granby Stafford, half-hidden in the shadows, looked like a strange meld of Banquo's ghost and specter-ridden Macbeth himself. He hadn't spoken a word from the time they all gathered, barely nodding in reply to the others' greetings.

Harris spread a map of Black Springs and another of Chupadera County on the mayor's desk. On the county map ominous black crosses marked the scene of each of the Apaches' known attacks and appearances. The circle was complete. There could have been more marks. These were the ones where survivors had managed to bring the news to town.

"For God's sakes!" Wilson Blaine said. "He must have a thousand men out there to blanket so much territory!"

"No," Jim said. "I know how many Mike Calico and I saw in the Black Range. Even if we were wrong, and even if he's picked up a lot more new recruits, he can't possibly have three hundred warriors." He bit his tongue then. He hadn't intended to say a word more than necessary now that they all knew the danger.

"But look at the evidence, McPherson," Wilson said.

"That's just generalship—and damned hard riding. Joe, could you mark in the approximate time of each of these attacks?"

The acting sheriff took the stub of a pencil from his shirt pocket and busied himself over the map. In a minute he looked up at the others. "McPherson's right. They been riding in a big circle around Black Springs. I'd guess they've dropped a permanent guard on the road up to the Mescalero and more at Stone Creek Pass—them being the only two ways we got of sending for help."

"That's got to weaken their main force a little," Wilson said. There was a different tone in the fussy little mayor's voice. If *he* could shape up and face things like a man, there might yet be hope.

"How many men did you muster this afternoon, Joe?" Dan Stone asked.

"Hundred and seventy-six with weapons, counting kids and oldsters. Eighty-two without."

"Well, at least in numbers it's pretty much of a stand-off. Whether they'll fight or not is something else. The Apaches will."

The silence was gloomy—and total.

"We've got to have a plan," Wilson said at last. "And a *man*, one man."

Jim looked around him: Joe, Matt Hendry, Dan Stone and the bald leathery foreman he'd brought to the meeting with him, Kelly the liveryman, old Dr. Lester Royston, the brutal-looking but meek and gentlemanly blacksmith Lathrop, red-faced Sam Riordan still half in the clutches of this afternoon's whiskey, Wilson Blaine—and the wraith indistinguishable from the shadows in the corner, Granby Stafford.

It was laughable to think that one of these could match wits and leadership and fighting skills with Corey Lane. Jim was so intent on studying the worried look on each face he was only half aware that, to a man, they were studying him. That he was undergoing a strange examination didn't dawn on him until he heard himself whispering, "No . . . no . . ."

"Mr. McPherson," Wilson Blaine was saying, "if you will accept the post, I am prepared to appoint you Commissioner of the Public Defense."

Even the whispered "No" died in his dry throat. Somehow he did manage to speak, and he heard himself say, "No, mayor, not me. I have far less competence in military things than almost anybody in this room."

"That may be, Mr. McPherson. But you've seen the

enemy. You recognized his intentions when all the rest of us were willing to ignore the facts. You have organizing abilities. And you have our confidence."

He realized that the others present were voicing their agreement—loudly. Only one man was silent, Granby, still a brooding haunt in his dark corner.

"Well, Mr. McPherson," Wilson asked, "will you be our commander? You'll have absolute authority. I guarantee it."

Jim looked at the circle of men once more.

"Yes," he said.

Almost all that night he rode the town and its outskirts with Joe Harris. Sam tagged along, and even though Jim would much have preferred the old-timer comfortable back at the Sacramento or at his sister's, he didn't have the heart to dismiss him. Gradually he grew at ease with the deference Joe showed his every suggestion and his every voiced thought.

A full moon revealed an entirely different town from the one he'd thought he knew, and the Chupadera County which abutted on Black Springs suddenly seemed as alien as the surface of that same bright moon. The gently rounded *lomas* which rolled away to the lower reaches of Cuchillo Peak, and whose bosomy billows had always signaled ease, comfort, and heart-warming beauty, were now dark threatening hiding-places, and the buildings of his town looked in the moonlight more like coffins than homes or stores.

Once he laughed aloud. It brought a puzzled look from Joe. Commissioner of the Public Defense! God bless and keep Wilson Blaine. Even when he finally capitulated and allowed that the peril was palpable and real, the last thing to leave the funny little mayor was his pomposity. Commissioner of the Public Defense indeed! He was more likely to be the Grand Architect of Defeat and Death. He didn't enlighten Joe Harris about the laugh.

"You were absolutely right about one thing, Joe," he said suddenly, "they will not attack at night." It surprised him when he said it. He had nothing to go on to utter such a statement in such sure tones. Or did he? Yes. He was right and he knew it, and he knew why he was right.

Corey wouldn't want to attack at night, never mind Apache custom. He would want to see every bit of the misery and suffering his warriors would inflict. The picture Jim had

formed of Corey in the *ranchería* was becoming even clearer
with time and distance. The nobility he had almost come to
take for granted Jim could see was submerged now in an
almost insane need for vengeance. Everything pointed to it.
The way the stage had been turned back at the pass; the
forbearance of the war-parties on the road up to Russell's
agency and in the attacks on the farms and homesteads—
everything except the slaughter of Will-Ed's people (and that
was easy to figure out, too), everything had been designed to
create as huge a charnel house as possible in the town of
Black Springs. They were all to die here under Corey's eyes.
Even now, after holding them back, he was probably whip-
ping his fighting men to a blood lust as deep and dark as any
in Apache warfare.

As before, Jim wondered where Victorio stood in all of
this.

None of these thoughts, he knew, could be voiced to
Harris, Blaine, or any of the others—not even Sam. Beyond
the statement of his conviction that the enemy would make
no move on them at night, he said very little to Joe until they
were back in the sheriff's office.

He stood at the door, looking out over the wagons and
carts parked in the plaza, and at the bodies huddled in lumpy
bedrolls on the ground itself. Frosted breath was rising into
the moonlight from the sleepers. Doubtless there would be
more of these refugees not long after dawn. It must be the
rational side of Corey's plan to crowd as many more eaters of
food and drinkers of water into Black Springs as possible
before he began however many assaults it would take to kill
them all. He would want to stretch their nerves like bow-
strings. Well, none of these shapes Jim looked at would suffer
the pangs of thirst or hunger very long before they died.
Somewhere a baby cried. That one might live. He recalled
with a shudder the two tormented captive girls in the Apache
camp.

He turned to Joe Harris. "We're going to have to give up
a large part of the town, Joe, if we're to have any chance at
all."

The sheriff nodded. "What have you got in mind, Jim?"
he said.

"Well, first thing, we've got to shrink the perimeter we
have to defend. I propose to turn the plaza and the buildings

face on it into a fort. There would only be the Estancia and
Frontera entrances to block off—whatever way we could. If
we post our lookouts on the roof of the Sacramento, along
with teams of the best riflemen, we can pretty much command the rest of the town, visually anyway.

"The buildings on the plaza are all commercial places
with nobody living in them, so they should house just about
the entire population, at least those not actively guarding or
fighting. We'll feed people out of a community mess we'll set
up in the Sacramento kitchen. Less waste that way. Of course
we'll have to commandeer all the foodstuffs in town. Put
Addie Hepburn in charge of it, if you can get the old girl to
leave that precious house of hers.

"Put someone else in charge of rounding up every barrel
and bucket that can hold water. Get a good supply into the
News office and lock it up. Make Tom Hendry water boy. Not
a drop of water we store in the *News* leaves there without a
written note from you or me. That's our last-resort water. See
that the Sacramento is stocked, too, and then put every other
container on the rooftops around the plaza. They'll try to
burn us."

He watched Joe as he talked, looking for signs that he'd
revealed his own astonishment at hearing himself talk this
way, with a deceptive crispness putting a sharp edge on his
words.

"The jail here," he went on, "will make a good arsenal.
Comb the town for every cartridge, every ball for the old
muskets, every keg—*hell*, every canister of powder. Get all
the dynamite you can find at Granby Stafford's and Noah
Strasberg's and anyplace else you can locate a stick of it. And
find me the best man in Black Springs for handling explo-
sives. Maybe he can rig us some kind of a minefield just
outside our lines.

"Take the best horses you can fit comfortably into the
stalls at Kelly's Livery and turn the others loose. We aren't
going anywhere for a while, and maybe the Apaches will busy
themselves for a little chasing the free ones down. Save a few
places at the livery for cows so we'll have milk for the children.

"You can call in the men you've sent out as scouts and
the ones you posted as sentries. We can't risk losing even one
of them before the real fighting starts."

There was more, lots more. The random plans which had

raced through his brain during his night ride with Harris were beginning to slow a little so he could catch them and put them in their place. He went over with Joe the maps the acting sheriff had brought from the mayor's office, and after they marked out the physical dimensions of the citadel forced on them by necessity, they divided the available men into combat units and tossed names back and forth as to who the leaders would have to be. "I want *you* near me all the time, Joe," he said.

He was exhausted when they finished, but there was still one more thing he felt needed saying.

"We'll have our biggest trouble, Joe, when the edge of town starts to burn. People might panic when they see the homes they slaved to build going up in flames. Some of them might try to go to them. We can't permit it. We'll have to stop them, even if it means threatening to shoot them. I'll tell them that when Wilson gets the word out I'm in charge."

When Harris left to start the tasks they'd agreed on, he put his head on the sheriff's desk and slept. When Joe awoke him two hours later as planned, and to take his own turn, Jim uttered a silent prayer of gratitude that he hadn't dreamed at all. He even wanted to forgo visions of Virgie until this was over. It was a blessing she hadn't come to him during the vulnerability of sleep. Her face was difficult enough to cope with during his waking moments.

The first attack came right after the noon meal, during a lull in the building of the barricades across the two openings to the plaza. It wasn't a serious assault, and Jim knew it wouldn't be when he saw only a score of warriors dismounting cautiously far down Estancia Street to advance on foot. Corey wasn't with them. Reassured by the watchers on the roof of the hotel that no other parties had entered town by any of the other routes, he'd gone to the half-finished bulwark for a closer look at the action.

The leader of the small force turned out to be the same Opera Hat he'd seen that day from the *malpais*. He hadn't caught sight of the man in the *ranchería* and had forgotten him till now.

The firing from the roof of the Sacramento was marvelously disciplined, held off until the last possible moment by Dan Stone, who was directing it, and proved more effective than Jim would have dared to hope. He could see two of the Apaches hit. A companion helped one back down Estancia Street toward the horses. Another, obviously in great pain, managed to make it by himself. Jim wasn't positive, but he thought he saw Opera Hat's body jerk from the impact of a bullet, too. In seconds all that remained of the marauders was a veil of caliche dust.

Glad cheering broke across the plaza, and Jim reflected ruefully that it was the greatest crescendo of sound he had heard in the old square since Corey had returned with Major Lattner from escorting the captives up to the Mescalero— some of them probably the very braves who had just retreated.

The exultation of victory bothered him. This foray was meaningless, just a probe, and perhaps he should mount the bandstand and tell them so, sober them again as he had with his short speech before lunch, when he'd told them what he'd told Joe Harris earlier about shooting anyone who tried to leave their makeshift fort. He decided against it. It might very well be the last thing any of them ever had to cheer about.

He was satisfied things were under control for the time being. When the column of smoke far down Estancia Street rose high enough to be seen in the plaza, there was some consternation and weeping among men and women whose homes were down that way, but none of them made a move.

A check of the barricade and of the sharpshooters on the Sacramento roof didn't turn up a single scratch.

They completed the breastworks across the two streets by suppertime, and except for the few folk worried about their houses and possessions, a mood of near-holiday gaiety prevailed across the plaza, on the roofs, and in the sleeping-quarters.

Jim ate with his lieutenants and Wilson Blaine in the Sacramento dining room. It was the same table he had shared with Corey, Virgie, Alicia, Sam Riordan, and the Martins. There was no wine on this occasion, although some of the armed men tearing into their food as if it was their last meal had whiskey bottles beside their plates.

"We do have one small chance of getting help," Matt Hendry said.

"What's that?" Joe Harris asked.

"When the stage don't make it into the stops up north,

maybe somebody will tumble to the fact that things ain't quite right down here."

"Don't count on it," Dan Stone said. "That northbound coach is two-three days late more often than it's on schedule. And even if somebody *does* wonder about it, they'd most likely send a patrol so small the Apaches would chew them up and spit them out."

Matt looked as if he was sorry he'd brought it up.

That night the sky was crystal clear and, if anything, the moon a shade brighter than during Jim's ride with Joe. If bad weather wasn't on its way to do its share, at least the visibility was good. He was still certain Corey wouldn't come in at night, but . . .

He went up to the roof of the Sacramento House and looked over the whole town. The watchfires of the Apache camp winked evilly at him from the high-ground watershed between the Concho and the Bronco. He strained to peer into the moon-washed swales beyond the mesa in the foolish hope he could somehow extend his vision to include the X-Bar-7. Nothing. Had Corey gone there yet? Would it even matter to Jim McPherson at this time tomorrow, or a day or two past that at the very most? He prayed he would have another dreamless night.

There was no cheering, no exulting either, during or after the attacks which began at dawn.

They came from six directions, and by ten it looked as if every house on the circumference of Black Springs was ablaze. The billowing smoke made it difficult to spot the Apaches in the brief time it took them to break through it and hide in the buildings nearest the ones which enclosed the plaza. Jim had wondered at first why they didn't torch everything they could reach. Now he saw they needed the cover of the unburned homes and sheds. He took himself to task for lacking the sense to fire them himself, creating a barren waste the attackers would have to cross under a withering fusillade. Well, if the townspeople got through this day, he would take care of that tonight. It would make trouble, particularly if the defenders had been misled into thinking they were winning, but he could face that when it came.

"Sure don't fight like any Apaches I remember," Joe Harris said. "Even Cochise and Mangas could never get their damned red devils to follow orders like real soldiers the way these bucks are doing."

"That's Corey, all right," Sam Riordan said.

Sam had been a wonder. It seemed to take him hours to reload his Navy Colt every time he emptied it, but he did it calmly and coolly, hardly taking the trouble to duck for cover as he worked. Jim wondered why Sam hadn't used the Winchester more frequently. Surely its accuracy and speed would stand the old rancher in better stead than the unwieldy slow-firing handgun. When he saw how low his own supply of ammunition was getting, he understood. It was the same with Dan Stone's men on the rooftop, with the ones Matt Hendry was commanding above the livery stable, and with the teams of riflemen at both barricades. The repeating rifles they had appropriated from the Strasberg storehouse were using up ammunition at a frightening rate. If things kept up this way for the rest of the day, and if the Apaches mounted more full-scale assaults tomorrow, tomorrow's noon would find them down to the Sharps and Hawkens and the even more ancient muzzle-loaders. Their only hope then would be that the enemy wouldn't see the trip wires running to the rudimentary land-mines Lathrop had rigged with the dynamite.

Surprisingly, Black Springs casualties had been light. By noon only six men had died and seventeen had taken wounds. Joe Harris had been nicked in the upper arm—his left one, fortunately. Wilson Blaine had turned his ankle carrying water to the crew at the Frontera breastworks. Jim smiled when the little man put a brave face on it and didn't complain at all, although it was obvious he suffered agonizing pain as he limped about his duties.

In his trips to the hotel roof and the top of the livery stable Jim looked in vain for Corey Lane. Perhaps the editor was relying too heavily on his growing conviction that until Corey showed his face the final rush would not begin. But he felt he was right. Corey would come in for the kill, and not before.

The Apaches withdrew at one o'clock. Was it too much to hope that they were calling it a day? That they had suffered a greater number of dead and wounded was clear from the bodies near the burning buildings, the men crawling off to die and the others being hauled away or helped. Some of their weapons were scattered in the open spaces in

front of the fires, and Jim had to veto a suggestion by one of
Dan Stones's ranch hands that they go out and get them. It
would mean dismantling Lathrop's explosive charges, and,
besides, they now were almost at the point where they would
have more guns than they had cartridges with which to stoke
them.

From the rooftop Jim saw that the Indians hadn't retreated far, certainly not all the way back to their encampment, whose fires he had watched the night before. He
thought they would come one more time today. Well, the
defenders could repel another attack as successfully as they
had the ones so far. After that . . . ?

They did come again, and with more unleashed fury than
before. He was sure he saw Victorio once, sitting his horse
atop a little knoll no more than half a mile away. With smoke
drifting across Jim's line of sight from several different places,
the Mimbreño chief looked ghostly. He seemed more ob-
server than combatant. In his hand there appeared to be a
long, brightly feathered lance. Jim thought of the spading-
fork which had seemed to become a lance like this one that
day in the Mescalero.

The second series of attacks was shorter than the first,
but far more damaging. Matt Hendry fell, pierced through
the upper lung. He would make it, Dr. Royston said when Jim
checked the wounded in the hospital set up in the dry-goods
store. Lathrop wouldn't. It was hard to believe that the tiny
hole in his belly Jim had seen when silent Granby Stafford—
who was working with the doctor and his half-dozen ladies—
pulled the sheet back could kill so big a man.

A dozen others didn't get as far as the dry-goods store.
They—among them the Luke who had tried to make it up to
the agency for Russell's help—were dead before they were
carried down from the rooftops or away from the barricades
where they had fought so hard. Three more of those wounded
in the morning had died, too. Soon Jim must decide what
should be done with the more than twenty bodies already
crowding the barroom of the Sacramento.

Clouds rolled in with the sunset, not thick enough to
promise any worsening of the weather, but an overcast which
would blank out the moon that had risen in the east even
before the day had faded. Jim made the rounds of the sentry

posts before he went to supper. With Matt Hendry in the hospital, there was an empty seat at table—two, as a matter of fact: he'd sent Joe Harris to check the fighting stations to see how the ammunition was holding out. The acting sheriff arrived, out of breath, before they were fairly started.

"Well, Joe?" Jim asked.

Harris looked doubtful, reluctant, as he eyed the rest of the seated men.

"Spill it, Joe," Jim said, "no matter how bad it is. No secrets here."

"Well, it's bad, sure enough," Joe said. "If they come tomorrow the way they did today, we can't last the morning. The Winchesters and the other repeating weapons will run out completely and we'll be down to the cap-and-ball guns and the muzzle-loaders—that and knives and hatchets."

There was silence all around the table.

Now was the time a real commander should bring up the subject of surrender. How could he tell these men the awful truth? Surrender was not only meaningless but impossible. That powerful force (he no longer saw Corey as a man) poised out there on the mesa between the run-outs would never give them terms. There could be no surrender to him. And Jim couldn't discount the one possibility remaining: they might just take enough of a toll in the very next attack to cause the enemy to break it off. There just could be a chance of that . . . if Victorio held any sway at all. They *had* killed a lot of the Apaches. Maybe Corey would fall from grace. But when he remembered the glimpse he had caught of the Apache chief in the afternoon (yes, he was sure now it was Victorio) he wasn't hopeful. Victorio hadn't looked like a man who led. Could that change if they stood firm enough?

Jim explained to the men at the table what he'd originally planned for the evening: to set fire to the buildings adjacent to the plaza. To his surprise, there wasn't a mutter of argument, and there was even enthusiasm when he went on to say he had changed his mind on one detail; the time.

"I think now we'll wait till morning. When they see the fires, it will give them something to think about. Might delay their first attack until some time after noon. We could make it through till dark again then, couldn't we?"

The other heads at the table nodded.

"Hey!" Dan Stone shouted. "Sure. Lots can happen if we

can last two more nights. Apaches get mighty restless in a long fight."

"They sure do," Joe Harris said. "Hell, I've seen them ride off in the middle of a battle they was clearly winning."

"Another thing," Stone said. "They don't know we ain't expecting any help. For all they know, we signaled Santa Fe days before they got here."

Thank God, Jim thought. The fighting will was still strong in all of them. Not that it would help in any real sense or in the long pull, but this show of spirit did make a difference.

"Look," Dan Stone said, "why don't I make one more try to break through to the Mescalero, or, better still, high-tail it right for Stanton? I been cussing them clouds we saw at sunset, but with no moon I should have a pretty fair chance to make it."

"No!" Jim ordered. "Too risky. Besides, we need you here."

"Look, Jim, if I get through, and if they send even one troop pounding down here, and if you can hold out till day after tomorrow, we could pull it off. Ain't like you was losing a man to use a rifle. We ain't got good guns and ammunition for the people we got anyway. I'll leave my Winchester and cartridges for someone else. Hell, I'll want to ride light anyway. Please, Jim?"

The logic was flawless, even if the chances were slim—or none. And it would keep hope alive.

"All right, Dan," he said at last, "you can try it."

They slipped Dan Stone out through the Estancia Street barricade at half past two in the morning, mounted on the best horse quartered in the livery stable. Even walking the animal until he cleared the edge of town, he disappeared in half a minute. They listened for ten, fifteen, twenty more to hear the dreaded sound of distant gunfire. Nothing, not even the wild creatures who usually patrolled the outskirts of town at night, broke the silence.

"By God," Joe Harris said, "I think he's going to make it."

Jim secretly doubted it. The best he could hope for was that when the shots did come, they would come from so far away that the defenders in the town, the wounded in the dry-goods store, the sentries on the rooftops, the women and children, everybody, would fail to hear them—and go on hoping.

At three fifteen the clouds rolled by and the moon sailed brightly away from them.

They didn't start the fire in the morning as Jim had planned. There seemed little point.

When the rays of the morning sun crept up the length of Estancia Street, one of the first things they lit was the naked mutilated body of Dan Stone, still streaming blood in a widening pool around the spot where the two swift Apache riders had dumped him, a hundred yards beyond the barricade.

They met in the bandstand, in full view of everyone.

"I think there's nothing left but to ask for terms, McPherson," the mayor said. "Now, look, I'm not taking back one bit of your authority. If you say we go on fighting, that's exactly what we'll do."

Jim looked at the others: Joe; Dr. Royston on one of his infrequent sallies out of the dry-goods-store hospital; Matt Hendry, bandaged across his entire upper torso and helped by son Tom; Sam Riordan, whose bloodshot old eyes were glazed to shiny blankness—and silent Granby Stafford.

"It isn't as though it was only heathen savages out there," Wilson said. "Corey Lane is a white man! There's got to be an appeal we could make to his decency."

Jim said nothing. Opening the eyes of these people had only resulted in the paradox of an even stonier blindness.

"We can at least hear what he has to say," Joe Harris said, "and it does buy us a little more time, Jim. If we don't get a deal we can accept, we can start your fires then. I got a man thinks he can hand-load the spent cartridges. They might jam the rifles, but at least we'd have time to try it."

The women and children had come out of the buildings where they had been holed up almost all the time the fighting had been going on.

"You could see if he'll at least give safe-conduct for *them*, Jim," Sam Riordan said. Jim hadn't expected to hear a word from Sam. "I can't believe Corey would refuse us that," Sam went on, "not the Corey I know."

Jim left the bandstand without a word. None of them followed him as he walked to the corner of the plaza and

mounted the Estancia Street barricade. The blood had dried
on Dan Stone's body, and in the calichi it was caked to a dull
red-brown. He would have to send a couple of men out to
bring the body in, or go himself.

He returned to the bandstand. None of the others had
moved.

"All right," he said, "I'll go out and sue for terms—but
only under one condition. If I come back and tell you there's
nothing doing, will that end it? Will you fight to the end?"

"You can count on it," Blaine said. It helped a little that
he could believe the mayor.

They rigged him a white flag on the end of a broom
handle, and he jammed it into the saddle holster which had
carried his rifle to Victorio's *ranchería* and back again. Here
was a strange, strange thing. All his life he had walked
without a gun; now he felt naked and desperate not to have
one with him.

He moved his horse to the gap they'd made in the
barricade to let him through, and as he reached it, he saw
Granby Stafford standing there. His back was a good deal
straighter than in recent weeks.

"Jim," the old man said.

"Yes, Granby?"

"Let *me* go."

"No, Granby. I'm sorry."

"Then let me go *with* you."

"No, I think it will be better if I go alone."

"But, Jim—" There was a faint cry of deep bone suffering
in the merchant's voice. It had been easier to turn down the
offers of Sam and Joe Harris and the others who had asked to
accompany him.

"Jim," the merchant said, "it may be *me* he wants, and
only me."

"No, Granby. That's final." He moved his horse through
the gap in the barricade, turned it about again. "Look, Granby,"
he said, "if I thought giving you to Corey Lane would save this
town and the people in it, I'd send you out there without a
qualm. Corey wants a good deal more than you."

IV

Come what may, this would be the last time he rode toward Corey Lane. He had done little else this past year, it seemed, except go on missions to or for that strange forbidding man. Why had he passed up the few chances granted him to go away from him?

There was no fear now. None at all. That would come later, when this mission failed, as fail it would. He had no doubt about that. Hadn't they all failed, one way or another?

For a few moments, as he had ridden through the charred and smoldering remnants at the end of Estancia Street, he had known a small flickering glimmer of hope. Actually, it was the brief exchange with Granby Stafford which had brought the glimmer to life. Of course Corey wouldn't be stopped by the sacrifice of the suffering merchant, but what about another offer—himself, Jim McPherson?

He might be an acceptable draught to slake Corey's raging thirst for vengeance. Without putting too fine a point on it, hadn't he been in large part responsible for most of the things which had gone wrong for the former lord of all this land? And now there was Virgie, too.

"I'll try not to be a hero." Virgie, I do remember!

Ahead of him he could see where the trail to the mesa left the ranch road leading to the X-Bar-7. Remembering how the Apaches had found Mike Calico on the hilltop, he guessed they would be upon him just about the time he reached the turn-off. Their lookouts must have seen him as he left the smoking ruins of lower Estancia Street. It would be a grim joke if whatever welcoming committee was waiting for him wasn't inclined to honor his white flag. Perhaps they were already marshaling for the morning's first attack, and would merely grind him under as they swept in on the plaza fort.

He was urging his horse to a little more speed when the next thought came: if the Apaches hadn't met him by the time he reached the fork in the trail, he could keep right on going. Maybe they were so preoccupied with getting ready for the assault they wouldn't see him if he set the spurs to his horse and raced straight for the X-Bar-7. He could gather up Virgie and the boy (she would never leave without him) and take them far across the mountains where there was no Corey Lane, no Black Springs, and no death.

Then he reached the split of the trail. He reined the horse to a stop. Far down the road he could see the last rise beyond which Virgie Lane waited for him.

He looked up the twisting length of the higher trail. There wasn't any sign yet of a captor escort. He could be free in a few more minutes. They hadn't seen him.

He shrugged his shoulders as if trying to shake from them a weight which wouldn't leave, and turned his horse up the boulder-guarded trace leading to the mesa.

The mesa was shaped like a huge tilted saucer, its northern rim overlooking a long gentle slope which spread down and outward like a great smooth fan to Black Springs' southern side, several hundred feet below and two miles away. Where Jim entered, on the lower edge, he could look back across the rise and all the way to the X-Bar-7. It would be the last chance he would ever have to see just where she was. Then he spurred his horse toward the center of the saucer.

Now he could see why none of them had come out to meet him. His guess had been right. The entire Apache force was assembled on horseback on the rim which looked down into the heart of Black Springs. The fires he had watched by night from the roof of the Sacramento House were now only blackened heaps. Hides and carcasses of what looked to be slaughtered mules were scattered helter-skelter. The two or three huts he saw seemed to be abandoned. There were a few ammunition boxes here and there, some in piles, others broken into kindling he realized would be used to start no more fires. The warriors he saw gathered on the edge of the mesa would not come back to this camp again. It was the beginning of the final onslaught.

Panic nearly shook him from his senses. They still hadn't seen him! They were all of three hundred yards away, and if they began their charge down the slope, he couldn't stop them. The precious minutes, perhaps as much as an hour, he had hoped to buy for Black Springs while he talked with Corey—and which was the only chance in Hell the defenders had—would be gone. He tried to shout, but his voice wouldn't come, and anyway he doubted if they could hear him at that distance and above the noise they must be making. Oh, dear God, if he only had his gun.

He lashed his horse into motion with the end of the reins, and in seconds the white cloth on his broomstick flagstaff was standing stiffly in the breeze. If the horse should stumble, break a leg, or even only throw him before he reached the Apache line or one of them chanced to see him . . .

In the center of the attackers he could see Corey Lane and beside him Victorio. He saw Victorio raise the lance he was carrying, and felt a sudden wave of black despair.

Then he heard the first whining ricochet come from the rocks through which his horse was racing. Someone on the ridge had seen him! He pulled the horse to a halt with all his strength, dropped the reins, and slid from the saddle. With his legs nearly buckling under him, he raised his hands above his head as Lane, Victorio, and the warriors nearest them turned to stare at him.

"Well, editor," Corey said, " we meet again. This, I think, will be the last time—or the next to the last at the very most."

Jim thanked whatever stars had watched over him for the few minutes during which Lane had dismounted, sat on a rock, and motioned for him to do the same. He knew that his trembling legs wouldn't have kept him erect a second longer. He hadn't spoken yet, and if speech had ever served him in his life, it must serve him now. He should try to talk, but every second he held his tongue was one more second of life for his embattled neighbors.

He looked at Lane. The man had changed again even in the ten days since Jim had faced him in the Black Range, but this time the change occasioned no surprise. The madness Jim had remembered from his last sight of Lane in the mountain *ranchería* was clearly a progressive thing. The eyes, wild then, were even wilder now. The primordial strength and passion Jim had noted then was even more pronounced, and it appeared to shake Lane in some fearful way, although outwardly he was as still as the rock he sat on. There would be no talking with this creature, no parley. All Jim could do was to play for time.

"You've fought well in there," Corey said. "Smart defense. Well directed. Who's running things?"

"We're all making our decisions together, Corey," he said. "I think you've been wrong all along about the skill and courage of these people." He could speak, after all.

"That well may be," Corey said. "Pity no one will ever know about it." He smiled. It was a smile Jim had seen many times before. This time he could scarcely bear to look at it. He looked around instead and found Victorio. The Mimbreño had dismounted, too, and stood twenty feet from them. The lance Jim had seen rested against the branches of a piñon tree. The Indian was watching Corey, but as Jim looked at him he turned those clear eyes on his. As in the mountain camp, there was no sign of recognition and none of the invitation Jim hoped for, the chance to talk with *him* if he failed with Corey. No, Victorio was going to hold himself well apart from whatever passed between the two of them. There would be no help there.

"Well, editor," Corey said, "let's get to the heart of things. Why have you come to me again with that white rag of yours?"

"To ask for terms, Corey."

"Terms?"

"Yes. Don't you think you've already proved whatever it is you want to prove?"

"No."

Lane stood up and turned his back. He took three fierce strides, turned back to Jim.

"No terms, editor. Tell them they'd better be ready to go on fighting."

"Will you let the women and children out safely, Corey?"

"No. The Apaches will have use for them. Slaves or ransom, one or the other. I don't care."

"Corey!"

Lane laughed. "Shocks you? Too bad you won't live long enough to get used to it."

"But why, Corey? Surely you can't hate the town *that* much."

Something strange happened to Corey Lane's face.

"*Hate?*" he asked. There was almost a puzzlement in his voice. "Hate, you say? This has nothing to with hate. I thought you, of all people, would know that. It seems you're as stupid as the rest of them." He fell silent. "No," he said in a minute, "nothing to do with hate or vengeance. They simply don't belong here. We're going to remove them as a surgeon would a growth. Nothing will be left. Not a stick or stone—not a memory. They go!"

"More will come, Corey."

"Then *they'll* die, too. This is only a beginning."

"You're mad, Corey. Don't these Indians, particularly Victorio, realize how you're using them?"

"Using them? Nonsense. I've given them a holy war. Ask them."

Jim looked at Victorio again. Certainly the man had heard every word, but his face betrayed no sign that he had taken notice. The other Indians were off the ridge now. Some of them had dismounted as had their chief. There was no impatience on the features of any of the warriors Jim saw, but then there was no sign of *anything* on those bronzed desert faces. He had been so intent on Corey until now—and to a slightly lesser degree Victorio—that he hadn't realized how many warriors there were. They must have added fifty or sixty to the number he had estimated in the *ranchería*. Corey had obviously used only a part of his effectives in the first attacks on Black Springs. When this horde swept down the slopes, whether they charged the barricades on horseback like white men or crept through the streets and alleys on foot, their attack would quickly become a holocaust. It was hopeless.

"All right," Corey said, "it's time for you to leave now, editor. We'll give you half an hour's start—and then we're coming."

All that was left was for Jim to make the offer.

"Corey," he said, "couldn't you be satisfied with *me*?"

Lane looked at him through narrowed eyes. He *had*

stopped him for a moment. Jim went on, "Don't I stand for the things you can't abide about the town and the other people there?"

Corey laughed. It was the beginning, only the bare beginning, of the same laugh Jim had heard in the mountains. But then Lane stopped it short. "Look! If killing *you* would do it, why, hell, editor, you'd be dead already. Don't think for a second that white flag would stop me. I take no surrenders—not one man or a thousand. Leave now. Tell them in Black Springs to fight to the last. You know, they should be grateful I'm giving them the chance to stand like men before they die."

Then—and if, against all odds, he lived, he never would know whether it was said in one last desperate attempt to buy a few more seconds for his town, or whether it was the only thing he could now use to wound this madman—Jim said, "Corey, remember this. I'll die, of course. You will live—but Virgie will be mine forever."

Lane stared at him. Then, deep in the man's throat a growl began. Before it was fairly started, though, it changed, and the mad laugh came—full and wild. It echoed off the rocks, rose in savage spirals of insanity. Just when Jim felt he could take no more of it, it stopped.

"*Victorio!*" Corey shouted. "Have this man's horse brought to him. He's ready to leave us now and prepare for battle."

It was done. Jim looked at the terrible face of Corey Lane and then turned to find the Apache chief. He expected no help. The tone Lane had used was one of almost contemptuous command.

But Victorio wasn't looking at them.

He and the warriors beside him were staring intently out across the mesa top, in the direction from which Jim had earlier made his frantic ride.

A drifting plume of dust was rising on the far southern rim, where the mesa tilted toward the X-Bar-7. Under the dust Jim could make out three horses galloping hard through the piñon and the rocks. One, a big buckskin, was some distance ahead of the other two. The rider was a woman, mounted sidesaddle, her full skirts flaring, rippling in the wind, a riding-crop rising and falling with unchecked fury.

"Alicia!" Corey said.

She sat her horse where she had reined it to a halt

before her son, but she didn't answer him. Virgie and little
Corey had pulled up beside her, or almost beside her. Their
horses' heads were only even with her saddle. She was the
leader here, as she always was.

Jim McPherson tried to catch the eye of the younger
woman, but she was looking at her husband, a look on her
dark face that he feared might never leave it, a look he might
never be able to caress away, even if that impossible chance
should come.

The boy seemed frozen. The face he shared with his
father and the older woman was suddenly one Jim didn't
recognize. There wasn't the fear in it Jim saw on the features
of his mother, only shocked wonderment—and the first signs
of a struggle for understanding a child should never have to
make.

Of the three, only Alicia looked like someone he knew at
all.

"Corey," she asked at last, "what are you planning here?"
Lane didn't answer her.

"I got the news just yesterday," she said, "about what
happened at the Martin place. Ernesto saw the butchery
there, and when I sent him to town last night to give the
alarm, he almost blundered into this encampment. At first I
couldn't believe him when he told me he'd seen *you* here.
What are you up to? Answer me."

It was incredible. She was as composed as if she were
making conversation in her own sitting-room instead of on a
barren mesa top surrounded by an army of deadly men. Her
head was tipped back in the same haughty way Jim McPherson had seen a hundred times, and her voice sounded the
sure notes of imperious confidence with which he had heard
her wither the clerks and merchants of Black Springs—and
himself.

"I was coming for you, Alicia," Corey said, "when I
finished my business there." His big hand gestured toward
the north rim of the mesa and the town hidden beyond it.
His voice was firm, purposeful. There were no concessions.
But it held none of the insanity of the laughter which still
dinned in the recesses of Jim McPherson's mind.

"You mean to attack Black Springs with these"—she
looked around her at the curious warriors who had moved in

closer to the little group—"animals?" A shudder, but of disgust not fear, passed through her slight rigid body.

"We *have* attacked. All that's left is the end of it. That will come today—in a matter of minutes, actually," Corey said. It was said with ingenuous, almost childlike pride. This madman was looking to her for approval.

She leaned toward him. The riding-crop was pointed at him as if she held a weapon in her hand.

"This must stop—*now*," she said, her voice still cool and under complete control. "You hear me, Corey?"

"It's too late to stop, Alicia."

"Rubbish!" She leaned back then and the riding-crop was tapping at her hip. "If you command here," she said, "you can stop it. If you *don't* command—you're not my son."

He gazed up at her, perched above him on the buckskin horse. His gaze was steady. "But isn't this what you've always wanted for me, Alicia?"

"No!" It was almost a scream, the first signal of the enormous tension this remarkable woman must be struggling under. "If you march on Black Springs, Corey, just *who* am I to pray for—the innocent people in there, or my son? I carried you and bore you. You're my flesh. My child! Yes, I wanted things for you—but what I wanted, and wanted you to want, was the honor of a soldier, not the shame of an executioner."

She shifted herself a little in the saddle, and the wide skirt which had blown up almost around the buckskin's neck fell in folds to her side. Jim saw the rifle stock jutting from the saddle holster.

"Will you stop this madness now, Corey?" she asked.

"I'm not sure I can, Alicia," her son said.

To Jim McPherson it sounded incredibly like a whimper.

"You'd best figure out a way, Corey," Alicia said. There was finality in her words. "I'm going in to Black Springs from here. I'm taking Virgie and little Corey with me." If her voice had been steel before, now it was forged from some new, even stronger alloy.

"If you and these savage brutes attack, you'll find me on the veranda of the Sacramento House," she said, "with this!" She put her slim hand, delicate even in the riding-glove, on the butt of the rifle stock. "I'll have to be killed, Corey— surely you know that—and I'll take a lot of killing. Maybe *you*

will have to do it. I won't live with my son a filthy renegade
butcher. Perhaps your wife and son will choose so to live.
They should make fine playthings for these new friends of
yours. When your usefulness to these devils ends, they just
might let *you* live and watch. Will you enjoy that?" She
snapped her head around. "Virgie, little Corey! We've another short ride to make!"

She slashed the side of the buckskin with the riding-crop
and the big horse bounded off.

In the half-second before Virgie and the boy got their
animals under way, Jim found the young woman's eyes. There
was love there, all right, but also fear for him—and beseeching.

No one moved to stop the three riders. Corey Lane
stared after them until they disappeared under the mesa rim.

Jim looked at Victorio. The face of the Apache chief was
dark. It had been as hushed as a church after the hoofbeats of
the three departing horses died away on the light upland
breeze. Now a counterpoint of new sound began coming from
the warriors gathered around their chief, heavy drumbeats of
muttering and low shouts. It was rising, swelling, until Victorio
raised his hand. The hush came again.

Corey hadn't moved; he still was staring at the place on
the rim where Alicia, Virgie, and the boy had vanished. He'd
paid no attention to the noise behind him, or the silence.
Now he motioned to the Apache boy holding the reins of the
chestnut.

He mounted, and the horse walked with him up the
slope leading to the rim. In seconds the horseman was poised
against the skyline, looking down into the town of Black
Springs. It was a familiar sight to Jim: Corey Lane towering
above the earth and its creatures—but with a difference.
Although he still looked splendid, it was a crippled splendor.

The breeze had stopped now, and it seemed that everything under the sky was waiting.

Jim McPherson wanted to pray, but his conflicting needs
blocked any attempt he might have made.

One thing seemed sure: he had been forgotten. Of course
he had ceased to exist for Corey. But for Victorio, too, and all
the other chiefs and warriors, and the boys too young to fight
who held the horses, he might well have been just another
rock.

Finally the mounted figure on the rim moved. He turned

the horse toward the waiting line and rode slowly down the
slope. It took forever, but at last Corey Lane stopped the
chestnut before Victorio.

"It's over, Victorio," he said. "We will not attack the
town—now or ever." It was the statement of a captain who
had no doubt that he was fully in command. Strangled wounded
cries revealed that at least some of the fighting men around
the Mimbreño chieftain understood the words, but on the
face of the Indian leader himself nothing showed.

The first outcries of shock had changed. Anger was rising
into the air as if the sun were pulling it up out of the ground.
Victorio looked at Corey Lane with glazed eyes.

Then the warriors around him began a slow surge forward and the Apache came to life again. He spread his arms
outward and stopped his warriors as if he had flung an invisible barrier across their path. His naked chest began to heave,
and the sinews in his neck stood out in heavy ridges.

"*You* have brought my people to this war," he said.
"Will you now turn your back on them?" The voice was
controlled and soft, but under it ran a current of passion.

The man on the horse seemed impervious to it. Corey
shrugged.

"They have no complaints, *viejo*," he said. "They've
killed some white men. I don't doubt they'll kill more another day." It was a dismissal.

He put the spurs to the chestnut's flanks and moved
through the line of warriors, down the slope in the direction
from which the two women and the boy had come. He didn't
so much as grant the Apache or his people a sidelong glance.
Corey Lane was going home.

The horse's pace quickened to a graceful lope, and as it
did, shouts of baffled rage broke from more than a hundred
Apache mouths. The man riding away didn't turn or show in
even the slightest alteration of his body that he heard them.

Victorio stared after him. Suddenly he ran swiftly and
lightly to where a boy held a pony. In one leap he was on the
startled animal's back. His heels kicked hard into its sides and
the pony reared, its front hoofs clawing at the air like the
forepaws of a cat. When they came down to earth again, the
rider spun the pony toward the piñon tree where the long
lance rested, and he seized the limber weapon as if he were

sweeping up a straw. He turned the pony down the slope, ran it hard for fifty yards, and halted it again.

Then he lifted his fine head toward the sky and loosed a sound that split the air the length of the mesa top. Jim McPherson knew then that something had been withheld from Victorio's chant that morning in the Mescalero.

This was the war cry of Victorio the Mimbreño, chief of men.

Down the slope the departing white man stopped his horse and turned. He looked back up to where the Indian was now as motionless as he had been himself on the mesa rim. For another half-minute they were linked silently by sight alone—and then the white man nodded.

The Indian began his charge with the pony walking as slowly and deliberately as the white man's horse had done. The tip of the lance, which had pointed straight for the heavens in the deathly quiet moments after the battle cry, now dropped level with his eyes. Gradually, without the changes clearly marked at any stage along the run, the pony moved from a walk to a light-footed canter and then to a lightning gallop, not running straight and true, but leaping wildly from side to side under the Indian's guiding hand.

Two hundred yards or more down the slope the white man's hand flashed to his hip and came up again with his revolver in it.

Why isn't he reaching for his rifle? The handgun wouldn't do him any good until Victorio was almost on top of him.

When only fifty yards separated the charging pony and the stock-still chestnut, the white man fired once and missed. At thirty yards he fired again. A spray, then a fountain of blood streaked from the left shoulder of the Indian. At ten yards the white man readied himself for the last shot he would likely make. The chestnut reared.

When its feet came down again, the point of the lance entered the white man's chest. The shaft drove straight on through until the hand that gripped it was almost buried, too.

Jim McPherson turned away.

As Victorio rode back up toward the others waiting on the slope, the point of the lance was lifted to the sky again. Jim was glad he hadn't watched the grisly business of getting it free from Corey's chest.

The Apache chief rode to where the riderless horses were being held, singled out Jim McPherson's mount, and took it from a boy whose head was hardly higher than the stirrups. Then he rode to where Jim was standing by his rock.

He didn't speak for a moment. The wound in his shoulder was streaming blood down over the hand that held the reins of the horse he led. The lance was glistening red, too, and the blood from it, Corey's blood, was thick on the other arm.

"Go and tell your people, Man of Words," he said, "that this war is over. Victorio will fight again—but in his own wars, not the wars of another chief, no matter how great he is!"

He held the reins in his left hand out for Jim to take them, and when Jim did he found the red-slicked leather almost too slippery for his hand.

Then Victorio turned and signaled to his warriors. One by one they mounted, and when they were all in the saddles or on riding blankets, he waved them out across the mesa toward the trail McPherson had taken that morning. The Apache chief was the last to go. Like the white man earlier, he didn't look back.

The mesa top was empty and silent when Jim McPherson mounted and rode to the body of Corey Lane. He kept his horse down to a slow walk. The chestnut was still standing over the body of its fallen master, and he didn't want to scare it off. He would need the big animal to carry the dead giant back to Black Springs—if he could manage to get the body across the horse's back.

When he reached the riderless horse, he leaned over and gingerly grasped its reins. Then he looked at Corey.

The blue eyes were turned straight up toward the sky. They were cold.

It was as if two oval drops of the wintry sky itself had fallen into the bearded face.

And Corey Lane looked surprised.

"Beat thou the drum, that it speak mournfully."

Epilogue

Puckett's Corners, New York, was in the last weakening grasp of a golden autumn. In a few more weeks winter would whistle across the border from Canada, and Jim McPherson would begin another long season away from the Ojos Negros.

Sitting at the desk in his father's old study, he looked down the back garden to where willows lined the brook marking the limit of McPherson property. The willows and the silver maples just this side of them were still holding the last of their yellowed leaves reluctant prisoners. The next determined November wind would whisk them all away.

The letter he had begun two days ago was still half-finished in front of him, but he would have to wait even longer before the tide of feeling subsided enough for him to go on with it. After a week of fighting back, he should have been proof against these attacks, but he wasn't. He read over what he'd written, for the twentieth time.

> *November 22, 1880*
>
> *Hon. Eloy Montoya*
> *7 Calle Pequeño*
> *Santa Fe, New Mexico Territory*
>
> *Dear Eloy:*
>   *Thank you so much for your letter. If I don't count a birthday note from young Tom Hendry (and an illegible scribble from Addie Hepburn) it's the first word I've had from anybody in Chupadera County since I left Black Springs the last of April. It's not*

that I feel people have been remiss; actually there's
no one left in the town with reason to write me any
more—now that Sam is dead. I'm glad you made time
to come down for the funeral, even if we didn't get
much chance to talk. Sam would have been happy if
he had known you were there—but perhaps he did.

Sam would have been happy, too, Jim thought, if he had
known in advance that he would go the way he had, standing
in his regular place at the mahogany bar of the Sacramento
House. There hadn't been much to make the old rancher
happy that last three months of life. Jim hoped the drink in
Sam Riordan's hand when the heart attack (that's what the
doctor called it) cut him down had tasted good to him. Not
many had for a long, long time.

I appreciate it, too, that you sent me the full
Territorial report on the battle at Tres Castillos.
The New York Sun *and the* Times *carried the story,*
but the details were sketchy and somewhat garbled.
One of the stories didn't even make it clear that it
happened south of the border, and that it was
Mexican troops involved, and not the U.S. Cavalry.
I suppose Colonel Terrazas and his soldiery are to
be congratulated on a splendid military operation,
but I must confess I had mixed feelings when I read
of Victorio's defeat and death, even though it prom-
ises to bring much needed peace to the Territory now.

Mixed feelings? No such thing. It was as if a lance had
been run through *his* heart this time. The news of the battle,
just five weeks ago, had left him in something close to shock
for days. Through the summer, despite all efforts to forget the
Ojos Negros Basin in every other way, he had followed
Victorio's trail of terror in the Southwest as he would have
followed magazine installments of a novel. What a chase that
magnificent man and leader had led the Mexican and American forces which had pursued him in the long months following the aborted attack on Black Springs. He often wondered
how Agent Russell felt. Did he, too, get some perverse
satisfaction from knowing that old Nana had somehow escaped the trap in the Chihuahuan wilderness and was now

raiding again with his tiny band in the Rio Grande Valley—
even if the old warrior's depredations were but a faint echo of
those of the great Mimbreño? Pity he had never actually met
Nana . . . or perhaps it was just as well.

> *Alicia Lane, I understand, has returned to the*
> *X-Bar-7. I think I knew she would. She is indomita-*
> *ble, and although her loss is a terrible one, the*
> *reserves of strength I discovered in my association*
> *with her will see her through.*
> *I had dinner with Virgie Lane and Corey Jr. in*
> *New York City two weeks ago upon their return*
> *from the extended trip abroad I'm sure you knew*
> *about. She plans now to spend some time with*
> *relatives in Kansas City. Then, counter to what she*
> *contemplated when she left the Ojos Negros—and*
> *in spite of all the painful memories—she and the*
> *boy will return to the X-Bar-7, too.*

This is where he had stopped. Could he begin again?
When he had written the name "Virgie Lane" two days ago,
his hand had begun to shake so he could scarcely finish the
page.

When he rode back into the smoky fearful town that
afternoon, trailing the chestnut with the lifeless body of Corey
Lane draped across its back, she had been standing with her
son on the veranda of the Sacramento House—behind Alicia
and her rifle. She looked first at the big horse with its
gruesome bloody burden, looked at *him* just once with eyes
so hollow and filled with pain he knew he would suffer
torture for days, no matter what the outcome of seeing her
again. Then she had gathered little Corey into her arms and
fled into the hotel with as much speed as Alicia had raced
toward the body of her son.

It was the last time he had seen her until in New York
two weeks ago. Letters, calls at the ranch, where he was
turned away time after time by María or Ernesto or one of
the other hands, nothing he did could bring him even a sight
of her. Then he had discovered she had left for Europe with
little Corey. It was almost as if she had died. In his agony and
desperation he would have bared everything to Alicia and
risked even destruction by enlisting her support, but the

older Lane woman had gone to Santa Fe to begin the six months' campaign to win the governor's pardon for her precious Corey.

Convinced at last that it was over, he broke the heart of young Tom Hendry by closing the *Chupadera County News.* He couldn't live one second longer in this unforgiving country without Virgie. Whether he could live *anywhere* without her he would have to wait and see.

Then, a month ago, probably at the very moment Victorio was dying in the gory rocks of Tres Castillos, the letter from London had come to Puckett's Corners. Would he meet her and little Corey in New York City?

He felt like Lazarus. His spirits soared like an Ojos Negros hawk—until they met. ˙

Never once was he alone with her. She was regal, beautiful—and distant. All the desire he'd known for her in the past was pale and weak compared to the way his need and overwhelming love raged now, but she gave him no opening at all. Finally, at dinner—and in front of the boy—he could hold it in no longer.

"What about us, Virgie?"

Suddenly she was Virgie again—for all the good it did him.

"I don't know, Jim. I just don't know. Of course I love you. I always will." For a glorious instant her old radiance came winging back, but then the dark eyes were far away again. "He's still there, Jim. I didn't get free of him the way I thought I could."

He kissed her—on the cheek—when he said goodbye.

Then, in the middle of a bright autumn week that seemed a bitter jest played out particularly for him, Eloy's letter had arrived. It was still as politely terse as the few Jim had gotten from the Concho man when he was in Black Springs, but Eloy's keen quick intelligence and warm affection danced above every line. Courteous as always, but insistent, the letter had demanded answers. He could almost hear again Montoya on the morning after the arrest of Granby Stafford, when he had walked into the office and softly challenged him, "Now I am here."

He had begun his answer, but when he'd reached the name of Virgie Lane he'd felt as stripped of life as the willows and the maples soon would be. For the next two days he had tramped the woods and valleys around Puckett's Corners.

Sam was dead. So were Will-Ed Martin and poor Valerie, and Jacky Jameson, Dan Stone, Mike, and Bill Talley, and countless other Ojos Negros people whose faces if not their names came all too frequently to mind. And Victorio! Essentially, Jim was dead himself. Virgie, too? For him—yes.

Had Corey Lane triumphed after all? Could that great gaping bloody hole in his broad chest have failed to bring him down to common clay? Would he and his overweening pride still rule the reaches of the Ojos Negros—and by default?

Jim McPherson sat at his father's desk and looked down toward the brook. The bright November sun had breathed away the frost from the fast-browning grass, turning it into gleaming amber. A quickening north breeze puffed another leaf from the nearest maple tree. He picked up his pen. Would it turn as treacherous as it had two days ago, and would his hand become palsied by memory again?

He began to write.

> *Now, Eloy, in answer to your questions. Yes, I am coming back to Black Springs, and yes, I will reopen the* Chupadera County News. *Like you, I appreciate the importance of the latter, but not, as you have been kind enough to suggest, the former.*
>
> *That many of my reasons for doing this are personal and private is a matter of indifference to you, I am sure. Enough to say that I will be back— and I will do what lies within my meager powers to efface some scars.*
>
> Con mucho respeto,
> *Jim McPherson*

The sun outside the window was bright enough, but not nearly so bright as the one which gave that strange wide country its daily bath of glory.

He knew what he would do when he reached his town, even before he faced the problem of the dark woman who was the other half of him.

He would go to the little tumbleweed-choked cemetery

at the edge of Black Springs and visit a certain grave. After he had poured a bottle of whiskey on the mound, he would talk with the old man who rested there.

"Old friend, I have gossip for you. That eastern greenhorn you despaired of ever teaching anything has come back to lay a ghost or two."

And then, because it would please him to grant himself a few moments of maudlin self-indulgence before he set to work, he would "sit upon the ground and tell sad stories of the death of kings. . . ."

★ WAGONS WEST ★

This continuing, magnificent saga recounts the adventures of a brave band of settlers, all of different backgrounds, all sharing one dream— to find a new and better life.

☐	26822	INDEPENDENCE! #1	$4.50
☐	26162	NEBRASKA! #2	$4.50
☐	26242	WYOMING! #3	$4.50
☐	26072	OREGON! #4	$4.50
☐	26070	TEXAS! #5	$4.50
☐	26377	CALIFORNIA! #6	$4.50
☐	26546	COLORADO! #7	$4.50
☐	26069	NEVADA! #8	$4.50
☐	26163	WASHINGTON! #9	$4.50
☐	26073	MONTANA! #10	$4.50
☐	26184	DAKOTA! #11	$4.50
☐	26521	UTAH! #12	$4.50
☐	26071	IDAHO! #13	$4.50
☐	26367	MISSOURI! #14	$4.50
☐	27141	MISSISSIPPI! #15	$4.50
☐	25247	LOUISIANA! #16	$4.50
☐	25622	TENNESSEE! #17	$4.50
☐	26022	ILLINOIS! #18	$4.50
☐	26533	WISCONSIN! #19	$4.50
☐	26849	KENTUCKY! #20	$4.50
☐	27065	ARIZONA! #21	$4.50
☐	27458	NEW MEXICO! #22	$4.50
☐	27703	OKLAHOMA! #23	$4.50
☐	28180	CELEBRATION! #24	$4.50

TERRY C. JOHNSTON

Winner of the prestigious Western Writer's award, Terry C. Johnston brings you his award-winning saga of mountain men Josiah Paddock and Titus Bass who strive together to meet the challenges of the western wilderness in the 1830's.

☐ 25572 **CARRY THE WIND–Vol. I** $4.95

☐ 26224 **BORDERLORDS–Vol. II** $4.95

☐ 28139 **ONE-EYED DREAM–Vol. III** $4.95

The final volume in the trilogy begun with *Carry the Wind* and *Borderlords*, ONE-EYED DREAM is a rich, textured tale of an 1830's trapper and his protegé, told at the height of the American fur trade.

Following a harrowing pursuit by vengeful Arapaho warriors, mountain man Titus "Scratch" Bass and his apprentice Josiah Paddock must travel south to old Taos. But their journey is cut short when they learn they must return to St. Louis…and old enemies.

Look for these books wherever Bantam books are sold, or use this handy coupon for ordering: